W9-BMK-685

EXILE

Anne Logston

ACE BOOKS, NEW YORK

This book is an Ace original edition,
and has never been previously published.

EXILE

An Ace Book / published by arrangement with
the author

PRINTING HISTORY
Ace edition / October 1999

All rights reserved.
Copyright © 1999 by Anne Logston.
Cover art by Jim Griffin
This book may not be reproduced in whole or in part,
by mimeograph or any other means, without permission.
For information address: The Berkley Publishing Group,
a division of Penguin Putnam Inc.,
375 Hudson Street, New York, New York 10014.

The Penguin Putnam Inc. World Wide Web site address is
http://www.penguinputnam.com

ISBN: 0-441-00669-8

ACE®
Ace Books are published by The Berkley Publishing Group,
a division of Penguin Putnam Inc.,
375 Hudson Street, New York, New York 10014.
ACE and the "A" design are trademarks
belonging to Penguin Putnam Inc.

PRINTED IN THE UNITED STATES OF AMERICA

10   9   8   7   6   5   4   3   2   1

To my honorary nephews (in order of appearance):
John, Michael, Jason, and Alex,
who remind Aunt Anne how important it is to dream.

NEVE SPENT AN IDLE MORNING KILLING dragons.

Well, to be quite fair, most of them died on their own with no help from her. She'd *seen* dragons aplenty, but she really had no idea how they worked on the inside, and therefore how they should be put together. Some simply dropped dead the moment she made them.

Others took longer.

At dinnertime Neve's mother, Dara, shook her head disapprovingly.

"It's horrible," she said. "I've told you about this sort of thing before, Neve. It's *wrong*."

"They aren't *real* dragons," Neve protested. "At least they weren't real until I made them."

"I don't care," Dara said flatly. "It's cruel. They feel pain, Neve, whether you made them or not. And look at the mess you're making on the beach. The one that exploded is splattered everywhere."

"There, you see?" Neve said, glancing at her father. "I need the practice."

Her father raised his eyebrows.

"Well, at least you made that one correctly up to the point of its fire-belching system," he conceded. "But you've got to let it vent the flammable gas, or—well, you saw. If you—''

''*Vanian,*'' Dara exploded, scowling.

The Guardian of the Crystal Keep sighed irritably.

''Oh, very well,'' he said. ''No more dragons, Neve. Your mother's right; you *are* making an awful mess, anyway. Do you have any idea how that beach is going to stink while those carcasses rot?''

Neve mumbled something into her lamb pie and Vanian looked at her sharply.

''What did you say?'' he said, and Neve winced a little at his tone. *Now* she'd done it.

''I said,'' Neve said, sighing resignedly, ''it wouldn't stink if you'd just make them all go away.''

''You see?'' Dara said pointedly. ''Do you see what she's becoming, Vanian? Is *that* what you want ruling the Keep in your stead?''

This time it was Neve's mother who'd gone too far; Vanian's eyes went cold and he abruptly vanished from the table. Dara scowled darkly and vanished just as abruptly, leaving Neve alone at the table. Neve returned to her lamb pie, torn between chagrin and amusement. Her father wouldn't get off *that* easily; Dara could track him to the far corners of the Keep, and she'd do it, too. On the other hand, Neve wouldn't get off that easily either. When her parents finally came back, no matter how angry they were at each other, they'd be twice as angry at her for starting the whole thing. And it was so unfair. It wasn't as if either of them had forbidden her to make dragons, after all, and she *did* need the practice. How would she ever make a proper Guardian if she couldn't create things?

Neve finished her pie, picked up another, and slid it into her pocket. Best to get away while she could. If her mother and father returned, they'd finish their argument all the faster without her presence; then, if matters followed their usual pattern, they'd go upstairs and make up in the bedroom with the door locked. Then they'd both be in a *much* better mood to confront their errant daughter. And there was one way Neve could sweeten their mood a little more . . .

Neve jumped back to the dragon-strewn beach and sighed, munching her lamb pie thoughtfully. Mother was right; it *was* a nasty mess, and this was the section of beach where they generally went swimming, too. Well, she'd think of something. She'd have to; the sight was absolutely ruining her appetite, and the smell was even worse.

Neve was still contemplating her problem at sunset. Bringing in all the gulls to gobble up the scattered bits had been the easiest part; getting rid of the large chunks and the whole carcasses was much more difficult. She'd tried pulling the tide in early, but even so the water was too shallow and the force insufficient to float the dragons away. She'd tried drawing in the water dragons to eat their kin, but the water was too shallow for them, too. There weren't any land predators in this pocket world large enough to haul the dragons away or push them deeper into the water. Father could have simply brought the dead dragons back to life, or made them vanish, or even made the corpses get up and walk themselves into the sea, but Neve had no idea how to do either. She could recede the shoreline, make the dragons simply tumble into the water, but her father would be *livid* if she tried world-scaping. Maybe if she—

"You're *making* it complicated."

Neve glanced over her shoulder at her father sitting on a rock. Her mother still jumped out of her skin every time somebody appeared unexpectedly (to Neve and her father's great amusement), but Neve had lived in the Crystal Keep her whole life and was utterly sanguine about such occurrences. Neve was relieved to see that her father wore a more mellow expression, and he'd newly combed and braided his straight black hair into a single plait down his back; that meant he and Dara had gotten past the argument and the sex.

"What do you mean?" she asked. "I thought about opening up the ground, but it's all sand, and it's too wet. It'd just cave right in."

Vanian shook his head.

"You can't seem to get away from large-scale creation and destruction," he said. "That's your problem. There's any number of simple solutions that you're completely ignoring. Come here." He patted the rock beside him.

Disgruntled, Neve sat down. Her father had a way of making her feel like an utter fool.

"Your problem is that you're thinking of them as *dragons*," Vanian said. "Contrary to your mother's tenderhearted opinion, they're not—not now, anyway. They're bundles of water and chemicals, the same things that go into anything else—trees, dirt, birds, thunderclouds. You should know that from the homunculi you've created. Transform the carcasses into something else, hopefully something that won't putrefy. Make them smaller and roll them down the beach. Take all the water out of them and they'll crumble into dust and blow away. Stop making it so difficult. It's always easier to work from the inside out.''

Neve flushed with shame and realization. She concentrated for a moment and the dragons dissolved in a cascade of sparkling red, blue, and green gemstones onto the sand.

Vanian hopped down from his perch and picked up a handful of stones, examining a few critically.

"Not bad," he admitted, tossing the stones back to the sand. "The rubies are especially good. Of course, it's going to become hard to have a private swim here once the mortals hear about a beach littered with precious gems, isn't it?"

Neve flushed again.

"Most of them will wash out with the next high tide," she said. "Or I could turn them into sand."

"No, leave it." Vanian chuckled. "It'll make things interesting." Then he gave Neve a sharper glance. "Where did you get so much experience with gemstones?"

Neve shrugged.

"I ran into a traveler in one of the pocket worlds," she said. "He wanted the largest diamond ever known. So I gave him one the size of a horse." She laughed. "Too bad he didn't think of wishing for a way to get it home with him, or something hard enough to break it up."

Vanian laughed, too, raising his eyebrows.

"And what did he trade you for it?"

Neve tried to imitate her father's mysterious-but-pleased expression.

"What I wanted," she said.

Vanian's smile turned to a grimace and he shook his head.

"Neveling, that's hardly equal value," he chided. "A beautiful girl like you, he should've been offering *you* jewels. Besides, do you have any idea what your mother would say about that sort of thing?"

"Oh, by the Nexus." Neve sighed. "Mother never said I

couldn't have lovers. She's never complained about any of the lovers I've made."

Vanian shook his head again.

"Homunculi conjured up out of clouds or flower petals or spring rain aren't at all the same as seducing mortal travelers," he said sternly. "I don't suppose it occurred to you that the fellow might have done you some harm?"

"Hah!" Neve lifted her chin. "I'd like to see one try. I'd feed him to the fell-beasts—*after* I turned him into a squirrel, that is." At least once she'd figured out how to make a squirrel . . .

Vanian sighed irritably, simply gazing at Neve.

Neve sighed, too.

"All right," she said. "How bad is it?"

"From now on," the Guardian said sternly, "You'll not attempt to create anything living again without supervision, not until we decide you can do it competently. And for three days you'll stay at the house, prepare our meals, and clean. No magic whatsoever."

Neve grimaced, not asking whose idea *that* had been. She knew one of her mother's punishments when she heard it.

"Not a word," Vanian warned when Neve would have protested. "Your mother said a week. I reduced it because you cleaned up after yourself. Now go home. *Walking*. The sooner you start your three days, the sooner it'll be over."

Neve hesitated.

"Are you coming?" she asked, hoping he'd say yes. If he'd unilaterally reduced her sentence, she'd far rather *he* be the one to tell Mother.

Vanian, however, apparently realized her ploy.

"No, thank you," he said. "I've borne quite enough of your mother's temper on your account today. And like you, *I* have responsibilities to attend to."

He vanished.

Neve sighed and started her long walk home. Once she left the beach, there was still the seemingly interminable distance down the long single hall of the Crystal Keep, past the doors that opened onto other worlds. How many were there now? Even her father wasn't certain. And new ones were being created all the time—each time a mortal entered the Keep, whether to seek answers of the Oracle or to beg a wish from the Guardian or to discover the secrets of the mysterious place or to prove themselves clever or strong enough to survive the place, whether they succeeded and left or whether they failed and stayed in the Keep or died, there would be a new door for each of them, a door leading to a new pocket world created from that mortal's memories or dreams, a world within a world. Sometimes, Neve suspected, the Nexus popped in another world just for the joy of it.

But no door for Neve, because she'd never come; she simply *was*. And because there was every likelihood that she wasn't mortal at all.

When Neve's mother had come to the Keep, it had taken her days (at least as far as time in the Keep could be measured) to walk from the entrance to the last door, the door that her own presence in the Keep had created.

But although the number of doors had increased greatly since then, it wouldn't take Neve nearly as long to traverse that same hallway.

She closed her eyes, finding the stillness inside her, the silent place. And within that—

The Nexus.

It wasn't cheating, not truly, the doors flashing by her like dry leaves in a windstorm. She wasn't using magic. The Nexus was simply . . . helping her. Because it liked her.

Because it recognized its own.

Neve stopped at the proper door without hesitation, although it looked like every door before it and every door after it. Like it or not, this little pocket world was *home*. It was unmistakable.

Inescapable.

The house was the same as always, simple and welcoming and surrounded by goats and chickens, dogs and cats, lines with drying clothes. Neve could smell bread baking in the outdoor summer oven, the hot yeasty aroma almost covering the less lovely odor of the animals and the garbage heap out back.

Dara stepped into sight at the kitchen door, drying her hands.

"There you are," she said. "What did you do, walk back?"

Neve nodded resignedly, picking her way through the

yard. Before her three-day punishment was over she'd have droppings aplenty stinking up her boots, but she planned to put it off as long as she could.

"Don't make such a face," Dara said, patting Neve on the shoulder. "Keep busy and the week will pass before you know it."

"Three days," Neve said quickly. "Father said three days." She saw the storm cloud gathering in her mother's eyes and added hastily, "It was because I cleaned up the dragons."

Dara scowled and sighed exasperatedly.

"Remind me to thank him," she said, "for making that decision without me." She glanced at Neve rather sharply. "Did he tell you anything else?"

Neve shrugged.

"No more making live things without supervision," she said.

Dara's scowl deepened a little.

"That wasn't what I—never mind." She sighed again. "I see he left me that delightful task, too. All right, come help me with dinner and we'll talk."

Neve resignedly chopped turnips, carrots, and parsnips, trying to remember to be careful with the knife. She *hated* working in the kitchen; it was hard to remember that things like knives and fires could actually *hurt* her, and she was forever burning herself or chopping off the tips of her fingers—and it hurt like blazes until Mother or Father grew them back. When she was finished with the vegetables she went out to the ovens and took out the finished bread, popping in the second batch, while her mother seasoned the roast.

"I don't suppose it occurred to either you or your father," Dara said, glancing over her shoulder, "to save some of that abundance of dragon meat? Most people roast it with a spicy sauce, but it makes a lovely hearty stew, too."

Neve thought of that gory beach and her stomach turned.

"I didn't save any," she said. "Anyway, the meat probably wouldn't have been right. The dragons certainly weren't."

She turned to her mother.

"Why don't you just *make* it?" she said. "For that matter,

why don't you just make the stew, if that's what you want?''

Dara sighed again, putting down the ladle with which she'd been basting the roast.

"Fine," she said. "So you wave your hand and have stew and all the trimmings, and bread and wine and dessert and everything else you could ever possibly want. Then what?''

"What do you mean, then what?" Neve said. "Then I eat it."

"That's not what I meant," Dara said patiently. "What I mean is, what do you do with your time, your life, that has any meaning? If everything's yours for the wishing, what's the point in anything? What gives your life purpose? What is there to want, to strive for, to dream of?''

Neve grimaced.

"I don't know," she retorted, "but I know it wouldn't be chopping vegetables and scrubbing dirty dishes. Even watching butterflies or just walking on the beach is better than *this*."

"Is it?" Dara cut a slice of warm bread, spread it thickly with butter, and handed it to Neve.

"I made that bread and churned that butter with my own two hands," she said. "I spent my time and my labor making tasty food to nourish and comfort the people I love. Every minute I spent kneading and churning and washing dishes I was telling you and your father how much I love you both. You'll live and grow strong on the food I prepared for you with so much love. So tell me, what good comes from your beach walking?''

Neve ground her teeth.

"I learned things," she said irritably, "that I bet you and your bread don't know. I learned that tiny crabs escape predators because they're exactly the same color as the seaweed or the rocks they live in. I learned that seawater is made up almost exactly the same as blood. I learned that there's lots and lots of creatures in the sea that make themselves look like stones or seaweed or beautiful flowers so that when fish swim close to admire them, they gobble the fish right down. I learned that the tides aren't made by the fluttering of a huge sea dragon's gills at all; they come from a strange power that pulls from the moon like a lodestone pulls iron shavings. I learned that pearls are valuable to people, but to an oyster they're just trash. Did *you* know those things?''

Dara frowned at the outburst, but she took a deep breath before answering.

"No," she admitted. "I didn't. All right, I'm glad to see you've tried to make your time useful. But what are you going to do with all those marvelous, strange facts you've learned? You've learned more about how things work, how they're made. All right, maybe that lets you use your magic more effectively. More magic, more free time, more walks along the beaches, more strange new knowledge so you can make more magic, which leaves you more free time, and so on. In the end it's just a circle that traps you inside, just as your father was trapped.''

"He's not trapped," Neve protested. "He's the Guardian. He can do anything, have anything he wants.''

"He could do anything but leave his huge, wonderful prison," Dara corrected. "He could have anything except everything he wanted most. In time, Neve, enough power— the power of the Nexus, I mean—and loneliness and imprisonment and despair will make a monster out of anyone. It almost made a monster out of your father. And we're afraid—both of us—that sooner or later that power and that imprisonment will make a monster out of you.''

"My father's not a monster!" Neve said hotly. "And neither am I.''

"No, you're not," Dara said softly. "Neither of you is. But, Neveling, it took your father's love for me, and mine for him, to pull him back from the edge. And because of the way you were born, you've always been close to the Nexus. A part of it, in a way, just as it's part of you. Someday when we're gone and the Keep becomes your responsibility, what—or who—will pull you back from that edge?''

"And chopping turnips and scrubbing pots will keep me from falling over that edge?" Neve retorted irritably. "Anyway, who's to say I'll need pulling back? If I'm part of the Nexus and it's part of me, maybe that's what I was meant for all along. My destiny.''

Dara was silent for a long moment.

"That's what Vanian believes," she said at last, sighing. "I don't know that I agree with him. But whether he's right or I'm right, the answer's the same. We're sending you to visit an expert.''

That got Neve's attention; she hunkered down pensively beside the hearth.

"An expert?" she said slowly. "What, an expert about the Nexus?"

Dara nodded.

"Kelara, the elf who opened the Nexus and created the Crystal Keep from its energies," she said. "And her mate Yaga, who was Guardian for most of the Keep's existence, before your father. We're sending you to visit them."

Kelara and Yaga. Neve remembered the names; she'd read about them in the histories her father had spent the last few years writing for her about the Keep. She'd seen some of that history in her father's magical mirror, too, even the actual creation of the Keep.

"But they're—" Neve swallowed. "They're gone. They're *outside*."

Dara chuckled a little wearily.

"That doesn't mean they've dropped off the edge of the world," she said. "They left the Keep not long after I met your father—you've seen that story in the mirror, I know—and went south, to the edge of the great southern sea. Yaga developed a fondness for those hot southern jungles while he was a dragon." Dara grimaced. "Well, there's no accounting for taste. Anyway, we've looked in on them from time to time through your father's mirror, even consulted them for advice once in a while. Such as when you were conceived." She glanced almost guiltily at Neve. "Between the four of us, we've made a simple enough map for you to follow when you—"

But Neve had heard enough. Before her mother could say another word, she bolted—not with her feet, but instinctively, with her mind. She didn't choose a destination, but something within her chose one for her. There was no door for Neve in the Keep, no place created particularly for her. But she had a special place where she went to be alone, to think, and it was there she found herself, sitting on sparkling white sand in a cave of purest crystal. In glistening crystal she saw herself reflected a hundred times, a thousand—straight black hair like her father's hanging loose over her shoulders, her father's pale skin (never browning even on the beaches), sharp angular features now set stubbornly, long black eyes cold and angry and rebellious. She'd come here a hundred times, a thousand, for this—the feeling of being surrounded only by the reflection of herself, no intrusions, no distractions. The only sounds here were the quiet drip of water, the gentle whisper of a breeze through the passages. It was a place of stillness, of clarity, of profound solitude and peace.

But there was no peace for Neve here now.

Outside. Her parents wanted to send her *outside*.

She wouldn't go. She *couldn't*. Every bone in her body, every drop of her blood rebelled against such a notion. She couldn't leave the Keep any more than she could stop breathing on a whim. The Nexus was a part of her, like her heart, her eyes. She couldn't simply walk away from it— could she?

She could feel the Nexus now as always, hovering on the edge of her awareness. With only the slightest effort she could reach out and touch it, feel—

In a desert pocket world two glorious gleaming-scaled dragons (Will I EVER get it right?) mated in a coupling only slightly less savage than combat, claws and teeth drawing blood, wings thundering—

Dara finished punching down her fourth batch of bread dough and wiped her hands on her apron, glancing out the window and swearing softly under her breath—

See—

A mortal visitor slogged through the swamp, cursing more loudly and openly (Oh, boy, he's headed right toward the fell-beasts. Should I—Father would kill me but—there, ripple the water just a little, let him take the warning or not)—

Fauns danced in a forest, cloven hooves striking the hard-packed earth precisely in patterns, in a ritual no living mortal had ever witnessed; they drew their small knives and fell upon their sacrifice, a young boar, blood spurting over an altar made of gold and human skulls—

Hear—

Rare blood orchids singing on a mountain peak, sweet siren song that would lull any mortal hearing it to sleep, never to wake as hair-thin roots slowly insinuated themselves through his flesh and into his veins to nourish the plants on his blood—

*Mermaids whistling victory as they converged on the
wounded shark, then attacked all at once, sunlight glistening
on their slippery skins, their teeth gleaming white, then red
as they savagely tore the thrashing creature to pieces—*

"I knew you'd come here."

This time Neve didn't turn when she heard her father's
voice, although it shocked her abruptly out of her commun-
ion with the Nexus; she resented his presence too bitterly to
acknowledge him. This was *her* place. The Nexus hadn't
made it for her, but she had claimed it for her own and
nobody had ever contested the claim. Father *had* a place
created for him. So did Mother. It was only fair that Neve
should have one place all her own. Only right.

"I was just—" She stopped. Her father hated it when she
messed with the Nexus.

"I know what you were doing." Vanian said it flatly, emotionlessly, and he was silent for a long moment. Then: "Do
you know why you come here?"

"To be alone," Neve said bitterly, and left it at that. Her
father didn't take the hint, however; when Neve wouldn't
turn to face him, he walked—*walked!*—around Neve and sat
down in front of her.

"You come here," Vanian said patiently, "because this
place feels special to you. And it feels special to you because
this is the place where you were conceived—or created, if
you prefer. Or both. Your mother always liked this cave, too,
which is why we chose it. She thought it was romantic."

Neve said nothing, gazing at her father steadily. His words
had somehow tainted her private place. She bitterly resented
the idea that her mother and father spent time in *her* cave,
that it could be special to them, but she'd make no sign of
that resentment. She knew her father's games. She'd show
him that she could play them as well as he—if not better.

"Your mother wanted a child very much," Vanian said.
"I myself doubted it was possible. Even in the admittedly
short time since she'd come here, Dara didn't age. She never
experienced a woman's moon days. Even staying in her own
pocket world, day and night came but the season never
changed, not for the world, not for her. Time wasn't time
here. And even lacking that, I was the Guardian, steeped for
centuries in the magic of the Nexus. Once upon a time I'd

been as human as Dara, but if I had any old portraits of myself, you could plainly see how much I'd been changed. There was every chance that I simply wasn't human enough anymore to father a child with her. Still, we hoped; it's said that sometimes even elves and humans can crossbreed.

"We tried for some time," Vanian said, shrugging. "The usual way. Of course, nothing happened. So we consulted Kelara and Yaga. They agreed with my concerns but thought there was a way it might be done—with what consequences, nobody knew."

He met Neve's gaze squarely.

"I used the magic of the Nexus to quicken my seed in your mother's body," he said. "I wove some of the Nexus's power into your very being. And because that magic answered my will, you could grow as a baby would grow inside its mother, be born, age as a child would age. But I knew there was a price; there's always a price. One day your own will would grow strong enough that that part of the Nexus within you—and possibly someday, through it, the Nexus itself—would answer to you instead of me. That time is approaching, as your mother and I knew it would. So we prepared for it as best we could."

Vanian sighed.

"When I came to the Keep, and later, your mother came, too," he said slowly, "we didn't understand how time passed outside as compared to within the Keep. That passage of time deprived us both of"—he closed his eyes briefly—"certain choices in the direction of our lives. Your mother didn't want you to have to face a world changed by time beyond all we knew. So together—she and I and the Nexus—we brought the Keep back inside time. We don't age, your mother and I and those who dwell here. We don't die. The seasons don't change in the pocket worlds. But one day inside the Keep is one day outside, and so it's been since you were conceived. It was the most difficult thing I've ever tried to do." Vanian shook his head, then grinned wryly. "But it's a good change. Before, sometimes it seemed that mortals invaded the place constantly. That wasn't true, of course; outside, years might pass, or even decades, between visitors. Now visitors seem much rarer, although that's only an illusion, too. But we did it for you, knowing that one day you'd have to make this journey."

"Nobody told *me* anything about any journey," Neve said sullenly.

Vanian shrugged.

"We decided not to mention it," he said negligently. "It might never have been necessary. Someone else might have become Guardian. You might have had no interest in the job or no talent for manipulating the Nexus. Your mother and I might have decided to take you and live outside, as Kelara and Yaga chose to leave. At one point we considered it seriously, especially your mother. There was a time Dara wanted that very much—a life with other people around her, friends, maybe more children."

Neve had never heard *that* before; somehow it disturbed her.

"Why didn't you, then?" she asked.

Vanian grimaced.

"I can't leave the Keep unless another takes my place as Guardian," he said. "Visitors came more seldom—at least in relationship to the passage of time inside—and none of them who might have wanted the job were fit to take it. I couldn't leave the power of the Nexus to just anyone. Besides"—he hesitated—"I wasn't so certain I could give it up anymore. Or even that I wanted to. The world outside has changed too much; everything that ever meant anything to me outside is gone, and I've changed too much, too. I didn't think—and still don't—that a normal mortal life outside would ever be right for me again, not after what I've seen, done, known here. I began to wonder whether I'd ever really want to step down. And then it became apparent that you had every intention of becoming the next Guardian." He fell silent.

"Well, what's *wrong* with that?" Neve demanded. "If I was *born* to hold the power of the Nexus, then that's what I'm meant to do. What I *should* do. What's the matter with that? Other than the fact that now you've changed your mind and you don't want to give it up, that is."

Vanian sighed irritably.

"You haven't been listening," he said impatiently. "Neveling, in many respects your mother and I never had a choice in the direction of our lives; it was chosen for us—by others, or by chance or circumstance or birth. We were determined that you *would* have more of a choice than we did.''

Neve scowled.

''It doesn't sound like that to me,'' she said. ''It doesn't sound like you're giving me any choice at all.''

''Ignorance isn't a choice,'' Vanian said pointedly. ''If a baby bird doesn't break the shell of the egg that contains it, it dies never knowing that it could have soared on the wind. You can't decide that the world outside the Keep holds nothing for you until you've seen it, experienced it. And your mother and I can't protect you from life forever. If you're old enough to take charge of your own destiny, then you must do it.''

He sighed, and to Neve's amazement, for a moment he looked almost *old*.

''You're right. I'm not certain I want to give up the Nexus now,'' he said. ''I'm not certain I'd want to live here under another Guardian, even—or maybe especially—my own child. I'm even less certain I want to live outside as a mortal. But if you're truly ready, and the Nexus was meant for you, then that's two to my one, and I'll step down. When Kelara gets to know you, she'll know the answer.''

''Alone?'' Neve said in a small voice. ''You're sending me outside alone?''

Vanian gazed at her soberly.

''I can't leave the Keep,'' he said quietly. ''Your mother could go with you, or we could make you an escort to protect you, but—'' He hesitated. ''Is that what you want?''

Neve swallowed. The idea of going outside, finding her way across the mortal lands to seek out two elves she'd never met—it was terrifying. But her mother had made such a journey all alone, and her mother had been a simple serving maid with no magic and no special talents. And after all, this was to prove that Neve was ready to become the Guardian of the Crystal Keep, fit to wield the incredible power of the Nexus. What kind of Guardian couldn't make a simple journey without someone along to hold her hand?

And in a way, it made a sort of sense. Nothing in the Keep came for free; value given for value received, that was the law. If she wanted the Nexus, she'd have to earn it. And if this journey was the price, the task the Guardian set her . . .

"All right," she said, as steadily as she could. "I'll go. Alone."

"You won't be entirely unprepared," Vanian said almost absently, as if he spoke to reassure himself more than her. "You've learned a great deal about the outside world watching in my mirror, and through what Dara and mortal visitors have told you. And no matter how you've disliked it, the skills Dara's taught you will help you survive outside. You'll have supplies and money and maps; it's more than your mother had when she made her long journey here."

Then he smiled rather grimly.

"There's never been much of your mother in you, not to look at you, but you're like her in one way at least. You're an utterly determined, incredibly stubborn little creature." He glanced at her sideways. "If the Guardian of the Crystal Keep couldn't stand against such an iron will, I shudder to think what the outside world has in store for it."

Despite her father's words, Neve *was* angry, and that anger carried her through the next days. Completely ignoring the rules of her supposed punishment, Neve spent her time in a frenzy of creation—clothing, supplies, weapons, most of which were utter failures because she'd simply never bothered trying to make such serviceable goods before, but she was too furious at her father to ask for help.

At last, however, it was Dara who came to her room with a sack and a peace offering of Neve's favorite cinnamon cakes and whipped honey butter, and she looked over Neve's creations with neither the disdain nor annoyance Neve had expected.

"These aren't too bad for a first try," Dara said gently. "But they wouldn't last you long outside. Tell me what you want and we'll work on it together. But—" She glanced at the pile again. "That's far too much to carry, you know."

"I was planning to take a horse, only I'm not allowed to make one," Neve said, trying to suppress her annoyance. Like it or not, she was going *outside*. She needed all the help she could get, little as she wanted to admit it.

"A horse is a good idea," Dara said, unperturbed. "And perhaps a pack mule as well. You'll be traveling through civilized land for the most part, so there should be good roads all the way down to the coast. I'd advise you to join a caravan; it's slower, but safer from highwaymen, and you'll eat better—won't have to catch your food, at least.''

Neve sniffed.

"I'm not taking the roads down," she said. "I'm taking the river.''

"The river?" Dara raised her eyebrows, her lips pursing.

"One of the visitors told me about it," Neve said, smiling inwardly. So much for her mother knowing *everything*. "Barges come up the Little Brother to trade as far north as Selwaer, and that's only a few days' ride from the Keep. I can take a trade barge south to Kent, where the Little Brother meets the Dezarin, and then buy passage on a ship all the way down the Dezarin to the sea. Other ships sail west along the coast to Zaravelle, and Kelara and Yaga live not too far from there. Father showed me on the map." Neve tapped the unrolled skin where she'd marked her route. "It's ever so much faster than traveling overland. I can be in Zaravelle in just a few weeks at the most. It'd take months by land."

"Well!" Dara took a deep breath, surveying the map. "I can see you've given this some thought. I admit I hadn't thought of boats." She laughed a little weakly. "I've never been on a boat in my life. I couldn't have afforded it anyway. And you're right, it should be faster and more comfortable, and probably safer—at least from highwaymen. A boat on the open sea, though—"

Dara shook her head, her brow furrowing, and Neve felt a momentary flash of satisfaction. Good. Let her parents worry about sea dragons and sirens and whirlpools and pirates. This whole trip wasn't *her* idea.

"Well!" Dara said again, as if at a loss for words. "After seeing all the planning you've done, I don't know whether this will be of any use to you or not, but here it is anyway." She pulled a thick leather-bound book out of the sack and handed it to Neve.

Neve opened the book, flipping through the pages idly.

"It's a grimoire," Dara said. She sighed. "More precisely, one I claimed when I first came to the Keep. It's very basic but has a good range of spells."

"Spells," Neve repeated. She glanced at her mother. "I don't use spells."

"You don't use spells *here*," Dara corrected. "Outside the Keep you can't simply make anything you want happen just by thinking about it. Magic doesn't work that way outside. You should know that. I'm assuming—"

Dara cleared her throat and, to Neve's astonishment, blushed. In all the years of her life, Neve had never seen her mother blush except with anger, usually when arguing with Father.

"I'm assuming," Dara repeated, "that you'll still have the ability to work magic when you leave the Keep. If that's the case, perhaps you'll find the grimoire useful. Or perhaps not." She hesitated. "You've had no real training in the sort of magic practiced outside. I thought you should learn it, but your father—he thought it best that you simply develop at your own pace and in your own way. Perhaps he's right. Training might have pushed you toward the Nexus too quickly. I don't know. Now I wonder whether we did you a disservice in that way."

Neve kept her mouth shut; her mother wouldn't much care to hear Neve's opinion on what disservices they'd done her.

"In any event, you've certainly taught yourself concentration and focus," Dara said hurriedly, as if to cover her earlier doubts. "You should be able to work your way through the spells if you start simply. And if you can't—well, you won't be any worse off than I was."

She turned back to Neve.

"Neveling, I wanted to ask—your father's mirror—"

Neve fought back a grimace.

"Don't watch me," she said. "Don't. I'd hate that, knowing you were watching me. And even if I was in trouble, there wouldn't be anything you could do, not if I'd gotten very far from the Keep, that is." She knew there was some cruelty in her request, but so be it. If she was going to be forced to make this journey, at least she wanted the satisfaction of knowing her parents had no idea—and no control, either—of what she was doing.

Dara sighed.

"I knew you'd say that," she said tiredly. "We'll try, Neve. That's all I can promise. We'll try not to look."

Which meant, Neve knew, that they'd look—her father would have done as he pleased anyway, despite whatever Neve or her mother said. Well, no matter. As she'd pointed out, she'd be well beyond their reach anyway. That thought was as reassuring in one way as it was frightening in another.

In the end Dara was right; a pack mule was a necessity, and Vanian agreed to supply the horse and mule. Neve was loaded with clothes, supplies, bedding, pots, her mother's grimoire—and a few secrets.

While Neve was checking the load one last time, Dara had come to give her a battered-looking leather purse.

"Your father and I made this together," she said. "Whenever you open it it'll contain ten silver pieces—Caistran coinage, that's the only one I really know. That's from your father and me. This is just from me." She clasped Neve's hands tightly, and Neve felt a warm tingling sensation flow through her fingers.

"I've taught you cookery," Dara said almost embarrassedly, "but many people can do that. Now you'll have a true talent for it. Should anything—well, if you lose the purse, at least you'll have a way to earn a living. With the talent I gave you, you should be able to get a position even in a High Lord's house if you need to."

Then she grimaced as if at a none-too-pleasant memory of her serving-maid years.

"But try not to lose the purse," she added wryly.

Neve had thanked her mother and tucked the purse into her tunic; she'd no sooner returned to her inspection than her father appeared.

"Ready to go, I see," he said cheerfully. "Did your mother give you the purse?"

Neve patted her tunic, nodding.

"Good. Don't tie it on your belt, especially in the cities and towns, or someone will steal it," Vanian said. "But you'll need something else in your travels."

He clasped his hands loosely around Neve's throat; Neve felt a slight tingling, as she had when her mother had taken her hands.

"Ever since I became Guardian," Vanian said slowly, "there's never been a man nor woman enter the Keep whose language I couldn't understand and speak. The Nexus does that, I think. Your mother didn't receive that gift, but somehow you did. Maybe it's because—well, I wasn't certain it would last outside the Keep. What I just did will make sure it does." He hesitated. "But sometimes words aren't enough."

He handed Neve a dagger. Like the purse, it was old and battered looking; it even looked *dull,* but when Neve started to test the edge Vanian snatched her hand away sharply.

"No!" he snapped. Then he flushed. "Never touch the edge or point. It's not a normal blade. It will kill anyone it cuts. You must always be very careful with it."

He shrugged rather sheepishly.

"Your mother and I never taught you much about defending yourself," he said, sighing. "That was probably a mistake, but you didn't seem to need it here. Outside it's different. You may not be able to rely on your own magic. But that knife—one cut is all you'll need. And if—hopefully—you never need it to defend yourself, it may at least come in handy hunting."

Neve took a deep breath and sheathed the dagger very, very carefully, forcing what she hoped was a grateful smile. Now she wondered whether she'd ever dare wear the thing. Maybe she could just bury it somewhere in the wilderness.

"Your mother would probably use that thing on me if she had any notion I'd made it for you," Vanian said wryly. "I can't even imagine what she'd do if she knew about this." He opened his other hand, displaying a shining crystal the size of Neve's thumbnail.

"A diamond?" Neve said, taking the crystal, suddenly thinking of the pouch of rubies she'd surreptitiously tucked into her spare stockings. But as soon as she touched the hard stone, a shock of pure recognition ran up her arm, and she knew it was no ordinary diamond she held.

"A small fragment of the Nexus itself," Vanian said. He grimaced. "You have no idea how much it hurt to create that for you. Hopefully it will let you retain some of the magic you've learned to use here. I don't know that it will. But there's no harm in trying, I suppose."

Then he scowled.

"Now, where to put it—"

"A necklace?" Neve suggested. "I can wear it inside my tunic, where nobody can see."

She well understood her father's concern. The Nexus was an incredible, immeasurable power; not only that, but her father—and Neve herself—were tied very, very closely to the Nexus. She couldn't imagine what might happen to either or both of them should that small fragment fall into someone else's hands or be destroyed.

"No, no," Vanian said, shaking his head. "Somebody might steal it." Then he sighed. "Sit down."

He pulled off Neve's boot, then unlaced the bottom of her trousers, pushing them up. He ripped open Neve's stocking behind her right knee.

"What are you doing?" Neve asked cautiously.

"Would you rather take your trousers and stockings off?" Vanian asked practically, raising one eyebrow. "I thought not."

He pressed the crystal against Neve's leg, behind and just above her knee; when he took his hand away it was empty. Neve reached behind her knee and felt; there was a crystal-sized hard lump there under her skin. Vanian ran his finger down the tear in her stocking and it closed seamlessly, but he left her to lace her trousers and replace her boot herself, sitting back on the bench.

"If you should happen to be robbed," Vanian said wryly, "the back of the knee isn't a place where an attractive young woman would generally be searched. But I don't know what will happen when you take a part of the Nexus out of the Keep. If it should cause you trouble, you might have to cut it out, so I didn't want to implant it too deeply, or anywhere vital." He grinned. "And do be careful which knife you'd use to cut it out!"

Suddenly Neve felt a pang of conscience. Her father hadn't even speculated what effect it might have on *him*—the Guardian sending a piece of the Nexus outside the Keep. It must be a great deal like tearing off a piece of himself.

"Maybe you shouldn't—" Neve said slowly.

Vanian raised his eyebrows.

"Nonsense," he said, waving negligently. "I think of it as a necessary experiment. If that fragment of the Nexus serves you, and if your mother and I leave here someday, I may want to take a piece of the Nexus myself. I've become rather accustomed to all the conveniences here, you know, and I was no mage at all outside.''

Neve didn't believe a word of it, but the deed was done and she knew her father better than to believe she could change his mind. His comments about her mother notwithstanding, she knew where the other half of her own stubbornness came from, and it *wasn't* the Nexus.

To Neve's gratitude, there was no teary farewell at the door, only her mother handing her a satchel with still-hot meat rolls and fruit pies and Father standing at the door tapping his toe impatiently. Neve said nothing; leading the horse and mule her father had made, she simply took a deep breath and stepped over the threshold—

And out of her world.

2

TO NEVE'S SURPRISE, IT SEEMED NO DIF-
ferent at first.

She emerged in the small valley that held the entrance to the Keep. Trees, brush, sky, weeds, grass, streams,
birds, game—she'd seen their like in many of the pocket
worlds. Even her first view of the outside of the Keep didn't
overly impress her; she'd seen far more awesome sights inside.

There was the ring of fog, of course, that guarded the
Keep; she could see it higher up the valley walls. Her mother
had shivered when she described it, but her father had told
Neve not to worry; what lived in the fog was actually relatively harmless, only meant to frighten away the faint of heart
before they reached the Crystal Keep.

There were no roads leading out of the valley, of course,
but Neve had no difficulty finding the faint trail her mother
had described and marked on the map. She stepped unhesi-
tatingly into the fog's moist, cool embrace.

Some fifteen to twenty years ago—neither Neve's father
nor her mother could say for certain, given the strange nature
of time and the Keep—Neve's mother had stumbled confused and terrified through this selfsame fog, blindly fleeing
its eerie inhabitants. Neve, however, walked steadily, untrou-

bled by the strange hollow sound of the horse and mule's hooves clopping against hard earth, the subtle rustlings and scrapings all around her, even the woody tendril that snaked up from the ground at one point to brush at her feet.

The horse and mule, however, plainly did not share Neve's sangfroid; they shied and danced at every strange sound, and Neve realized to her dismay that she really knew very little about horses and how they behaved. By the time she reached the end of the band of fog, she was fighting hard to hold them, and she wished she'd troubled herself to learn more. The animals seemed so big and strong and not nearly as docile as the ones Father or Mother had conjured up to teach her to ride—could they actually be dangerous? If they stepped on her hard enough, could she actually be hurt? Even killed?

Neve was beginning to develop a grudging respect—and maybe, little as she liked to admit it, perhaps just a bit of fear—for this world outside.

The horse and mule, however, settled down again when Neve emerged from the fog. Neve tied them relievedly to a bush. There was one last thing she wanted to do before she went any farther, just to be certain, now that she was completely outside the Keep's magic. Neve picked up a pebble and cupped it in her hands, reached out—

Nothing happened.

A shock of pure fear ran through her, and she rigidly suppressed it. She took a deep breath and focused tightly on the pebble, concentrating *hard*. No dirt-crusted pebble was stronger than her will, her power, the will and power of the Guardian of the Crystal Keep's daughter, child of the Nexus!

Slowly, grudgingly Neve felt the pebble respond at last. It was difficult, terribly difficult, but the pebble shifted in her hand, and at last a ruby gleamed up at her. Neve gave a sigh of satisfaction, wiping sweat from her brow with the back of her hand and tossing the ruby away. Yes, it was difficult— but *she* was stronger. Stronger than stone. Stronger than Outside.

Neve climbed into the saddle with a new sense of confidence, knotting the mule's lead rope around the saddle horn, and urged her horse westward.

She was ready.

She rode through the midday sunshine, through the lengthening afternoon shadows, and when dusk fell she stopped, going over the steps in her mind. Unsaddle and picket the horses; they were real animals now and needed to eat and drink or they'd die, and she wasn't certain she could make more. Set up the tent; she'd practiced that several times in the last few days. She didn't really need a fire—it was warm out and her food was already cooked—but she gathered wood, cleared an area of dirt, and made one anyway with her flint and steel, just to prove she could.

It was after darkness fell that the world around her began to feel different at last. She couldn't see outside the circle of light of the fire, and that bothered her. She'd been similarly blind when she'd made fires in the pocket worlds, yes, but that was different; she knew her way around many of them, certainly the ones where she'd made a camp, knew the terrain, the inhabitants . . . and of course she'd never been stupid enough to camp in a *dangerous* world.

Now, though, the night seemed full of unseen watchers, unknown dangers. Neve shivered involuntarily, then forced herself to stop. Her father and mother might be watching in the mirror right now, and damned if she'd let them see her quailing like a frightened rabbit. Besides, as her mother had told her often enough—

"Fear's a warning that you've been caught unprepared," Dara said firmly. *"It means you haven't done something you should, or that you've done something stupid. Don't sit there and be afraid; fix what's wrong and go your way."*

Well, if coming to the outside world was the stupid action Neve had taken, there wasn't much she could do about it but go crawling back home, and that she'd *not* do. What else could she fix?

Neve banked down the fire and lit her lantern instead, hooding it and letting her eyes adjust. Now she could see fairly well in the moonlight and the land around her assumed a less threatening image. Then Neve realized what she'd done wrong.

I'm right out in the open, she thought sourly. *Anybody, anything might've seen my fire and crept up on me while I was night-blind. Tomorrow I build a smaller fire, and I find cover before I make camp so the light of it can't be seen half a league away.* She laid her dagger—still carefully in its sheath—ready to hand beside her pallet and felt a little better. *One cut, that's all I need. Father was right. I can manage that even if I'm completely outnumbered and overpowered.* With that, she could lie down and rest, and each sound she successfully cataloged—crickets, tree frogs, owl, breeze—whittled away a little of her remaining unease, and at last she slept soundly.

In the morning Neve crawled out of her pallet and groaned. An hour or two of horseback riding in one of the pocket worlds hadn't prepared her for the consequences of her first daylong ride, and those consequences had probably been exacerbated by an unaccustomed night's sleep on the hard ground. Biting back a whimper—her parents *might* be watching, and she'd never give her father the chance to direct that lofty chuckle at *her* again—she got up and forced down a cold breakfast. It was tempting, so tempting, simply to keep her camp for an extra day while she—uh—acclimated to the outside world, but Neve sighed and struck camp. Her parents wouldn't be fooled, and besides, she'd only just acknowledged the mistakes of her first camp anyway. Wearily she packed up her belongings, pulled herself painfully into the saddle, and rode on.

By the time Neve met her first caravan she thought she'd gotten most of the mistakes ironed out. She'd learned not only how to set up camp but how to choose a proper campsite; not only how to build a fire but how to select the proper wood to burn slowly and how to conceal the fire—and what to do when a burning log unexpectedly exploded, sending sparks flying everywhere, or rolled out of the fire and almost onto her feet. She'd met up with the road, exactly where it was marked on the map, and was making fair time toward Selwaer.

She'd made her first real, intentional kill, a rabbit she'd snared, and when the animal was roasting over the coals, Neve scrubbed her hands with sand again and again and again in the creek beside which she'd camped, doubting sickly whether she'd actually be able to bring herself to eat any of the meat. Thankfully the snare had killed the rabbit, so Neve hadn't been forced to finish the job, but she wondered whether it had been a mere oversight or a deliberate omission—probably for her father's amusement—that her parents had never taught her the disgusting process of skinning and gutting her prey. Neve had nearly vomited when she saw all the nastiness inside a rabbit, nastiness she had to pull and scrape out with her own two hands. She thought of her dragon-strewn beach and fought her gorge down again. Well, no doubt about it—next time she'd have a far better idea of exactly how animals were made up inside!

When the smell of the roasting meat reached her nose, however, fragrant with the herbs and spices from her cooking pouch, Neve found that her squeamishness couldn't quite compete with her appetite. She could barely wait long enough for the rabbit to cook through; then she burned her mouth tearing into the succulent meat. Pain didn't stop her either, and her kill was rapidly reduced to a pile of bare bones.

After that it was easier, and since then Neve had managed another rabbit, a fat little thing she guessed was a woodchuck, and a couple of fish with nary a heave. The second rabbit hadn't been quite dead, which gave Neve a chance to test her father's knife. A single prick dispatched the creature with a neat quickness that her softhearted mother would have appreciated. In fact, Neve had begun to think in terms of trying to cure the furs instead of burying them with the offal, or perhaps even trying something larger, like a deer, which would mean staying in a camp long enough to smoke and dry the meat. She really had no idea how to do *that,* and no concept at all of butchering beyond cutting her prey open and scraping out what she didn't want to eat, but how hard could it be?

Before she made the experiment, however, Neve came upon the caravan near sundown. It was headed west, just as she wanted, and from the look of it had only just stopped for the evening. She rode in slowly, then stopped a good distance away, sliding off her horse and holding up her hands to show that she was unarmed.

"It's always best to meet a caravan in a city or town," Dara said. *"They're edgy once they're on the road on their own. But if you want to join one on the road, wait till they stop for the evening and all the guards are deployed. Give*

plenty of advance warning and expect a lot of questions. For all they know, you're an advance scout for a party of brigands planning to ambush them—or, at best, a thief working alone, wanting a chance to cut their purses and maybe their throats while they sleep."

"Hello, the camp!" Neve called out, feeling very vulnerable and stupid and excited. She was about to meet her first mortals outside the Keep—and, for the first time ever, more than one mortal at a time.

Heads popped out of wagons and three guards trotted up—one with sword drawn, two with bows. One of the archers was a woman, and Neve felt obscurely anxious; fewer women came to the Keep than men, and Neve had never actually met a woman besides her own mother.

"What do you want?" one of the men with a sword said shortly.

Neve took a deep breath.

"I'm riding to Selwaer," she said as humbly as she could manage. "Alone. If you're headed that way, I'd like to join your caravan. I'll pay a fair price, or—" Another deep breath. "Or I'll work. I'm a good cook. *Very* good."

The woman archer edged a little closer, bow still at the ready, and looked over the horse and the mule with a skeptical eye.

"You're carrying a lot of goods for a young 'un alone out here," she said. "And what's a girl well-to-do enough to afford so much doing out here on her own, hey?"

Neve hesitated, then decided.

"I'm coming from the Crystal Keep," she said.

The bow wavered a little, and all three guards' eyes widened.

"You say you're coming *from* the Crystal Keep?" the first guard demanded. "Not many dare go in, but almost none ever come out. What was your business there, eh?"

"I—" Neve forced a confused expression. "I can't remember much," she lied. "Every day I seem to forget more. I must've had a wish."

She shrugged.

"Guess I got it," she said. "I mean, here I am." In retrospect she regretted her lie; as far as she knew, she'd never lied before. She was probably as bad at it as she was at creating dragons.

The female guard lowered her bow slowly.

"You're bound to Selwaer, then?" she said. "And what's your business there?"

"To catch a boat," Neve said. "Down to the coast. I'm going to visit some friends—elves, if you must know."

That widened their eyes again; the leader backed up to join the other two, and there was a murmured conversation for some moments. At last the third guard, who had remained silent throughout Neve's questioning, trotted back toward the camp. The other two stayed where they were, guarding her. Neve began to feel a little annoyed.

"Look," she said. "You can see I'm alone. There's no cover at all for miles back along the road, so nobody could be following me and watching." Then, more impatiently: "You haven't even told me if your caravan's going to Selwaer."

"It's not our destination," the leader said brusquely. "But we'll pass through. What weapons are you carrying?"

"You can see the bow on my saddle," Neve said, gesturing. She touched the dagger at her hip. "This, another knife with my cooking pouch, and my eating knife. That's all." She grimaced. "Oh, and some fishhooks and a fork, I suppose. Do they count?"

The woman scowled.

"Quite the joker, hey?" she said. Then she barely turned her head. "Ah, Dwyer. What's the word?" The third guard had returned.

"Wagonmaster says all right." He turned to Neve. "We got a cook, but you'll help out. Fourteen Moons. And you camp with Mora here, where she can watch you."

Neve bit her tongue to stifle an outraged retort. From what she had heard from travelers, the price was outrageous, especially if they expected her to work, too. Then she hesitated. The guards seemed awfully jumpy, more so than her mother had led Neve to believe was normal. There must be a reason—most likely a band of brigands in the area. Neve didn't want to meet those brigands at all, much less alone on the road. Besides, the gathering clouds threatened rain, possibly a storm. She drew her purse out of her tunic.

"I don't have Moons," she said. "I have Caistran silver. And I've only got ten." She opened the purse to show him. "But if I help your cook, you'll be glad you let me come."

Another brief conference; then the first man who had spoken shrugged and nodded, taking the coins. The woman Mora took the horse's reins from Neve and followed the others, leaving Neve to fall in awkwardly beside her.

"My name's Mora," the woman said after a long moment of silence.

"I know," Neve said, mildly annoyed. "The other guard said so." Did the woman think she was deaf or simply stupid? Then she grimaced. The woman was making polite conversation, the way mortals talked to each other when they really didn't have anything worthwhile to say. Neve wasn't used to that, but if she was going to spend weeks among mortals, she'd better learn.

"Pardon me," she said. "I'm Neve."

Mora glanced at her with an expression somewhere between surprise and annoyance.

"You're a strange-looking bit," she said shortly.

"I'm not," Neve said indignantly. "I look like my father, mostly, and he's"—she closed her mouth quickly before she could say "the Guardian of the Crystal Keep."—"he's very handsome, or at least my mother says so," she finished a little awkwardly.

Mora snorted and gave Neve an infuriatingly pitying glance. Neve bit her lip *hard* and shut up. Whatever this rough, grubby woman thought was of no consequence, none at all.

The caravan wagons had already been unhitched for the night, and several men and women were pitching small tents that attached to the sides of the wagons; other wagons themselves held straw mattresses for more comfortable rest. Neve hoped one of those was meant for her and the surly guardswoman, but Mora dashed her hopes immediately.

"We doss under there," the guardswoman said shortly, gesturing at one of the cargo wagons. "You can throw your bags in the back, then tie your horse and mule with the rest. Be quick about it. I'll tell Cook you're on your way."

With that she left Neve to her own devices; now Neve was really outraged as she unloaded her gear, then had to pull her horse and mule through the camp, past curious and suspicious stares, until she finally located the other horses. She tied her horse and mule with the others, in easy reach of the feed that had been put out for them; since Mora hadn't said anything about picketing her animals out to graze, this nasty prickly lot could damned well feed them, especially at the price they were charging her.

Somehow Neve had expected Cook to be a woman (most likely because of Dara's stories of her youth and services in the high house of Caistran), but in fact he proved to be a rather elderly man, not unkind but apparently uninclined to conversation. When Neve started to fetch her pouch of cooking herbs and spices, it was not the cook, Tarson—she had to wring his name out of one of the guards as he showed no inclination to tell her himself—but a guard who told her brusquely that she'd use the supplies Cook had brought and nothing but. Neve resentfully returned to the firepit, sneering at the guard behind his back. If they thought she intended to poison or drug the food, what kind of fools were they to make her do this work anyway?

Tarson had nothing like the selection of herbs and spices that Neve carried, but at least he gave her free use of what he had, and it wasn't long before the savory aromas drifting from the cooking fire attracted a circle of hungry-looking guards, merchants, and servants.

"Not bad," Mora acknowledged (rudely, with her mouth full, to Neve's disgust).

"So tell us about the Crystal Keep, girl," another of the guards demanded, dribbling grease on his beard.

Neve pointedly finished chewing and wiped her lips before answering.

"As I told *her*," Neve said, gesturing at Mora, "I don't remember much about it. That's part of the Keep's magic, you know." She glanced around, imagining this loutish lot tramping through the halls. "I remember something about monsters," she said. "Terrible monsters roaming the place, hideous creatures that—"

"Can't be that bad," a middle-aged woman said, grinning. "Not if a slip of a child like you could get through it."

Neve favored her interrupter with an icy glare.

"I was *clever*," she said flatly.

"How d'you know, if you can't remember nothing?" Mora asked mildly.

"I'm alive, aren't I?" Neve retorted.

"Well, if you forget everything when you leave," Mora countered, "how do you know you weren't just lucky?"

If I was lucky, Neve thought sourly, *I wouldn't be here with the likes of you, would I?*

"Luck," she said with great dignity, "might get you past one monster, or five, or twenty. But it wouldn't solve the mysteries of the Keep for you, nor would it save you from the tricks of the Guardian. You have to be brave and clever and—"

She shut her mouth abruptly. Why was she giving these people advice about the Keep, much less *true* advice? Her father wouldn't much appreciate his daughter giving away the secrets of the Keep, and he'd be right. After all, it would be *her* Keep someday, and the fewer rude louts like this disturbing her there, the better. In fact, maybe she'd best plan on imposing some newer and better defenses. Unlike her father, Neve rarely found the hapless visitors very amusing.

"I heard tell of a fellow who went in there 'bout five years ago," one guard mused. "Right ugly he was. Said he was going to find a spell to make him comely so he could win a lass's heart. Wonder whatever became of him?"

"How would I know?" Neve said irritably. In fact she knew for truth that the aforementioned youth was now a unicorn in one of the pocket worlds—undeniably the handsomest unicorn in the herd.

"Sounds like you don't know much of any use," someone muttered sourly.

"I've already paid silver and cooked your supper," Neve snapped. "Nobody told me I was expected to be a bard and a teacher, too."

A few sour grumbles circulated through the group, and Neve abruptly found herself without her audience. Undismayed, she helped herself to the stew and hurried off to eat it in private before somebody decided she was supposed to scrub the pots, too.

By the time she finished, it was full dark. Except for the guards on watch, everyone had gathered at the fire; Neve could hear laughter, occasionally not-very-melodic song. She scowled and located the wagon Mora had indicated, finding her packs and spreading her pallet underneath it. If they didn't have the courtesy to invite a guest to share their fire, especially after she'd extended herself to give them extra-tasty fare to feed their loutish bellies, so be it. At least that spared Neve their prying questions and boorish manners—

Not to mention their invasive presence. Until she'd left the Keep, Neve could have counted the number of humans she'd ever met on the fingers of her two hands. Now she was surrounded in one night by more people than she'd met in her entire life. She'd had no idea that when people gathered in groups, they were so rude, so noisy, so overwhelming. So smelly.

More laughter from the fire, and Neve rolled over on her side, grinding her teeth. How was she supposed to sleep through that racket? Why, the chickens and geese at home were quieter. And probably cleverer, too.

Neve finally fell into an uneasy doze; she woke with a start late in the night to find that Mora had apparently rolled over against her back. Neve stiffened and jerked away; nobody had ever touched her without her invitation, much less her consent, before. The guardswoman was snoring, too, resoundingly; even the rain that had started to fall couldn't cover the noise. Neve hurriedly retreated as far as the shelter of the wagon would allow, groaning and wrapping her arms around her ears.

Ten silver pieces for this*? I'd have been better off on my own, taking my chances with brigands. At least they've probably learned to be quiet.*

"There it is," Mora said flatly. "Selwaer."

Neve said nothing, staring at the first human settlement she'd ever seen (in the flesh, at least) with a mixture of relief, disappointment, and consternation.

She'd somehow thought it would be . . . bigger. Grander. Cleaner.

The little cluster of thatched wooden huts couldn't have housed more than a hundred souls. The road—if the tiny track through the middle of the town could be called such—was a squelching strip of mud and dung that buzzed with flies. There were no shops in the small plaza that Neve assumed was the marketplace, only a few carts and a few more men and women peddling their wares from baskets and trays.

"Well, here you are in Selwaer," Mora said. "Fare you well."

Neve stared blankly as the guard turned her horse away, preparing to rejoin the caravan continuing down the road past Selwaer.

"Wait!" she called, alarmed. "What do I do now?"

Mora glanced over her shoulder at Neve, then shrugged.

"You paid for passage with our caravan," she said indifferently. "Not nursemaiding. Good luck to you."

Neve set her teeth grimly and turned toward Selwaer. Four days of traveling with the caravan apparently hadn't endeared her to the others, but that didn't particularly bother her, either.

Fine. Fine. *I hope they* do *run into bandits on the road. And wolves. And maybe a good hard thunderstorm, too.*

It was actually easy enough to find the barges; Neve simply followed the main road through town to the river, ignoring the grubby townsfolk who glanced up curiously as she rode past. There were several barges tied up at the docks—some loading, some unloading.

Well, if this is as far north as the barges go, then the ones loading up are traveling back south.

She picked out a dignified-looking middle-aged man who appeared to be watching the barges quite closely, hoping he was the wharfmaster.

"Excuse me, sir," she said. "I'm looking for passage on a barge to Kent. Could you tell me if any of these folk will be traveling that way soon and might accept a passenger?"

The wharfmaster (apparently) looked Neve up and down.

"Can't take the horse and mule, you know," he said shortly.

"Yes, I know," Neve said, forcing a smile. "I'll sell them in town. But could you tell me—"

"Might try Pickerd at the north end," the man said.

Neve glanced upriver.

"Is he the one loading the barrels?" she asked.

The man shook his head.

"Naw, Pickerd at the north end of town," he said. "He might buy your animals."

Neve gritted her teeth.

"Yes, thank you, I'll talk to him," she said, keeping her voice even. "But about passage—"

"He'll give you a fair price."

"I'm sure he will," Neve said, unable to keep an edge from her voice now. Was the man a complete idiot or just pretending? "But, sir, I have no desire to sell my horse and mule until I've found other transport. Can you tell me which of these barges will pass by Kent?"

The man chuckled.

"They all do, girl, if they're going any distance at all," he said. "Ain't no other way to go."

Neve gave up.

"Thank you," she said between clenched teeth, "for your assistance."

"No trouble atall," the man said amiably.

One at a time Neve approached the loading merchants. The first snapped brusquely that he had no room for passengers. The second told her, more politely, that he never took passengers at all. The third informed Neve that he was going only a short distance downriver on a special commission, and her odds of catching another barge there were poor. Neve began to suspect that her entire journey was cursed. Was this her father's idea of a joke?

"Eh, miss?"

Neve turned to find a tall, lanky man leaning against one of the dock posts, smoking a pipe and watching her with apparent interest.

"You say you're looking to ride a barge to Kent?" he asked.

"Yes, I am," Neve said warily. "Do you know of one?"

"Aye, the *Skipper,* right there," he drawled, gesturing with his pipe at a barge where Neve could see no activity at all taking place. "She's mine. We're bound for Kent. We got room for you if you want. We'll be leaving first light tomorrow."

"Wonderful," Neve said relievedly. "How much do you want for passage?"

The man looked her up and down.

"Three gold," he said.

"Three—" Neve said, outraged. "That's ridiculous!"

The man shrugged amiably.

"Looks like you ain't got a lot of choices, though," he said, grinning. "Well, if that's too much, guess you ain't interested, eh?" He turned away and walked back toward the *Skipper*.

"Wait!" Neve swallowed. "Listen. I—I don't have any gold, not unless I can get gold for the horse and mule. But I'll pay you in silver, Caistran silver."

The man turned back, shaking his head pityingly.

"Girl, local silver ain't no good on the river. Ten, twenty leagues downriver, nobody knows who's adulterated their coin and how much. You won't find a captain who'll deal in aught but gold or gems."

Gems! Neve hurriedly rummaged in her pack and pulled a ruby out of the pouch.

"Here, then," she said, holding the gem out. "What about this?"

The man took the gem, eyeing it critically. He grinned slowly, exposing yellowed teeth. Neve fought the instinct to cringe away.

"Right, then," he said, chuckling. "You've got passage, girl." He glanced up at Neve. "I can't give you no change for this, though, till we reach Kent and I sell my cargo."

Neve shrugged.

"Where am I going to spend it in between?" she said practically.

The man started to tuck the ruby into his pocket, but Neve shook her head firmly, holding out her hand.

"When we leave," she said.

For a moment she thought the man might refuse; after a long moment, however, he handed the gem back reluctantly.

"Be here before first light or we sail without you," he warned. "The river don't wait, and neither do I."

"I'll be there," Neve said grimly. Her only possible ride? She'd be there, all right.

The first step was to sell her horse and mule. Several peasants gave her conflicting directions, but at last she found "Pickerd at the north end," a farm with a goodly number of horses and mules in pens and on pickets. Neve was hardly surprised when the owner came out of his house and she recognized the very man she'd mistaken for the wharfmaster not long before. And she was hardly surprised by the ridiculously low price she was offered for the animals; he already knew she had to sell, and quickly.

What Pickerd hadn't reckoned on, however, was Neve's temper.

"Never mind," she said shortly. "I wouldn't sell you the dirt off my shoe for two gold. They're worth ten times that"—at least her father had said so, and he should know—"and you know it."

Pickerd chuckled in that infuriating, indolent way.

"Well, lass, I'm the only one in the market for horses," he said. "And they ain't going to let you take them aboard a barge."

"I'm aware of that," Neve said icily, looking him straight in the eye. "But I don't like being tricked and played with, and I'll damned well *give* them to the first beggar in the streets before I'll be cheated by you, too, sir."

She must have looked angry enough to do it, too, because Pickerd looked rather alarmed—and well he might, Neve reflected; her father took pride in his magic, and the horse and mule were fine animals.

"No need to be so prickly, lass," he said hurriedly. "I'd never had it said about town that I was mean enough to cheat a pretty child like you."

Half an hour later Neve pocketed her thirty gold pieces. She briefly considered calling up some sort of misfortune for Pickerd—dry rot for his rafters or maybe woodworms in the barn—but her pride in her successful bargaining outweighed her annoyance, and she decided it wasn't worth the trouble. She walked back into town smiling smugly.

Her smile, however, didn't last long. She quickly learned that Selwaer, despite its river traffic, had nothing like the inns Neve had heard about, and the few rooms for rent were already occupied. The best she could find was a choice between a pallet on the floor in a room with three others, or a hay-filled barn loft to herself. Remembering Mora's snores, Neve chose took the barn loft, not even quibbling over the additional silver for a bath and another for the privilege of having the back room with the tub to herself for half an hour. It was only money, after all, and she had plenty more.

A bath, a bowl of vegetable soup, and a piece of hard

bread later, Neve curled up in her surprisingly comfortable hay bed, trying to ignore the noise and smell of the animals below, moderately pleased with herself. It was nasty outside the Keep, worse than she'd supposed, but she was managing, and she'd continue to manage.

She was her father's daughter, after all.

3

"**N**O CABINS?" NEVE REPEATED, DIS-
believingly. "What do you mean, no cabins?"
Captain Warten chuckled in that conde-
scending manner Neve already found intolerable.

"Miss, don't know what you were expecting, but this is a
plain cargo barge, not some nobleman's luxury transport.
There's a shallow hold below for the cargo. Most of the men
hang their sling beds there rather than sleep on deck and risk
the weather. You're welcome to do the same, or doss on top
of the crates if you like, but I wouldn't recommend the floor;
there's always a little water, and there's rats about, too.
There's a tiny little galley aft, and there's my cabin forward.
Unless you want to share that, that is." He chuckled again
in a way Neve found distinctly disagreeable.

She did not even dignify that last comment with a reply.
If the men slept below, then she'd most certainly sleep on
deck. The sky was clear and the temperature pleasant anyway, and it was only a couple days to Kent.

After considerable weighing of her options, Neve had
picked a spot up against the galley wall that seemed slightly
sheltered, and there was even a thick coil of rope she could
use for a makeshift pillow; when she started to lay out her
pallet, however, a voice said, "Wouldn't do that."

Neve whirled, saw nobody, then realized that the voice had come from above and behind her. She whirled again and saw a slender figure sitting on the galley roof, gazing down at her with unmistakable amusement. For a moment annoyance almost made her turn away again; then she got a better look at the speaker and curiosity replaced some of her anger.

He was short, not much taller than Neve herself, and slender, unlike the other burly sailors who manned the barge, although his wiry muscles spoke of hidden strength and agility. He was darkly sun-browned, and his teeth were startlingly white in his face. His brown hair was bleached pale by the sun and indifferently pulled back into a tail behind his head, his features angular and pleasant rather than handsome, and his eyes were an unusually dark blue, but strangely slit-pupiled like a cat's.

What drew Neve's stare, however, was his feet.

His feet were hands.

No, not hands exactly, although the digits were long and probably able to grasp and hold, and although the most inward digit was obviously a sort of thumb. She'd seen such extremities before, but only on monkeys in the hot jungle pocket worlds of the Keep, never on a man. Not that she'd seen that many men.

"Passing strange, aren't they?" The man chuckled, and Neve hurriedly forced her gaze away, flushing hotly, humiliated that he'd caught her rudely gaping at his deformity.

"Pardon me," she said stiffly. "I didn't mean to stare."

The man shrugged and hopped down from the galley roof.

"Doesn't matter," he said. "Everyone stares." He held out a hand. "Ash."

Neve noted the grimy condition of the hand with some distaste, but took it gingerly; it was the least she could do after her poor manners.

"Neve," she said.

The hand was withdrawn after a cursory shake; Neve suppressed an urge to wipe her own hand on her trousers.

"Well, Neve, you don't want to flop there," Ash told her, his eyes sparkling. "It don't get much traffic now, but come dusk you're going to have sailors stepping back and forth over you and yanking that rope out from under your head.

They're going to tie up ashore tonight, and that's one of the anchor ropes.''

"Oh." Neve hurriedly picked up her pallet, then hesitated. "Ashore? I thought they sailed through the night."

Ash nodded.

"Usually they do," he said. "That's how I got hired on—got great eyes, especially at night, so I'm good for night lookout. But Captain thinks one of the brandy casks down in cargo's got a slow leak, so we'll tie up, move everything around, find the guilty cask, see if we can plug it. Find it fast, and if it can be plugged, we might move on tonight, but I don't figure that to happen."

"Oh," Neve said again, grimacing. A night ashore would certainly lengthen the journey, especially at the slow pace of the heavy barge.

"Don't look so glum." Ash chuckled. "Captain Warten's type generally manages to find at least one leaky cask whenever he carries brandy. He'll likely say it can't be plugged, just pour it off into skins and share it out, and then we'll have a jolly supper ashore. Anyway, at least you can sleep on dry ground tonight."

Well, there was that. Neve rolled her pallet and tied it securely.

"First time on the water?" Ash asked, leaning casually against the galley wall.

Neve bit her lip, stifling her irritation at his prying. Shifty as this fellow looked, he was by far the least disagreeable person she'd met since she left home.

"Yes," she said shortly. "How could you tell?"

Ash chuckled.

"It shows," he said. "Just leave it at that. Most drylanders'd be hanging over the rail by now, though, puking up yesterday's breakfast. Good for you that you've got a tough stomach."

Neve briefly considered asking the sailor whether he'd ever stood on a beach strewn with dragon entrails and kept his breakfast down, but suppressed the impulse.

"Thank you," she said at last, choosing to take his words as a rather crude compliment.

Ash laughed again, then turned away and swarmed up the rigging like a monkey up a vine, and Neve lost some of her irritation in marveling at his feet once more. It *was* rather clever of him, to have chosen a trade that turned his strange feet into an advantage.

There was little else for Neve to do but watch as the day wore on. She shifted from one spot to another, trying to get out of the way of the rude sailors who simply pushed her aside as they went about her business. At last she climbed rather clumsily up to Ash's galley-roof vantage point. She felt her skin burning under the sun, but stayed where she was; a single short visit to the hold earlier in the day had convinced her that the dank and foul-smelling space below-decks, so shallow that Neve could barely stand upright, was far better suited to the vermin inhabiting it than to her. Despite the heat of the sun, Neve liked sitting on deck and watching the sailors work, watching the world pass by at the slow, steady pace of the river. As she'd told her mother, she found value in simply sitting and looking, and here there were endless new things to see. She put on the stylish leather cap she'd paid most of her thirty gold pieces for (the matching gloves and shoes were in her pack), uncorked the skin of excellent wine she'd spent the *rest* of the thirty gold on, and settled herself comfortably.

Around noon the cook came out of his galley and passed around mugs of ale and surprisingly tasty meat pies. Neve claimed her share and returned to the galley roof; not long after she climbed up, Ash joined her, dropping down from the rigging.

"Been watching you," he said without preamble. "You're an odd bit, aren't you? Most passengers—not that Warten takes many—come in groups, or if they don't, they pester the crew. You just sit there alone, though."

"I didn't come aboard for companionship," Neve said, shrugging. "I like being alone." She hoped the sailor would take the hint, but he didn't, only grinning and biting into his pie. Thankfully, however, he didn't press her for further conversation, and Neve was able to ignore his presence and resume her pastime of watching the sailors, watching the river, watching the land pass by.

Ash drew her attention when he jumped to his feet, brushing crumbs off his trousers.

"You're a quiet little thing," he said rather approvingly,

and without further ado jumped from the galley roof and returned to his duties.

The sun sank slowly. Neve's reddened skin stung, but she ignored it. She'd sat just as motionless on the beach many times, watching crabs or anemones, and by morning the burn had always faded, leaving her skin as pale as ever. She watched the sun dip down over the trees. The sailors drew in fish lines she hadn't noticed them casting; judging from the catch, Neve looked forward to plentiful fish for dinner.

Toward sunset, true to Ash's prediction, Captain Warten ordered the barge turned to the shore. They drew closer to the wooded shoreline, closer—then the barge jolted as anchor lines were cast and pulled tight. Neve sat unmoving, watching the sailors scramble about securing the ship. A long bridge of rope and boards was unrolled, stretched between ship and shore, and secured; other sailors brought up casks from the hold, probably looking for the leak.

Neve jumped down from her perch when there was a clear path to the shore and disembarked. There were any number of good sites where the sailors might choose to make their camp, and she saw no harm in picking her own spot first. She found a hollow at the base of a large tree just big enough for her pallet, far from any likely location the others might choose.

The men came ashore one or two at a time, carrying food, blankets, and a cask that Neve supposed was the brandy. She wasn't surprised. Judging from what she'd seen of the sailors, she imagined that any excuse to broach a cask of brandy was good enough. She'd be lucky if they didn't find a new leaky cask every evening. The prospect of a night ashore was considerably dampened by the idea of spending it within earshot of drunken sailors who were certainly loutish enough when sober.

When she smelled the cook fire, however, Neve abandoned her self-imposed exile and wandered over. The cook was stirring what appeared to be a very thick and chunky fish stew that smelled dismayingly bland.

''I've got some spices,'' she offered rather awkwardly, wondering whether she should have said anything at all. Mother tended to get prickly whenever Neve or her father suggested that her cooking could be improved upon.

"Huh?" The cook, a burly fellow with truly horrible teeth and even nastier breath, glanced up. "What's that?"

"I said, I've got spices," Neve said, embarrassed now. "Some would be good with the fish. You're welcome to use them, or I could—I mean—"

The fellow's eyes narrowed, and Neve was certain now that she'd offended him, but he only sat back on his heels, gesturing at the pot.

"Do what you want," he said.

Most of the crew had debarked from the ship and gathered in the camp by the time Neve had finished seasoning the stew; she was less than surprised when they hung back, swigging their brandy, plainly expecting her to eat the first bowl. Well, that suited her fine. She ladled out a generous bowl, accepted a hunk of bread from the cook, and settled herself at the edge of the cleared area, eating as quickly as good manners would allow. She didn't observe when the others helped themselves from the pot, but by the time she'd finished her meal they were deep into their own bowls, their rude grunts and lip-smacking the only thanks or compliments Neve seemed likely to receive.

To her surprise, however, Captain Warten filled his bowl a second time and walked over, sitting down beside her.

"You got a good hand at a cook fire," he said, swigging from a mug that smelled of brandy. " 'S good to have a hidden talent." He gave Neve a look just short of a leer. "Got any others?"

Neve felt ice flow through her blood.

"Nothing worth mentioning," she said flatly.

"Mmmm. I figured maybe otherwise." Captain Warten was still watching her rather closely. "I mean, ain't many bits who can throw around rubies for boat passage. Don't figure you came by that kind of money cooking."

Neve ground her teeth.

"Maybe I'm just a *very good* cook," she said as coldly as she could.

Captain Warten chuckled.

"Well, seeing that you've made such a dashed good living," he said, "I expect you can afford a little increase in the price of travel."

The ice had seeped into Neve's stomach.

"What," she said slowly, "are you talking about?"

Captain Warten shrugged.

"Costs go up," he said. "Having to stop here tonight, it slows us down, cuts our profits—"

"That's hardly *my* fault," Neve snapped. "I didn't touch your leaky barrel."

The captain shrugged again.

"Got to recoup our costs," he said. "I figure if you got rubies to throw around, stands to reason you can afford a little more."

Neve's eyes narrowed further.

"You still owe me change from the ruby I gave you," she said. "You quoted me a price of three gold pieces. That ruby's worth at least ten—"

"More like twenty," Captain Warten said idly. "Burket, one of my boys, he knows a bit about gems."

"Fine," Neve said through clenched teeth. "Twenty. Nevertheless you quoted me a price of three—"

Captain Warten grinned.

"We're still a long ways from Kent," he said. "Fancy walking the rest of the way?"

Neve took a deep breath, forcing down the anger that would serve no purpose at the moment. It wasn't the money; she had gems aplenty and could make more if she liked. It was the sheer gall of this rude unwashed lout sitting here and baldly extorting money from *her*, Neve, daughter of the Guardian of the Crystal Keep and heir to all its power. Why, she could—

She could—

Neve smiled slowly, a cold smile.

"Fine," she said. "You needn't give me the change you owed me. Paying my fare six times over should certainly cover any . . . increase in your costs."

Captain Warten chuckled again, sitting back and gazing at her amusedly.

"Don't guess you've quite taken my point, girl," he said, glancing at a point somewhere over Neve's shoulder. "But let's see if I can make it clearer."

Suddenly a pair of steel-hard hands clamped over her arms, hoisting her roughly to her feet. Neve gasped and grabbed for her knife, but her wrists were immediately wrenched painfully upward behind her back. Neve understood the unspoken message quite clearly and immediately stopped her struggles, but the iron grasp eased only slightly. She did not turn to look at her captor, but kept her eyes on Captain Warten.

"What I figure," Captain Warten said, smiling lazily, "is we'll just have a look at how much you can afford to pay, and then we'll talk about the price. Eh, men?"

"Aye, Cap'n," someone said behind her, and this time Neve did look around, hoping against hope that someone would intervene. Sometime during their discussion most of the crew had gathered around them. There were only a couple still by the fire, watching—the little fellow, Ash, was there. He glanced at Neve, shrugged indifferently, and turned back to the fire, dishing up another bowl of fish.

Rough hands groped over Neve's body, finding her purse at her belt, and in her tunic, the little pouch of rubies she'd hidden in her breastband.

"What've we got here?" Captain Warten said, opening the little pouch. He dumped the contents out in his hand, poking through the rubies. "Now, this is more like it, girl."

He poured the rubies back into the pouch and shoved it into his shirt, then opened the purse, spilling out the coins. He scowled, tossing the purse aside.

"Ten pieces of silver? That's all?"

Neve said nothing. By dint of holding carefully still otherwise, perfectly passive in her captor's grip, she'd managed very slowly to work her hand down near the hilt of her dagger. Just a little more—

"Ten pieces of silver?" Captain Warten repeated suspiciously. "That's what you had when—"

There!

Neve flicked the dagger upward, cutting lightly at the hands trapping her arms. There was a howl behind her, then a gurgling moan that choked off abruptly; the hands holding her loosened and fell away.

Neve whirled, slashing out wildly with the dagger, but the men danced back, glancing at their fallen comrade. Neve, furious beyond all thought, pursued, stabbing, slashing—

Then something hard crashed into the back of her head,

and Neve embraced hard earth, watching the deadly dagger falling toward her, falling, falling . . .

But the darkness came to claim her before she saw it land.

Murmur of voices. Darkness, but this time it was the darkness of night. There was a glow of firelight somewhere off to Neve's left, but she could not manage to focus her eyes, and turning her head sent a series of earthshaking explosions through her skull. Neve stifled a moan and lay still, assessing her injuries. Besides the ache in her head, one eye was swollen almost shut, her lips felt huge and sore, and her entire body felt bruised, as badly as the time she'd fallen out of a seaside tree and rolled all the way down the rocky slope. Had those sailor scum actually beaten or kicked her while she was unconscious? Probably.

Her hands were bound behind her, connected by a short rope to her bound ankles; a brief experimental movement indicated that she was tied *to* something as well, maybe a tree or root. Her clothes were torn, but she still had her trousers more or less on; she hoped that meant that at least she hadn't been raped. But the pain and wetness at the back of her right knee, the emptiness in her soul where the Nexus had once been, testified to a worse injury.

The crystal. They'd taken the crystal.

"I say kill 'er now," a cold voice asserted. Neve didn't recognize the voice. "Dorn's dead. Kill her and leave her."

"Killing's too good," another voice said. "I say we cut her up. Slow."

"That's stupid." This time Neve recognized the voice; it was that little fellow with the strange feet. Ash.

"Stupid?" Captain Warten was the speaker this time. "We got her piddling silver, we got the gems. What use have we got for the girl now?" He chuckled. " 'Cept maybe one, and after what she did to Dorn, don't know as I'd value her much for that. She's a strange-looking little bit, anyway, even when she wasn't so knocked around. So what's the use in keeping her?"

"You've got the rubies," Ash said patiently. "You've got the big diamond, and you've got ten silver pieces. But what if that isn't all she had?"

"What?"

"You said she sold a horse and a mule, and you said they looked like quality animals—that's why you first thought she might be rich, even before you saw the ruby. So where's the money from the horse and mule?"

Silence; a few mumbles.

"She spent one night in town. Now, Pickerd would've paid forty gold for a horse good enough to be a nobleman's mount—"

That lying, cheating scum—

"—and probably another ten for a high-quality mule, and another ten or fifteen for good tack—"

To think it was too much trouble to put dry rot in his wood!

"So where's the money?"

Silence again. Then Captain Warten spoke up.

"Oh, what's the difference?" he said impatiently. "We got the rubies, we got the big diamond. Next to that, a few gold don't matter none."

Ash sighed patiently.

"Captain, if she's managed to hide sixty pieces of gold, who's to say that's all she hid?"

"Maybe she swallowed it." Somebody chuckled. "I wouldn't object to cutting her open to find out."

"Of course," Ash said sarcastically. "She *swallowed* sixty gold pieces. She hid it somewhere, you idiot. She came ashore before the rest of us and she stashed it somewhere. And why would she bother to hide sixty gold pieces but leave rubies on her person for us to find? That means she's got something even more valuable, probably."

"Fine," Captain Warten said indifferently. "You think so, *you* bring her around and try to get something out of her. Maybe she'll bite you and *you'll* drop dead. But I'll tell you, you better do it fast, son. Come sunrise, we pull anchor, and damme if I'm leaving that poisonous little bit alive when I do."

Mutters of agreement, then the voices seemed to retreat. Gurgle of liquid being poured, clink of mugs; then the voices, more distant now, got louder. Sudden rustling nearby, very close; Neve grudgingly opened her eyes and found herself staring at the widest pair of boots she'd ever seen.

"Well, you're in a bit of a mess, aren't you?" Ash said mildly, crouching down. "They all want you dead for killing

Dorn. Can't say I blame you, as you'd probably have been in for a jolly tumble with the lot of them if you hadn't done it, and then they'd probably have just killed you anyway afterward. Still, I wouldn't want to be in your place.''

"Save yourself some trouble," Neve rasped out hoarsely. "There isn't any gold hidden. I spent it on a cap, gloves, slippers, and some very nice wine."

Ash shrugged.

"I'd watch saying that," he said mildly. "Right now it's about all that's keeping you alive."

Neve cleared her throat.

"Why do you care?" she spat.

Ash was silent for a moment.

"I'm a fair-to-middling sailor," he said at last. "I was once a damned good thief. But I ain't no murderer."

Neve heard the scrape as a knife was drawn from a sheath and decided almost numbly that the strange fellow was at least going to spare her a much nastier death at the hands of the crew; to her amazement, however, she felt the knife cut carefully, surreptitiously, at the rope binding her wrists.

"Stay still," Ash muttered. "Don't move till the others go to sleep. Won't be long now; they're deep into that cask of brandy. You can creep off easy enough then, get a good start by dawn. They won't bother trying to track you far."

Neve might have been surprised, even grateful, had her head not throbbed so miserably. She wondered whether it was the blow on the head or the absence of the Nexus's familiar presence that ailed her.

Yes, she could creep away. She'd have nothing but the torn clothes on her body, no knife, no money—nothing. She could probably make it back upriver to Selwaer. She might—*might*—be able to find somebody to take her back to the Crystal Keep for a promised reward; legends about the Keep were tempting enough that someone could probably be persuaded.

Then she could return to her father and tell him she'd failed.

"What's the captain giving you?" she rasped.

Ash had stood up; now he glanced down at her.

"Hmm?" he said absently.

"How much," Neve said more slowly, "is the captain giving you out of what he took from me?"

Ash shrugged.

"One of the rubies," he said. "I'm not rightly part of the crew; I just joined up to get from Selwaer to Kent, where I could sign on with one of the big ships, so I wasn't rightly entitled to a share. But after I found that diamond back of your knee, the captain said he'd cut me in for one of the rubies."

Neve stifled a surge of anger.

"I can give you more," she said. "Gems, I mean."

Ash slowly squatted down again.

"You *have* got more?" he said. "Hid them somewhere around, I suppose?"

Neve shook her head; the ground reeled under her and she instantly regretted the motion.

"Not hidden," she said. "Made. By magic."

Ash scowled dubiously.

"Made?"

"I made all the rubies in that pouch," Neve told him. "I can make more. As many as I want."

Ash raised an eyebrow.

"If you're such a mage," he said, "how come you're still tied here? Why haven't you magicked them all dead or you far away?"

"I'm not—" Neve considered. "The diamond, the one from the back of my leg. I need that to work my magic. It's like a focus-stone. I can't do the magic without it."

"Not a proper mage, then, eh?" Ash said, shaking his head. "Well, if the magic's in the stone, what's to stop us making rubies for ourselves?"

Finally fear—Neve couldn't imagine what might happen if one of these louts tried to tap into the power of the Nexus.

"You can't use it," she said, hoping fervently it was true. "Nobody can use it but me. You wouldn't have the faintest idea how to try, even, would you?"

"That's true," Ash admitted. "And why should I believe *you* can do anything with it, either?"

"I can prove it," Neve said quickly. "I made things with it—the rubies in the pouch—"

"They're just rubies. That doesn't prove anything."

"The knife," Neve said. "The one that killed that fellow with one cut. It's magical—"

Ash shrugged again.

"Proves nothing. Could've been a clever poison."

Neve racked her brain frantically. Then—

"The purse," she said.

"Hmm?"

"The purse," she repeated. "The one the silver pieces were in. Captain Warten dropped it on the ground. Is it still there?"

Ash stood, walking away. Neve thought desperately that he'd simply abandoned her, but after a moment the wide boots returned and Ash squatted down again. The purse was in his hands.

"So?" he said, inspecting the purse critically. "What about it?"

"Open it," Neve said.

Ash gazed at her steadily a moment, then opened the purse. He stared down into it silently, then gazed at Neve again.

"There's silver in there," he said slowly. "But I saw Warten take it all out."

"Ten pieces," Neve said. "Take them out and close the purse again."

Slowly Ash obeyed, tucking the silver absently into his sleeve.

"Now open it again."

Ash opened the purse. His eyebrows raised.

"Magic," he murmured. "A magic purse."

"That's *nothing,* " Neve said quickly. "I just wanted silver I could spend without arousing suspicion. But I made those rubies for emergency money. I can make more, as much as I want. As much as you want."

Ash was silent for a long moment.

"In exchange for what?" he said slowly. "I already cut you loose."

"I can't make any rubies," Neve said patiently, "without the diamond. I need it back. Steal me back the diamond, and my dagger and gear"—she considered, then decided—"and see me safe to Kent, and I'll give you a ruby for every day it takes to get there."

Ash squatted there silently, staring at her, for a long moment. At last he nodded brusquely.

"Done," he said. "Don't try to creep off on your own, then. Stay still till I come for you. Got it?"

"Absolutely," Neve said grimly. That would pose no difficulty. Her entire body ached, not to mention her head. She was far from sure she could move at all.

Ash rose and his boots disappeared again. Neve sighed and lowered her head to the ground, closing her eyes. Her feet were numb, but her newly freed hands tingled painfully with returning sensation. She ached *everywhere*, and she could feel insects crawling into her clothes. Her skin stung and burned from the day's sun, and her head throbbed sickly.

Father, when I tell Mother about what's happened to me on this journey you wanted me to make, she's going to flay the skin off your bones, Guardian or not, and make herself a new hearth rug out of it. And when I'm Guardian I'll—why couldn't you have taught me some magic? Maybe something useful, like healing myself?

Despite her discomfort she fell into an uneasy doze; she woke to the faintest moonlight and the sound of footsteps approaching. Ash crouched beside her again, and this time his knife cut through the ropes binding her ankles.

"Right," he said. "Up. We're gone."

Neve pushed herself to her feet, then nearly fell again. Ash swore.

"Stay quiet, will you?" he hissed. "Do you want the lot of them waking up? What's the matter with you?"

"What do you think?" Neve whispered furiously. "My feet are *numb*."

Ash muttered an oath and pulled Neve's arm over his shoulder, then futilely tried to find a way to fit his bundles under his free arm.

"Wait," Neve whispered. "Give me the crys—the diamond."

Ash glanced at her, scowling.

"Later," he said.

"*Now*," Neve said flatly. "If you think I'm going to run off, keep the purse, keep the rubies—I'm sure you took them, too. Just give me back the diamond. I'm not moving without it."

Ash cursed under his breath, but fished the crystal out of his tunic, handing it over. Neve clenched it tightly in her hand, feeling the presence of the Nexus wash through her once more. She tucked it securely into her breastband.

"I can carry some of the load," she whispered. "Just help me walk."

With one of the sack straps looped over her shoulder and one over Ash's, Ash's arm around her waist and her arm over his shoulder, they walked slowly, painfully slowly, out of the camp. Neve couldn't see much; she could only follow Ash's lead and hope his night vision was as good as he'd said. Sensation quickly returned to her feet, agonizing hot prickles, but she bit her lip and kept moving, kept silent. She was the heir to the Crystal Keep, child of the Nexus. Nothing, *nothing* would master her—not this ridiculous test her father asked of her, not a dozen drunken loutish sailors, and certainly not her wretched *feet*. At last Ash paused, straining his ears.

"Nobody's coming," he muttered. "Guess we got away clean." He dropped his sack, slid out from under Neve's arm. "Sit," he said, gesturing at a log.

Neve frowned.

"Shouldn't we go further," she said slowly, "before we—"

"Shut up," Ash said shortly. "Sit."

Neve sat, swallowing an angry protest. Then she stifled another protest as Ash bent over her, roughly yanking her boots off. To her amazement, he knelt before her, rubbing her left foot briskly, then the right. Neve yelped at the extremely unpleasant sensation.

"Shut up," Ash repeated, continuing his rough massage. At last he shoved her boots back on. "Better?"

Neve nodded, not trusting her voice to answer. When Ash shouldered one sack, she stood, taking the other. Without another word, Ash set off again into the darkness and Neve followed. His vision must have been as good as he'd said; she had to hurry to keep up, but she didn't complain. If a monkey-footed mortal could travel at such a pace, *she* certainly could.

After some time, however, Neve abruptly realized that she could no longer hear the river.

"Wait," she said. "Aren't we following the river?"

Ash stopped.

"No," he said impatiently. "We've been heading east, away from the Little Brother. Warten and the others will be following the river, so obviously we won't want to."

"You said they wouldn't bother coming after us," Neve reminded him.

"They won't," Ash said shortly. "They'll be following the *Skipper*. I cut the anchor ropes. She'll probably ground half a league south; there's shallows there. But that'll keep them busy until we're long gone, and then they'll have to hurry south or lose a lot of their profit. And the revenge won't be worth the time lost. That's why I *didn't* take the damned rubies."

Neve gaped, struck silent. For the first time it occurred to her that she might have made a very, very lucky choice—albeit possibly a dangerous one—in buying this man's service. His greed was obviously tempered by a very canny wit.

"You left the rubies?" she repeated. That meant that until she could make more, the only money she owned was the silver in the purse—which Ash still held.

"You said you could make more," Ash said mildly. "And I'll take my pay every day, by the way. And if you don't—" He shrugged. "I'll take the diamond instead."

"The only way you'll take that," Neve said coldly, "is from my dead hand."

Ash shrugged again.

"If you prefer," he said.

He was *threatening* her! Her!

"If you had any idea who you're dealing with—" Neve said, her voice shaking with anger.

"I know I'm dealing with a rich bit stupid enough to flash high-priced horseflesh and gemstones on a public wharf in front of strangers and agree to a passage fee five times what any idiot would pay," Ash said flatly. "But I've seen the knife and the rubies and the purse. Those things and the fact that so far you've had the sense to keep your eyes open and your mouth shut is all that's keeping me from leaving you here and now. So I'd advise you to start moving your feet instead of your lips if you want to get to Kent." With that, he turned and strode off into the darkness again.

Shaking with anger, Neve picked up her sack and followed.

By the time Ash stopped and dropped his pack again, her anger had gradually faded, replaced by utter exhaustion. Her bruised body still ached and her battered head throbbed wretchedly with a sick pain that made her want to vomit. As furious as she'd been with Ash earlier, now she could muster only a dim gratitude when he pulled two blankets out of his sack, tossing one to her.

"Get a little sleep," he said shortly. "We'll have a hard day's walk tomorrow and I want an early start."

Wordlessly Neve wrapped the blanket around her and curled up against the base of a tree; despite the hard ground, despite her discomfort, she was asleep almost instantly.

Neve woke slowly, grudgingly. Her entire body was one huge ache, dwarfed only by the positively *gargantuan* pain in her head. She was cold and stiff from sleeping on the hard ground in the spring-night chill. She smelled something, a cooking sort of smell, and, groaning, raised her head.

Ash was squatting beside a tiny fire, stirring something in a small pot. He glanced at her and dipped some dark liquid from the pot, thrusting the cup at her.

"Drink that," he said.

Neve slowly forced herself up to a sitting position, accepting the cup. The warmth in her hands, the smell of the hot liquid was wonderful. She glanced upward. Although the morning chill still lingered, the sun was high; surely it couldn't be earlier than midmorning.

"I thought you wanted an early start," she rasped.

Ash grunted, dipping out a cup of the hot liquid for himself.

"Looked like you needed the sleep," he said, shrugging. "If you fall down in a faint on me, I ain't carrying you to Kent on my back."

Neve tentatively sipped the liquid in the cup, immediately making a face at the horrible bitterness.

"That's *awful*," she gasped. "What is it?"

Ash chuckled.

"It's *cai*," he said. "Expensive stuff, that—imported all the way from Bregond. Drink it. It'll put you on your feet."

He tossed something at her; reflexively, she caught it. It was a skewer of some kind of fish. "Eat up."

Neve forced down the hot, bitter liquid; it tasted awful but the heat of it was marvelous, and by the end of the cup she found that the taste had grown more tolerable, strangely satisfying. Ash was right; it woke her up fast and even drove some of the ache from her head and limbs. The fish was dry and bland and overcooked, but she said nothing; it was better than dried meat and hard bread, and that's what she would have gotten if Ash hadn't woken up early to catch, clean, and cook their breakfast.

Ash finished his breakfast before her. He kicked dirt over the fire and bundled up their pallets without a word, handing one pack to Neve as soon as she finished.

"Let's go," he said shortly. "It's a long walk to Kent."

"Wait," Neve said. "Let me change my clothes, at least. I had a spare set in my pack."

Ash shrugged.

"Didn't bring 'em."

"*What?*" Neve choked disbelievingly. She threw down her pack and rifled it frantically. Not only were her clothes gone, so was most of her gear—her other pots and pans, her spare boots, her utensils, her wine, even—oh, gods—then she sighed when her fingers closed around the pack of her cooking spices. That and her grimoire were almost all that was left of the gear her mother had made her. She rounded on Ash furiously.

"My gear," she ground out. "You left most of my gear behind."

Ash raised an eyebrow.

"Look, girl, you got neither horse nor mule here," he said. "You can't carry twice your weight in luxuries. For the weight of one extra pan, we can carry a good bit of food. We got what the two of us can carry and still make good time. You want to go back and ask Warten and his men nicely for your pretty underthings, you go right ahead."

He pulled a scrap of cloth out of his pack and gestured vaguely at her.

"Push your trousers up," he said. "I'll wrap your leg. I can see it bled during the night. Unless you're mage enough to heal it?" He added that last almost mockingly, and despite her fury Neve could see why; she was bruised and battered, and if she'd had any healing magic, quite obviously she'd have used it before this. Not trusting her voice, she pushed her trouser leg up and let Ash bandage it neatly.

"I guess it doesn't need stitching," he said, "which is a good thing, as I've never done it and don't have a needle nor thread." He glanced at her. "You planning on sticking that diamond back in there?"

"No," Neve said shortly. If Ash had thought to search there, others probably would, too. She shivered a little, wondering where else the sailors might have searched while she was unconscious.

She didn't ask Ash.

"Best not," Ash agreed. "I wouldn't swallow it, either, not unless you want to poke through the chamber pot for it later. You really want to sew that thing into you, find a place it won't make a lump." He raised an eyebrow, sweeping Neve's body briefly with his eyes. "I could probably suggest somewhere."

"No, thank you," Neve said from between gritted teeth. "If *you* know where it is, there isn't much point in hiding it, is there?"

"There's that," Ash agreed, apparently unoffended. He stood, shouldering his pack. "Let's go."

Neve slung her own pack over her shoulder and yelped, dropping it immediately. She touched her shoulders disbelievingly, then stared at her forearms, seeing what her bleariness and confusion had made her miss earlier. Her skin was bright red, blistered in spots, and excruciatingly sensitive. She couldn't see her face, but judging from the hot tightness over her cheeks and nose, that skin, too, had suffered a like fate.

"What's the matter?" Ash said mildly.

Neve gritted her teeth. She didn't want to tell him that she'd sat out in the sun all day on deck the day before because she'd blindly assumed that her sunburn would simply fade away as it always had back home in the Crystal Keep. She couldn't explain to Ash why she'd made such an assumption, and he'd only laugh at her for being too stupid to get in out of the sun. And she'd dive into the mouth of a swamp-fell before she'd give this scruffy mortal an excuse to laugh at her. She shouldered her pack carefully, gritting her teeth against the pain.

"Nothing's the matter, Ash," she said shortly.

Neve followed Ash silently through the woods all morning, wondering how he found his way. The river was out of hearing, of course, and there were no stars or particular landmarks . . . after a while Neve supposed he was following the position of the sun, making allowances for the changes as the day progressed. Or maybe he'd just been here before and knew his way.

"Where were you born?" she said suddenly.

Ash glanced rather irritably over his shoulder.

"What's it to you?" he said.

Neve shrugged, refusing to be intimidated by the surly fellow.

"Dellhaven," he said briefly at last, leaving it at that.

"I don't know where that is," Neve said.

"Capital city in Arawen, east of Agrond," Ash said grudgingly. He glanced over his shoulder again. "You?"

Neve ignored the question.

"Why are your feet and eyes like that?" she asked. "Were you born that way?"

This time Ash stopped in his tracks, scowling.

"You're paying me to get you to Kent," he said flatly, "not answer your damned questions."

"For a ruby a day," Neve said sourly, "you should do both and polish my boots, too."

"Well, pardon me, Your Highness," Ash said sarcastically, sweeping an exaggerated bow. "I guess you should've put that in the agreement when you made it." He turned and stalked off through the underbrush; Neve, gaping and frozen in surprise, had to run to catch up. She was so angry that she thought sourly, *It's probably a good thing he's still got my knife right now, or I'd stick it in his back.*

And speaking of that—

"I want my knife back," she said.

Ash stopped again.

"What?" he said impatiently.

"I said," Neve said deliberately, "I want my knife back. And my purse. That *was* in the agreement."

"You're right. It was." He shrugged. "Later."

"Now," Neve insisted.

"Later." Ash grinned. "Maybe when I see you're going to pay me like you promised. Or maybe when we get to Kent." He turned and walked off again.

This time Neve was too furious to reply; she simply strode after him, venting her anger in activity, charging blithely through thickets even Ash skirted, occasionally dashing ahead and waiting for him to catch up.

Neve thought they might stop at midday, but Ash continued on, probably because of their late start that morning. She felt no inclination to object despite her bruised body, aching head, and feet to match. The sooner they got to Kent, the sooner she'd be rid of her infuriating guide, the sooner she'd make her way to Zaravelle and then home again.

Besides, she'd rot in a swamp-fell's stomach before she'd let this lout think she couldn't keep up with him.

By late afternoon, however, Neve had begun to regret her initial burst of energy. Her feet hurt abominably, her headache was worse, and for some reason her legs itched furiously. She kept stubbornly quiet, however, until Ash stopped near sunset beside a small stream to refill their waterskins. While he accomplished this, Neve ducked behind a bush and cautiously pulled the legs of her trousers above her low boot tops. She was horrified to see her calves covered with an ugly, oozing red rash; judging from the itch, her legs were covered from just above her knees to her ankles. Squeamishly she pushed her trouser legs back down and walked shakily out from behind the bush.

"May we—" Neve swallowed her pride. It went down in a hard, bitter lump. "May we please stop for the night?"

Ash glanced at her.

"Done in, eh?" he said.

"My feet hurt," Neve said, forcing out the words. "And there's—there's something wrong with my legs."

Ash raised his eyebrows, gazing at her a moment longer. He put down the waterskin.

"Sit," he said. "Let's have a look."

Silently Neve obeyed, unlacing the bottom of her trouser legs with trembling fingers. She could hardly bear to look at the nasty rash. Ash swore, impatiently pushed her trouser legs higher, then swore again.

"Gods, girl, I knew you were a green bit," he said sourly, "but I didn't think you fool enough to go strolling through thickets of itchweed."

Neve bit her lip, daring a glance at her legs. The sight turned her stomach. Exploded dragons were one thing, but this—this was *her*.

"Itchweed?" she said in a small voice.

Ash rolled his eyes, muttering something that Neve could only assume was insulting. He stood.

"Right, then." He sighed. "Off with 'em."

For a moment Neve felt a surge of panic—did he mean to cut her legs off?

"Come on," Ash said impatiently. "Off with the trousers, unless you're wanting me to do it for you."

Trousers! Utter relief, then embarrassment. No fear. *Nobody would touch me with my legs looking like that, not even those awful sailors.* She had to force herself to peel the garment off.

"Just sit there," Ash said. "Don't touch it. I'll be back." To Neve's alarm, he picked up their cooking pot and vanished into the bushes bordering the stream.

To distract herself, Neve pulled off her boots; her soles and heels were blistered, too, but they were just plain blisters from walking. She wondered dismally how she was going to walk tomorrow.

Ash returned several minutes later, his hands full of leaves and the pot full of slimy black mud. He sat down at Neve's feet, smashing the leaves between his hands and then working the pulp into the mud. To Neve's amazement and disgust, he then proceeded to slather the mixture thickly over her legs, covering the rash completely.

"This'll take most of the itch out," Ash said shortly. "A couple nights'll take care of it. Do me a favor, from now on stay out of the itchweed."

Neve bit her lip.

"I'll try, if you'll show me what itchweed looks like," she said embarrassedly. The mud was surprisingly soothing, and thank the Nexus it hid that awful rash from her sight.

"There," Ash said, wiping his hands. "Now I'm sorry I didn't tote along some of those fancy linens. They would've made dandy bandages. Never mind, just put your trousers back on and lace them up tight over the mud. Now let's see the feet.''

After Ash's previous contempt, Neve expected mockery when she showed him her blistered feet. There was more sympathy than annoyance in his expression, however, as Ash shook his head, reaching for his pack.

''That I can do something about,'' he said. He pulled out a clay jar and rubbed some rather smelly, greasy substance over her feet. ''One thing sailors know, it's blisters.''

''What, you're not going to laugh at me again?'' Neve said sourly.

Ash snorted.

''What, because you've got tender feet?'' he retorted. ''Any rich bit green enough to go marching through itch-weed's going to wear her feet raw walking all day. Can't say I'm used to it myself—all the walking, that is—but my feet are tough as old leather. I have to say, you're a tough little piece to keep going so long in your state, and without grip-ing, either. And those are sensible boots, better'n I'd have expected on a noble girl. There, that'll do you. Unless you know how to make something better.'' This last accompanied by a half-raised eyebrow as he pulled off his own boots, liberating his strange feet with a sigh of relief.

''Make something—'' Neve hesitated. ''What, you mean like a potion or something?''

Ash nodded.

''I saw all those herbs,'' he said. ''That's why I brought 'em.''

This time it was Neve who snorted with suppressed laugh-ter.

''They're for *cooking,*'' she said.

''Cook—'' Ash rolled his eyes and sighed. ''Right. *That* figures. I got to be traveling with the one noble mage in the world who uses her herbs for *cooking* instead of magic.''

He handed her her boots.

''Grab a blanket and settle yourself,'' he said, shaking his head resignedly. ''I'll get wood. Then if you can make a fire, maybe I can catch something for you to use your herbs on.''

Ash disappeared, returned with firewood and tinder, and departed again. Neve debated attempting to light the fire by magic, but decided that the humiliation of failure wasn't worth the risk and simply used flint and steel. The thought of magic, however, reminded her that sooner or later Ash was going to demand the first of his rubies, and when she had the fire burning steadily, Neve drew out her piece of the Nexus and found a couple of pebbles. When she'd done this before, the Nexus had actually been under her skin—almost part of her—and she didn't know if she'd have more difficulty now. In any event, she preferred not to let Ash watch her make the transformation, lest he start getting the notion he could do it himself.

To her surprise (and gratitude) neither her temporary loss of the Nexus nor its removal from her body had affected her ability to use its power. Still, it wasn't easy; changing the first pebble wearied her, and the second left her almost exhausted, her headache renewed to its full sickening force. Neve tucked one of the rubies into her bodice with her fragment of the Nexus; she needed to start building up her store of emergency money again, and judging by the way the magic drained her, she'd better do it a little at a time.

Ash returned with a couple of fair-sized game birds. Neve tried to ignore the strange man's rather insulting surprise when she proved she knew how to pluck and clean the birds; he salved her ego somewhat, however, by the appreciative noises he made as he wolfed down the seasoned meat with appalling speed. Neve, who had walked all day on a cup of *cai* and a skewer of overcooked fish, found it hard enough to eat neatly and slowly that she couldn't entirely fault him. When Ash, without being asked, fetched her blanket and a couple armloads of dry leaves to serve as bedding, she decided she could forgive his manners. At least he'd limited himself to a few curses and mild contempt; compared with the other boorish peasants she'd met, that made Ash a paragon of etiquette.

"This is yours," she said when she'd settled herself down, holding out the ruby. "First day's pay."

Ash took the gem, inspecting it critically in the firelight. He nodded noncomittally.

"Good enough," he said. "I set a couple eel lines when I was down at the creek. With any luck, we'll have something fresh for breakfast." He chuckled. "Not much left of the birds, unless you've got a taste for bones and skin."

"Eel would be good," Neve said cautiously, not wanting to admit that she had no idea how to clean an eel. Still, if he could catch and clean it, she could cook it—at least she could be confident of *that*.

"Right, then." Ash pulled his own blanket from the pack. "Get some sleep. We're up at dawn."

For once Neve was not troubled in the least by Ash's rude abruptness; she was so exhausted that she was asleep before he had finished banking the fire.

4

NEVE GROANED, CLUTCHED AT HER
stomach, and staggered into the bushes again. When
she emerged, Ash was nowhere to be seen, but he
stepped out of another set of bushes a few moments later.

"Damme, girl, next time you'd better be more careful with
those herbs of yours," he muttered.

"It wasn't my herbs," Neve said with dignity. "It was
those mushrooms you picked. I *told* you they tasted wrong."

"Yeah, well—" Ash looked uncomfortable. "I can't say
I've spent all that much time in the woods, and then it was
back in Arawen." He ducked his head. "I suppose it's just
possible I picked the wrong ones."

" 'Just possible,' " Neve growled. "My vitals say there's
no 'possible' about it. We're lucky you didn't kill us."

"Look, girl, it's another half day's hard march to Kent, at
least," Ash snapped. "Am I going to have to listen to you
gripe the whole time?"

"Only when I'm not in the bushes retching up breakfast,"
Neve retorted. "Which probably won't be long. Now, shall
we move on, or do you want to turn that hard half day's
march into another day on the trail together?"

"Not damned likely," Ash muttered, and stomped off
down the trail. Neve set her teeth and followed, wishing for

the hundredth time that her parents had seen fit to teach her how to use the power of the Nexus for something other than creation and transformation.

Healing, for example.

She'd wished that constantly on the trail while the itchy rash on her legs had healed—although she had to admit that Ash's mud-and-herb paste had certainly helped, and had proven equally effective on bee stings when she had blundered into a nest of the horrible little monsters. And, yes, her blisters had quickly subsided under the salve he'd used on them. But there was no salve to heal her mortally wounded pride.

Up until Selwaer she'd thought she was doing at least reasonably well.

Well, even my parents didn't count on me being robbed and mauled by sailors, nor having to flounder around in the woods without horses, most of my gear, or even a road, and with only this bumbling idiot sailor for a guide, Neve thought sourly. *I'm sure neither of them would have done any better. Oh, by the Nexus, when I'm the Guardian, they're going to be sorry for this. I'll put a swamp-fell in their privy, stuff their mattresses with itchweed, fill their well with dragon piss—*

Thunder rumbled overhead, and the first splatter of rain plopped right into Neve's eye.

And put leaks in their roof, she added grimly. *BIG, gaping, dripping leaks.*

Scattered droplets quickly turned to a sprinkle, then a shower. Then a deluge. Ash stopped under a tree, pulling Neve under the sheltering branches.

"Don't suppose you can do anything about rain, eh?" he shouted over the downpour. "Or at least a waterproofing spell or some such?"

Neve hesitated. Could she? Hadn't she seen something about weather magic in the grimoire her mother had given her?

"I don't know," she shouted back. "I can try."

Ash gave her a rather dubious look, but he squatted down patiently while Neve pulled out the grimoire and flipped through the pages.

"*To draw a storm aside, and thus render the weather*

clement.'' That looks like what we need. Wonder why it's so far back in the book with the adept stuff? It looks like a simple enough spell. All right, then.

Neve clutched her crystal firmly, focusing her concentration, feeling the power of the Nexus uncoil. The chant was simple and short, the patterns uncomplicated, directing the power here, *here* into the storm, more power to nudge it like *so*, shift the currents, more power, energy rising, winds shifting—

No, wait, that wasn't what I—

Flashing patterns of energy coalescing, cold meeting heat and lightning born from their union, more power uncoiling, wind rising, whipping sharply now and Neve tasted the first raw hint of panic as the power of the Nexus and the storm rose together, Neve stretched in the middle like a taut and fraying cord, fighting to keep her grip on both forces as raw magical power fed from the Nexus into Neve into the storm and back again.

I've got to cut it loose before it—but I can't, I can't—

Then something struck her wrist, a numbing blow, and a shock more profound than pain flashed through her body as her connection with the Nexus was abruptly severed. She collapsed, stunned, only dimly aware of the chaos around her, a sense of jolting movement for some interminable time, then a sudden jarring impact. Mud was slimy and gritty in her nose and mouth and there was a heavy weight on top of her, but Neve made no protest because the earth was shaking under her and a roaring louder than an exploding dragon was in her ears.

But strangely the sound and the shaking became more remote, quieter, and Neve felt as though she was sinking slowly, comfortably into a soft warm bed, so gentle—

So dark . . .

''Wake up, girl!''

Neve groaned in protest. She ached everywhere—*But I thought we left the sailors far behind*—and her eyelids seemed far too heavy to lift.

''Come on, damn you! Wake up!'' Potent liquid was forced between her lips and burned in her throat; she sputtered and coughed, but forced her eyes open, swallowing some of the brandy despite herself.

It was dark, very dark, and there was no fire. As far as Neve could tell, she was under a rocky overhang. The ground was cold but dry, which was a blessing since her clothes and the blanket around her were damp.

"Wuh—where are we?" Neve said stupidly. Her tongue felt thick and clumsy and her lips didn't want to work properly.

Ash gave a short bark of derisive laughter.

"About half a mile from where we were," he said. "And lucky at that, or we'd be in the next kingdom instead. You napped through a whirlwind, girl."

"Whuh-whirlwind?" Neve repeated blankly.

Ash snorted.

"Remind me never to ask you for a waterproofing spell again," he said sourly. "Don't know whether you conjured it up or just pulled it in, girl, but the great-grandpappy of all whirlwinds just barely missed sucking us up and spitting us back out. Probably would've had us, too, if I hadn't knocked that damned stone out of your hand—nah, don't fret, it's in your pocket there. Traveling's going to be interesting tomorrow. There's trees and branches down everywhere and more falling all the time, and the creek's flooded out of its banks. If it doesn't go down somewhat by morning, we may be stuck here anyway."

Neve stared at him dumbly. Had she done that, conjured a whirlwind almost on top of them, wrecked the forest, nearly killed them? She had only the dimmest memories of her spellcasting, that terrifying sense of the power growing out of control, trying to hold on but feeling it doing its best to shake her loose as if she clung to the tip of a dragon's tail while it bucked and flew.

Neve felt a hot tear wind a path down her icy cheek and bit her lip *hard*. No, the heir to the Crystal Keep would *not* weep like a mewling babe, no matter *what*, no matter—

Then she *was* crying, silently and without fanfare but crying nonetheless, crying bruised and stung and itchy and cold and exhausted beyond measure, crying lost and lonely and afraid and hating herself for her tears.

Ash sighed.

"Oh, hush up, girl," he said gruffly. "We're alive, that's what matters. Look, never mind. We'll get to Kent tomorrow and it'll be all right and all over, see?"

Neve shook her head despairingly, not explaining. It *wouldn't* be over and it *wouldn't* be all right, but Ash couldn't understand. He didn't know that she was the heir to the Crystal Keep, that this was her test and she was failing it already.

Ash sighed again; then Neve jumped in surprise as his arm went around her shoulders, squeezing comfortingly.

"Look, you're just cold and done in, that's all," Ash said not unkindly. "I'd make a fire if there was any dry wood to be had, but there's none. So now I know you're not going to die on me, let's just get some sleep, and things'll look better in the morning."

Neve nodded numbly, but she jolted awake again in surprise and distrust when Ash took the blanket from her, making one pallet with the two blankets. Ash saw her expression and chuckled.

"Relax," he said. "I'm thinking of our cold asses, not my loins, girl. We're both chilled through. Anyway, I've seen donkey turds looked prettier'n you do now, and that's the truth."

To her amazement Neve found Ash's insult rather reassuring. She made no further argument but curled up beside the wiry sailor, letting him tuck the blankets around them both. As their wet nest warmed, Neve slowly relaxed, not fighting off sleep any longer.

Well, at least if he assaults me during the night, she thought drowsily as sleep claimed her again, *I'll probably never notice.*

Neve woke to the smell of hot *cai* and burning meat and the sound of Ash swearing. She sat up stiffly, rubbing her eyes.

Ash had not exaggerated the damage to the forest. There were gaping holes in the canopy where huge trees had been ripped up by the roots or snapped off like twigs and flung about like discarded toys. The muddy ground was littered with fallen branches. Apparently Ash had found enough dry wood for a fire, however, for he was placing several rather blackened skewers of meat on a piece of bark, which he carried over like a tray.

"Eat up," he said. "Last time you get breakfast in bed from me."

Neve took one of the skewers and nibbled at it gingerly, trying not to grimace. Ash had clearly dipped into her bag of herbs, and just as clearly had *no* knowledge of how to use them. The meat was well burned and tasted so awful that she couldn't even ascertain what manner of animal, fish or fowl, it might have come from. But Neve couldn't bring herself to complain, not after Ash's clumsy reassurances of the night before.

"Well?" Ash said, staring at her.

"It's good," Neve lied, forcing herself to take another nibble. "Wonderful."

Ash snorted.

"It's burned dogshit," he said.

Neve stopped eating and dropped the skewer, her gorge rising, and Ash laughed at the expression on her face.

"That's a *joke,* girl!" he said, grinning. "It *was* rabbit, not that you'd know. Never mind. This afternoon you'll be eating proper food in a public house."

Neve forced a smile and laid the piece of bark aside.

"All right," she said simply. "Let's go. Please," she added.

They walked through the ravaged forest, and thankfully they soon came across a road that led toward Kent. The road, too, was littered with fallen branches and trees, but it was more easily navigated than the forest. The road cleared as they drew closer to Kent, and by the time Neve got her first look at the small city, there was no sign of the whirlwind's passage.

The sight of Kent reassured her; it more nearly matched her expectation of a city than Selwaer had. For one thing, there was a stout wall around it, and even from a distance she could see the tiny figures of guards walking the top occasionally. Wagons, carts, and pedestrians came and went through the nearest gate, although everyone seemed to be coming from or going to roads other than the one she and Ash had taken—*Well, of course, if the whirlwind went through behind us, nobody would be going through there—*

and from her hilltop vantage point she could dimly see the riverside docks on the other side of the city, and several ships anchored there. Farther south, she knew, the Little Brother met the great river Dezarin as it wound its way down to the great southern sea. And one of those ships would carry Neve on that journey—with a *cabin,* if you please!

At the center of the city Neve could see a fair-sized market, and she knew from the books she'd read, from her mother and father's stories, from what she'd seen in her father's mirror, that where there were trade ships and wagons and a good market, there would be inns and taverns aplenty. And *that* meant a soft bed, a hot bath, a proper meal, and by the Nexus, clean clothes.

Neve and Ash walked in silence to the gate, and Ash rapped sharply with a huge iron knocker. Shutters opened from inside a barred window beside the gate, and a young man gazed out dubiously at them.

"What's your business in Kent?" he said.

"Just passing through," Ash said. "Looking for passage south for her, and a sailor's berth for me."

The young man squinted.

"Where's your horses?" he said suspiciously.

"Got none," Ash said. "Just what you see. Met up with a whirlwind last night."

The young man's eyebrows shot up.

"You saw it?" he said. "Every mage in town was out casting last night. It was headed straight for Kent, I'm told, and then it just veered right off and plowed into the forest. Saved the city. Every mage in town's taking the credit."

Neve and Ash exchanged startled glances; then Ash barely smiled, and Neve, to her amazement, found herself shaking with suppressed laughter.

"Hell of a thing," Ash said with a straight face, although Neve could see his lips twitching. "Well, you going to let us in or not?"

"Sorry," the guard said, withdrawing from the window. Presently the gate creaked slightly open. "Welcome to Kent, travelers," the guard's voice said from somewhere inside.

Neve stopped just inside the gate, taken aback. Selwaer hadn't prepared her for the noise, the bustle, the smells of a fair-sized and prosperous city. Even more than in the caravan or on the ship, the sight and sound and smell and *presence* of all these people seemed to close in around her in an attack of sorts. It was impossible to ignore them, impossible to avoid them. She fought down her instinct to retreat back out the gate.

"Well . . ." Neve turned and found Ash gazing at her with an unreadable expression. "Here you are in Kent, just as I said. You going to be all right from here, girl?"

Neve took a deep breath, fighting down panic. *Of course. That was our bargain. Just to Kent, that's all. I'm the heir to the Crystal Keep. I don't need a nanny.*

"Yes," she said with more assurance than she felt. "Yes, thank you. I can manage now."

She reached into her bodice and found the largest of her little cache of rubies by touch. Creating the rubies had gotten easier with practice, and she'd quickly replenished her emergency reserve. The largest stone was almost twice the size of the others and had taken her a great deal of effort to make, and she'd planned to save it for a dire emergency, but . . .

Hiding the ruby in her clenched fist, Neve held out her hand.

"Thank you for your help," she said rather stiffly.

Ash took her hand, his expression not changing as Neve opened her fist and dropped the ruby in his palm. Gazing into her eyes, he held her hand just a moment longer than necessary, then released it and unobtrusively tucked the ruby away, nodding.

"My pleasure," he said, but the twinkle of his eyes made it a joke. "Well, you're a fine cook at least. And the toughest little rich bit I've ever seen. You'll go far, girl." He pulled her dagger and purse from his pack and handed them over. "These are yours, I guess."

Neve swallowed, taking the dagger and purse.

"Neve," she said. "My name's Neve, not 'girl,' not 'rich bit.' "

Ash grinned that saucy, infuriating grin.

"Right you are." He chuckled. "Well, smooth water, girl."

With that, he turned and vanished into the crowd, leaving Neve gaping behind him.

Neve clutched at her dagger and purse, trying to stop her

shaking. What, was she afraid of a lot of noisy mortals? Not her! She was alone, yes, but she *liked* being alone. And there was certainly nothing to fear. She had money and she was in a proper city at last.

All right. Clothes first, or no inn will have me, she thought grimly. *Then food and drink.*

Finding the market was easy enough; most of the roads seemed to lead inward to it, like the spokes of a wagon wheel. In the market, however, Neve soon confronted problems she hadn't expected. The first merchant and the second looked at her Caistran silver and laughed politely, directing her to a moneychanger. The moneychanger inspected the silver critically and finally agreed to convert it to local coin, at what Neve suspected was a miserable rate—but given her bedraggled appearance, the man probably took her for a thief anyway, and she didn't dare flash one of her rubies until she was dressed more respectably.

Neve had thought she'd enjoy her first *real* marketplace, but she quickly found it completely disagreeable—she refused to use the word "frightening" even to herself. She'd never *imagined* so many people in one place in her life, all of them assaulting her with their smell, their noise, the sheer proximity of their bodies even when they weren't elbowing her or bumping into her or stepping on her toes. Several times Neve was forced to retreat—strategically, of course—into a shop or an alleyway to catch her breath, amazed and dismayed to find herself shaking. But there was nothing she could do but venture out again and bear the chaos as long as she could; there was nobody to shop for her, and in any event, she'd have to wade through the living morass again just to find an inn.

Several transactions later, bathed, well dressed, and with a ruby's worth of gold in her purse and two changes of linens in her sack, Neve opened the door of the Spiral Horn. The tailor who had taken her measure for another new set of travel leathers had told her that the Horn was a clean, respectable place for a lady of good breeding, and Neve willingly exchanged one of her gold pieces for three nights' board and supper—after that horrible marketplace she'd have paid twice the price for a flea-infested closet just to get away from the noise and bustle.

She flopped limply onto a thick, soft feather bed and sighed contentedly. Now *this* was more like it! There was scented water and perfumed soap on the washstand, soft slippers for her feet, candied violets and a bottle of sweet wine on the bedside table, and a bell rope to summon a servant to draw her bath and "attend to her" if she wished. And the room was wonderfully, blessedly *quiet*.

Two hours later Neve was hopelessly bored and unaccountably disappointed.

She'd luxuriated in the soft sheets and thick quilts, she'd nibbled at the violets and sipped the wine, she'd called the attendant and enjoyed another hot bath even though she'd already had one only a few hours earlier. The lad had scrubbed her back and rubbed her shoulders skillfully, but despite the invitation in his glance and the rather wistful way he'd asked if there was anything else she needed, Neve found that she really wasn't in the mood for a tumble, not after her awful day in the market, and sent him away.

When the boredom became too much, Neve wandered downstairs to the public room for supper. A few lords and ladies were already there, eating, drinking, chatting, and listening to a pretty young girl playing a small harp and singing, and Neve cheered up immediately. An evening of fine food in polite—but not too numerous—company was just what she needed.

Again, however, Neve found herself disappointed and irritated, too. The lords and ladies glanced at her, raised their eyebrows, and pointedly turned away without a word of greeting, excluding her from their company even more decisively than the peasants in the caravan. Neve felt her cheeks burning and sat down at a back table, fuming. How *dared* they! Why, she was the heir to the Crystal Keep. Not a one of them could boast such lineage or such holdings or power as she could. Why, they—

Neve scowled.

But of course none of them knew that. Neve, who had shopped with a mind to travel, was wearing a tunic and trousers and boots, albeit expensive and high-quality ones, rather than the fine gowns and silk slippers of the noble ladies who did their traveling by carriage rather than horse or ship or—gods forbid—on foot. Neve wore no crest or arms of any noble house, not even any jewelry, and compared with the people she'd seen so far, she was probably judged an "odd-looking bit" here, too, with her pale skin and sharp, narrow features. As far as any of the nobles knew, Neve was simply a traveling peasant who'd lucked into a little money, or maybe stolen it—and for her own safety, she couldn't prove otherwise.

Fortunately for her temper, the three glasses of wine she'd gulped while pondering this monstrous injustice took effect quickly, reminding her how exhausted she was and how soft and comfortable that feather bed upstairs had felt. Neve gulped down another glass of wine and a marvelous supper she was suddenly too tired to enjoy, then stumbled upstairs to bed.

In the morning, well rested and of much more cheerful temper, Neve braved the market again to finish resupplying. She claimed her second set of travel clothes, another set of linens, a sturdy cloak, and a marvelous leather pack with a waterproofing spell, and was just about to start on travel food—or should she wait until she debarked from her ship to buy that?—when she remembered she hadn't yet booked passage on a ship to Zaravelle.

Neve asked for and got directions to the wharf, where she found three good-sized ships at anchor. Upon inquiry she learned that while all three were traveling south as far as the coast and were accepting passengers, only one, the *Waver-unner,* was going all the way west down the coast to Zaravelle. Remembering Ash's comments about the fare she'd paid in Selwaer, Neve haggled the price until she hoped she'd allayed any suspicions, then paid in gold. She considered leaving her goods on the ship and spare herself carrying the heavy bundle back to the inn, but the ship wouldn't depart until day after tomorrow, and after her adventures so far she preferred to keep her belongings close.

Cheered by the simplicity of the transaction, Neve nonetheless found herself lingering on the wharf, surveying the other ships; after a while she admitted to herself that she was looking for Ash among the sailors. Well, that was only natural, she told herself defensively. He *had* saved her life—twice over, probably—and in a strange way she'd rather liked him despite his rude tongue and irritating manner.

There was nothing so strange in her concern that he'd fared well after they parted ways the day before.

Her curiosity justified to herself, Neve went back aboard the *Waverunner* and asked whether Ash had come there looking for work. The captain nodded immediately when Neve described him.

"Oh, yes, my lady," he said. "He came aboard. But I'm at full complement this trip. You might try down at the end of the wharf, the *Sea Dragon.* I know Alain was hiring, and he's due to weigh anchor at first light tomorrow, so you'd better ask while the sun's still high. He doesn't like his men ashore last night in port, so he'll probably pull the gangway come sunset."

Neve made her way down the wharf to the *Sea Dragon,* and after some difficulty—the last of the cargo was being loaded and that dock was bustling with activity—located the captain.

"Oh, yeah, he hired on," Alain said sourly. "Lot of good it did me. Word is he ran into trouble with the law as soon as he went back into town on some errand."

"The law?" Neve said slowly. "What sort of trouble?" Ash had mentioned that he'd once been a thief, but surely he wouldn't have turned to stealing again, not when he'd just found work and had a pocketful of rubies, too.

Alain shrugged.

"Don't know, don't care," he said. "All I know is if he ain't got them monkey feet back on my deck before sundown, he can damned well find himself another berth."

Neve slowly walked back into town, found a jeweler, and sold another ruby for gold. Whatever manner of trouble Ash had gotten himself into was hardly *her* affair. She should go back to the inn and have a nice dinner, then force herself to make one last trip into the market to finish her shopping and—

And—

Neve sighed and found a guardsman, asked for and got directions to the city prison, buying some roast chicken and a pie or two to eat on the way. If she didn't find out what trouble Ash had gotten himself into, she'd never sleep that night for curiosity.

Neve regretted her curiosity, however, when she arrived

at the prison. It was a nasty place, foul smelling and noisy—
even worse than the market. The rude guard confirmed that,
yes, a man fitting Ash's description had been arrested that
morning, but professed ignorance of the details, or of where
Neve should go to learn more—at last Neve realized what
was going on and handed over a gold piece, after which the
guard grudgingly showed her to the magistrate's office. Two
more gold pieces got her an immediate appointment with a
genteelly dressed older man.

"Yes, he's been sentenced to have his hands struck off
tomorrow," Magistrate Levan said indifferently. "Thievery,
you see. If he was guilded, I suppose the Thieves' Guild
might ransom him, but he's just a transient."

"What did he steal?" Neve asked, scowling. And *why*?
Ash had had *plenty* of money; she should know.

"Oh, several gems," the magistrate said, consulting his
ledger. "Complaint was filed by his shipmates. There's no
question of his guilt; we found the gems on his person, and
they matched gems his captain showed us."

Neve took a deep breath.

"He didn't steal them," she said.

"Hmm?" The magistrate glanced up, peering at her suspiciously.

"He didn't steal them," Neve repeated. "I gave them to
him in payment. They were rubies like this, weren't they?"
She fished out one of her remaining rubies, handing it to the
magistrate.

Magistrate Levan's eyebrows shot up as he examined the
gemstone.

"My lady, this complicates matters considerably," he said
slowly. "I think I'd best hear the whole story. Sit down. I'll
have the prisoner brought in."

Neve sat down, disgusted to find herself shaking hard.
Stop it! she told herself fiercely. *What's the matter with
you?*

The magistrate returned and sat down, saying nothing; a
few moments later a guard hauled Ash into the room, and
Neve couldn't suppress a wince of sympathy. Ash was, if
anything, dirtier than he'd been before; he was manacled
hand and foot, and numerous bruises and scratches suggested
that he hadn't been treated with any great gentleness. One

eye was swollen shut, but the other one widened in amazement when he saw her.

"This young lady," Magistrate Levan told Ash, "says she has new evidence in your case. Would you care to change your story now?"

Ash glanced at Neve, sighed, and shook his head, saying nothing.

"He says, you see, that he found those rubies," Magistrate Levan said, leaning back in his chair. "Not much of a story, since the gems matched those his captain had. Not that I'd have believed them his either, not to look at him. So tell me, my lady, if you would, what's your version?"

"I booked passage in Selwaer aboard the *Skipper*," Neve said. She flushed. "I'm new to travel, and didn't have any gold on hand, and I paid the captain of the *Skipper* with one of the rubies." She fought down anger at the magistrate's chuckle. "The *Skipper* put ashore that night, and the captain and crew beat and robbed me and would have killed me, too. I offered Ash payment if he'd help me escape and see me safe to Kent. He agreed, and he did, and I paid him in rubies. That's 'my version,' and that's the truth."

The magistrate was silent a long time, gazing at Neve, then Ash; then he shook his head.

"I'd like to believe you," he said slowly. "But if Captain Warten and his men robbed you, where'd you come by the rubies to pay this rogue?"

"She didn't," Ash said, speaking for the first time. "As I told you—" The guard clouted him sharply on the back of the neck, and he fell silent, glaring at Neve.

Neve took a deep breath.

"I didn't come by the rubies," she said. "I made them. By magic."

Magistrate Levan's eyes narrowed.

"A mage, eh?" he said. "But you'd have to be a mighty powerful mage to do such a thing. You're young to be that powerful. And if you're such a mage, how did you end up bested by a bunch of drunken sailors?"

Ash was giving her a look of warning, but it was the slight trickle of blood that ran down his cheek that made her decide.

"I'm not a mage—exactly," Neve said slowly. "I'm the daughter of the Guardian of the Crystal Keep."

Silence. The magistrate sat back in his chair, his lips narrowed. Then he chuckled.

"You'll have to do better than that, I'm afraid, my lady," he said.

"It's true," Neve insisted. "I don't know much magic except the transformative sort; I'm still learning. But I made the rubies, and I can prove it."

The magistrate's eyes narrowed.

"I believe I'd like to see that," he said.

"All right." Neve glanced around. There were no pebbles on the stone floor, but at last she found a chip of stone that would suffice. She'd made the transformation so often that it was almost effortless now; she left the crystal where it was hidden in her bodice, and held the stone chip in her open palm so the magistrate could watch it change.

This time the silence was longer as the magistrate examined the gem.

"I see," he said slowly. "Well, my lady, there's no doubt that you've shown me better proof than Captain Warten. I suppose I'll have to release this scoundrel, though I'd like to give him a flogging for lying to a magistrate—not that I'd have believed him if he'd told me the truth. But I already returned his rubies to the captain. Will you be wanting to make charges against him and his men? I can send out the guards for them, but likely they'll be quick out of town now that they've got what they want."

"I certainly—" Neve began.

"Don't," Ash interrupted. "I'm sure they're long gone by now, and my lady has more important business." His eyes telegraphed a warning to Neve.

"Hmm." The magistrate scowled at Ash. "I'll have the guards look about for them nonetheless. As to these—" He held up the ruby Neve had given him at first, and the one she'd just made.

"I know those are evidence," Ash said quickly. "Why don't you keep them safe here until the matter's investigated to your satisfaction?"

"I believe I'll just do that," the magistrate said slowly. "And you, my lady, where can I reach you in case more questions arise?"

"I'm staying at the Spiral Horn," Neve said, glaring at

Ash. Who was he to deny her her justice and her property? "But I've booked passage aboard the *Waverunner* day after tomorrow."

"That's fine, that's fine," Magistrate Levan said absently, making a notation in his ledger. "Good enough, then. Guard, unlock his chains. The two of you can go."

Neve winced again when she saw Ash's wrists and ankles, raw where the manacles had rubbed his skin, but Ash was already pulling her out the door as quickly as he could—presumably before the magistrate changed his mind. She didn't object until he yanked her down a filthy alley, then around a corner into another, then another—

"Wait a minute!" Neve said hotly, pulling Ash to a halt. "What are you doing?"

"Probably saving your damned life," he said sourly. "Listen, girl, just this one time could you *please* just do what I say without a fuss?"

Neve scowled ferociously—how *dare* he act like this when she'd just saved his hands! Why, the lout hadn't even bothered to thank her!—but she had no time to argue; Ash was already dodging through the maze of alleys as fast as he could drag her. Neve was breathless when he finally stopped, leaning against the wall of a building.

"All right," he said, panting himself. "Guess we got away clean."

"Got away from *what*?" Neve demanded. "There weren't any guards after *me*."

"Not yet, there weren't," Ash said exasperatedly. "Whatever made you tell that story to the magistrate?"

Neve drew herself up proudly.

"It was the truth," she said.

Ash rolled his eyes and sighed.

"That's what I was afraid of," he said ruefully. "Come on, then."

This time he moved at a more reasonable pace, leading her through twisting alleys until she was totally lost. She could tell by the waning light that it was growing late in the afternoon, but the tall buildings above her blocked enough of her view that she couldn't tell which direction she was going. At last the alley ahead seemed to open into a clear space, and through that opening Neve saw to her surprise that they'd worked their way all the way south to the docks again. When she would have stepped out, however, Ash pulled her back into the alley.

"What are we waiting for?" Neve demanded.

"Just a minute, will you?" Ash hissed. He poked his head out just enough to glance around.

"We can't stay back here forever," Neve said practically. "Besides, your ship will leave without you. Look, you can see they're ready to pull in the gangway."

"That's what I was waiting for," Ash said grimly. "Come on."

He pulled her after him, hugging the side of the buildings until he reached the *Sea Dragon*. To Neve's amazement, he pulled her up the gangway with him, towing her along until he found Captain Alain conferring with the cargomaster.

"Oho, so you're back, eh?" Alain chuckled. "Clear up your little problem with the guards, did you?"

"False accusation," Ash said shortly. "Listen, Captain, do I still have my berth?"

Alain shrugged.

"I suppose," he said. "But you'd better get your friend there off the ship. We're about to draw in the gangway."

"She wants passage to Strachan," Ash said. When Neve started to protest, he silenced her with the fiercest look she'd yet seen from him.

"Hmmph." Captain Alain eyed Neve appraisingly. "A lady, eh? I've got one cabin left, but it'll cost, especially this being so last-minute. Eighteen gold."

"Thirt—" Neve began, but Ash cut her off.

"Done," he said.

Neve waited until they'd left the captain's range of hearing before she rounded on Ash.

"What do you think you're doing?" she demanded. "I don't want to go to Strachan, I want to go to Zaravelle. And I've already got passage on the *Waverunner*."

"I know," Ash said wryly. "As you've gone to the trouble to announce it. Forget that. You can catch a ship to Zaravelle just as easy from Strachan."

"And eighteen gold!" Neve protested. "I only paid fifteen on the *Waverunner*."

Ash gave her an impatient glance.

''What's it matter?'' he said. ''You can make all the money you want.''

''That's not the point,'' Neve growled. ''Besides, I've only got twenty gold pieces left, and then I've got nothing to spend but Caistran silver. And it isn't *easy* making gemstones, you know.''

Ash gave a bark of derisive laughter.

''Easier than trying to get to Zaravelle with your throat slit,'' he said. ''Here, this one looks to be empty.'' He opened the door to a tiny cabin and threw her bag on the narrow bunk. ''Sit down.''

Biting her lip, Neve sat. Ash latched the door firmly and sat down beside her.

''That true, what you said?'' he asked. ''That you're the Guardian of the Crystal Keep's daughter?''

''Of course it's true,'' Neve said impatiently. ''You don't think I'd lie to a magistrate, do you?''

''No, but I was hoping.'' Ash sighed. ''Girl, you got any idea what kind of trouble you'd be in now?''

''You're the one who was in trouble,'' Neve retorted. ''*I* was doing just fine, thank you.''

Ash shook his head.

''You got any idea how valuable you are?'' Ash said patiently. ''Gods, just the fact that you can conjure up gemstones whenever you want—''

''It's not that—'' Neve began.

''It doesn't matter,'' Ash said firmly. ''You had to tell it all to a greedy magistrate and a common guard. Even better, you had to let them know that while you can make gems, you can't do nothing to defend yourself. Best you could hope for is that the magistrate would want you for himself and send a couple guards to wait for you near the Spiral Horn or the *Waverunner* to pick you up on the hush-hush, since you so nicely told him where you could be found. Worst case, word gets out on the street and every two-copper thug in Kent'll be out looking for you. Maybe, if you're *really* lucky, they'd just take you as a hostage home to Daddy to see what they can get out of you. But more likely they'll find you a nice dark cellar somewhere where you can sit around all day making gems for them.''

Neve swallowed. She hadn't thought about that.

"I didn't know," she said in a small voice.

Ash sighed again.

"Doesn't much matter," he said grudgingly. "Now that the captain's pulled in the gangway, we're safe enough. And like I said, you can get to Zaravelle easily enough from Strachan. So no harm done." He grinned. "Leave much at the Spiral Horn?"

Neve sighed.

"Just two changes of linens," she said wistfully. "But I paid for three nights. With baths."

"Well, those three nights and your two changes of linens will hopefully keep anyone from checking the *Sea Dragon* before she's out of port," Ash said wryly, glancing down at his own clothes and sighing. "I wish I'd had a chance to buy a few things myself before all my gems got confiscated and turned over to that scum Warten."

"Why didn't you want me to make charges against them?" Neve asked curiously.

Ash chuckled.

"Same reason I didn't want you telling the magistrate the whole story," he said. "The fewer folks who know there's a green, rich young mage who can make gemstones in town, the better."

Neve swallowed her surprise with some difficulty.

"You mean," she said slowly, "you'd have let them cut off your hands rather than tell the magistrate the truth and have them hunt me up for my testimony?"

Ash shrugged.

"Probably wouldn't have come to that," he said indifferently. "I told you, I used to be a damned good thief. I'm a fair hand with a lock. I was just waiting till nighttime to make a try at getting away." He grinned. "Anyway, I said I'd see you safe to Kent, and you paid your side. I figure my side doesn't include getting you in trouble the minute we walk through the city's gates. Warten and them, they were my problem, not yours."

Neve frowned. Somehow she felt more indebted to this strange man than she had the night he'd cut her loose and helped her escape Warten and his men. That thought made her profoundly uncomfortable.

"That was . . . very good of you," she said, trying not to sound too stiff.

Ash shrugged again.

"Well, it was decent of you to come forward and help when you found out I'd been locked up," he said cheerfully. "So we'll call it even."

"It's not even," Neve insisted. "All the rubies I paid you—why, you don't have anything at all now. And it's all because of me."

"No, it's not," Ash said, shaking his head. "I told you, Warten and them were my problem. I should've known they'd have made it to Kent well before us. They knew we'd be coming here, and they were bent on revenge."

"Well . . ." Neve took a deep breath. "Where are you going after Strachan?"

Ash shrugged.

"Who knows?" he said. "I'll see when I get there. Meanwhile, unlike you, I've got work to do." He swept an exaggerated bow. "Enjoy your cabin, milady."

Over the next few days, Neve hardly saw Ash except from a distance. The *Sea Dragon* carried cargo, yes, but it had also been built to ferry passengers from Kent to the coastal cities, and Neve was only one of several nobles rich enough to occupy the tiny cabins, in addition to a number of other passengers sleeping in bunks and sling beds in the cargo hold, or in pallets and makeshift shelters on deck. Neve tried not to spend too much time in her claustrophobic little cabin, but between passengers and crew, she found herself hard-pressed to find any peace or privacy on deck. At last she found sanctuary and a good vantage point at the bow.

Neve had enjoyed Ash's compliments on her "toughness" when she'd traveled on the *Skipper,* but hadn't really taken them too seriously. Now, however, Neve noticed to her amusement the large numbers of passengers—peasant and noble alike—who spent most of their voyage hanging over the railings and spewing their bile into the mighty Dezarin. One or two of the more arrogant nobles actually seemed to resent the fact that the "odd-looking northern bit" suffered not the slightest discomfort, no matter how the deck rolled and pitched; it was possible, too, Neve had to admit, that she'd been less than careful in hiding her own amusement at their plight. So she avoided the other passengers and they avoided her, and apparently the sailors had been told to leave the passengers be, so Neve was happy to find herself left alone to sit and watch.

She was a little surprised, therefore, the third night out when Ash dropped unexpectedly from the rigging and landed beside her, settling himself comfortably. Both he and his clothes appeared much cleaner; Neve speculated that he'd pulled in buckets of river water to wash.

"Found another spying spot, eh?" Ash said jovially.

Neve wondered if that was a veiled insult, decided it was, and ignored it.

"Aren't you supposed to be working?" she said pointedly.

Ash shook his head.

"Not yet," he said. "I've got night watch in the crow's nest." He pointed up at the walled but open-topped platform built high above the deck.

Neve surveyed the perch with interest.

"Is there a good view up there?" she asked. "Could I go up to look?"

Ash laughed.

"I've got to say I like that about you." He grinned. "Nothing much shakes you, does it? That noble lady, the one with the dark red hair, she watched me climb up yesterday, turned green, and spewed her supper right there on the deck. And on her, too."

Neve indeed remembered that particular lady; the first night out at supper, she'd pointedly taken the seat farthest from Neve at the table. Neve found a certain satisfaction in picturing the haughty lady soiling her fine skirts with vomit.

"Nothing makes me sick," Neve declared. "Except your mushrooms, that is. You didn't answer me about the crow's nest."

Ash shrugged.

"Captain would probably have my hide," he said amiably. "But if a noble lady wants a look up top, who am I to say no? Wait a bit, till the sun goes down, and you can climb up with me. Maybe nobody'll notice."

He disappeared again then, back into the rigging with his strange feet and his night eyes, and Neve went down to the galley and ate her supper with the others and then came back up and sat and watched again. But as soon as the sun slipped below the tree line, Ash landed beside her again, a loop of rope clutched in one hand.

"Tie this around your waist," he said, not asking whether she was afraid or had changed her mind. Neve liked that. She tied the rope securely around her waist.

"Over here," Ash said, showing her where to start up the rigging.

"Should I look up or down?" Neve asked, testing her grip on the knotted ropes.

"Peregard's balls, no." Ash chuckled. "Look at where you're putting your hands and feet."

Neve climbed a few feet. It was more difficult than it had looked because the ropes weren't perfectly taut.

"Stop there a moment," Ash said. He scampered up the rigging with an agility Neve envied, holding the other end of the rope. Presumably he tied it off somewhere above; she couldn't see exactly what he was doing in the fading light. Then he was back beside her.

"All right," he said. "Go on up. Slow."

Neve climbed slowly, three limbs securely anchored before she moved one. The wind swayed the rigging; the river swayed the ship. It was farther up to the little platform than she'd thought. She climbed up into the nest through a little opening cut in the platform. Ash climbed up after her, pulled up the rope that had secured her to the mast inside the platform, and closed a small trapdoor over the hole, bolting it securely.

"Well, here you are," he said. "I've got to say, I never really expected you to make it all the way up. How do you like the view?"

The swaying up here was strong; Neve thought with a chuckle that there probably wasn't a passenger on board who wouldn't heave their supper over the side here. She stood up and looked out. The moon was up, and it blazed a silver trail over the Dezarin. The stars shone from sky and water.

"It's good," she said. She wondered whether she could create a platform like this in one of the pocket worlds of the Keep, maybe by the sea, to watch the stars shine on the water from as high up as a bird might fly.

"So," Ash said idly, leaning against the railing beside her.

"Your father's the Guardian of the Crystal Keep. Fancy that."

Neve thought about that for a moment.

"No," she said. "The Guardian of the Crystal Keep is my father."

Ash was silent for a moment, and Neve wondered whether he'd understood the difference or not.

"Nobody believes in the Crystal Keep anymore," he said. "It's just a legend, just hearthside stories."

"It's real," Neve said. "When I've finished my journey, I'll be the Guardian."

"So what *are* you doing out here, then?" Ash asked her.

Neve shrugged.

"It's a test," she said. She didn't expect him to understand.

"What, you've got to get to Zaravelle and back?" Ash said after a pause.

"Something like that." He didn't need to know that her worthiness would be judged by someone else.

Ash scratched his head.

"So why didn't you just pay some mage in Kent to Gate you to Zaravelle?" he said. "You could've afforded it."

Neve scowled at him.

"It's a *test*," she repeated. "There are *rules*."

Ash chuckled.

"I don't hold much with rules myself," he said.

Neve made no reply to that. She stared at the moon on the water.

"Why are your feet like that?" she asked after a while. "And your eyes?"

This time it was Ash who fell silent. When he spoke, his voice was flat.

"I don't remember much about my early childhood," he said. "I know I had a lot of brothers and sisters. I know we were really poor. I was always hungry. A man came when I was very young. He gave my mother some money and took me away with him. His name was Harod. I can't say I really missed my family. Harod gave me plenty of food and clean clothes and a bed of my own, and he didn't beat me. There were other kids, too. Plenty. And when we were old enough, he started training us as thieves—cutpurses at first, snatch-

and-run in the marketplace, that sort of thing. I was good at it, quick on my feet. Wily. He liked that, said I had talent.

"I must've been eight or nine when he took me to the mage, said he had special training for me. The mage gave me something to drink and I fell asleep. When I woke up—"

He glanced down at his feet.

"After that I did inside work," he said. "I could go in from roofs, through upper-story windows—shops, nobles' houses, and the like. I was good, damned good."

Neve thought there might be more to the story, but Ash shook himself, as if waking from a dream, and gave her a rather forced smile.

"Anyway, these feet and these eyes have gotten me jobs like this," he said. "And if people point and stare a bit, well, what do they know? They've probably never seen the river the way a bird sees it. The way I see it."

The way I see it, Neve thought.

"Come with me to Zaravelle," she said.

Ash's eyebrows jumped.

"What?"

"Take me to my friends," Neve said. "They live not far from Zaravelle. I'll pay you like I did before. You'll be rich again."

Ash chuckled.

"I half expected you to ask me to see you all the way back home," he said, "and promise me some fantastic reward when you're Guardian."

"Is that what you want?" Neve asked, surprised.

Ash stared at her a long moment, no longer chuckling.

"No," he said. "No, I don't think I do. If the legends about the Keep are true, there's a price for everything. And it scares me a little, what that price might be."

"There's a price for everything here, too," Neve said flatly. "Only nobody says so straight out. They pretend there's not."

Ash glanced at her sideways.

"I suppose that's so," he said. "You know, just then you sounded as streetwise as any of Harod's kids."

Neve sat down on the platform.

"Do you want to couple with me?" she said.

Ash's eyebrows jumped again.

"What?" he said, laughing disbelievingly this time.

"I said," Neve said patiently, "do you want to couple with me? It's been a long time since I've had a lover."

Ash laughed again, a little bitterly, but he sat down next to her nonetheless.

"What, you want to see how it is with a freak like me?"

"You're not a freak," Neve said, surprised. "I've seen lots of stranger things than you. You're something new and different. There's nothing wrong with that. I like you."

Ash stared at her a moment, then leaned forward, his lips barely brushing the side of her neck.

"You're a strange bit," he whispered. "And there's nothing wrong with that either."

"No," Neve agreed into his hair. She felt him smile against the skin of her throat.

"So what's this going to cost me?" he murmured as his hand slid over her waist and up to cup her breast.

Neve said nothing, pulling loose the laces on his tunic.

"And this." His hand slid inside her tunic, over her shoulder, fingertip tracing her collarbone. "What's this going to cost me?"

Neve reached for him and touched him in a way that made those strange eyes open wide.

"I'll show you," she said.

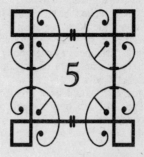

5

"SO HOW DID YOU LIKE YOUR FANCY trip traveling with the nobles?" Ash said as they carried their packs down the gangway to the dock.

Neve considered.

"I suppose it was all right," she said. "Comfortable. Rather boring."

"Boring!" Ash scowled slightly.

Neve chuckled.

"You asked me about traveling with nobles," she reminded him. "You aren't a noble."

"Oh. Well, there's that," Ash admitted, mollified. "Well, seeing as we're here on the docks, you want to see about a ship to Zaravelle now, or find an inn first? Probably ought to be ship. The storm season's coming up here on the south coast; won't be too many more ships going out for a few weeks, so we'd best book your passage while we can."

"Ship," Neve said firmly. She was, in fact, finding the land rather uncomfortable at the moment. She hadn't been aboard the *Skipper* very long; the Little Brother had flowed rather placidly, and the wide, shallow barge hadn't pitched like the *Sea Dragon* on the Dezarin. Now, however, Neve was finding that although she was quite at home on the water, getting back on land was another matter. The dock seemed to roll and sway under her, to her profound embarrassment. One of the debarking nobles smirked, although he walked no more steadily, and Neve glared viciously.

"Right, then." Ash tucked Neve's hand firmly under his arm and walked down the dock, apparently untroubled.

"You'll get your land legs back soon enough," he murmured more quietly. "Happens to everybody who ain't used to water travel. If you want, you can sit down somewhere while I find out what's what."

Two weeks ago Neve would have bristled at the suggestion. Now, however, she felt only vaguely embarrassed by her own infirmity.

"All right," she said. "Find me someplace where I won't get stepped on."

Ash found her a quiet spot against the side of a warehouse, and Neve gratefully crouched down with their bags. One of the ships was being loaded, which Neve knew meant it would be departing within the next day or two, but that didn't mean it was going to Zaravelle. There were other coastal cities to the east, in the wrong direction. Still, she saw Ash head for that ship first and smiled. It was what she would have done.

If, of course, she hadn't been dazzled by her first glimpse of the great southern sea.

It wasn't her first experience with an ocean, of course; there were seas in several of the pocket worlds, and Neve had visited them all, marveling at the fascinating differences in the seaweeds, the shore plants, the tidepool creatures, even the type of sand from one sea to the next. Were they different seas or just different parts of the same one? Could there *be* more than one body of water so vast? But still Neve had known that these were just creations of the Nexus modeled after someplace outside the Keep's walls, that these reproductions were somehow finite. That somewhere there had to be an end to it.

And this sea was different. No nexus created it; no Keep defined it. Neve's first sight of the huge expanse of it at the river mouth had struck her silent with awe. She was gazing at it now; up and down the coasts, the pale beaches only pretended to bound so much open sea. There might very well be no end to it at all. The concept of something larger than the Nexus made Neve profoundly uncomfortable, and she looked back at the ship again.

She turned a closer eye to what was being loaded. She recognized the smaller casks as containing brandy, and the larger ones oil. There were sacks of grain, barrels of salt meat, and bales upon bales of garishly colored cloth, then smaller boxes of—

"Looks like we got a ride," Ash said, appearing at her side as if by magic. He looked mightily pleased with himself. "Good thing we checked when we did. Captain says the *Albatross* is the last ship out before the rains, and she's running late or she'd be gone already. Just had the one cabin left, too."

One cabin? Neve squirmed slightly, uncomfortable all over again. A few tumbles here and there didn't give Ash the right to presume—

"Oh, don't give me that look," Ash chuckled. "I got a berth for night watch as usual."

Neve was surprised—no, astonished.

"I'm giving you a ruby every day," she said, "and you're going to *work* on the ship to Zaravelle?"

"Damn right I am," Ash said almost fiercely. "Last time you give me a bag of rubies I ended up with nothing and nearly got my hands bobbed into the bargain. Besides, I need every copper I can get."

"For what?" Neve asked curiously. "Are you going to buy a ship of your own?"

Ash stared at her a moment, then chuckled.

"Never mind," he said. "It's no trouble of yours anyway. Listen, the *Albatross* won't sail until tide goes out tomorrow, and that's three hours after dawn, so we can sleep ashore tonight if we want."

"I'd rather sleep on the ship," Neve muttered, although the dock had nearly quit pitching under her. Still, she couldn't help remembering the trouble she'd run into in Kent.

Ash laughed outright at that.

"What, and miss your chance at a nice, wide, soft bed and a hot bath?" he said. "Besides, you can buy more frilly linens."

Neve pointedly ignored that, but she admitted to herself that a big, comfortable room with a big, soft bed would be pleasant. And a hot bath would be *wonderful*.

Apparently Ash had asked one of the captains for a rec-ommendation and directions, for he led Neve unerringly through the streets to an inn bearing no name but a sign depicting a tankard spilling over with ale. To Neve's relief, despite his apparent miserliness, Ash didn't make the arro-gant assumption that he and Neve would share a room. Neve didn't have enough coin left to pay for the rooms, but the innkeeper of the Brimming Mug was content to hold their packs and direct them to a moneychanger.

It wasn't until they left the inn that Neve realized that Ash had talked to the innkeeper as easily as he'd talked to the ship captain in Kent; she had taken her own linguistic ability so much for granted that it amazed her to realize that Ash apparently knew several languages all on his own, with no magical aid whatsoever. Then again, she had no idea how long he'd been a sailor, but the implication was that he'd traveled extensively. Obviously he'd either have to learn sev-eral languages—at least enough to get along—or spend a good bit of money on translation spells.

Strachan was about the same size as Kent, which surprised Neve, considering that Strachan was the gateway city be-tween the Dezarin and the sea; Ash explained, however, that Strachan was, after all, only a transfer point. Most cargo and passengers that arrived here only moved to other ships bound east or west to the larger coastal cities.

"What's flash powder?" Neve asked as they walked.

Ash shrugged.

"It's a gray powder alchemists make," he said. "When you light it up, it makes a bang and a big flash of light. Why?"

"They were loading a lot of boxes of it on our ship," Neve told him. "I just wondered what it was for."

"Oh." Ash shrugged again. "I told you, the rainy season's about to start. That pretty much shuts down the coastal cities because the ships can't get through. Most of them have one last big festival before that happens. I'm sure Zaravelle does, too. That stuff's probably for displays the mages put on for entertainment, big illusion-and-flashing-light displays."

"Oh." Neve thought about that. "Will we get there in time to see it?"

Ash chuckled.

"The stuff's on the ship we're sailing on, remember?"

Neve grimaced. Ash had the most infuriating way of making her feel incredibly stupid sometimes.

"My father," she said coolly, "wouldn't need any of those things. And I imagine he could create a display more impressive than any of those mages could."

"Probably could," Ash agreed, unruffled. "But who'd be to see it?"

Neve glanced at him.

"There are people in the Keep," she said. "Plenty of them."

"Oh, yeah?" Ash grinned. "Somehow you made me think you'd hardly met a human being in your life."

"I hadn't," Neve said. "Not many. But I never said all the people in the Keep are human."

"Oh, yeah?" Ash stopped. "Elves, you mean?"

Neve considered that.

"No," she said. "At least I don't think so. Not since Yaga and Kelara—the friends I'm going to visit—left. Just people. Some of them were transformed when they came to the Keep. I don't know, maybe some of them were never human to begin with."

Ash gave her a suspicious glance and started walking again.

"Now you're joking me," he said. "There's just elves and humans, that's all. And shifters, but they don't count."

Neve snorted.

"You don't know anything," she said. "I've seen creatures I read about in books of legends, and I've seen creatures humans have no names for."

"What sort of legendary creatures?" Ash asked dubiously.

"Oh, there's the fauns," Neve said, shrugging. "There's lots of them. I used to have a friend, a faun named Skivvit, when I was little, but when I started getting older Mother wouldn't let me go into his pocket world anymore, and Father agreed with her. I don't know why."

"Fauns." Ash snorted. "I suppose you're going to tell me now that mermaids are real, too."

"Of course they're real," Neve said, shrugging. "Everything's real, at least in the Crystal Keep. I suppose they're real here, too, because if somebody hadn't seen them some-where, I don't know how they'd exist in the Keep.''

"You *saw* mermaids?" Ash demanded.

"Of course I saw them," Neve said, mildly insulted. Did Ash think she'd say something was real if she hadn't seen it for herself? "They're common enough in reefy places in the seas, where they nest in caves. They follow packs of sea dragons, too, and eat up the leavings from the sea dragons' kills. And I'll tell you something—they aren't just 'maids' either. There are males, too." Nor, despite their legendary status, had Neve found them to be particularly shy. Quite the contrary. *That* sea was one Neve stayed out of.

"You *saw* mermaids," Ash repeated, shaking his head. "The beautiful sea ladies every sailor dreams about—"

Neve chuckled.

"Then sailors are stupid," she said. "Or not very picky. Or else they're thinking of sirens. Sirens live in lonely places, like the sea, and they usually look like beautiful women; they're actually predatory demons who drown and eat anyone they can lure in close enough.

"Mermaids aren't demonic—although you'd never know it to look at them. They're *ugly*, and not very smart, either. Their whole language is only a couple dozen gestures and a few whistles that'll split your ears, most of them meaning 'fish' because that's what they eat—raw. So you can imagine their breath."

"Their . . . breath." Ash's voice was flat.

"Well, all right, they don't breathe air," Neve said crossly. "Their smell, then." She glanced around her. "Listen, you didn't want me to tell a magistrate who I am. Now we're standing in the middle of a public marketplace and you're asking me about mermaids."

Ash scowled.

"You're right," he said. "It's just—no. You're right."

A jeweler bought five rubies from Neve and, to her surprise, gave her what Ash told her was a decent price. She divided the gold with Ash so that neither of them were carrying temptingly bulging purses.

To Neve's surprise, she found the marketplace in Strachan more tolerable in Ash's company than she had in Kent, alone. Ash didn't seem to intrude on her the way other people did;

he didn't touch her (except of course when she wanted him to), he kept quiet most of the time and talked only when he had something real to say. His unobtrusiveness was somehow reassuring among these people who blithely jostled Neve or elbowed her, stepped on her feet, shouted in her ears until she hardly knew which way to turn, violating her with their very presence. When Neve thought she couldn't take it another minute, Ash would touch her shoulder lightly and almost mystically steer her to a less crowded spot.

Slowly Neve relaxed; by midday she'd even begun to rather enjoy the newness and variety of the marketplace. She could distract herself with goods she'd never seen before, clever trinkets, exotic new fruits to sample.

Neve chuckled at a memory, gesturing to a basket of fruit when Ash raised his eyebrows.

"We ate ourselves sick on those once, when I was little." She chuckled again, touching the green and orange-skinned fruits her father had called "monkey apples" because of the way the creatures wolfed down the sweet flesh. "Mother and Father and I."

The merchant, a middle-aged lady of ample girth, favored Neve with an icy glare.

"You must be . . . mistaken, young woman," she said flatly. "These fruits were only recently discovered by a ship exploring westward, and this is the first cargo of them to reach port."

Neve gave back a glare just as cold and hard.

"They grow on a tall tree with very long, oval leaves," she said. "The flesh is golden orange and a little grainy. There's a very large, flat seed in the middle, and the flesh clings to the seed, so it's hard to cut out. And if you pick them before they're quite ripe, they make a *lovely* tart." She stared the merchant woman straight in the eye. "And I don't *lie*."

"That's true," Ash admitted, chuckling. "She don't. Even when she ought." He took Neve's elbow, steering her firmly away from the stall. "Come on, girl. Calm down. If you put the back up on every merchant in the square, where are we going to get our dinner?"

"Not *there*, that's for certain," Neve muttered darkly. *Stupid woman! It'd serve her right if every one of those fruits was wormy.* Then, to her amazement, she felt a strange shudder go through her, a sort of internal wobble, and she stopped where she was, clinging to Ash's arm dizzily.

"What?" Ash said, stopping too. "Look, girl, it's not that big a thing if—"

"Seram preserve us!" someone choked behind them, and Neve heard gasps, a small shriek of horror.

Ash glanced over his shoulder, then froze. Neve turned more slowly, somehow dreading to look, but even so her jaw dropped in amazement at the sight.

Worms were welling up out of the basket of monkey apples, wriggling out of the fruits and up between them, spilling over the edges like ale out of an overfilled mug—long worms, short ones, pale and dark and ringed and smooth, earthworms and maggots and cabbage worms and—

"Peregard's balls," Ash swore, swallowing heavily. He grasped Neve's arm more tightly and pulled her away at a fast walk, then a trot. At last he ducked around a corner, pulling her with him, and pushed her roughly up against the side of a building. "Did you do that, girl? Are you that stupid?"

Neve swallowed, too, still stunned.

"I—I don't know," she said in a small voice. "I didn't mean to. I mean, I didn't *try* to."

Ash held her there a moment, his strange eyes searching hers. Then he took a deep breath and slowly eased his grip on her arms.

"All right," he said slowly. "All right, then. Listen, you just tell me one thing. This magic you use, has it ever done anything without you meaning to?"

Neve shook her head firmly.

"No," she said with certainty. "Never." At Ash's dubious gaze, she added, "Sometimes when I try to do something new, that I'm not sure of, it doesn't come out the way I meant it to—like the whirlwind, you see? But nothing's ever happened without me even trying. Not ever."

Ash's eyes stayed riveted on hers.

"So you don't think you did that?" he asked softly.

Neve swallowed.

"I don't see how I could have," she said. "Not without stopping and concentrating and working at it. And practice."

But the Nexus could, a small voice within her said. *The Nexus has always been . . . helpful . . . to me. It molds its power to my will. Or maybe just to my thoughts? Can I really be sure?*

Ash slowly released her.

"All right," he said. "As you say, you don't lie. Still and all, probably best to find another part of the market, eh?"

"Probably," Neve agreed, still shaken. Someone else could have produced the worms—another mage, maybe. But how? Why? And just before it had happened, she'd been thinking about worms, thinking—

No. No. Nothing happened to that annoying fellow, Pick-erd, and I wished everything but Whore's Rot on him. And the crew of the Skipper—*why, they came out better than I did. The Nexus knows I've ill-wished enough rude people since I left the Keep, and nothing happened to any of them. It's just a coincidence. Of course I felt wobbly. I've felt wobbly since I stepped off the ship. It's only natural.*

Neve put her troubling thoughts aside, especially when Ash bought her a bowl of spiced spiderclaws in a red sauce Neve assumed was wine until she took a bite and the fiery taste seared her mouth. Ash chuckled while Neve sputtered and gasped and frantically swallowed the ale he handed her. Apparently her mother's vast knowledge of cooking had not extended to incendiary southern peppers. Neve swallowed more ale and ate more spiderclaw even as the tears ran out of the corners of her eyes; when she was finished, nothing would do but Ash must find her a spice merchant so she could include in her cooking pouch all the exotic new seasonings available here.

There were other foreign goods for sale here, too, and Neve wrinkled her nose when Ash bought more *cai*. Well, hopefully they wouldn't be doing any more camping, and he could keep the foul-tasting stuff to himself.

By the time they returned to the Brimming Mug, Neve had almost put the worm incident out of her mind, and the bountiful supper there restored her to calm. After supper, when she inquired of the innkeeper about a bath, however, Neve was puzzled when the innkeeper absentmindedly gestured her toward a door on the main floor.

"What, even for a gold piece a night we can't get a bath

in our rooms here?'' Neve muttered darkly to Ash.

Ash chuckled.

"Steamhouses," he said. "All the best inns in Strachan have 'em. Never done that, hey?''

Neve hadn't, and she made no objection when Ash followed her in and showed her how to ladle water over the red-hot rocks in the central grate, sending up great clouds of steam. Neve stripped a little reluctantly, although they'd latched the steamhouse door firmly behind them; somehow it seemed unsafe to be naked in a room where she couldn't see more than a couple handsbreadths in front of her nose. The hot, soggy air was disagreeable, too, even worse than the steamiest jungle pocket world in the Keep. Neve slumped down on one of the benches, breathing hard and wondering how long she was expected to put up with this misery.

Ash sat down behind her on the bench and rubbed her shoulders, digging his fingers skillfully into the muscles.

"Relax," he said. "That's what these places are good for.''

Neve let her head roll forward, leaning back against Ash's hands.

"What are you doing?" she murmured.

Ash chuckled.

"Right now, just rubbing your shoulders. Here, stretch out.''

The wood of the bench was smooth, almost polished against Neve's cheek. Neve closed her eyes, almost dozing in the heat under the delightful pressures of Ash's hands.

"Where did you learn to do this?" she said.

"Oh, back when I was on the streets, I used to spend time with a girl who worked in a fancy whorehouse," Ash said easily. "She taught me a thing or two. Like this.''

Neve sighed contentedly as his thumbs dug into her lower back. The tension seemed to melt out of her body.

"Is that all she taught you?" she mumbled.

Ash chuckled, his hands sliding over her wet skin.

"Well—she taught me this, too.''

"Mmmmmmmmmmm."

"And this.''

"Ooohhhhhhhh—''

"And this . . .''

* * *

There were disadvantages, Neve mused wearily in the morning, to having a real human lover who actually spent the night in one's bed (as opposed to conjured homunculi who could be dismissed with a wave afterward, or visiting mortals whom she could simply leave when she was done). Lovers snored, pulled the covers off their bedmates, rolled and kicked and elbowed and kept their partners awake, and took far more than their fair share of the pillow. They also made Neve chide herself for paying the extra money for another room.

And if they were sailors, they got up ridiculously early, blithely rousting their bedmates with them even though there was no breakfast to be had yet, and were entirely too perky at an hour of the morning when even the sun wasn't properly awake.

Leaving the inn so early also meant that they ran into the coming-to-market crowd, pedestrians and carts and wagons all bound inward to the central plaza, while Neve and Ash had to try to push outward to the docks. To Neve's surprise, Ash preferred to brave the crowds rather than cut through the alleys as they'd done in Kent.

"Back alleys are no place for a noble girl, especially one with a fat purse," he said briefly when she made the suggestion.

"I was still a noble girl with money in Kent," Neve said, a little nettled. "And you hauled me through the alleys there."

"Yeah, well, in that particular case the law was more dangerous than the criminals." Ash chuckled. "Come on, noble girl. Our ship's waiting."

So it was that Neve boarded the *Albatross* tired and without her breakfast, glad to drop her bags in her tiny cabin and flop down on the narrow bunk. She felt a brief moment of spiteful glee in knowing that while she could now rest, Ash was just beginning his day's work, and the ship wouldn't even leave port for another couple of hours. Well, *she* certainly hadn't kept *him* awake all night.

Neve woke just in time to find a comfortable vantage point between posts on the forward deck and watch the *Albatross* leave port, the docks fading behind them with gratifying rapidity. For the first time she understood what Ash loved about the sea. After the noise and fuss of the city and the stink of the wharf, the fresh, clean sea air and the relative quiet were a welcome change.

Neve had hardly settled herself, however, when an unexpected complication arose. Captain Corell, after glancing at her several times, finally walked over, holding out one callused hand.

"I'm Corell, lady," the tall, muscular woman said politely. "The captain."

Neve grudgingly took the proffered hand.

"Neve," she said shortly.

"Lady Neve," the captain said, a little more stiffly, "wouldn't you be more comfortable in your cabin?"

"No, thank you," Neve said, shrugging. "I'm quite comfortable here."

She thought that would be the end of it, but to her dismay, the captain showed no sign of leaving.

"Lady Neve," the captain said, still politely, "my men are very busy here. I'm sure you would be more comfortable in your cabin."

This time Neve got the message, and she didn't like it.

"I'm not in the way here," she said between gritted teeth. "Nobody's even come near me but you. I won't bother the sailors or get under anybody's feet."

Captain Corell didn't budge.

"We need the decks as clear as possible," she said.

Neve glanced pointedly at the deck passengers, and Captain Corell shrugged.

"They have nowhere else to go," she said.

"You mean to say," Neve said coldly, "that deck passengers can sit out here in the fresh air, but I'm confined to my cabin like a prisoner?"

Captain Corell smiled remotely.

"I'm sure I wouldn't put it in those terms," she said. "However, you *did* pay for a cabin, my lady. Not a space on the deck."

She hates nobles, Neve realized angrily. *She thinks I'm a weakling who'll only get underfoot and hang over the rail spewing my breakfast. If I'd had any breakfast, that is. By the Nexus, the nobles don't like me because they think I'm a peasant, and now the peasants don't like me because I'm a noble!*

Neve got up, her eyes never leaving Captain Corell's.

"I'm not some weak-bellied idiot," she said icily. "And I'm not going to be kept shut in my cabin like a prisoner all the way to Zaravelle." She turned on her heel and walked back to her cabin, slamming the door resoundingly behind her. *I'd like to see you hanging over the rail puking for the whole trip, you arrogant bitch.*

Then she sat down on the bunk, suddenly glad of its stability as her stomach lurched. *Oh, by the Nexus, don't let me be getting ship-sick like those weak-kneed nobles who sneer at me. We're barely even out of port.*

She lay down, and to her relief the unsteadiness passed in a few moments.

Thank the Nexus. I couldn't bear that rude captain laughing at me all the way to Zaravelle. Never mind, I'm just tired and upset. It's nothing.

Nevertheless Neve didn't venture out of her cabin, except to claim her dinner and supper, until the sun set. The *Albatross* was well out into open water by then, and Neve hoped that as on the previous voyages, nighttime meant fewer crew on board. Maybe Ash would have time to talk to her; he'd be on watch now, maybe up in the crow's nest again.

But when Neve crept quietly up onto deck she found a rather hectic flurry of activity going on; one glimpse at the sky told her why. Clouds completely covered the moon and stars, and faint, distant rumblings of thunder warned of coming rain. That entirely banished any thoughts of a pleasant evening's socializing and sightseeing, and Neve hurriedly ducked back into her cabin. At least it was an outside cabin, where she could push aside the curtains over the porthole and see out. She did hear thunder that night and saw the occasional flash of lightning, and she could hear rain, but the sea never became too rough and by morning the sky was clear again.

To her surprise and delight, she ran into Ash in the galley the next morning over breakfast. The sailor looked rather bedraggled and tired, and Neve speculated that he was just coming off watch.

"You look like you got the worst of it last night," she

said. "The storm didn't seem that bad to me."

Ash managed a weary grin.

"Oh, it wasn't too bad," he said. "But it was kind of confusing up top without the captain, and the sailors were worried about storms without their mage."

Neve frowned.

"Where was the captain?" she asked. "And what happened to the ship's mage?"

"Same answer to both questions," Ash said, shrugging. "Captain Corell *is* the ship's weather mage, and she's down sick. Pretty bad, I hear. Some say she ate some bad pork back in port, maybe. She just keeps heaving and heaving."

Neve's heart gave a great lurch in her chest and a wave of cold seemed to sweep through her body.

"What?" she said, very softly. "When did that start?"

"Oh, not too many hours out of port," Ash said, shaking his head. "I guess she'd bought a pork pie on the docks just before we sailed out. That's no joke, bad pork. I wish we had a healer on board. I sure don't like the thought of being on the high seas just a week out of storm season without captain and mage both."

Neve swallowed.

"What if she did eat bad pork?" she asked. "What happens then?"

Ash shook his head again.

"No telling," he said. "She could be up on her feet and fine tomorrow, or she could be dead in a few days if she can't keep at least liquids down. Meanwhile that bloody idiot of a first mate, Arden, is trying to run the ship and making an awful mess of it, and we got no mage to scry out the weather and find us a clear path around it. I don't like it a bit. There's already been a couple fellows suggest turning back, but Corell and Arden won't hear of it."

Neve closed her eyes, shivering.

She just keeps heaving and heaving.

"What about the passengers on deck?" she asked. "What did they do last night during the storm?"

"Ah, wasn't much of a storm," Ash said dismissively. "If it'd been bad enough we'd have brought them in, wherever we could fit 'em—crew's quarters, the hold, you name it. But it never got that bad last night."

Neve was silent for a long moment.

"What happens," she said very slowly, "if—if really bad weather comes?"

Ash hesitated a moment.

"Hard to say," he said. "I got to admit, turning back now, we'd be going against current and wind both, and there's no good anchorage along the coast now—all reefs and cliffs and the like, most of the way to Zaravelle. It'd be hard enough even getting a scow ashore. Push on, I guess, and hope for the best."

He hesitated, then spoke again very softly.

"Don't suppose you've got anything in that book of yours that might help the captain?"

Neve tried not to wince at the question.

"I—I suppose there might be a healing spell in there," she said, just as softly. "But what if I tried to cast it and it went wrong, like the whirlwind?"

"Mmmm." Ash glanced down into his mug, grimacing. "Well, better start reading anyway. Things get bad enough, it might come to risking it."

Neve returned to her cabin, deeply troubled.

I'd like to see you hanging over the rail and puking for the whole trip, you arrogant bitch.

She just keeps heaving and heaving.

Neve began to tremble.

By the Nexus, I couldn't have. I couldn't.

Then she took a deep breath.

No. It's by the Nexus that I COULD.

Her hands shaking, Neve pulled the crystal out of her tunic, clasped it tight, trying to remember what the grimoire had said about spellcasting. She cleared her mind, stilled her emotions, focused her thoughts.

I want the captain to be well, she thought firmly. *I want her stomach to settle. I want her to feel fine and strong. I want her fit and able to run this ship and protect us. I don't want her harmed. I don't want her sick. Do you hear me?*

Nothing. No tingle of magic, no strange internal wobble as she'd felt in the market and in her cabin the day before. No tiredness such as she'd felt when she changed the pebbles into rubies. Neve felt unhappily certain that that meant nothing had happened.

She pulled out her mother's grimoire. Like the weather spell she'd tried, the healing spell looked deceptively simple, but it was closer to the front of the book, which meant it was a more elementary spell.

Neve pulled out her knife—her sharp eating dagger, *not* the one her father had given her—and gingerly cut her finger slightly. A simple superficial wound—that would do to start. She read the spell again. Yes, simple enough, direct—

But—

The whirlwind. The gore of misbegotten dragons littering the beach.

Neve closed the book and her eyes at the same time.

I don't dare. I'm a coward. I—just—don't—dare. What if it goes wrong? What if I do something horrible to myself, something as horrible as making someone vomit and vomit and vomit until they die?

Now *she* felt sick. What kind of Guardian was she, gifted with the power of the Nexus but lacking either the skill or the courage to use it? How could she ever face her father knowing that she could use the power of the Nexus to slaughter dozens of dragons and conjure up a whirlwind huge enough to devastate a forest, but couldn't bring herself to heal so much as a cut finger?

Desperately she opened her cooking pouch, fingered the smaller sacks of herbs and spices inside. There was mint, and mint made a tea that soothed the stomach.

I'd like to see you *hanging over the rail and puking for the whole trip, you arrogant bitch.*

Neve shook her head. Mint tea wasn't going to do it this time.

Maybe Ash was right, she thought desperately. *Maybe it was bad pork. Maybe it's just a coincidence.*

Neve thought sickly of the worms. No. Much as she'd like to, she couldn't quite manage to believe it was a coincidence.

How? How can I do it without even trying, but I can't do it when I do *try?*

Neve shook her head to clear it. The plain fact was that until she had more skill, or at least more practice, in using her power, anything she tried might well do more harm than good. A *lot* more harm.

Well, the one advantage of the captain's illness was that

Neve could now sit on deck with impunity, and she decided that sunshine and fresh air was exactly what she needed. She made her way back up to the deck, eager to reclaim the vantage point she'd found earlier—

Then she stopped, scowling. A decidedly grubby child of indeterminate sex had curled up in *her* comfortable nook, nibbling a piece of dried meat as she—he?—watched the sailors, the sea, just as Neve had.

Neve stood there rather blankly, angry but at the same time somehow caught off balance. She'd seen mortal children before in Selwaer, in Kent, in Strachan—from a distance. She'd never actually met one.

The child turned its head just enough to glance at Neve out of the corner of its eye, then turned more—enough to stare. That bit of rudeness doubled both Neve's anger and her confusion.

"Are you a noble lady?" the child asked. Neve reassessed the child, adding in the evidence of its voice, and decided it was male.

"Yes," she said. "I'm a noble lady."

The child digested this information rather indifferently; at last it—he—spoke again.

"Is this your place?"

Neve folded her arms.

"Yes."

The child appeared unimpressed, but he slid out from between the posts, vacating the spot. Neve hesitated just a moment before reclaiming her vantage point.

"Noble ladies," the child announced, "don't sit on deck."

"This one does," Neve said shortly. "This one doesn't like being shut up in little cabins." She started to turn away, dismissing the child—then she remembered the nobles in the inn who had turned away from her in just that way. Neve turned back. The boy was still there.

"What's your name?" Neve said.

"Ruper," the boy said, settling himself nonchalantly against the same post Neve was leaning against. "What's yours, lady?"

Neve fought to keep from reflexively backing away. The boy was dirty but thank the Nexus she couldn't see any vermin.

"Neve," she said, trying to sound friendly.

"Are you sure you're a noble lady?" Ruper asked curiously. "I've never seen a noble who didn't wear fine clothes and their house crest."

Neve thought that over.

"Well, if I wore fine clothes, I couldn't sit out here," she said. "And I don't think my family has a crest."

"All noble houses have crests," Ruper said, wrinkling his nose.

"Well, mine doesn't," Neve said shortly. "I guess we're not like other noble houses." She smiled. "We have powerful magic."

"Magic?" Ruper's eyes widened. "Your family's mages?"

"Something like that," Neve said after a moment's thought. "My father probably has the most powerful magic in the world."

"Can *you* do magic?" Ruper asked immediately.

Neve winced slightly.

"Yes," she said. "But not as well as my father does."

"Then do."

Neve scowled.

"What?"

"Do it," Ruper said eagerly. "Do some magic."

Neve hesitated. The very thought made her cringe, but the eagerness in that child's eyes was a challenge, almost a demand. No Guardian-to-be would ever admit to a grubby mortal child that she was *afraid* to use her own magic!

"That," Neve said, gesturing at a bracelet of chipped wooden beads around Ruper's wrist. "Give me that."

Ruper narrowed his eyes suspiciously, but he untied the knot on the bracelet and handed it over.

Neve slid one bead up the string by itself and clenched it tightly in her hand, closing her eyes. *This* she could do. *This* she was sure of, and that alone felt good.

She handed the bracelet back, and Ruper fingered the transformed bead.

"It's red," he said, surprised. "It's stone."

"It's a ruby," Neve said. "It's valuable. Very, very valuable. If you want, when you go ashore you can sell it for plenty of gold."

Startled brown eyes searched Neve's; then Ruper grinned.
He was missing two teeth in front.

"Thanks, Lady Neve," he said. "Wait'll my mama hears
I met a real noble lady, a mage, too." He hesitated. "I won't
sit in your spot again. I promise." He scampered off, tying
the bracelet back around his wrist. She saw him rejoin an
equally ragged family in what was apparently *their* spot
against the galley wall.

Perversely Neve was sorry to see him go; filthy and rude
though the child was, he was certainly the most agreeable
human she had met, apart from Ash. To her surprise, she'd
rather enjoyed the company.

At midday Neve left her "spot" just long enough to fetch a
little dinner, then settled in again. She caught sight of Ash
from time to time, usually high in the rigging, but although
he must have seen her, he did not approach. That worried
Neve slightly.

More worrisome were the clouds gathering rapidly overhead and ahead of them. Neve was no weather mage, but she
knew a good-sized storm in the making when she saw one;
there were several pocket worlds in the Keep where it
seemed to do nothing *but* storm.

Neve stared out to sea, scowling as the first drop of rain
spattered her cheek. Could they avoid the storm by moving
to deeper water? Moving closer to shore would be dangerous,
if Ash was right about cliffs and reefs, but surely in open
water—

Neve gasped. Had she seen—had she really—oh, by the
Nexus, surely not—

There it was, that flicker of movement, that swell that
wasn't a wave. Neve had spent too much time watching the
seas within the Keep to doubt what she saw.

By the Nexus!

Neve bolted to her feet, glancing around frantically. There
was Ash in the rigging, far overhead. She waved both arms,
but he apparently didn't see her. She waved again, more
desperately; this time Ash's eyes flickered down and she was
sure he'd seen.

Come down here, Neve thought as if the force of her will
alone might sway him. *You know I have something important*

to say or I wouldn't say it. Come down *here!*

And thank the Nexus, down he came, sliding down a long rope to the deck.

"What is it?" he said with none of the impatience Neve had expected. "We're kind of busy right now, you know."

"I know." Neve swallowed. "I saw a sea dragon."

Ash went still, very still.

"Where?" he said, lowering his voice almost to a whisper.

Neve dropped her voice, too.

"Out to sea," she said. "Far enough that I wasn't sure at first. But it's there."

Ash took her arm, strolled with her over to the rail almost casually.

"See if you see it again," he said. "Don't point, just tell me."

Neve scanned the horizon. Nothing.

"Shouldn't we tell the others?" she murmured.

"Not yet," Ash said just as quietly. "If the passengers panic, there'll be a riot, and we'll *all* be dragon food."

Neve took a deep breath, straining her eyes. Maybe she'd been mistaken. It could've been anything. Something else. Anything else.

No.

"There," she whispered, her mouth dry. "I'm facing it."

Ash was silent for a long moment.

"I see it," he said. "Just the one?"

Neve shook her head.

"I only *saw* one," she said. "But sea dragons swim in packs. I've never seen a pack of less than six or eight." She glanced at Ash. "Do you think—are they following us?"

"Oh, you'd better believe they are," Ash said grimly. "The good news is they probably won't attack as long as we stay reasonably close to shore; they're open-water animals and need depth to set up for an attack. The bad news—"

"Is that we don't want to be close to shore if there's a storm," Neve said. She felt her hands shaking and clenched them hard around the rail. She took a deep breath and glanced at Ash.

"Are we desperate enough yet," she said slowly, "for me to—"

Ash bit his lip, probably thinking of the whirlwind.

"Not yet," he said. "Listen, go back to your cabin and wait there. Look through your book and think about what you could do. I'm going to talk to Arden, and then I'll come and talk to you."

This time Neve was grateful to return to her cabin; the rain was coming down harder now, but it wasn't the rain that made that chill deep in the pit of her stomach.

There's a pack of sea dragons following the ship, there's a storm coming in, and we have no captain and no mage— and whose fault is that? Mine. Come on, Neve. There's got to be something *I can do. What would Father do?*

Neve shook her head, slouching on her bed. Father would simply banish storm and dragons both with a wave of his hand. Or, more likely, he'd simply transport himself off the ship.

Well, that's not much use, Neve thought sourly. *I can't do any of those.*

She leafed through the grimoire, assessing one spell, then another. They all *looked* simple, but Neve knew how deceptive that was. Thunder crashed abruptly, much closer than she would have expected, and she shivered.

I can't turn a storm, she thought, feeling the first hint of desperation. *The last time I tried that, I brought it right down on top of me.*

Her door opened; Neve was so relieved to see Ash that she barely noticed that he'd forgotten to knock.

"What's happening?" she asked.

"Well, the dragons aren't no closer," he said with a sigh, running his fingers through his wet hair. "But the storm is. Looks like we're in for it."

"And the captain?" Neve asked reluctantly.

Ash shook his head.

"No better," he said. "She wanted to be brought up on deck, but Arden said there's no point, and he's right. She can't even stand up, much less cast a spell or run the ship. She'd just be in the way."

Neve swallowed.

"So what are we going to do?" she asked softly.

Ash shrugged wearily.

"The only thing we can do," he said. "Forge on ahead.

To turn back, we'd have to steer out to sea to get out of the current, and then there's the dragons. We can't put in to shore, and even if we could anchor, the storm would just bash us to splinters against the reefs anyway. So we push on and pray a lot. The storm's coming in from the sea, so it's hitting us sideways instead of head-on; that's something. But we're stuck between sea dragons to port and reefs to starboard, and I don't like those reefs so close with bad weather coming in.''

Neve fought down panic.

No. I'm the heir to the Crystal Keep. I told the captain I'm no weak-bellied idiot, and I'm NOT.

"All right," she said as steadily as she could. "Tell me what I can do."

Ash nodded, half smiling as if he was pleased with her.

"Good girl," he said. "First off, bundle everything you've just *got* to have in a little, light pack and keep it on you. If we have to get into the longboats, won't be time to go back for your goodies, nor room for much baggage.

"I told Arden about your magic," Ash continued, grimacing slightly. "He doesn't think it's worth taking the chance of making things worse. I don't know that I agree with him, but he's in charge. Listen, though. I had another thought. What you seem to be good at is solid things, right?"

"Well—maybe," Neve said cautiously. "What kind of solid things?"

"The hull." Ash stomped on the deck demonstratively. "The worst danger we've got is leaks and breaches in the hull, and that's what a mage is best for in a storm that can't be stopped and can't be avoided. Think you could mend a hull breach?"

Neve caught her breath.

"I don't know," she said, a cautious hope blossoming in her heart. Wood she knew. "I think so. Let me try."

She searched the wall of her cabin until she found a knothole. Clutching her fragment of the Nexus tightly, she focused tightly on the hole, concentrating.

Wood is solid, seamless, sturdy, Neve thought firmly. *Tight enough to hold water without leaking. Strong enough to weather storms. Solid. Solid. It lived, grew, changed. It can grow now to be what it's supposed to be.*

Wood flowed, shifted, sealed. Neve sighed with relief. She poked the place where the knothole had been, gingerly at first, then harder. At last she drew her dagger and chipped at it hard. It was solid; there was no sign there had ever been a hole there.

"Yes," she said, and the word was a celebration. "Yes. I can close holes."

Ash scowled.

"That puts you down in the hold, though," he said. "I don't much like that, especially if we got something a mite more important than leaks—like sea dragons making a rush. Can you fix a hole you can't see?"

Neve started to shake her head, then stopped.

Wait. I built dragons—never mind that they weren't right—and the Nexus knows I'd never seen the inside of one. Remember what Father said? It's always easier to work from the inside out.

"I don't know," she said carefully. "Let me try."

She laid both hands against the wooden wall, closing her eyes.

I know how the ship's built, or pretty much so; that's more than I knew about the dragons. There's a rightness to shapes, a wholeness, a balance. Feel that balance, wood and strength and pressure and water, all bound together in this creature called a ship—

Without knowing precisely how she did it, Neve felt the shape of the boat, the precise way the ribs balanced against the pressure of the water, the way the rudder slid against the current, the weight of the boat and yet its lightness in the water—

"Got it," she said, a little breathlessly, this time with hope instead of fear. "Yes, I think I can mend a breach even from deck."

Ash sighed raggedly, and Neve was relieved to see some of the anxiety leave his face.

"All right, then," he said. "We'll want you there on deck, then, if you can take the weather. If there's an emergency, won't be no time to go fetch you."

"Yes," Neve said. She hurriedly bundled her coin purse, her gold and gems, her fragment of the Nexus, and her daggers into a scrap of cloth; when she dumped the spices out of her cooking pouch, she could pack her valuables tightly inside and lace it securely to her belt. She grabbed her cloak and followed Ash out onto the deck.

The storm had gotten worse even while they talked. Rain lashed down heavily now, and the thunder was almost continuous. Flickering lightning illuminated the deck brilliantly, then left Neve blinking helplessly with dazzled eyes in the darkness. She saw the deck passengers clustered as close to the middle of the ship as they could get, huddling under waxed skins.

"Wait," she called out over the storm, halting Ash. "Hadn't you better get the passengers in? It'll clear the decks, at least."

"Right!" Ash called back. "I'll get the cook to start bringing them down to the hold. You meet me up at the bow." He vanished into the rain.

Neve hesitated—*The hold? But if there's a leak, or worse*—then decided. She had to push her way past sailors and confused passengers, but she managed to struggle to the galley, working her way around the outside wall. She almost stepped on Ruper; he was huddled, along with the rest of his family, under a large waxed skin.

"Lady!" He laughed when he recognized Neve. "What're you doing out here in the rain?"

"I told you, I don't like being shut up in little cabins," Neve said, feeling a sudden warmth in her heart. "Listen, Ruper, you take your family down to my cabin. Just go down that hatchway. It's third door on the left. There isn't much room, but there's a couple dry blankets. Go on, now. Fast."

Ruper's eyes widened, but he grinned.

"Yes, lady," he said. "Thank you, lady!"

Neve started to turn away, but a hand clutched at her wrist and she whirled, almost drawing her dagger by reflex alone. She found herself gazing into the wide eyes of Ruper's mother and hurriedly forced her hand away from her dagger hilt.

"Thank you, lady," the woman said, loudly over the rain. "We're in your debt."

You'd better believe you are, Neve thought in a moment of perverse amusement. *Just wait till you sell that ruby.*

"Never mind that," she said. "Just take your children

belowdecks. I'm told it's going to get worse before it gets better.''

She didn't wait to see if Ruper's family obeyed her instructions; passengers were starting to head for the hatches, and Neve hurriedly pushed her way forward. Ash was waiting for her near the bow, his arms full of cork floats linked on a rope.

''Tie this around you,'' he shouted over the rain. ''Good and tight. Then tie one end to the mast, but keep a knife where you can get to it fast in case you have to cut loose. That way I'll know where you are. I've got to go keep lookout—''

Neve glanced up at the crow's nest and her heart lurched.

''You can't go up there!'' she gasped. ''The lightning, the wind—what if it just blows you off?''

''I ain't fool enough to go up there,'' Ash returned impatiently. ''Even if I saw something in this mess, nobody could hear me call down. I'm going starboard and up the rigging just a bit. Don't worry.'' He picked up one foot, wriggling the long toes. ''I can hang on good and tight, believe it. Now stay here, hold on, and be ready with your magic if we need it. Right?''

''Yes,'' Neve shouted. She pulled her cloak on, drew the hood up. ''I'll be here. I'll be ready.''

Ash said nothing else, but he squeezed her hand, just a little, before he turned away, and Neve felt reassured. She hurriedly tied the floats securely around her waist, then anchored the end to the mast, making sure that her ''safe'' dagger was within easy reach in her boot. Then there was nothing to do but hold on and watch—watch the sailors scramble to secure the sails and get the passengers belowdecks, watch the increasing swells of the sea, watch the growing fury of the storm.

Then lightning gleamed on wet glistening scales, closer than before, much closer. Neve froze in awe and fear as the great leviathan slid so sleekly through the water, so beautiful, nearly as long as the ship and ever so much more graceful. She realized suddenly that *they* were the trespassers in the dragon's world, and she forgot to breathe as the long snake-like neck and head shot up from the water and a roar that was half music, half thunder split the air. Lightning glistened on long silvered teeth and golden eyes.

Am I going to die to feed that creature? Neve thought with rather surprising detachment. *There's a kind of balance to that, after I killed so many dragons on the beach. What would Father think?*

Then the great glistening bulk slid under the water again and Neve sucked in a great heaving breath, hearing for the first time the screams of passengers and even some of the crew pushing their way violently down belowdecks as most of them saw the gigantic monster for the first time.

That's silly, Neve thought idly. *This ship's no protection at all if the dragons make a rush on us; they'll crush it like an eggshell.*

A groaning sound below, a grating—*The reef?* Neve laid both hands on the deck and focused her mind, dismissing the dragon, the storm, with some difficulty. Yes, she could feel the stress *here* and *here,* timbers beginning to yield under the pressure.

Neve took a deep breath. *Make the shape whole again. Restore the balance.* She let the power of the Nexus flow outward, guiding it by instinct more than thought, reinforcing the structure where it was about to buckle, more pressure outward *here,* more strength *here,* careful—

Then a snapping sound—*Below? No, above*—that seemed to rip through the fabric of the universe, a flash that dazzled Neve's eyes and shocked straight through her as a piercing tongue of pure energy shot into the structure she'd sent her awareness into, and she slumped to the deck, reeling dizzily and half-stunned.

"What?" she whispered to no one in particular. "What?"

Dimly she heard screams, scrambling footsteps, a crackling sound that should have meant something but didn't; all Neve was certain of was the wet deck beneath her cheek. Slowly the dancing blue spots in her eyes faded and she shook her head, trying to clear it. The icy rain helped.

Lightning, she thought dully. *We were struck by lightning. What I heard must have been one of the masts snapping—*

There was something about that, and Neve tried to follow the thread to some conclusion.

Lightning.

Mast.

Then Neve pushed herself upright, blinking tears and rain out of her eyes. She cut loose the end of the rope tied to the mast.

"Ash!" she screamed. "Ash!"

She stumbled over the deck, pushing heedlessly past milling passengers, panicking crewmembers. She stumbled over a fallen, smoldering sail and tangled her feet in rope and went on anyway, dragging the end of the string of floats behind her. Where was everybody going?

The longboats!

Oh, by the Nexus! Neve realized, finally recognizing the crackling sound, the dim red glow. *The ship's on fire!*

The deck was clearing rapidly as one longboat, then another plunged down to the frothing sea, but for the moment Neve had no thought but her friend. She scanned the deck desperately through still-blurred eyes; at last she literally stumbled over the strange man. He was crumpled to the deck, his head bloody. A section of mast lay over him.

He's probably dead already, some small horrible part of her mind said practically. *And the boats are leaving. There aren't nearly enough boats for all these people. I'd better get going* now *before I'm trapped here to burn or drown or go down a dragon's throat.*

Then Neve knelt and laid her hand on the mast and wood became water and flowed aside. And Ash's eyes stayed closed, but yes, he was breathing. Neve half dragged, half lifted him, pulling him to the rail even as the last longboat dropped into the water.

"Wait!" she screamed. "Wait, we're here!"

Then another crackle from somewhere below and almost without thinking Neve pulled in the length of rope and floats and looped them around Ash, once, twice, again, and tied it tight as she realized—

Fire.

Brandy and oil and flash pow—

And suddenly the world grew very, very bright.

Neve must have lost consciousness for a bare moment, but awareness quickly returned as salt water burned her eyes and nose and filled her mouth. She was icy cold—

Well, of course, you idiot. You're in the sea.

The cold shocked the sense back into her. Someone was struggling against her, jabbing her with knees and elbows—oh, yes, Ash, of course. He sputtered and spewed water into her face.

"What—" he gasped. "Where—"

"We're in the water," Neve said needlessly, struggling to clear her eyes. "The ship was on fire. I think—I think there was an explosion—"

Ash stiffened.

"The dragons!"

"Don't worry," Neve shouted over the storm. "I think we're probably too small to notice. Can we make it to shore?"

Ash struggled to get his head above the waves to look, then slumped back.

"How good a swimmer are you?" he shouted. "The current's pulling us out, not in!"

Oh, by the Nexus, not like this—

Wait!

Sea dragons! Reefs and—

Neve coughed and spat seawater, clearing her mouth as best she could, then doubled her tongue and whistled as shrilly as she could. Again. Again.

Come on, you smelly scavengers! This is your kind of territory; maybe the weather's not so nice, but look, there's a sea-dragon pack out here which means lots of juicy scraps, and you'll see the fire, and you're ever so curious! By the Nexus, hear me! HEAR ME!

She thought she'd asked too much, almost decided there'd be no answer, when strong scaly hands grabbed her hard enough to bruise, horny claws piercing through her clothes. A shout of surprise and fear from Ash told her that he had also felt the presence of their rescuers. Neve had to rack her brain to remember the right squealing whistle, but thankfully she had a rather small vocabulary to choose from and her gift for languages held true; the claws, the hands did not tighten further, but held Neve up so she could keep her head above the water, and she was sure she could feel the speed of their movement through the water.

"Neve!" The sound of Ash actually calling her by her

name instead of "girl" momentarily shocked her silent. "What—"

"Don't worry!" she gasped, spitting out more water. A rotten fishy odor filled her nostrils. "We're being rescued—I think."

"You *think*?" Ash choked. "By the gods, these aren't— they *are*!"

The strong hands around Neve's waist grew rather more inquisitive than she'd have liked; she pushed at the strong, slippery fingers ineffectually.

"Damned smelly slimy—" Neve grumbled, squirming in her bearer's grip.

"Hey!" Ash yelped. "Let go of that! Tell 'em—"

Neve started to whistle "no" and abruptly realized that might be misinterpreted as a request for release; she sorted through the few whistles and gestures that made up the mermaids' language and settled on "unsuitable mate." At that whistle, however, a scaly gray head popped up from the waves, bulging eyes gazing into hers, sharp-toothed mouth gaping in what Neve interpreted as incredulity, followed closely by vast amusement, before the head disappeared under the water again. Several whistles and squeaks reverberated through air and water between who knew how many mermaids bearing them. To Neve's gratitude, however, the grasping hands became more polite.

Dimly through the storm Neve could see the coastline now, closer than she'd have expected; either the ship had drifted nearer shore than they'd thought or the mermaids were carrying them shoreward more quickly than even she would have believed. Never mind; either way she'd feel dry land under her sooner, and that was good enough for her. She held still and let the mermaids do the work. The strength seemed to drain out of her limbs as the numbing cold of the sea soaked into her skin.

"No!" Ash's hands pawed at her, shook her. "Keep kicking. Keep your blood moving."

Neve tried, really tried, but she was so cold, so tired—

Then she jolted violently, her eyes wide, at a rude pinch on her buttock.

"Keep kicking," Ash shouted grimly, "or I'll show 'em where *else* to pinch. Got it?"

Anger momentarily overcame exhaustion and chill and Neve kicked, thrashed with her arms—mostly hoping she'd hit Ash a good solid thwack in the face—until she realized they were rapidly approaching the rocks. Then she pulled in arms and legs, feeling Ash doing the same, hoping fervently she wouldn't lose a limb to the rough coral heads. She saw a gaping hole in the cliff face and realized the mermaids were propelling them toward a cave of some sort.

"No!" Ash yelled. "Not in—tell them not in the cave!"

Once again Neve had to sift through the inadequacy of the mermaids' language, but again she managed to convey her intended message and the mermaids turned up the coast. At last Neve felt rock under her feet and she scrambled over it, barely feeling the sharp coral as it abraded her numb fingers. Ash was tangled in the ropes with her, impeding her progress but scrambling along nonetheless.

"Got to get farther up," he panted. "A good wave comes in, it'll wash us right back out. Keep climbing!"

Neve was too tired and cold and shocked even to manage thought now; she barely noticed when Ash drew a knife and cut the rope binding them together. The only thought in her mind was that she wanted to get as far away from the sea as she could; by the Nexus, a thousand leagues wouldn't be far enough.

They climbed over coral heads, boulders, jagged shelves, and crumbling slopes, but at last Neve felt gravel, then sand under her. She collapsed limply, still tangled in rope and cork floats and her cloak. She half roused as Ash tugged insistently at her arm.

"Come on," he grunted. "Can't stop yet."

"Why not?" Neve groaned. By the Nexus, all she wanted in the world was to curl up and sleep right here and now, even with rain pouring down her face.

"We're both half-frozen," Ash said. "We've got to get under cover of some kind. Come on, little girl. Not much further."

"Little girl" was enough to stir the dying embers of Neve's anger and she forced herself to her feet. Ash was no steadier than she—of course, she remembered, she'd just come ashore from a ship again, not to mention chills and weakness—and they helped each other stumble and stagger along.

Neve barely noticed the first scrawny, wind-whipped vegetation, but she did note with gratitude the large rock with the jutting shelf, a shelf just large enough to shelter two sodden travelers below it. Ash crawled under and Neve followed, uncaring of water or muck or possible inhabitants. She would have collapsed then, but Ash insistently pulled at her cloak, huddling tightly against her body and pulling the cloak snugly around them both.

Neve had barely enough time to note the warmth slowly building between them, enough to stop her shaking, before exhaustion claimed her at last.

6

NEVE ROUSED SLOWLY, PAINFULLY, groaning in protest as she was dragged from blessed darkness. Her eyes, nose, and mouth were crusted with salt and sand; salt still stung in what seemed to be hundreds of cuts on her hands and knees. Every muscle in her body ached.

Oh, by the Nexus, not AGAIN, she thought wearily. The last time it had taken a troop of robber sailors to beat her this badly. This time the sea had done it.

Gradually it occurred to her that she had more room in her cloak than she'd had before, and that her head was pillowed on sand instead of Ash's shoulder. She forced her eyes open, wincing as sunlight stabbed twin daggers into her skull. The storm had ended and Neve was alone in her sodden bed— unless, of course, she counted the seeming thousands of sand lice who had joined her in the night. Her stomach gurgled ominously and suddenly she was mortally certain she was going to vomit.

Neve rolled out from under the rocky shelf and forced herself to her knees, crawling a few feet before she retched up what felt like gallons of seawater, retched again and again until she had nothing left to bring up.

''Here.'' Suddenly, miraculously Ash was there, easing

her over to her side and supporting her, pressing something to her lips. Almost uncaring, Neve bit, chewed, swallowed some kind of sweet, juicy fruit. It was the most wonderful thing she'd ever tasted in her life, and she reached eagerly for more.

"Slow, now," Ash said warningly. "Your gut's likely to be a bit tricky yet."

Neve ate, waited, ate, waited, and ate a little more; then Ash let her have the fruit and she gobbled without dignity, smearing the juice over her salty cheeks.

"You all right?" he asked at last. "Nothing broken?"

Neve wiggled fingers and toes, then flexed her arms and legs, wincing as her ankle twinged sharply and other muscles protested.

"I don't think anything's broken," she said. She glanced at him, noticing for the first time that he was naked except for his linen trousers and a makeshift bandage around his head. The bandage was heavily stained, but otherwise Ash appeared remarkably clean. "Are you all right? Your head?"

Ash grimaced.

"Well, I've felt better," he admitted. "Even after too much brandy the night before. Got a hell of a knot on my head and the nastiest bruise on my hip where the mast smacked down on me, and a whole bunch of other scrapes and bruises and cuts from who knows where. But nothing permanent, I guess."

He was silent for a long time, and finally Neve forced herself to speak.

"The ship?" she asked softly.

Ash shook his head slowly.

"I've seen debris wash ashore," he said. "Most of it burned pretty bad. No sign of the longboats. I haven't seen no . . . no bodies or anything, though."

Neve closed her eyes, feeling suddenly sick again. The current had been going out from shore, not in. And away from shore was the dragons. And for those who hadn't managed to reach even the poor safety of the longboats, there had been the explosion. The fire. Then the sea. Neve thought of Ruper and his family and fought down her gorge. Had it been the fire or the dragons? They'd been in her cabin, probably hadn't made it to the longboats. Probably the explosion, then. She could only hope it had been swift and painless.

Ash laid a gentle hand on her shoulder.

"Listen, don't think about it," he said softly. "Right now we've got more'n enough to concern ourselves, just staying alive. Come on. There's fresh water and more fruit a little further inland. Let's get you cleaned up."

Ash had to help her to her feet, and Neve leaned heavily on him after she discovered that her sore ankle was bruised and swollen, probably sprained. To her surprise, there was a narrow path or trail into the increasingly dense foliage—a game trail, she decided as they stumbled along. The sounds of the sea faded slowly behind her, but those sounds were rapidly replaced by the wet chuckle of yet more water. They emerged at last into a good-sized clearing around a clear pool, fed by an insignificant waterfall running off the hillside above. Ash helped Neve to a boulder beside the pool.

"Sit down and strip off," he said. "I'll slosh the salt and bugs out of your clothes and then lay them out to dry a bit while you scrub off. I found a plant that looks a bit like soaproot—lathers up like it, too. Probably'll eat our skins off in a couple hours." He chuckled sourly.

Even if Ash had never been Neve's lover, modesty would have vanished under the horrible sensation of sand lice crawling through her clothes and hair. Neve pulled off her wet clothing disgustedly and willingly handed it over to Ash, taking the pounded roots he offered her and wading eagerly into the water. Despite all the seawater she'd swallowed (and then vomited up) and the fruit she'd eaten, she found that she was achingly thirsty; she swallowed sweet fresh water, slowly at first, then more when her stomach accepted the liquid gratefully. After drinking deeply and soaping herself so vigorously that all her cuts and scratches stung anew, Neve began to entertain the hope that she might survive after all.

Ash finished spreading the last of her clothes on the rocks to dry in the sun and sat down on a rock, holding out a piece of fruit Neve didn't recognize.

"Hungry?" he asked.

Neve waded out and took the fruit, sniffing at it skeptically.

"I've never seen this," she said. "Are you sure it isn't poisonous?"

Ash chuckled.

"I ate three before you woke up," he said. "Haven't killed me yet. Relax. I've sailed southern waters before. I don't know a name for these things, but I've seen folks eating 'em before. Sit down in the sun and dry off. It takes out some of the ache."

Neve sat down and ate, gingerly at first, then voraciously. The sun and the fruit were wonderful, almost as marvelous as the sensation of cleanliness.

Ash handed her the pouch she'd filled on the ship.

"I didn't get into this," he said. "Let's see what you've got that might be of use."

Neve unwrapped her belongings, grimacing to herself. At the time she'd packed the pouch, she'd thought her rubies valuable and necessary. But money was only good where there were people to accept it. Here in the wilderness gemstones and gold and magically lethal daggers had precious little use. Her ordinary sharp dagger and her piece of the Nexus were the only useful objects she'd brought.

"I feel so stupid." Neve sighed. "I didn't even bring a *candle*."

Ash chuckled.

"Don't kick yourself too hard," he said, pulling out his own pouch. "I knew better, and I *still* brought the damned rubies. Left the gold, though—too heavy. But I got a few more useful things—flint and steel, fishhooks, leather cord. I found the rope we were tied up with and unraveled it for string. With those, we can fish and make snares and traps. With daggers and a couple good branches, we can make spears and hunt or fight if we need to. Listen, that magic knife of yours, the one you used to kill Dorn, if we kill something with it, reckon we can eat what we kill?"

"Yes," Neve said. "I've eaten game I've killed with it before. It's magic, not poison." True, she had eaten game killed by the dagger—but not since she'd killed a human being with it.

Well, she'd cleaned it since then.

"Right." Ash nodded with some satisfaction. "That knife'll make a prime good spear, then; all we need is one little poke even if something big attacks us. And it's good you brought the gold. I can tie it on fish line for weights easier than stones. So we're not so bad off." He sighed. "Only thing we don't have is a skin to carry fresh water with us. I don't much like that, but if we can kill something big, we can clean the bladder, maybe."

"I can do that," Neve said suddenly.

Ash glanced at her.

"Hmm?"

"I can make a waterskin," Neve said with certainty. "I'll need some time and practice, but that's easy enough, easier than wood or stone. I can make most simple things."

Ash chuckled.

"Right," he said. "I forgot about that. Now, *that's* going to come in handy, girl. Tell you what we'll do. You sit here and dry off a bit with your clothes, rest that ankle, and work on making us a couple waterskins. I'm going to scout up the coast a ways, see if I can figure where we are, but I'll set a few fish lines first. I'll cut something you can use as a crutch, too, while I'm out. Then when I come back we'll figure what's what. All right?"

"Yes," Neve said, relieved beyond measure that Ash seemed to know what to do in these circumstances. All right, she'd probably have come to the same conclusions, but she'd have had to think and figure a lot longer. Of all the contingencies she had planned for, shipwreck on the south coast was not one of them.

While Ash was gone, Neve found some large flat leaves and practiced transforming them into stout leather waterskins. She'd tried making such ordinary items—it seemed like ages before, back in the Keep, with far less success. Now, however, despite having only a fragment of the Nexus's power at her disposal, it seemed ever so much easier. Well, of course; she'd had more practice since then, and she'd been working with stone up till now, and stone was the least mutable substance Neve knew. Wood had seemed easy by comparison, and leaves and leather were easier still.

After the waterskins, a stout pack was a natural next step. That was far more complicated, and it took several tries before Neve succeeded, but after she had finished that, soft but sturdy leather straps to bind up her ankle were positively simple. Neve found a straight sapling and stripped it down to use as the shaft of a spear, borrowing some of Ash's leather cord to lash the dagger securely in place as a point. She picked up a branch to use as a temporary walking stick as she hobbled around the clearing; she wasn't putting her hand anywhere near that dagger!

By the time she'd finished these projects, her clothes were dry, and Neve was more than happy to dress again. The warm sun was nice on her skin, but walking around naked in this strange land made her feel just a little too vulnerable. Neve made a mental note to herself to practice making clothing at the first opportunity; traveling through dense jungle, she and Ash were liable to make rags of their garments in record time, and besides, there might not always be convenient pools to wash their clothes in.

Neve estimated she'd slept through to late morning; the sun had passed its zenith and was low on the horizon by the time Ash returned, sunburned and stiff but proud, carrying a string of fat fish over a sturdy length of wood.

"Well, there's good news," he said slowly, laying down his burdens, "and then there's not-so-good news. Want the worst first?"

"Yes," Neve said, taking a deep breath. After storms, fires, shipwrecks, and sea dragons, she wasn't certain she could take too much more bad news.

"Well, I didn't see no sign of any of our shipmates, alive or dead," Ash said, shaking his head dismally. "Now, that could be good or bad. I mean, I walked west, and who knows, they may've landed further on, or maybe back east. But what it means for sure is there's no help in sight.

"At my best guess, we're a good long walk from Zaravelle, but an even longer one from Strachan, so we might as well push on, I guess. I could be wrong, but we'd had a good wind and a strong current at our backs, so I figure we're past the halfway point." He glanced at Neve hopefully. "Don't suppose you can do anything like scrying?"

Neve sighed.

"I've never done any scrying myself," she said apologetically. "My father had a special mirror that I always used if I wanted to see something. There were scrying spells in the grimoire, but I didn't even try to save it. It was so big and heavy—and it would've just been ruined in the seawater, anyway.''

Ash sighed, too.

"Well, I didn't expect no better," he said resignedly. "Never mind. Keep going west, we're bound to run into Zaravelle sooner or later.

"Rest of the bad news—no nice sandy beaches in sight, just more cliffs and rocks. That means even hugging the coast we're pushing through jungle. Now, that's not all bad," Ash added hastily. "Trees mean shade and fruit and fresh water. But it'll slow us down some. And I doubt water'd be a problem anyway—rainy season's coming on, and this part of the coast gets lots of rain anyway, or so I'm told.''

He glanced down at his bare feet, grimacing. Neve could see that his feet were already bruised and cut, and she winced inside. If only she'd learned something as practical as healing back at home!

"Wish I'd had my shoes," he said softly.

That perked Neve up.

"I can make you shoes," she said quickly. "At least *something* to protect your feet. It might not be a very good job, but it'll be better than nothing.''

Ash grinned.

"Good girl," he said. He glanced down at the waterskins, pack, and spear Neve had made, then picked them up one at a time, inspecting them critically.

"Good job on these," he said, raising his eyebrows, and Neve felt a glow of pride.

So much for Mother and the joy of making things with my own two hands, Neve thought grimly. *If we waited till we killed some large animals, skinned them, scraped and cured the leather and found some way to stitch it, we'd both be dead of old age.*

"This should do you as a crutch," Ash said, handing her the stick. There was a fork in it at just the right height. "We'll tie some cloth around it to pad your arm a bit." He glanced down at her swollen ankle and sighed, and Neve heard what he didn't say. With her hobbling on a crutch, jungle or no jungle, they'd make precious little distance in a day.

"Well!" Ash took a deep breath and smiled, although

Neve thought it looked just a bit forced. "Next thing is some shelter for the night, and a fire to cook my catch. I'll fetch some wood, and if you'll take care of supper, you can sit still while I make us some kind of camp, eh?"

"Yes," Neve said quickly. "I can take care of the fire and the fish." Somehow she positively *burned* to feel useful again, as if she had somehow to atone for her ankle.

Well, I've got a lot more to atone for than an ankle, but Ash doesn't know that.

"Good girl." Ash said nothing more, just shuffled off rather tiredly. He returned just long enough to drop off an armload of wood, then claimed Neve's cloak and disappeared again.

Neve cleared a small area of ground and, with the help of Ash's flint and steel, managed to light a tiny fire, wet wood notwithstanding. The fish were simpler but messier, and Neve hated that she had not so much as a pinch of spices to cook them with, but she was hungry enough that this didn't bother her for long. As soon as Ash returned, they sat impatiently, watching the fish cook, and the second it was done they pulled it off the sticks and wolfed it down greedily, with a liberal helping of fruit to follow. By the time they'd finished their meal and smothered the fire, it was full dark, but the stars were bright and Neve hoped the clear skies meant no rain before morning.

Ash had managed to lash several branches of large leaves together into a sort of lean-to, with more leaves hanging down at the sides which would hopefully fend off some of the biting insects that seemed to thrive in this part of the world.

Neve crawled wearily into the makeshift shelter, wrapping part of her cloak around her (tomorrow night she'd have to work on a proper blanket), and Ash crawled in beside her. Despite the heat, she was glad of his presence, and she scooted closer, curling up against his side.

Ash rolled over, propping himself up on one elbow.

"Hey," he said. "One question. Those mermaids, merfolk, whatever—" He hesitated. "I mean, everybody's heard the stories, and they did seem kind of grabby. Would they really—"

Neve chuckled.

"I don't think so," she said. "As I told you, they aren't very smart and they don't have much of a language. But the best I can puzzle out, since they have tails and we don't, they're curious to see what we have instead. That's probably where your sailor stories come from. But when they were pulling us in to shore, I told them we wouldn't make very good mates, and one of them all but laughed in my face at the idea."

Ash shook his head, chuckling.

"You know, though," he said, "it'll make fine telling, won't it, at the taverns? Groped by a mermaid."

Neve chuckled, too.

"Are you sure it was a mer*maid*?" she said.

Ash laughed outright this time. "If it's all the same to you," he said, "I'd rather go on believing it was. And the prettiest of the slimy lot, too."

Suddenly Neve felt better, almost cheerful. She slid her hand across Ash's chest, enjoying the solidity and warmth of his skin.

"Want to pretend I'm a mermaid?" she murmured.

Ash laughed and captured her hand, rolling back over and pulling her half on top of him.

"Not a chance," he said. "One look, one sniff, and I'll never gaze wistfully out to sea again, I tell you that. How about we just pretend we're not bruised, battered, and worn-out?"

Neve laughed.

"I think we can manage that," she said.

In the morning there was fresh fruit for breakfast, and then they bundled up their few belongings and trudged off down the coast. True to Ash's word, there was little choice but to contend with the verdant jungle, because it grew right up to the edges of the crumbling cliffs.

Ash stepped along almost merrily, his feet cradled in the sturdy (if clumsy) sandals that Neve had managed to conjure up. He wore only his linen trousers and had hacked those off at mid-thigh; apparently the clouds of biting insects didn't like the taste of him.

Neve stumped along miserably. Her ankle throbbed and ached even when she barely put weight on it, and her shoul-

der, neck, and back quickly protested the strain of the crutch.
The hot, wet air, only occasionally refreshed by a breeze off
the sea, was stifling, and the insects seemed to like her flavor
just fine.

Despite the discomfort and inconvenience of their slow
journey, however, Neve was comforted that they didn't seem
to be in any real *danger*. The sky stayed clear, and Ash
mused that there would probably be few large predators at
the edge of the jungle. As he'd indicated, there was plenty
of fruit and fresh water. Still, by the end of the day Neve
knew they'd covered only a short distance and she thought
miserably that the little progress they'd made was hardly
worth the misery of it.

Ash, apparently pleased with the day's travel, laughed at
her discouragement.

"Zaravelle's not going anywhere, girl." He grinned. "If
you're in that much of a hurry, why don't you magic us up
a couple of horses? Not that they'd get through this tangle
much faster than we can. Or maybe we can make a raft and
you can get those pretty mer-people to tow us along up the
coast, hey?"

Neve ground her teeth.

"I promised my father," she said icily, "that I wouldn't
try to make living things until he said I was ready." She saw
no need to tell him about the dead dragons. Besides, that
train of thought led her back to the sea dragons, and the ship,
and from there to other, darker thoughts Neve would much
prefer to avoid—such as worm-ridden monkey apples and
sick captains.

Ash turned to glance at her.

"What's chewing at you today?" he said mildly. "You
were in good enough spirits last night."

"What's chewing at me," Neve snapped, suddenly furious, "is this cloud of biting things. I wish these damned bugs
hated me as much as they seem to hate you!"

Then she stopped, glancing around puzzledly. There was
not one gnat, not one annoyingly whining biter circling
around her head or darting in at her face, not one fly tickling
her cheek. The air around her had suddenly gone utterly silent, completely empty. There was a familiar flutter in her
stomach; then that, too, faded away.

Ash stopped, raising his eyebrows.

"What?" he said patiently.

Neve swallowed.

"The insects," she said. She reached out with her hand, waved it in the air. "They're gone. As soon as I said that, they were gone."

"Oh, yeah?" Ash scowled slightly. "How'd you manage that, hey?"

"I—" Neve hesitated. "I don't know. But I think I did . . . something."

Ash's scowl deepened.

"Those worms in Strachan," he said. "You said you couldn't have done it. Are you still sure about that?"

Neve swallowed again.

"Maybe not," she almost whispered. "Maybe I did it after all, but without meaning to. But how could that be?"

Surely not. She didn't want to believe it, and everything she knew argued against such a possibility. Her mother had told her time and time again that magic required concentration, focus, careful deliberation. Her father's magic sometimes seemed almost effortless, true, but he had the whole power of the Nexus behind him; he was the Guardian, after all. And even so, Neve had never seen him do anything by accident. Magic simply wasn't that capricious.

Ash glanced around, picked out a fallen tree, and sat down.

"I don't know," he said slowly. "Those worms, and now this. That kind of thing could be dangerous, girl. I've got to know. You sure it's never happened before?"

Neve closed her eyes.

I can't. I can't tell him about the captain. He'd hate me, even though I didn't do it on purpose, even though I'd have undone it if I could. He might even leave me here.

"Using magic was much easier back in the Crystal Keep," Neve said slowly and carefully. "Every time I've made something here outside, even simple things like those sandals, I have to *work* at it. I have to think hard about what I'm doing, have to *understand* what I'm making. It makes me tired, too, afterward. I don't think even my father could create living things like worms, or banish insects, without even trying." Then she dropped her eyes. "But I'm not like my father. Not exactly."

"You mean because you're not the Guardian?" Ash asked her.

Neve shook her head.

"I mean I'm not exactly—human," she said faintly. She couldn't look at Ash, didn't want to see his expression.

"My father was human once," she said hurriedly. "When he came to the Crystal Keep, before he became the Guardian. Over the years he was Guardian, the magic of the Nexus became part of him. Changed him."

She took a deep breath.

"Mother's human," she continued. "But she and Father couldn't have children as normal people do. So Father used the magic of the Nexus and . . . and made me. Out of the Nexus. I look human, but I'm not. Not really."

Silence. Neve couldn't bring herself to raise her eyes, dreading what she might see in Ash's expression—contempt, disgust, or worse. She didn't think she could bear it if he hated her.

Then a rough hand touched hers gently and Neve jumped in startlement, glancing up despite herself. To her amazement and dismay, Ash was grinning, although there was a certain grudging sympathy in his eyes.

"Well, Peregard's buttocks, girl, that's no surprise," he said, chuckling. "Everybody *knows* the Guardian of the Crystal Keep's some sort of demon, so it just stands to figure you're a strange creature yourself. You bleed and puke same as normal folks, so I guess that means you aren't too awful far off, are you?"

He squeezed Neve's fingers.

"Something new and different, that's what you said," he said more gently. "Nothing wrong with that, remember?"

Neve swallowed. Ash's acceptance was an amazing relief, but not quite enough to overcome that awful niggling fear.

"I know," she said. "But maybe I'm different enough that—that maybe things happen that I don't do consciously. Like the worms."

Ash thought about that for a moment, then sighed and shrugged.

"Well, you haven't done any real harm with it yet," he said. "So I wouldn't fret about it. We don't know anything for certain anyway. Listen, I don't know why the damned bugs don't bite *me*, either.''

Haven't done any harm? Neve shivered. She was far less certain of that than Ash. *Mother said I could become a monster. Is that what I'm doing, becoming some dangerous creature? But she thought my leaving the Keep would prevent that. What if leaving the Keep causes it instead? What if I need the power of the Nexus to keep my magic under control?*

Worse, there wasn't much she could do about it either way. She couldn't exactly tell her parents, ''Sorry, there's a problem, got to come home now.'' And the middle of a strange jungle was hardly the place for Neve to safely explore this new ''gift''—if indeed the magic had worked as she feared. What she needed was time and quiet and possibly the opinion of another mage—or perhaps some sort of communication spell that would let her consult her father. And, if the worst were true, a Gate home.

All of those things meant Zaravelle. And to *get* to Zaravelle probably meant using her magic, at least from time to time.

Well, maybe the practice will help me get it under control, Neve thought grimly. *I certainly* hope *so. If I put worms in our food or cursed Ash or me with the never-ending spews—* She shuddered at the thought.

Neve kept her thoughts to herself as she helped Ash set up camp as best she could. As before, he left her to make the fire while he ventured out in search of food; Neve was more than happy to get off her aching ankle. Despite her misgivings, she set grimly to work until she'd produced a stout waxed-cloth tarpaulin that would make a better shelter than branches and leaves, and a good-sized blanket, too. Encouraged by her success and by the increasing ease and sureness of her endeavors, Neve splurged and made a copper pot. Let Ash laugh.

To her delight, not only did he *not* laugh at her ''luxuries,'' but he promptly cut three stout poles to form a tripod from which to hang her pot. He'd had no success fishing, but he'd brought back a shirtful of hard-shelled shore creatures—some ugly crawly things disturbingly like giant spiders, which Neve realized with a shiver were the spiderclaws she'd eaten so blithely, and clams and oysters and a few less recognizable creatures that Ash assured her were quite edible. Neve had some doubts herself, especially when one large spiderclaw came at her with clicking pincers, but she dispatched that particular specimen into the hot water with considerable satisfaction. A little later, digging out the sweet meat, Neve admitted to Ash that she couldn't have asked for better—although with some thick cream and butter, maybe a bit of thyme—

Ash chuckled at her wistful tone.

"When we get to Zaravelle," he said, "you can buy all your nice spices again, and I'm telling you, I'm going to make you cook me a big dinner with all the trimmings. For all you seem to know what you're doing, I've still never had anything out of your pot but stringy game and the like."

"Wrong." Neve sniffed. "There was that night we came ashore from the barge and I made the fish stew."

"Well, there's that," Ash admitted. "And it was mighty fine, too. But I can't wait to see what you can do with a plump goose or a tender suckling pig."

Neve felt a flush of pride, then winced almost reflexively. *Oh, wonderful. Wonderful. I thought Mother was the turnip chopper in the family. Now just look.*

Still, she had to admit to herself, if grudgingly, she'd rather be a cook than a monster. When the gathering clouds finally loosed a heavy evening shower, however, and she and Ash huddled cozily under the watertight waxed canvas cloth, wrapped warmly in the blanket, Neve revised her opinion.

Better a cook than a monster, yes. But better a Guardian than either one.

In the morning they set out again. To Ash's disgust and Neve's utter dismay, they found the cliffs rising higher and higher above the level of the sea, looming more and more steeply above the rocky shoals below. That meant not only a steeper climb as they walked, but it put an end to Ash's fishing and tidepool gathering, too. This time they had to stop for a rest at noon; Neve's ankle simply wouldn't bear her another minute. To her gratitude, Ash looked as ready for a rest as she felt; she remembered what he'd said about not walking much over long distances, and she realized on reflection that his long-toed feet were really meant for climbing, not for hiking.

Ash wiped sweat from his brow and flopped onto the ground, leaning back against the fallen tree on which Neve was sitting.

"Sorry, but I got to ask," he panted. "You sure you couldn't magic up a couple of mules?"

Neve grimaced.

"I wish I could," she said apologetically. "My father made the horse and mule I rode to Selwaer on. I wasn't really up to living things even back at the Keep, and I've got a lot less power now. Trust me. You wouldn't want to see the mistakes."

Ash sighed.

"Well, I'd be much obliged if you could just manage a new pair of sandals, then," he said, holding up one foot illustratively. Neve's makeshift shoes were literally falling apart, and his poor cut and bruised feet made her wince. She privately resolved to master the art of bootmaking before the next morning, even if she had to sit up all night to do it.

They stumbled into a bit of luck after their rest—a narrow game trail that wound along the fringes of the jungle at the top of the cliff. That made the walking a bit easier, although the way still led upward. Ash said nothing, but Neve began to worry about the availability of fresh water. They hadn't crossed a stream since morning, and water flowed downhill, not up. When she took only a meager sip from one of the waterskins, however, Ash shook his head reassuringly.

"Drink up," he said. "Don't worry, we'll find water before nightfall."

"Are you sure?" she said doubtfully.

"Dead-on certain," Ash said with assurance. "Look at this jungle, girl. This much green needs a powerful lot of water, and every game trail in the world goes to water sooner or later. If we don't come across a spring or stream, it doesn't much matter. Look at those clouds—we'll be lucky to make sunset without rain."

The ground leveled out by midafternoon, and by evening Neve was certain they were beginning to move slightly downhill again. True to Ash's prediction, they crossed a small stream spilling over the cliff near sunset, and to her delight, he called a halt for the day. Once they'd picked a campsite, Ash pulled off the tatters of his sandals and simply plunged his feet into the stream, sighing with pleasure.

"Don't suppose we could get by on fruit and such tonight?" he asked wistfully. "My feet are just about done in, and that's the truth."

Neve smiled smugly.

"Lend me your hooks and string," she said. "I'll get supper tonight."

Fishing in a stream Neve could do, and when she'd set her lines carefully, the cool water downstream felt just as good on her aching ankle as it probably felt on Ash's battered feet. The memory of those feet made her scowl; after debating with herself for a long time, she took out her "safe" knife resolutely.

I've got to learn sometime. What if Ash fell and broke a leg? I can't carry him, not all the way to Zaravelle. And if I can hurt, I can heal.

Gingerly she cut the tip of one finger ever so slightly, contemplating the cut gravely.

It's no different than the wood in the ship, she told herself sternly. *Except that it'll probably be easier because flesh is softer. I'm not making anything new. I'm just reminding my skin what wholeness feels like, reminding it how to be what it already is. It'll be simple.*

And to her utter amazement it was. The cut closed almost effortlessly. Neve could hardly believe it; she had to try it again. By the time she was sure of herself, she had healed almost every cut, scratch, and bruise on her. That left only—

Neve unwrapped her ankle slowly. This was different than a simple cut or bruise; she didn't really know anything about how muscles worked or what a sprain really *was*.

No, she told herself. *It's no different. I don't know how skin heals either. I'm just reminding it. Don't think so much.*

To her surprise she was right. At first she could hardly bring herself to let her power uncoil, touch the throbbing joint; when she did, however, the swelling went down with gratifying rapidity and the pain ebbed just as fast. Neve stopped short of healing it completely; she didn't know what might happen if she did too much. But at least tomorrow she could walk without a crutch and her boot would fit properly.

Her fish lines were just as successful, and Neve enjoyed Ash's wide-eyed grunt of surprise when she brought her catch home (although she thought later with a chuckle that not so long ago she'd have taken offense at his assumption that she couldn't fend for herself). When her catch was scaled and gutted and wrapped in leaves to bake in the coals, however, Neve contemplated an even better surprise. She lifted one of Ash's feet into her lap, careful of the bruised and abraded skin.

"I think I can help," she said simply. "Shall I try?"

Ash raised one eyebrow.

"Well—if you're sure," he said hesitantly. "I mean, that foot's odd enough now."

Neve took a deep breath, and before doubt could begin to creep in, she let the power extend, flow over Ash's sole, mending the torn flesh, easing the bruises. It wasn't as easy as healing herself, but neither could she have called it difficult.

"There," she said, sighing. "Better?"

Ash turned his foot up, poking hesitantly at the unmarred sole. His other eyebrow shot up and he broke into a slow grin.

"Girl, I'd have been glad for that the morning after we landed," he said. "Never mind; I guess if you'd worked up the nerve before, you wouldn't have been hopping along on a crutch, hey?" He lifted his other foot into Neve's lap. "Got enough juice for one more?"

"Just watch," Neve said loftily.

Supper was a celebration; even the heavy storm that roared in to shore while they were eating and drowned the fire couldn't dampen their spirits. They retired to their tent and finished their fish and fruit, then laid out their blanket and celebrated more energetically. Later, resting comfortably together, Ash grimaced at a peal of thunder that shook the ground.

"We should've made camp on the other side of the stream," he said with a sigh. "It may be hard crossing tomorrow."

"We'll manage," Neve said drowsily. "I bet I could make a bridge."

Ash chuckled.

"Yeah? Well, while you're getting so ambitious, you give them mules a little more thought," he said amusedly. "It's still a couple days' walk to Zaravelle, more than likely."

Neve only chuckled to herself. Mules wouldn't make any better progress through this tangled mess than Ash and herself—probably less, in fact.

In the morning they set out almost merrily—Ash in stout new sandals, Neve without her crutch. The stream was as swollen as Ash had predicted, but they found a fallen tree large enough to use as a bridge, and Neve was doubly glad of the previous evening's healings. With her wobbly ankle and Ash's battered feet, one of them would have ended up in the water for sure.

They were walking downhill now, too, which would be easier—or at least so Neve thought. She quickly learned that prolonged downhill travel only strained a different set of muscles. She also learned that people walking on a steep downhill slope after heavy rains were quite likely to slip on muddy trails and go sliding headlong down muddy hillsides. At one point the path became so steep that they were forced to stop and cut vines and tie them to trees to anchor their descent, Neve being too tired and unsure of herself to trust any rope she might create at that time.

At midafternoon, however, they stopped, gazing disbelievingly at the first real obstacle they'd encountered since the shipwreck.

"Well," Ash said slowly. "No fallen tree's going to do the job here, I guess."

Neve had to agree.

The ground seemed to drop away in front of their toes; the rocky chasm plunged down so deep that Neve, cautiously gazing over the edge, could barely see the bottom.

"Forget mules," Ash said, chuckling ruefully. "How about tame dragons to fly us over?"

Neve grimaced.

"I'm afraid I'm not very good at dragons," she said, fighting down a chuckle of her own. "And I don't think climbing down and back up is much of an option either."

Holding on to a vine, Ash leaned out so far over the gorge that Neve panicked and grabbed wildly for his belt. After a moment he pulled himself back to firmer footing.

"Going around isn't much of an option either," he said with a sigh. "It goes as far back as I can see, and I can't see any better place to get down."

Neve scowled.

"Leaving what choices?" she said.

Ash shrugged.

"Not many," he said. "We can go back up the coast to lower ground, try to get around in the sea. Or we can head off into the jungle and hope there's someplace we can get across."

"Or, let me guess, I can create something to get us across," Neve said wryly. "Listen, Ash, do you really want to trust yourself over that chasm on my amateur effort at a bridge? Even a rope bridge?"

"Not really." Ash grinned. "But I don't want to spend the rest of my days in this jungle, either, and Zaravelle is on the other side. So that kind of tips the scales a little bit. Still, it might be a good idea to go inland a bit, see if there isn't a narrower place to cross. And camp to give you a bit of practice at ropes, eh?"

Neither the prospect of detouring inland nor of trying to conjure up ropes sturdy enough to get them across such a chasm appealed to Neve, but the idea of camping was a welcome one.

"All right," she said. "But find some water. I'm all over mud. If I'm going to risk my neck, I want to at least be clean when I do it."

They walked inland for nearly an hour before Ash found them a fair-sized pool. Neve scrubbed herself off, trying not to think about the setback. They'd think of something. But neither she nor Ash had any inclination to go far hunting dinner, and they listlessly ate fruit and went to bed. Rolled up in the blanket, however, with both of them too depressed to consider anything but sleep, Neve pondered their predicament.

What crossed chasms? Dragons and birds flew over, but humans had to build bridges, bridges of wood or stone or rope at least. And to bridge a chasm this size meant starting from *both* sides. But if one could start from the other side, why bother crossing?

Neve scowled, suddenly angry. It wasn't *fair,* not fair at all, that she'd come so far, gone through so much, only to be halted by an oversized ditch. By the Nexus, she *hated* this horrible hot steamy jungle and all its insects and mud and bother! If there was something living here big enough to make game trails, why couldn't there be something big enough to hang a bridge across the chasm, too, something she and Ash could cross on? It was downright infuriating, when she thought about it.

She sat upright, startling a sleepy groan out of Ash, who rolled over and went back to sleep. Neve ground her teeth, for a moment so angry that she felt physically ill. No! Her journey was *not* going to end this way. She was born to be the Guardian of the Crystal Keep, and she *would* find a way across that crack to Zaravelle—

Thunder boomed overhead, breaking her train of thought and startling her out of her anger. A moment later the rain poured down again, and Neve sighed.

Another muddy day's walk, she thought with a sort of sour amusement. *Oh, well—if we can't cross the crack, maybe we'll just sit right here and keep dry.*

Sighing again, she slid down in the blanket, curled up against Ash's back, and fell asleep to the sound of rain dripping through the canopy of trees onto their shelter.

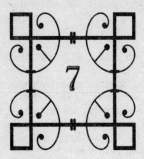

7

"I SEE IT," ASH SAID, VERY QUIETLY, VERY slowly, "but what *is* it?"

Neve shrugged uncomfortably.

"A little luck," she said. "A bridge."

But it wasn't a bridge, not in any sense Neve had ever known. What stretched across the chasm looked more like a network of ropes, each as thick as Neve's wrist, strung tautly between the cliffs on either side. She could see more ropes vanishing into the fog below at odd angles, probably anchoring the upper strands more firmly.

They'd woken up to a dense fog that hadn't burned away with the dawn, but had finally lightened a little. Now it lingered in the depths of the chasm. They'd walked only a short distance inland before Ash spotted the strange structure. He was puzzled; he thought he'd seen this far up the chasm the day before, but he certainly hadn't seen anything like this then. He'd shrugged it off after a moment; the chasm wasn't perfectly straight, and his view might have been blocked. Neve was less certain.

It happened again, she thought, unable to suppress a shiver. *I was thinking about a bridge—no, about* something *making* a bridge across, *and . . .*

She fought down her own unease. Yes, she was almost

certain that once more the magic of the Nexus had acted—perhaps not against her will, but certainly without her conscious direction. But this time, unlike the others, it had done something positive, something helpful. That had to be an improvement.

But if that's so, a tiny voice insisted, *why not a regular bridge, a proper bridge of wood or stone?*

Neve grimaced and pushed that nagging voice to the back of her mind. They could stand here and question their good fortune until the flesh rotted from their bones, or they could take advantage of the bridge that luck—or the Nexus—had placed in their way.

"I've never seen a bridge like that," Ash said, echoing Neve's thoughts. "Still—" He nudged the nearest cable with his foot, gingerly at first, then harder. It didn't move in the least.

"It looks sturdy enough," Ash concluded rather doubtfully. "Anyway, I doubt we're going to find anything better."

Neve squinted down into the chasm. She'd have felt better about the whole thing if she could see the full extent of the structure, gauge exactly how sturdy it might be. But there *was* one precaution they could take.

"I can make a rope," she said slowly. "A very *long* rope, long enough to reach the other side. We can anchor the rope and cross one at a time."

Ash chuckled.

"That won't be much use," he said. "If that crazy network of lines broke, we'd just swing down on your rope and bash ourselves into jelly against the cliff wall. Still—" He shrugged. "If we tie a rope off over here, and then I cross and tie the other end off there, that'd give you something a little less chancy to anchor onto when you cross over."

"I'm lighter," Neve said quickly. Somehow she felt she'd rather trust her own life to this creation of the Nexus than Ash's. Hadn't her father said that magic was less likely to turn on its creator?

Ash stripped off his sandals, wiggling his long toes.

"Yeah, but I'm the better climber," he said flatly. "Listen, girl, to me this is just more rigging. You get started on your rope while I figure out how I'm going to do this."

To Ash's impatience, Neve insisted on testing every foot of the rope she made, looping it over a branch and both of them hanging on it section by section. This was a slow process, since both she and Ash agreed that one solid piece of rope long enough to cross the chasm was more reliable than several pieces tied together; consequently it was midafternoon before the rope was pronounced sturdy and Ash tied it securely to a large tree on their side of the bank. He looped the rope around a second tree before knotting the free end around his waist. Neve made two shorter sections, giving one to Ash and laying the other aside for her own climb.

"I hope like hell I won't have no use for this, because if I do, I'm probably finished anyway," Ash said wryly as he tied one end of the second, shorter rope around his waist. "Listen, the fog's burned off enough that you should be able to see me all the way across. You keep braced here at this tree and let the rope out as I go. The less slack the better if I end up swinging at the other end of this. If I fall, don't try to pull me up; even if you could do it, I can climb faster than you could pull. Just dig in good and let me do the work. All right?"

Neve nodded tensely, taking the rope where Ash indicated. Glancing around, she located a stump she could use as a second anchor point if she had to.

"Now, I'm going over as quick as I can," Ash continued. "But don't *you* do that. When I'm across, give me a little while to secure the rope over there and check the area out a bit, make sure nothing's going to sneak up while we're busy. I'll give you a good loud whistle, like you did with the mermaids, but you may not be able to hear me if the wind's up, so wait till I wave with both arms before you start across. Check the tension on the long rope and the knots on your short rope real good and go slow and careful, just like you did on the rigging. Got it?"

Neve licked her lips.

"Yes," she said. She would far rather have taken her chances crossing with Ash; she didn't want to think what her fate might be alone in this jungle if something happened to her companion. But Ash's response when Neve had tentatively suggested a joint crossing had been sufficiently flat that she knew she had no chance of convincing him.

"Right." Ash grinned, patting her hand. "Don't fret, girl. This won't be exactly a pleasure, but it looks safe enough if a bad wind doesn't come up. Just remember, I go fast, you go slow. Now hold tight on that rope, if you please. I got no ambition to explore the bottom of that crack, especially head-first."

Ash slid down under the thick cable, holding on with both knees and one elbow while with the other he looped his short rope over the cable. He tied the free end around his waist, but using this time a quick-release knot ("Never know when I might need a quick out," he'd said), and without hesitation began working his way out over the chasm hand over hand. Neve watched anxiously, her mouth dry, her hands clenching spasmodically around the rope.

By the Nexus, I didn't make this on purpose, she thought sickly. *But I certainly hope I made it RIGHT.*

Ash's figure receded with dismaying rapidity, pausing only to unfasten and retie his short rope when he reached a cross cable, leaving Neve alone clutching the rope tightly, doling out slack an inch at a time.

If I wish for him to make it across safely, would the Nexus help him? Protect him? Or would it go all wrong? She swallowed, thinking of the Captain Corell vomiting away the last hours of her life on the *Albatross.*

No. No. It's too dangerous, too uncontrolled. I don't even know how I do it. If he falls, let it be because of something he does *or just plain bad luck. Not because of something I do wrong. Not that.*

Neve swallowed hard. Her hands were sweating; the rope felt slippery. Biting her lip, she daringly released the rope with one hand, wiping her palm roughly on her tunic, then switched hands, then grabbed the rope again, more tightly. Ash was still progressing steadily across the gorge. Neve grudgingly let out a little more slack.

Does Father ever feel this way? Afraid of his own power? Neve was certain he didn't. There was absolutely no uncertainty in Vanian, Guardian of the Crystal Keep. And he wouldn't have much appreciation of it in his daughter and heir, either.

Is this what Mother wants, me questioning everything I think and do and am? Is that why she wanted me to make this journey? Neve grimaced. She still couldn't believe that any part of this was her father's idea. *Is she trying to kill in me everything she doesn't like in Father?*

Something inside her hardened in resentment.

Well, I'm not out here to be molded into something more acceptable to my mother, she thought. *I'm here because the Guardian set me a task, and by the Nexus, I'm going to complete it no matter what. The power of the Nexus serves me—me, its child no less than that of my father and my mother. Maybe more. And I* will *master the power of the Nexus, the power I'm going to control as its Guardian. I'm going to be what I was always meant to be, whether my mother likes it or not.*

For the first time in days Neve felt completely firm, resolved. Strong. She set her feet firmly, renewed her grip on the rope—the rope *she* had made, and quite competently on the very first try, thank you—and let out a little more slack. Ash was almost to the other side of the chasm.

One more thing done right. It's a good sign.

Still she held her breath until she saw the now tiny figure scramble up onto the ground on the other side. Sighing with relief, Neve let out the rest of the slack on the rope and watched Ash untie the end from around his waist. Although she could hardly see what he was doing, from his motions he seemed to be tying the rope securely to a stout tree—yes, he was tugging hard on the rope, testing the knots.

He vanished briefly into the jungle on the far side of the chasm but reappeared only a few moments later. Neve listened, straining her ears for his whistle, and shortly she heard a thin, reedy sound barely audible over the wind blowing through the gorge. But the signal was confirmed immediately as Ash waved both arms vigorously.

Taking a deep breath, Neve tested the knots on the anchor rope again, pulling at it vigorously. Stepping to the edge of the chasm, she tied one end of the short rope around her waist, looped it over the anchor rope, then secured the other end around her waist tightly as well. She didn't know any quick-release knots; she'd just have to use her knife if she needed to get loose in a hurry. She reminded herself to use her dagger at her hip, not the magical knife, now liberated from its spear shaft, in her boot sheath.

As she'd discussed with Ash, Neve had no intention of going hand over hand as he'd done. Setting her feet on the strange cable and her hands on the anchor rope, she inched out over the void below. *Should I look up or down? Gods, no. Look where you're putting your hands and feet.* Neve chuckled in spite of herself, grateful for the fog in the chasm. She didn't want to see how far down it was.

She scooted out slowly, moving one hand, one foot at a time, just as she'd done on the rigging. The cable under her feet was almost rock steady, but the rope in her hands swayed and yielded slightly under the pressure of her weight. Neve wondered briefly whether she might not have been safer taking Ash's way after all. But no. Her arms and legs weren't as strong as his; she'd wear herself out before she was half-way across. She forced her feet to start moving again; they kept wanting to stop where they were. Her hands wanted to grow roots into the rope.

I'm the heir to the Crystal Keep, Neve thought grimly. *I am not going to freeze up like a panicky rabbit. This is no different than the rigging. Ten man-heights or two hundred, if I fall I'm just as dead. The good news with two hundred man-heights is that the fall will kill me straightaway. At ten man-heights I might not die right off. I'd have time to suffer, time to scream. So stop it, Neve, and get moving!*

Perversely the thought of a quick death was comforting, and it was enough to goad her reluctant limbs into motion. She worked her way out more quickly, with more assurance. The edge of the chasm was slowly receding behind her, but the far edge didn't seem the slightest bit closer. The wind grew stronger as she moved away from the edge, from the jungle—wild drafts coming from below her, above her, all around her. The cable seemed to vibrate occasionally beneath her.

Someday, Neve thought, *when I'm Guardian, I'm going to find some way to give myself wings and fly out over a chasm like this, ride those crazy drafts of wind. Fly out over the sea in one of the pocket worlds, too. Maybe I could become a bird, a seagull or—no, something more formidable. Predatory. Safer. A hawk, maybe. Or—maybe a dragon?*

The cable beneath her feet was definitely vibrating, more strongly now—not constantly, but rhythmically. The wind?

Neve forced herself to move a little faster. She was still only about a third of the way across, even by her most optimistic estimate.

I can do this. I can do this. Ash's done it already, and I've got a second rope that he didn't have. What's stopping me? Nothing. Nothing but pitiful cowardly fear. Are Father and Mother watching me in the mirror? I hope they are. I hope they're watching right now. *Let them see how much danger this silly journey of theirs has put me in. Let them see how clever I've been just to get this far. Let them believe I made this cable on purpose to get across this chasm.* Those thoughts lent her feet steadiness, and she almost chuckled. *Let them argue and argue and argue over whose stupid idea it was for me to leave the Keep. Right now I bet Father's already trying to figure out how to bring me back, and Mother's telling him why that won't be nearly soon enough. I bet—*

Suddenly the cable under her feet jarred sharply, and Neve grabbed frantically at the rope to steady herself. For a moment some of her weight hung on the short rope around her waist and she felt a brief surge of panic before she found her balance again. Now she wished she'd taken off her boots and stuffed them in the pack Ash had carried across. Her toes were hardly a match for Ash's, but right now she wouldn't sneer at anything—*anything*—that might give her surer footing.

The cable under her feet was vibrating again, more strongly this time, and suddenly a faint sound reached her ears. For a moment she couldn't place it; the wind and the fog and the chasm made every sound seem to come from all around her. At last she recognized Ash's whistle, and holding on tightly to the rope, she turned her head—*just* her head— and finally glimpsed him at the end of the rope. He was waving his arms frantically, gesturing wildly at something below her.

Neve froze. *Is the cable fraying, breaking, or the rope, or—* Her heart pounding, she forced herself to drop her eyes, slowly, slowly—

And her heart stopped.

The fog had receded. Not much. But enough. She saw other cables beneath her, some vertical, some horizontal, others angled crazily, each joined to others here or there in a structure that would have been immediately familiar if she'd seen more than the veriest edge of it. The edge she was standing on.

The edge of the web.

But what was scuttling up it from below was no spider, not even one from Neve's darkest nightmare. It was many-legged like a spider, yes, but at that point all resemblance to any insect she had ever seen ended completely. It had more legs than a spider, at least twelve or so, although Neve neither could nor wanted to count them at the moment. But this creature had neither the horny carapace of some spiders nor the strangely hairy body of others she had seen. This spider seemed to be carved from solid gold liberally sprinkled with brilliant gemstones that sparkled in every rainbow color; the reflections from its moving legs and body were nearly blinding. Its eyes were multifaceted prisms. It was beautiful, incredibly beautiful.

And incredibly huge. It could have given any of the sea dragons Neve had seen a good fight. And it was coming straight up at her. It was almost upon her.

And Neve had the sinking suspicion that the heir to the Nexus was only a light snack to that incredible beast.

Flee. Flee where? She could barely move, and even at her best she could never outdistance the huge sparkling deadly creature approaching with wonderful terrible speed. Neve's hands clenched on the rope.

I could cut myself free, she thought with sudden, almost numb clarity. *I could jump. Better the fall than . . . that. I could draw my knife and—*

My knife.

Dreamlike, Neve reached down, finding her boot sheath, finding the hilt. She drew the blade slowly, carefully. *Mustn't cut myself, oh, no.* The monster was almost on her now. Despite its size, it made no sound whatsoever; its silence was more terrible than any whistle or chitter or cry it could have made. She could see its mandibles now, sharp and gleaming, opening and closing in anticipation. She could see a stinger, too, far below, long and exquisitely sharp, dripping clear venom.

Doesn't need that for me, Neve thought detachedly. *It*

could just take my head off with one sweep of those jaws.
One hand still grasping the anchor rope firmly, tightly, she
brought up her knife, raising it before her face as if in challenge.

Come on, then, she thought with no emotion whatsoever.
*I'm just a tiny little thing, just a soft, juicy little mouthful.
But this tasty little bite has a stinger of her own. One of us
is going to die here, monster. I made you—somehow, some-
way I made you—and I'm going to unmake you, too.*

It seemed to come so slowly now, but a part of Neve
realized that that was just time stretching out. Some part of
her mind registered another sound, cries maybe, and out of
the corner of her eye she could see Ash scrambling across
the cable, no rope around his waist to protect him, just clam-
bering along as fast as he could.

He should've taken time to tie himself off, Neve thought
with that same cool clarity. *He won't get here in time anyway.*

And then it was upon her, gold and jeweled shell gleaming, prism eyes sparkling, jointed legs dancing; a drop of
clear fluid flew from the working mandibles and splashed
against her arm and burned there but Neve ignored it. She
swept out with her dagger at the nearest gleaming leg, slashing not desperately but deliberately, completely calmly—

And inside she went utterly silent, utterly still as the dagger glanced harmlessly off the thick shining shell plating it.

The creature never felt the blow, apparently, for it did not
even pause; only the sweep of Neve's stroke, which over-
balanced her and threw her around to the side, pulled her out
of the way as those mandibles clicked in the exact space
she'd occupied only a second earlier. For a moment Neve
flailed wildly, unwilling to relinquish either her grip on the
rope or the knife, and then her feet slipped off the cable and
she plunged—

Neve swung wildly at the end of the loop of short rope,
her feet dangling over empty space, the breath driven out of
her as all her weight hung on the rope around her waist, but
the fall saved her again; the spider was simply too big to
maneuver quickly enough to compensate for her quick
change in position and once again overshot her. Dimly Neve
heard Ash shouting again, closer now but still too far away,

and this time as the spider-monster moved forward, trying to turn, to find her, its gleaming belly loomed right in front of her face.

Sitting and watching, Mother, sometimes you learn the most amazing things— Coldly, precisely, Neve struck out with the dagger again, not taking the easy target of the broad belly but instead the softer, flexible tissue between the two sections of its body, thrusting the point inward with all the strength and poor leverage she could manage as she swung over the foggy chasm, one hand still uselessly clutching at the anchor rope. And still the creature made no sound, but even as Neve buried the dagger deeper into its body, a shiver went through it, only that, as some foul liquid poured down her arm and over her shoulder, spattering her face. And then the monster stiffened, went utterly still, wrenching the dagger from Neve's hand.

And then, still silently, it fell—*Thank the Nexus, not on top of me*—backward, so slowly, like a dead leaf drifting slowly downward on the currents of air. Neve watched it fall, hanging limply now. Little spots were dancing before her eyes, bright at first, then gray. She felt heavy, so heavy.

Well, of course. I'm hanging here—

So tired.

"Wake up. Wake up, damn it!"

Neve groaned and forced her eyes open as she was shaken violently. Air rushed into her lungs in a joyous explosion.

"What?" she mumbled. "What?"

Whack!

This time her eyes flew open wide, her hand coming up—*By the Nexus, what is that horrible smell? And why does my arm burn like that?*—to cover her stinging cheek.

"You *hit* me!" she said disbelievingly.

"Never mind that," Ash snapped. "You awake?"

"I—I think—" Suddenly Neve realized where she was, and simultaneously realized that the strangling comforting grip of her safety loop was gone from around her waist. She screamed and clutched frantically, at Ash, at the rope, at thin air—then Ash hauled her hands back to the anchor rope by main force.

"Hang on," he said sharply. "Look at me. No—" He

punched Neve's shoulder hard as Neve's eyes dropped. "Look at *me,* damn it!"

Neve forced her eyes up to meet his. Her teeth began to chatter.

"Listen to me," Ash said slowly, gazing into her eyes. "I had to cut your safety rope. You were tangled in it, choking. And I haven't got mine. So you're going to do just what I say, real nice and slow, got it?"

Neve clenched her teeth hard to stop their chattering. She nodded; she didn't trust her voice.

"You just hold on tight," Ash said, still speaking slowly as if to a child. "I'm gonna have to lean on you a bit while I take our belts off—"

Neve swallowed.

"My pants will fall off," she said in a small voice.

"I still got the cord in my pocket," Ash said, nodding. "I'll tie 'em up. The last thing either of us needs is to be tripping now, hey?"

Images flashed through Neve's mind—she falling flailing through the air, her pants and hose down around her knees; she letting her pants drop away into space (be fair, they were filthy anyway now) and edging across the chasm naked from the waist down—Neve chuckled involuntarily and suddenly felt just a little better.

Ash pulled her belt off, tying her linens, hose, and pants up with cord; then, more awkwardly, he repeated the process on himself. He fastened the two belts together, tugging at them before passing the ends under Neve's arms and then around the anchor rope.

"Now, that ain't the best arrangement in the world," he said quietly. "Those belts don't leave a whole lot of room. So if you feel yourself falling, for Peregard's sake don't throw your arms straight up or you'll just slide on through."

"But—what about you?" Neve whispered.

Ash chuckled.

"Girl, it's been a lot of years since I've needed a safety line on the rigging," he said. "Now let's get moving, shall we?"

Neve started back the way she'd come, ever so slowly, but a gentle tug from Ash brought her to a stop.

"Uh-uh," he said firmly. "We're going over."

"But—the other side's closer," Neve protested. Right now the only thing in the world she cared about was getting *off* this web.

"Not much. Come on, now. Just do like you were, nice and slow. Slide your feet, watch your hands."

Muscles knotted tightly, Neve inched her way along the cable even more slowly than before. Ash showed no impatience until she realized she was halfway across the chasm, realized how far away either edge was, and slowed to a stop, shivering.

"Come on," Ash said, a slight edge creeping into his voice. "You're not planning on camping out here, are you? No room to pitch the tent, girl."

Neve shivered again. She felt absolutely helpless to move. "I—I need to rest for a minute," she whispered.

"Uh-uh." Ash laid his hand over hers and squeezed hard, hard enough to hurt. "We're going to keep moving. You can rest when we get to the other side. Get going and I promise I'll catch you something fat for dinner."

"Just a little while," Neve begged.

"Speaking of dinner," Ash said patiently, "you want to wait around and see if your friend the big bug had invited a cousin over for a snack?"

That did it. Neve started moving again, so fast that Ash had to slow her down several times. This time she didn't look at either edge; she simply concentrated on moving her hands, her feet. Soon she had a rhythm that was comforting, almost reassuring. Left foot, right hand; right foot, left hand; scoot the belt over; left foot—

"Doing good," Ash murmured. "We're almost there."

Startled, Neve glanced up and realized that he was right; the edge of the chasm was only a few feet away. Relief weakened her legs; it was only as Ash's hand steadied her and the belts tightened under her arms that she realized that she'd better not count herself safe yet. Taking a deep breath, she scooted the last few feet to solid ground, stood shaking a moment longer—just long enough for Ash to slip the belts off her—then quietly collapsed where she was. She sat there shaking silently, not crying, not speaking, just shaking, clenching her aching hands.

Ash said nothing, just grabbed her under her arms and

pulled her a few feet farther back from the edge. He retrieved their pack from under a bush and pulled out the blanket, then draped it around Neve's shoulders, sat down beside her, and held her with one arm until she stopped shaking.

"Are you all right by yourself for a few minutes?" Ash asked at last. "Just long enough for me to find some water, maybe a campsite."

To Neve's disgust, the very idea of Ash leaving her, even for a moment, caused a surge of undeniable panic. She clenched her teeth hard.

"Go ahead," she said. "I'm fine."

Ash chuckled.

"You *are* a tough little bit," he said. "All right. Just relax there." He vanished into the jungle.

Neve found herself shaking again, and she pulled the blanket more tightly around herself. Her gooey tunic slid wetly against her skin, and suddenly she realized that she was positively drenched in whatever noisome fluid had spurted out of the spider-creature. Shuddering, she flung the blanket aside and fumbled at the laces of her tunic, her trousers; her aching, trembling fingers wouldn't seem to obey her. At last she drew the dagger from her hip sheath and cut the laces, hurriedly stripping off her tunic and trousers. Thankfully the goo hadn't reached her linens, and Neve used the clean sections of the blanket to wipe her skin clean as best she could. She found, to her dismay, that her left arm between elbow and shoulder was a mass of oozing blisters, so painful that she couldn't bear to touch it. At last she threw the blanket aside with her outer clothes, pulled her cloak out of the pack, and wrapped it around her. Then there was nothing to do but sit and wait and try to ignore the horrible smell from her slimy hair.

True to his word, Ash returned before long. He glanced at the pile of Neve's clothes and blanket, shrugged, and kicked them over the edge of the chasm.

"Think you can walk now?" he said. "It's not far. I can carry you if I have to."

"I can walk," Neve said immediately, although she was far from sure she spoke the truth. But she pushed herself to her feet, and with Ash's arm to lean on she managed. The camp wasn't far; there was neither a pool nor a stream, only a small spring coming out of a rock face, but Neve couldn't have cared less—at least until she remembered her gooey hair.

"Well, we've had better," Ash sighed. "We're going to miss that blanket tonight. Unless you can make another one?"

"I can make one," Neve said. Somehow she'd manage. "I just need to wash and eat and rest a little while."

"Well, eating and resting's no problem." Ash chuckled. "Washing's going to be a bit tricky, though. Hmm." He helped Neve over to a rock beside the stream, then placed their cooking pot under the flow of water. The pot filled slowly, and he handed her a cup.

"Just pour that over your head," he said. "There's no soaproot, but I guess you can use sand if you have to." He glanced at Neve's blistered arm and scowled. "Better leave that be. I'll see what I can do with it when I get back." He emptied their pack and took it with him, vanishing into the jungle without another word.

Neve stripped off her linens and made the best toilet she could; she was glad of the gritty sand to scour every last trace of goo from her skin and hair. After a thorough sanding, and after drinking an amazing quantity of sweet cold water from the spring, she felt recovered enough to build a fire and replace their blanket and her clothes, and while she was at it, she made some long strips of linen to bandage her arm. She simply didn't feel competent enough at the moment to attempt healing herself.

Ash returned with a sturdy stick over his shoulders, the pack bulging on one end. At the other end of the stick was suspended the carcass of an animal Neve had seen in one of the pocket worlds—a plump deerlike creature no bigger than a medium-sized dog.

"Lots of goodies tonight," Ash said cheerfully. He opened the pack and pulled out several different kinds of fruit, a few tubers, and a handful of strange thick leaves.

"I've had these roots aboard ship before," he said. "They're tasty."

Shortly the strange small deer was roasting on a makeshift spit, the pot set underneath it to catch the drippings, the tubers wrapped in leaves and baking in the coals. While the food cooked, Ash carefully examined Neve's blistered arm.

"Better wait to heal this till you're a little better rested," he said, shaking his head. "It doesn't look any worse, so I guess whatever poison it was has stopped burning in." He dipped out some of the grease from the dripping pot, let it cool, and mashed it with the leaves he'd brought into a slimy, viscous paste that he plastered thickly over Neve's arm. The slime was surprisingly soothing, and the leaves Ash wound around her arm before bandaging it kept the goo from soaking into the bandages.

When the meat was cooked it was so plump and tender that Neve gorged herself; after a brief hesitation she followed Ash's example and cut up the tubers, dipping them in the meat drippings before eating them, licking her fingers as noisily as he did. Somehow she couldn't seem to remember a better-tasting meal in her life.

"Well, if I pack this in the pot and put it under the spring, maybe we can keep the rest of the meat to work on in the next day or two," Ash said wryly, suiting actions to words. "You just curl up and rest, though. Sleep's what you need."

Wrapped comfortably in the blanket, however, watching while Ash put the meat away and buried the fire, Neve felt no desire to sleep despite her bone-deep exhaustion and aching muscles.

"Thank you," she said at last, rather stiffly.

Ash turned to her, raising his eyebrows.

"For what?"

Neve shrugged uncomfortably.

"For taking care of me," she said. "I'd have been dead if you hadn't come back out there for me."

Ash chuckled.

"Oh, don't put too much on that, girl," he said. "I never seen nothing like that in all my days—a little bit like you, taking on that monster with nothing but a dagger. And you put it down, too, right proper, didn't you? Toughest little piece I've ever seen, there's no denying."

Neve sighed.

"The dagger my father made for me," she said miserably. "It's gone now."

"Well, I can't hardly think of a better way to lose it." Ash grinned. "Anyway, girl, I figure I'm safer with you and your magic around than without. Besides, you die, who pays me?''

Neve grinned back faintly, both amused and slightly disappointed with Ash's glib response. But when Ash crawled into the blanket with her, he pulled her close, his fingers stroking her hair with a gentleness she'd never felt from him before.

''You know,'' he said softly in the darkness, ''that was really something, you and that gigantic thing. That moment, the moment when you killed it, there was this look on your face, so calm, almost cold. At that moment I guess that's the first time I could actually imagine the Guardian of the Crystal Keep—imagine *you* as that Guardian. I guess I figured if there really was somebody with all that power, he'd look just like you did at that moment.''

Neve was inwardly pleased, but she chuckled wryly.

''The look of suffocation,'' she said. ''I doubt my father ever found himself in the position of wondering whether he'd have time to soil himself before he died.'' Then her grin faded. She was mortally certain that her father had never frozen up, never lost his courage as she had out there over the chasm.

Ash raised up on one elbow, squinting at Neve in the darkness as if reading her thoughts.

''You did great out there,'' he said flatly. ''I've seen strong men get weak in the spine their first time on a high rigging, much less over a big crack like that. And I'll bet you the stoutest warrior in Zaravelle would've turned tail if he saw that thing coming—you better believe *I* would have! Don't kick yourself too hard if you got a few quivers afterward.''

I didn't do anything, Neve thought, suddenly depressed. *It was a magical dagger. I didn't actually* do *anything. Except panic and have to be rescued, that is.* And she wondered miserably whether her father had ever felt quite so humiliated.

In the morning there was potted meat and fruit, and after a night's rest Neve felt confident enough to try to heal the burned skin on her arm. Burns, she quickly discovered, were more complicated to heal than simple scratches or cuts—or possibly this injury was more difficult because it was inflicted by a creation of the same magic. Still, the skin grudgingly healed, thankfully without scarring, and Neve was marginally cheered by her success.

Then, too, there was the fact that the gorge was behind them now. They still had to walk back to the coast, which meant most of another day with no progress west toward Zaravelle, but even so, this success, too, was cheering. Neve tried not to think that there might be another such crack between here and Zaravelle, but the possibility haunted her nonetheless. Horrible as that monster insect had been, they could never have crossed the chasm without its web. Would Neve dream another such monster into being if they had to make another such crossing? Could she even manage to set toe tip on that web if they did? They had no magical dagger now, and Neve had no illusions of her chances against such a monster in a second encounter.

The sight of the coastline was a welcome one. They were still walking downhill, and progress was faster at the edge of the jungle where the growth was less dense. The sea breeze, too, helped dissipate some of the steaminess of the air. Ash perked up considerably, whistling as he walked. Still, Neve couldn't manage to be cheered.

At first I could ignore this problem, my magic doing things I didn't try for, she thought. *It wasn't dangerous, just . . . annoying. But this is the second time I've almost gotten us killed—not to mention all the innocent people I did kill. And Ash doesn't even know it. What would he do if I told him? He'd leave me here, abandon me. By the Nexus, I couldn't blame him if he did. I don't even know if throwing the stone away would help. And it might hurt Father, or me, if anything happened to it. What can I do? And I can't even ask Ash for advice.*

After several hours of silence, Ash turned around, stopping to gaze at her.

"What's bothering you now?" he said. "You still fretting about what happened back there?"

Neve shook her head.

"In a way," she said. "I lost the dagger Father created. It was our best weapon."

Ash shook his head, too.

"Not a bit of it," he said flatly. "It was a weapon, and a pretty decent one—maybe a little too dangerous to carry around, to my way of thinking. But it wasn't our best. The best weapon's your wits, girl. You got those, then you've still got a weapon no matter if you're bare-assed naked. Lose 'em and you're lost. Just keep your wits about you, girl, and we'll do well enough."

Perversely Neve felt comforted by his words. She might have lost her nerve, but she'd never yet lost her wits.

And then, near sunset, something that truly raised her spirits—a ship on the horizon.

"Fishing boat," Ash said, nodding happily when Neve pointed out the speck she could barely see against the setting sun.

"Does that mean Zaravelle's close?" she asked hopefully.

"I'd say so," Ash said more cautiously. "Usually I'd say no; sometimes these ships are out for weeks on end, going way down the coast. But it's too close to storm season, so they'll be hanging around close to port. I'd say another day or two should see us to Zaravelle now."

"You don't suppose," Neve said tentatively, "that if we lit a big fire, that ship would come in and pick us up?"

Ash shook his head.

"They can't come in amongst these reefs any more than the *Albatross* could," he said. "Besides, if they're out working this close to storm season, they're out to get their last profits in the hold. I doubt they'd stop their run just to come ashore and check out a fire. No, just take it for what it is—a sign that the walk's nearly over."

They found a good-sized stream, complete with a small waterfall, to camp beside that night. There was fruit and tubers to eat with the last of the potted meat without the need to hunt down supper. They made a celebration of it, and Neve, after considerable effort, managed to conjure some wine, which, heavily mixed with honey that she also created, wasn't too bad.

They were both more than half-drunk by the time they stumbled to the water, dug and pounded soaproot, and stripped for a real bath. The water was deliciously cool, and for the first time since Strachan, Neve felt really, truly clean. She picked up some soaproot, lathered it, and scrubbed Ash's back, rather enjoying the solidity of his skin. She'd never bathed with any of the lovers she'd made, nor with the few travelers she'd seduced. It was surprisingly intimate, pleasant. When she'd finished, without a word said between them, Ash turned around and scrubbed her back, too. Neve closed her eyes, sighing.

"You know," Ash said speculatively, "sometimes to talk to you, you sound a bit like some noble's spoiled child. Sometimes I have to look at you to remind myself that you're a full-grown woman."

"Oh, thank you," Neve said sarcastically.

"Hey, you're a strange bit, and I've never said otherwise," Ash said easily. "But who am I to talk about strange? Don't take it wrong. If I didn't think much of you, I'd've left you on your own back in Kent. You pull your weight, you don't love the sound of your own voice, and you're the hardest little thing to rattle I've ever seen in my life."

"Thank you," Neve said again, this time more confused than offended.

There was a long moment of silence that should have been awkward but wasn't. At last Neve spoke again.

"Ash, will you answer one question for me? Those rubies . . . what *do* you need all that money for?"

Ash's hands stopped their motion, and Neve wished she hadn't said anything. Then slowly he resumed washing her back, almost absently.

"Don't suppose it makes any difference to say it," he said. "I want to hire a mage to fix what was done to me. You know, the feet and the eyes. That'll cost a good bit of gold. Transformation spells come dear." There was a long pause. "Unless you could . . ."

"I can't," Neve said hurriedly. She turned to face Ash. "I wouldn't dare. That isn't healing a wound. That's outright transformation magic. I'm nothing but an amateur in using that on living things. Believe me, you wouldn't even want me to try, not if you saw what happened to the failures. Maybe with all the power of the Nexus, with lots of practice, I could, but not now."

Ash's expression never changed; if Neve hadn't been looking closely she might have missed the bare flicker of disappointment in his eyes.

"Well, can't say I expected it," he said, shrugging.

"Ash, I—" Neve laid her hand on his arm. "I'd do it for you if I could, if I wasn't afraid of doing more harm than good. Truly I would." She hesitated. "If you want to come back to the Keep with me—even if my father doesn't turn the Keep over to me right away, I'm sure he'd feel he owed you a debt for all you've done for me. I'm sure I could persuade him to help you." In fact, under the laws of the Keep, it was entirely possible that her father would be *obligated* to help him.

Ash grinned wryly.

"Everybody's heard the stories about the Guardian of the Crystal Keep and his tricks, no offense to you and your father," he said. "I don't know how much of what I've heard is just lies, but none of it was very complimentary, if you get my meaning."

Neve thought of the tricks her father—and she herself, there was no denying it—had played on visitors to the Keep, just for the amusement of it, and flushed slightly. Whatever her father's reputation in the mortal world, it was not exactly undeserved.

"There's also the little fact that taking you back to the Crystal Keep puts me in exactly the wrong part of the world," Ash said gently. "I'm a sailor now, remember? I don't need to go countries out of my way for what I can buy in any good-sized city."

This time Neve felt decidedly disappointed. Somehow she'd harbored a hope that Ash would stand by her for the whole journey, all the way back home. But why should he? He was a sailor, as he'd said, not a guard. He was doing her a service in exchange for pay, and because to some extent their interests coincided. She could certainly understand that. In a way she was almost relieved. Value given for value received; that was the way things should be.

Neve turned around and Ash resumed washing her back. Suddenly she felt neither as drunk nor as joyful as she'd felt a few minutes before.

"I think between one thing and another, I missed paying you for a few days," she said at last. "I'll make sure you're caught up before we reach Zaravelle."

The hands paused again; then abruptly Ash turned her around to face him.

"You know what?" he said, a strange expression on his face. "I never thought I'd say this about you, but—you talk too much."

"What—" Neve said, just before Ash claimed her mouth with his own, silencing her.

It took them two more days to reach Zaravelle; their progress was somewhat hampered by the increasing frequency of violent downpours; Ash thought the rainy season had officially begun by now. They saw one or two more fishing boats, but not many; Neve agreed with him that they were probably afraid of the storms, too.

More alarming, twice on their journey the earth had started shaking under their feet. The first time Neve was sure a dragon was coming, or some other such predator, and nearly fled into the jungle. She'd been utterly humiliated when Ash had explained that earthquakes were quite common in these parts. True to his words, the shaking had stopped after a few minutes with no harm done, although Neve had seen a few rocks crumble from the cliff, and from that point on she made it her practice to stay well back from the edge.

Neve was surprised at how abruptly jungle gave way to city; in Selwaer and even Kent there were signs of civilization well in advance of the cities—farms, cottages, roads. Here, however, she and Ash stepped out of the jungle and found themselves on the bank of a wide river; the riverside docks of Zaravelle were on the other side. Farther to the south Neve could see the seaside docks; a number of ships were already well secured there, and there was almost no activity at the docks now. Zaravelle itself was much higher on the cliffs.

"Yeah, there's a few farms and a few roads," Ash said in response to her surprise. "But they go inland, not along the coast here. Nobody travels by horse or wagon along the coast. Most of the traffic's shipping anyway, either along the coast from Strachan or the other port cities, or by raft along the Willow River. This really isn't farmland, you know. Floods out regularly during the rainy season. If Zaravelle weren't up so high it'd just wash away. Now let's figure out how we're getting across that river.''

Neve stared blankly.

"Isn't there a ferry?'' she asked, surprised. She'd never heard of a city built next to a river but lacking a bridge or ferry.

"Why would there be?'' Ash said patiently. "There's nothing but jungle this side of the river. Folks might cross to do a bit of hunting or pick fruit, but I bet they've got their own small boats or rafts.''

"Well, then,'' Neve said irritably, "we'll just have to make a raft or a boat.''

Ash snorted.

"You got any idea how long that'll take?'' He chuckled. "Especially without an ax or—'' Then he stopped, glancing at Neve. "Oh. *Make* a raft, eh?''

"*Make* a raft,'' she agreed.

In the end it took several hours of labor almost as intensive, Neve suspected, as making a craft by hand would have. She knew nothing about rafts; the logs and rope were simple enough, but arranging them properly was considerably more complicated than she'd thought. By the time she'd re-created the structure several times to take Ash's specifications into account, she was exhausted. Finally, disgusted, she gave up and tried a small rowboat instead, and to her surprise, it was a great deal easier. Of course—she'd had *plenty* of experience with the structure of a boat now, the hows and whys of its shape, and oars were simple, too. The rowboat leaked slightly, but Ash reassured her that it would get them across the river.

Neither Neve nor Ash, however, had tried rowing a boat across the strong and complicated currents of a river dumping into the sea; Ash had always traveled on larger boats, and Neve had never rowed in her life. At first their inexperienced efforts only spun them around in circles as the current tried its best to sweep them out to sea, but at last they managed to coordinate their movements. It took both of them, pulling as hard as they could, simply to fight the seaward pull, and several times they almost lost their progress through sheer exhaustion. By dint of downright hard work, at last they reached the docks and wearily pulled themselves up out of the boat. The boat drifted off toward the sea as soon as they released it.

So it was that Neve stumbled into Zaravelle bedraggled, sweaty, and utterly exhausted, too tired even to take note of their surroundings. She simply staggered along at Ash's side and let him find an inn, then staggered up and collapsed into the bed, completely oblivious.

When she woke, it was midmorning and the sun was streaming in the window on her face. Neve opened crusty eyes and sat up. She was lying alone in a wide, comfortable bed—stark naked. Ash must have undressed her—must have washed her off, too, for the sweat and grime of her journey was gone. Her first reflex was to scrabble around wildly for her fragment of the Nexus; she found it immediately, tucked under the pillow.

The room was pleasant and clean and spacious, but far less luxurious than the room she'd rented in Kent. The pack Neve had made, presumably still with its contents, judging from the way it bulged, lay at the foot of the bed, her soiled clothes in a heap beside it. Ash was nowhere to be seen.

Neve scooted out of bed, stumbled over to the washbasin, and scrubbed her face vigorously. She pulled a cover from the bed and wrapped it around her, then leaned out the window.

The air was surprisingly fresh, with very little stink from the streets—of course, the sea breeze kept the air cleaner. This window faced the sea, and she could see it over the roofs, over the city wall, past the masts of the ships anchored at the docks.

The street below her window was bustling with traffic—pedestrians, donkey-drawn wagons, goat carts, but surprisingly few horses. It was the people themselves, however, who drew her attention immediately.

They were all so different from each other, as varied as the visitors who came to the Keep. There were dusty-haired easterners like Ash, bronze-skinned warriors from the middle plains, swarthy dark-haired southerners, slender pale red-haired merchants. And elves, too, such as Neve had seen in pictures or in the mirror—golden-haired and tall, browned by the sun. Everyone dressed in bright colors as though some festival were under way, and she remembered what Ash had

said about celebrations before the storm season, but there was
no other sign that today was anything but ordinary.

Neve was well rested enough that creating a clean set of
clothing was relatively simple. She found her rubies and
gold—to her amazement, Ash hadn't touched them, even to
take what she still owed him—pulled on her boots, and
walked downstairs. She only dimly remembered arriving at
the inn the night before, but she recognized the common
room at the bottom of the stairs. Ash was not there, nor was
anyone else; it was too late for breakfast, too early for dinner.
Neve finally located a middle-aged man, presumably the innkeeper, in the kitchen, stirring up pie pastry.

"Excuse me," she said politely. "My companion—the
man I came in with last night—did he leave any message for
me?"

"What, the fellow with the strange eyes?" the man said,
grimacing. "No. He ate his breakfast and went on out. Your
room's paid for three days."

Neve's mouth went dry. Had Ash left her, then, as he had
when they'd reached Kent? There was nothing obligating
him to stay. He had the rubies she had already given him.
He'd fulfilled his side of their bargain. He'd probably decided that it was easier just to leave than to go through the
messy business of saying good-bye.

Neve swallowed, rigidly fighting down the sudden ache in
her heart. She had nothing to be disappointed about. She'd
certainly received value and more; why, she hadn't even paid
Ash all he was due. Now she was on her own.

"I came here looking for two friends, Kelara and Yaga,"
Neve said quietly. "They're elves. I understand they live a
short distance from the city."

The innkeeper shrugged.

"I don't know the names," he said. "There's elves
aplenty here. You might ask in the marketplace. If they live
hereabouts, somebody'll know them."

Neve grimaced. Markets again. It would be miserable
without Ash. Then a thought occurred to her.

"Sir, if you please, who's the best mage in town?" she
asked, surprised when the innkeeper gave her a mocking
laugh.

"The best mage?" he said, shaking his head. "The *only*

mage, you mean. That's Rhadaman. He's got a place south-east of the market. Anybody can tell you the way. Oh, there's a few charlatans in town, and a madman some say can tell the weather, but Rhadaman's the only one worth the price.''

Neve sighed and started toward the marketplace. The streets, thankfully, were not too crowded now; gathering clouds above told the reason. The citizens were probably getting ready for the seasonal storms. She began to wish she'd brought her cloak.

The market was still fairly busy, and for a time Neve found some distraction in the unfamiliar goods, exotic spices, and tempting-smelling foods. She heard at least six or eight languages spoken, which startled her; Zaravelle wasn't very handy to any of the large trade cities, and there wasn't even a direct road or river route to Allanmere, the largest trade city of all.

At last, however, Neve asked a spice merchant where she might find Rhadaman's shop and received directions. The shop was farther from the market than she'd expected; it was as if the mage wasn't especially looking for customers. Strange, if he was the only mage in the city! The shop itself was a rather understated building; the only marker was a somewhat faded sign hanging on the door depicting a flask full of some liquid. But as Neve watched, a couple of customers emerged from the building, and another walked in. She hesitated only a moment longer, then opened the door and stepped inside.

The interior of the building was as unremarkable as the outside, although Neve was hit by the strange combination of smells as soon as she walked through the door. To look at the jars and flasks on shelves lining the walls, she could have been in any herbalist's or spice merchant's shop—at least until she read the labels on the jars. She'd never seen sea dragon bile, ice-newt liver, or basilisk eyes in any herbalist's shop she'd been in. There were a few chairs, all presently empty, and the room was bisected by a counter. There were more shelves, holding more ingredients and a few thick books, behind the counter. The only other feature of note was Rhadaman himself.

Neve's first thought was that the mage must be ill himself, or suffering from some kind of curse. He was pale and gaunt,

his strong bones standing out sharply under his skin. But
further observation made her question her initial judgment.
The mage's long-fingered hands as he worked a mortar and
pestle were strong and sure, and his eyes were bright and
lively; he was tall, which contributed to his appearance of
thinness, but not stooped, and his neatly trimmed dark brown
hair and short beard were thick and lustrous.

"There you are," he said, handing a small vial to the
woman at the counter. "We'll try this one more week. If
you're still having the headaches after that, we'll have to try
something else."

Neve waited until the other two customers in the shop had
been served before she approached the counter. Rhadaman,
writing something in a ledger, glanced up absently, then laid
down his quill, gazing at her more interestedly.

"Good morning, my lady," he said. "I don't believe I've
seen you about town before."

"No, my friend and I just arrived yesterday," Neve said
a little hesitantly. Yes, she knew she was very pale and startlingly dark-eyed, and her features were set strangely in comparison to the people she'd seen, but . . . well, everybody *did*
call her strange looking. She wasn't sure whether to take
offense at the mage's interest or not.

"That's very interesting," Rhadaman said, closing his
book. "The last ship came into port days ago."

"We were on the *Albatross* out of Strachan," Neve said,
feeling somehow that she'd been put on the defensive. "It
caught fire in a storm and sank. There were sea dragons in
the water, too. As far as I know, my friend and I are the only
ones who made it ashore."

Rhadaman went very still, very quiet.

"The *Albatross*?" he said softly. "Captain Corell?"

Neve nodded.

"The ship was struck by lightning in a storm," she said.
"The ship exploded. I know some people got into the long-
boats, but I think the sea dragons—" She saw the look in
Rhadaman's eyes and quickly changed directions. "My
friend and I swam ashore several days' walk east of here.
We just made it to Zaravelle yesterday."

Rhadaman shook his head sadly.

"What a tragic occurrence," he said quietly. "We thought

the *Albatross* had decided not to leave Strachan because of the early storms. What a dreadful thing. Captain Corell was a good friend, a competent, if limited, mage.''

Now Neve felt a little sick.

"I'm sorry," she said tentatively. "She seemed like a good captain, too."

Rhadaman barely smiled.

"I'm sure you're being kind," he said. "Her bad temper and dislike of the nobility were well known. Still." He held out his hand. "I do thank you for the news and your concern. Welcome to Zaravelle. May it prove worth your trouble. I'm Rhadaman."

Neve took his hand. It was warm and strong.

"I'm Neve," she said. "Thank you for your welcome."

"So, my lady Neve," Rhadaman said, the interest in his eyes sharpening, "what can I do for you today?"

"Two things, actually," Neve said, grinning wryly. "Neither of them requires magic, I'm afraid, though I'm glad to pay for it. First, my friend Ash was going to look for a mage, so I'm sure he'd come here. He needs some transformation magic—"

"Ah, the fellow with the unusual feet and eyes," Rhadaman said, nodding. "Yes, he was here not two hours ago."

Neve felt a pang of disappointment. She'd missed him, then.

"Were you able to help him?" she asked softly.

"Mmm." Rhadaman scowled slightly. "I told him to consider his request carefully and come back another time if he still wished such magical assistance. Strong magic can be very dangerous in this part of the world. The magical fields in the aether are badly out of alignment because there's no single power center here, very difficult to manipulate properly, and magic easily becomes distorted. So far as I know, I'm the only mage in the city currently able to use such powerful spells, and even so, I'm very cautious. I've had more than one spell go terribly wrong, and transformation spells aren't my strong suit. I mislike to use them for purely cosmetic purposes, since failure could be so disastrous. I'd be less reluctant to risk it if he were actually maimed in some way."

"Oh." Neve was momentarily taken aback. She'd never

thought that another mage would have the same uncertainty she'd had. She quickly recovered. "Well—I'm also looking for some friends of my family. I thought they were mages themselves—two elves, Kelara and Yaga. I was told—"

"Oh, really?" Rhadaman raised his eyebrows. "Yes, I've made their acquaintance. They visit the city from time to time. I've never been to their home—I don't own a horse, and I rarely find it worth the risk to cast a Gate hereabouts—but I could draw you a rough map, and I understand it isn't a long ride. Or if you prefer, I could do a farspeaking, contact them and have them come for you."

"No!" Neve felt suddenly shy, so close to her destination now. She wanted to arrive unexpected on Kelara and Yaga's doorstep, well dressed and prepared as if she'd never lost control of this journey, not have them come for her like a feeble child to be rescued. "No, thank you. I'll make my own way. I'd rather."

"Yes, of course." Rhadaman hesitated. "You're a mage yourself, are you not?"

"Well—" Neve hesitated. "Something like that."

Rhadaman smiled gently.

" 'Something like that'? Would you care to join me for dinner, perhaps?"

"Dinner?" Neve asked blankly.

Rhadaman chuckled.

"Yes. The meal ordinarily taken at midday, after breakfast but before supper."

Neve flushed, embarrassed, but Rhadaman's eyes twinkled charmingly at her, as though they shared a joke.

"I'm sorry," she said. "I'm not used to being asked to dinner."

"You should be." Rhadaman gazed at her speculatively. "Well? Do you accept?"

Neve hesitated. She wondered whether she should check back at the inn, to see if Ash had come back, or look in the marketplace, perhaps, or check the local Guild of Thieves—no. *He'd* left *her* in their room, without a word. So far as she knew, he wasn't coming back and didn't want to be found. It was a slight twinge of resentment that made Neve smile and nod.

"Thank you," she said. "I'd be delighted to dine with you."

Rhadaman closed his shop and took her to a pleasant little tavern, the Grapevine, as tucked away from the public eye as Rhadaman's own shop. Neve began to wonder what else was hidden in this strange city. Apparently the proprietors of the Grapevine were accustomed to Rhadaman's business, because the moment he guided her to a quiet screened booth in a corner, a serving maid appeared with a bottle of wine and a tray of cheese and fruit, smiling at Rhadaman and giving Neve a more formal curtsy.

"Afternoon, sir, lady," the maid said. "We have a nice fish pasty today, or if you'd rather, there's venison in wine."

Neve hadn't tired of fish yet and followed Rhadaman's lead, choosing the pasty. The wine was fair, though she'd had better—but certainly never created better, so she supposed she shouldn't complain.

"Your friends are interesting people," Rhadaman said conversationally. "They keep very much to themselves. I don't believe they even visit much with the other elves. Most of the eastern elves who come this far west have grown rather—cosmopolitan, I suppose. If they mind the society of humans, they don't tend to leave the elven cities at all."

Neve squirmed slightly. She had no idea what Kelara and Yaga had told this mage, if anything, about the Crystal Keep, and it was really none of his business.

"I don't know them myself," she said after a moment's thought. "They were friends with my father and mother, but that was before I was born. My parents suggested I come visit them." She grinned. "It's been rather more of an adventure than I'd expected."

"It sounds so to me." Rhadaman peered at her intently. "I'm surprised that with two mages on board—Captain Corell and yourself—the ship was lost. But then—" He frowned slightly. "You *aren't* exactly a mage, are you?"

Neve drew back, feeling a pang of fear.

"What do you mean?" she said, keeping her tone light.

"I'm not sure myself." Rhadaman tilted his head slightly, and Neve had the oddest impression that he was gazing at her with a pair of eyes she couldn't see.

"Interesting," he said, very softly. "No, you're not a

mage at all. Rather you *are* magic—a magical creature your-self, like a demon or a homunculus.'' He leaned forward over the table eagerly. ''Will you confide in me? You may as well; otherwise I'll just go home and scry it out for myself, you know. I don't believe you intend any harm here, and if that's true, I'll tell no one, I promise you.''

Neve hesitated, shivering. She was trapped, well and truly trapped. She should have thought more carefully before con-tacting such a powerful mage—well, to be fair, she'd never planned on doing any such thing; she'd had a map to begin with, and if she'd needed to ask him for directions, hopefully she could have sent Ash to get them. What Rhadaman said, however, was the simple truth: he could probably scry out anything he wanted to know about her. Scrying couldn't pen-etrate the walls of the Crystal Keep, and that might provide her some protection, but not nearly enough. Neve knew no spells to prevent that, nor to silence him, nor even to defend herself against whatever use he might choose to make of his knowledge. She wasn't used to being at the mercy of some-one else's magic, and the position made her distinctly un-comfortable.

But Rhadaman's eyes seemed open and honest; there was something straightforward about him that rather reminded her of Ash. And he *could* have simply used his scrying, rather than buying her dinner and asking her politely. She and her father were often less . . . courteous . . . to visitors in their land.

''My father,'' she said, barely audibly, ''is Vanian, the Guardian of the Crystal Keep. I was born there.''

Rhadaman was silent for a long moment. He pressed his fingers to his lips, his eyebrows raising.

''Ah!'' he said, very softly. ''How very strange and won-derful. Yes, that *is* a secret. And the elves you seek?''

''They were both Guardians,'' Neve said. ''Kelara was the first Guardian. Yaga came later, and Father took his place.''

''I see. They never told me, of course,'' Rhadaman said slowly. ''Understandably so. Then they are older than I'd thought. Much older. That explains their isolation and aloof-ness. They must be well accustomed to their solitude.''

He ate for a while in silence, with an appetite that belied

his gaunt appearance. After a while, however, he paused again.

"And are you planning to settle in Zaravelle, then?" he said.

Neve shook her head quickly.

"Father and Mother wanted me to come visit with Kelara and Yaga," she said. "I suppose they wanted me to see the world a bit. I don't think any of us expected me to see quite so much of it." She chuckled. "I asked them not to scry after me while I was gone. If they've done it after all, I'd love to hear the arguments about whose idea it was that I make this trip."

Rhadaman only gazed at her silently for a long moment.

"What are you, then?" he asked softly. "Not human?"

Neve felt her amusement melt away as if it had never been.

"I don't know what I am," she said. "Mother and Father couldn't have a child the normal way. I'm a creation of the Nexus, I suppose. A part of it. Or maybe it's a part of me. I don't know."

Rhadaman reached out very slowly, as if afraid Neve might bolt like a frightened fawn, and touched her fingertips very gently.

"No seed of man and woman, at least," he murmured, as if to himself. "Perhaps the seed of your Nexus, then."

"Maybe," Neve said warily. This man's intensity and curiosity were beginning to alarm her.

Then Rhadaman sat up, shaking his head ruefully.

"I'm sorry," he said. "As I'm sure you've heard, there are no other real mages in these parts except your friends, and they live like hermits. My mind very seldom has anything interesting to work on. Please forgive my rudeness. I don't mean any harm."

Neve slowly relaxed.

"That's all right," she said. "But I'm a little curious myself. How did you end up being the only mage in Zaravelle? And why would you come here at all, if magic doesn't work properly here?"

Rhadaman shrugged.

"I didn't come here," he said. "My father did. His name was Duranar, and in his time he was known in the east as a mage of astounding power. He took a notion to see what there was to see in the westward lands; hardly anything was even mapped west of Allanmere then. His wanderings brought him south to Zaravelle, where he met and married my mother, a lyric poet. Zaravelle desperately needed a mage powerful enough to work despite the magical distortions, so he settled here. Mother died not long after I was born, bitten by a poisonous snake when she was out walking. Father stayed on, having nowhere better to go—and me to raise and train, of course. But working against such powerful distortions is terribly draining over time. He died before he'd quite finished my training.''

Neve swallowed.

''I'm sorry,'' she said softly. She couldn't conceive of her parents being dead and gone. ''I didn't mean to pry.''

Rhadaman smiled.

''Oh, not at all, my lady,'' he said. ''It was long ago— I'm older than I look. Mages tend to be long-lived. At any rate, I stayed in Zaravelle and took up my father's work.'' He chuckled. ''And Zaravelle's been good to me. It's easy to prosper as a mage when you're the only mage in town.''

Neve smiled, understanding. In his own way, Rhadaman had become Guardian of Zaravelle. Not a bad position.

''Listen,'' she said awkwardly at last, ''I really should get back to the inn. But if my friend calls tomorrow, would you tell him—''

Then she stopped. Tell Ash what? Beg him to see her again? No. They'd had a bargain. He'd fulfilled his part and more. If he'd decided that was the end of it, then there was nothing more to say.

''Tell him?'' Rhadaman prompted gently.

''Nothing,'' Neve said abruptly. ''Nothing, really. Just help him if you can. He thinks he's cursed and ugly. A monster.'' She felt a sort of bitter amusement, remembering the spiderlike monster, Captain Corell's endless vomiting, the worms . . . *Ash, friend, you have no idea. And just as well.* ''Nobody should feel that way.''

''Of course,'' Rhadaman said gravely. He hesitated. ''But—I wish you'd come visit me again at my shop tomorrow. I'll draw you a map to your friends' home. I've never been there, as I said, but I can scry out the path easily enough.''

"All right," Neve said, suddenly feeling unaccountably shy. *The end of my journey. It's almost in sight. Thank the Nexus. Then I can go home, where things make sense again. Where the Nexus is waiting for me.*

"Yes," she said more decisively. "I'll come tomorrow. We can have supper again if you like."

Then she grinned.

"But tomorrow I'll pay. It's the least I can do, taking so much of your time and not even hiring a single spell cast."

Rhadaman chuckled.

"Lady Neve, that's quite unnecessary," he said. "But I won't argue. I'm happy simply for the pleasure of such fascinating company."

All in all, Neve thought as she walked back to the inn, the visit with Rhadaman, though tense at first, had gone better than she'd expected. Still neither her success nor the fascination of the market much cheered her.

When she opened the door to her room, however, her heart gave a great lurch and she froze momentarily. Ash was there, sitting on the bed, a truly ferocious scowl on his face.

"You're—" Neve swallowed. "I thought you were gone. Really gone, I mean."

"I was just thinking of going," Ash growled. "Where have you been all day?"

Neve bristled. How *dare* he take that tone with her when he'd disappeared without so much as a word, a note to let her know he'd be back at all?

"I went to the market," she said. "And I met a mage named Rhadaman, and we had supper together."

Ash's scowl deepened.

"That mage? What in the world did you want with him?"

"I was hoping he'd know Kelara and Yaga, or at least how to get to their home," Neve said, more impatiently now. Then she took a deep breath. She mustn't become angry with Ash. Anger was dangerous.

"Besides," she admitted, "I thought you might go there. He's the only real mage in town, after all."

Ash's expression softened slightly.

"You were looking for me?" he asked hesitantly.

Neve flushed.

"Well, of *course* I was," she said. "You left without a

word, without—well, I mean at least you could've said you'd be back.''

Ash glanced down at the floor.

''I'm sorry,'' he said awkwardly. ''You were so exhausted, I thought you'd just sleep most of the day. I figured to be back before you woke up. Thought I'd buy us both some new clothes so you wouldn't have to make any more, tired as you were. And I wanted to find a mage, talk to him.''

''He told me,'' Neve admitted. ''Maybe you should wait, Ash. After what he said about spells going wrong around here—''

''Ah, it can't be that bad,'' he said, shrugging uncomfortably. ''I mean, you managed without too much trouble.''

Did I? Neve wondered. Could she blame her magical mishaps on the distortion effect Rhadaman had mentioned? *No. I can't. I really can't. As Ash said, it didn't seem to affect me much when I was making our supplies. Besides, things started going wrong back in Strachan, and there were no distortions there.*

''I don't know if that's the same,'' Neve said cautiously. ''I think the magic of the Nexus may work differently. Maybe—''

She took a deep breath.

''Maybe you ought to visit Kelara and Yaga with me before you decide,'' she said slowly, not meeting Ash's eyes. ''They're both powerful mages and both very experienced in transformations. They were Guardians for centuries, after all. I'm sure they could do it more safely than Rhadaman. And maybe they wouldn't charge you anything, as a favor to me. Really, you should—''

''All right.'' Ash spoke so softly that Neve wasn't certain he'd said it at first.

She glanced up, surprised.

''What?''

''I said, all right,'' Ash repeated, louder. He grinned wryly. ''I've come this far, right? Guess I couldn't stand not knowing how it comes out. Besides, can't hurt to have the heir to the Crystal Keep owing me a favor, hey? You never know, someday—''

Neve chuckled, too, surprised by the wave of relief that almost weakened her knees. She hadn't realized how much she'd relied on Ash's support, the simple reassurance of his presence, to see her through the last of it. It disturbed her a little, the degree to which she'd made herself vulnerable to this man. He knew all her weaknesses, all her secrets.

Well, no. Not all of them. He doesn't know about the magic that's gotten out of control. And hopefully, after I talk to Kelara and Yaga, he never will have to.

"So—" Ash hesitated again. "Did you get your directions?"

"Rhadaman's going to make me a map," Neve said quickly. "I have to pick it up tomorrow. I—I said I'd buy him supper. That's a cheap enough price, I guess. Why don't you come?"

Ash scowled again slightly.

"Nah, I don't want to, not if I'm waiting to decide about the spell," he said resignedly. "Besides—"

He shrugged, sighing.

"I've got to start looking for someplace I can doss down for the rainy season," he said. "No more ships going out till after the storm season's over, so I guess I'm stuck here. You might give that a bit of thought, too. I doubt there's going to be much going upriver, and even if there was, that's a nasty trek back across land that's hardly even on the map, hundreds of leagues west of where you want to be. Unless you're planning on Gating back or something like that."

Neve swallowed. She hadn't actually thought ahead that far. She hadn't known anything about ships and stormy seasons, and she was almost certain her parents hadn't, either. It had never occurred to her that she might be stranded in Zaravelle for a whole season. But her father had said she was to journey to Kelara and Yaga's house and back on her own. That meant no Gate. Would her father change his mind if he knew what had happened to her since she left home? Did she want to ask the elves to contact her father and find out? Neve swallowed again.

"I don't know," she said. "I suppose it'll depend on what happens when I visit Kelara and Yaga."

She hesitated.

"I'm glad you're going with me, though," she admitted.

Ash chuckled.

"Oh, well, guess I can hold off buying new boots for a

few more days," he said. "I can't say I like the idea of my feet maybe ending up even worse off." A fleeting expression crossed his face; Neve wondered whether it had been pain.

"What?" she asked softly.

"Well—" Ash shrugged. "Remember that time in the jungle when you learned you could do healing? You know, I think you're the first person ever touched my feet since they've been like this."

Neve scowled. She strode to the washstand and poured water into the basin, snatching up soap and a cloth. Plumping herself down on the floor beside the bed, she pulled off a vastly startled Ash's sandals and scrubbed one foot thoroughly, then the other. She dried both feet off, then lifted them into her lap.

"There's nothing *wrong* with them," she said, tracing her fingertips over his long toes. "They work just fine. Better than fine. If I'd had toes like yours, that big insect wouldn't have come so close to dropping me down the chasm. And if you *hadn't* been so quick climbing out to help me, I'd probably be dead."

Ash grimaced.

"They're ugly," he said. "Look how long they are." The toes of his right foot curled illustratively around her finger.

"Why does that make them ugly?" Neve said practically. "There were women in the market with bigger breasts than mine and women with smaller ones. Which size is ugly, bigger or smaller?"

"Bigger or smaller, that's one thing," Ash said patiently. "But these are downright strange."

"*Different,*" Neve corrected. "Different's usually better. You're different from other people I've met, and that's good, because if you were more like them, I wouldn't like you a bit. You don't know how lucky you are. I saw sailors in the market today with hooks for hands, or peg sticks for legs, or missing an eye, and you feel sorry for yourself because you've got eyes and toes that work better than anybody's. I suppose that makes me a *real* freak, doesn't it?"

"Well, you're an odd-looking little bit, and I've never denied it." Ash chuckled. "But I wouldn't go so far as to call you a freak."

"But I am," Neve said softly. "There probably isn't another person in the whole world like me. Even my father was human to begin with. But me—Rhadaman could tell the difference, you know. I'm not a mage; I'm a magical creature, like a demon or an homunculus. A true freak.''

Ash sat gazing at her for a moment, then reached down, pulling her up off the floor and onto the bed beside him.

''All right, fellow freak,'' he said, grinning. ''Guess the likes of us got to stick together, hey?''

''We've done all right so far,'' Neve said, feeling suddenly shy.

'' 'All right'?'' Ash mocked, pulling daringly at the lace of her tunic. ''How about 'damned good'?''

Neve lay back on the bed, grinning.

''We'll see,'' she said.

8

"**W**ELL—" ASH HESITATED. "IT'S— homey, I suppose."

Neve just stood staring blankly.

Kelara, creator and first Guardian of the Crystal Keep, and Yaga, a powerful mage and past Guardian, who had once lived as a dragon, now dwelt in a simple stone and wood cottage.

Not a particularly big one, either.

It *did* have a nice view of the sea from the hilltop on which it had been built; one could see all the way to Zaravelle, two hours' walk back along the coastline. And there was a gorgeous garden planted all around the house in beds of frothy color, there was no denying. Dara would have loved it instantly.

Neve was utterly disappointed.

"You must be Neve. At least I hope so."

Neve whirled at the unexpected voice, then winced inside. She'd never have startled like that back at home, where she was accustomed to people popping in and out. The tall elf stepping out of the bushes, plainly dressed and a bit disheveled, that must be Yaga. Father had shown her images of the slender golden-haired elf before, but in those images his skin had been fair, his clothing immaculate, his air dignified. This tanned and rather rumpled fellow was barely recognizable as the same elf.

Belatedly Neve took the dirt-stained and callused hand extended to her.

"Yes, I'm Neve," she said apologetically for her staring, swallowing her astonishment and dismay. "And you're—"

"Yaga, of course, at your service," the elf said gravely. He glanced down at his hand and grimaced. "You'll have to pardon me. I was chasing the cat, you see."

"The—" Neve shook her head hesitantly. "The cat?"

"Yes. She ran off with one of Kelara's bracelets, the hateful beast. Sometimes she buries things under bushes—the cat, I mean, not Kelara. So I was—" Yaga grimaced again. "Never mind. Pardon me. I'm babbling. I'm ever so glad to see you. Your father told me you were coming, but it's been so long since then, I've worried endlessly. I'm glad you're all right. And your friend?" He tilted his head slightly at Ash.

"Oh, I beg your pardon," Neve said hurriedly. "This is Ash, my friend and traveling companion. Ash, this is Yaga, Guardian before my father."

"My pleasure," Ash said easily, apparently unfazed by the prospect of meeting an elf who was both a powerful mage and a past Guardian of the Crystal Keep.

Yaga shook Ash's hand almost absently, glancing around the garden.

"Kelara's somewhere about," he said. "She wanders a bit. But perhaps—"

He hesitated, glancing searchingly at Neve.

"Do I feel what I think I feel?"

Neve fished in her tunic and pulled out the crystal.

"You mean this?" she said.

The oddest expression flitted across Yaga's delicate features—longing, almost greed, then revulsion. He closed his eyes, shivering.

"Put that away, please," he said in a fading voice.

Neve blinked.

"But—"

"Please." Yaga nearly choked the word out.

Slowly Neve tucked the crystal back into her tunic.

"I'm sorry," she said. "I didn't know it would bother you."

Yaga smiled rather weakly.

"No. Of course you couldn't. Just as I couldn't anticipate that you'd be bringing a part of the Nexus with you. Listen, young one, if I might ask you a very great boon, I'd much appreciate it if you could put that in—in something. I've got a box that might work. Kelara couldn't bear that presence."

"All right," Neve said doubtfully. Why in the world should the presence of part of the Nexus trouble either of them? They'd lived with it for centuries. "Whatever you like."

When Yaga had disappeared into the house, however, quite rudely leaving them alone in the garden, Ash nodded sympathetically.

"I've seen that look before," he said.

Neve glanced at him, surprised. For a moment she'd almost forgotten his presence.

"What look?" she said.

"The way he looked at that crystal," Ash said wisely. "People in Arawen used to buy dream dust, a drug that gave them wonderful dreams—still do, I guess. After a while they couldn't get by without it. Didn't want it—hated it, even, but couldn't stand to go on without it. I've seen folks sell their children to buy more. They looked at that dust the way that elf just looked at your stone. You're smart, you'll keep that thing well away from him and his lady, too. They might decide they can't do without it anymore either."

Neve touched the lump of the crystal through her tunic, troubled. Yes, her father had said something about that, hadn't he? That he was no longer sure he could give up the power of the Nexus, yes. And Yaga and Kelara had been Guardians far, far longer than her father had been. How had they been able to walk away from the Nexus, surrender that power to another?

Yaga returned presently with a small box that looked as though it was made from silver, but when he handed it to Neve, it was surprisingly heavy.

"That should do it," he said. "I keep my most delicate magic in those boxes, to insulate it from the distorting effects hereabouts."

Neve reluctantly took the crystal out again, placing it in the box and closing the lid. Immediately the presence of the Nexus was gone as if it had never been; gasping, Neve opened the box again, sighing with relief when she saw the crystal there. She forced herself to close the box again, then tucked it into her pocket hurriedly. Thankfully Yaga made no indication that he'd expected her to give it to him.

"Thank you," Yaga said softly. "Thank you very much."

He reached toward Neve, then drew back his hand, grimacing slightly and shaking his head.

"I can still feel it on you," he said. "Well, that's to be expected, I suppose, under the circumstances. It's unfortunate. I'd hoped to invite you to stay with us here while you're in Zaravelle."

"Oh, no," Neve said hurriedly, glancing at the house. She was mortally certain there was no extra bedroom in it. "I never expected to presume on your hospitality. I mean, all my gear is back in Zaravelle. Ash and I are staying at an inn there."

"Well—" Yaga ducked his head, but not before Neve saw the relief in his eyes. "Why don't you go in the house, make yourselves comfortable. I'll find Kelara and prepare her a bit before she meets you. I think that's best. There's wine and cheese and fruit on the table. Please, make yourselves at home." He hurried off into the bushes again, leaving Neve gaping after him.

Ash chuckled, startling her again.

"If your kinfolk are anything like their friends," he said amusedly, "guess you're not so odd after all, hey? Come on, dream-dust girl. I'm hot and my throat's dry."

The house was no more impressive on the inside than it had been outside. It was less than half the size of the house in Dara's pocket world, where Neve had been born. It was light and clean and pleasant enough, colorful and fragrant with cut flowers in cups and growing flowers in pots all around, but there was not even a rug on the wooden floor.

Ash poured goblets full from the pitcher on the table and cut wedges from the golden wheel of cheese. He perched nonchalantly on the edge of the table, ignoring the stools, and sipped the wine.

" 'S good," he said. "Have some."

Neve sighed and took a goblet, perching on a stool. The wine was delicious, and the cheese creamy and rich, but she felt profoundly dismayed. *These* were the past Guardians of the Crystal Keep, the powerful mages her mother and father had spoken of, now living like this? *They* were going to judge Neve's worthiness to succeed her father as Guardian?

And what gave them any basis to judge anyway? Kelara's soul had been torn from her when she created the Crystal Keep; she'd lived for centuries in an unknowing haze until Neve's mother had found the way to return her to herself. She'd never been a real Guardian at all. And Yaga had forgotten himself, too, lost his key and most of his memories and been trapped in the form of a dragon in one of the pocket worlds for centuries until Dara had freed him, too—and then he and Kelara had left the Keep together. In Neve's opinion, they were miserable failures as far as Guardians went. Her father had done better than either of them—at least he'd managed to keep his memories and his own form. So what did these elves know, anyway?

Yaga stepped through the door, drawing after him an elven woman who Neve presumed was Kelara, although she found Kelara no more recognizable from the images she'd seen than she'd found Yaga himself. The leaf-green eyes were the same, and the flowing golden hair, but that hair was tangled with crumbled leaves and bits of twig, the delicate features thinner, and there was a scratch across one tanned cheek. The green eyes darted to Neve's face, then away again, like a frightened animal.

"Kelara," Yaga said gently. "This is—"

"Neve. I know." The soft, musical voice was barely louder than a whisper. Kelara stepped a little closer, but stopped still out of reach of the hand Neve had half raised.

"Welcome, Neve," Kelara said unconvincingly.

"Thank you," Neve said awkwardly. She gestured at Ash. "This is my friend Ash."

"Lady," Ash said softly.

Kelara afforded him another of those darting glances but said nothing.

Neve cleared her throat.

"My father," she began, "sent me to see you because—"

"I know why you've come." Kelara glanced at Neve again, then away. "You're not ready. Not yet."

Instantly Neve was on her feet, her cheeks hot with anger.

"How can you say that?" she demanded. "We've only just met. You don't even know me! You've hardly spoken to me! By the Nexus, how can you possibly—"

Kelara winced visibly, as if Neve had struck her. She held up a shaking hand almost pleadingly. Yaga gave Neve a chiding look, sliding an arm around Kelara's waist comfortingly. Shaking with anger and confusion, Neve sat back down. She clenched her fists hard.

"Why do you think I'm not ready?" she said, forcing a steady tone. "You don't know what I've been through coming here, the things I've done—"

Kelara held up a hand again, not meeting Neve's eyes.

"You have had many trials," she said softly. "But the real test is still ahead of you."

Neve bit her lip.

"Another test?" she said, fighting to stay calm. "My father said if I came here and—"

"This test comes not from me, nor the Guardian," Kelara said softly. "Perhaps it comes from the Nexus, or from you yourself. I don't know what it is, nor where, nor when, nor why. Only that it lies ahead." She sagged in Yaga's arms as if wearied.

"Come back in a month," she said abruptly, stepping back out the door. Before Neve could gather her wits enough to protest, she was gone. Yaga gave Neve an apologetic glance, then vanished out the door after Kelara.

Neve sat gaping blankly after them until Ash sighed and stood up, reaching for her hand.

"Come on," he said resignedly. "Best get going."

"A month!" Neve said disbelievingly. "Come back in a month!"

Ash shrugged, grinning wryly.

"Don't much matter, does it?" he said practically. "No ships to take you back east or upriver anyway. Come on, girl. Let's think on our feet on the trail. These folk put the hairs on my neck up. Too strange for me by half."

Silently Neve followed Ash through the lush gardens. There was no sign of either Kelara or Yaga, although at one point a sleek cat darted across the path, a sparkling gold bracelet in its mouth. Neve almost laughed as it disappeared into the bushes again.

A month! she thought disgustedly. *But why? What could happen to me in a month in Zaravelle stranger than all that's happened since I left home? And what test could there be worse than what's already happened to me? And Kelara didn't even want to hear about that. At least they could've asked me if I needed help, if there was anything I needed. At least they could have helped me contact my father. He wouldn't want me to be gone so long. He'd have told me to just come home, I'm sure of it. Kelara or Yaga could've made me a Gate. At least they—*

Then something occurred to Neve, and she gasped, stopping in her tracks and turning to Ash.

"Oh, Ash," she said contritely. "I meant to ask them about your feet and your eyes, ask them to help you, and I just forgot. I was so surprised when I saw them, and they weren't at all what I expected. It all happened so quickly."

Ash shrugged again.

" 'S all right," he said. "I can hold off for another month before making a decision. There's always that mage Rhadaman if I get too desperate. Besides—" He grimaced. "Your friends didn't seem quite even in the keel, if you get my meaning, to be messing around with transforming parts of my body."

"No, they didn't," Neve said, troubled. Yaga was eccentric at the very least, and Kelara, to all appearances, was completely mad. Rhadaman had said nothing of such strange behavior, nor had Neve's parents, and that troubled her, too.

She sighed.

"I'd never met Kelara and Yaga myself," she said. "Father never said they were—like that. Sometimes I've seen people go mad in the Keep, mostly visitors who've been trapped there for a while, but—why would Father send me to them? I don't know what to do now. How can I prove myself to Kelara if she won't even talk to me?"

Ash patted her shoulder comfortingly.

"Don't worry about it now," he said. "Look, things aren't so bad. Short of a Gate you'd be stuck in Zaravelle anyway, so might as well make the best of it."

Neve sighed.

"I suppose so," she said. "I suppose there are worse things than being stranded in a large city with comfortable inns, good food, and plenty of money."

Ash chuckled.

"What, like jumping off exploding ships?" he teased. "Or dangling over chasms with monster bugs?"

Neve had to chuckle reluctantly in return.

"Or being beaten half to death by greedy sailors," she agreed. "Or strolling through forests during whirlwinds. All right, all right. Things could be worse, I admit it. What about you? Did you find a place to spend the rainy season?"

"Well—I did find a place, sort of," Ash admitted. "A nice quiet bunch of rooms for rent over a chandler's shop. Couple bedrooms, a kitchen, sitting room, the lot. I thought it was a bit big and fancy for just me, but—"

He glanced sideways at Neve.

"Might not be so bad for two," he said slowly. "We could go halves on the price, I mean," he added hastily. "Don't get me wrong—you'd have your room and I'd have mine, go your own way and all—"

Neve felt a surprising warmth in her heart, and she found herself smiling.

"Yes," she said. "I'd like that. I could share some rooms with a friend."

Ash gave a sigh of relief.

"Right, then," he said, back to his usual cheeriness. "You'll like the place. It smells good, from the candles, you know."

And it did smell good, warm and spicy. The rooms were spacious and clean, and if Neve craned her neck painfully she could see the sea from one of the bedrooms' windows. According to Ash, the chandler and his family had lived in these rooms until the birth of twins had made larger quarters a necessity. The street was fairly affluent, and the money-changer's shop a few doors down meant that guards patrolled regularly. Neve approved.

"You know, somehow I didn't imagine you picking anything this fancy," she said, checking the draft over the kitchen fireplace.

"Well—" Ash shrugged, grinning. "You know, I never

had a chance to live too high. And now, seeing's I had lots of money, I thought I'd just make myself comfortable for a couple months. The chandler's daughter said she'd come up now and again and tidy up, even cook a bit.''

"I see." Neve turned around. "This chandler's daughter, is she pretty?"

Ash chuckled.

"If you like 'em real big both fore and aft," he said. "My guess is the chandler's wife must be some good cook, to look at the whole family. Bet you their new house hasn't got a steep, narrow stairway like this one."

Neve stifled a grin, inexplicably pleased. Yes, she could bear this for a month.

"I suppose we'd better fetch our things from the inn, then," she said. "But—what am I supposed to *do* for a month?"

"Don't know," Ash said, leaning against the window frame beside her. "Wait around for this mysterious test, I guess." He slid an arm around her waist. "I could think of a few things to pass some time, maybe."

Neve scowled impatiently.

"I can tell you one thing from living in the Keep," she said. "Nothing comes to you if you just sit around waiting for it."

Ash sighed.

"All right, then," he said resignedly. "If you're supposed to be proving to her you'll make a proper Guardian, then I guess you'd better be doing what a good Guardian'd be doing so she'll see you can do it right. And what would that be, hey?"

That made Neve pause and think.

"I—I don't know," she said slowly. "The Guardian controls the magic of the Nexus. My father greets the visitors, tells them the rules of the Keep, sets them a task or bargains with them for what they want. I don't know how I can do any of that here."

"Well, it all comes down to magic, doesn't it?" Ash suggested after a moment's thought. "Controlling this Nexus thing, using its magic properly. Maybe you could use some practice there, eh?"

"Well—yes," Neve admitted. "I suppose so. Yes, that

makes sense. But practice what? I mean, I can make things, yes—not living things," she added hastily. "But still—"

"There's all kinds of magic, right?" Ash told her. "So practice different kinds."

He chuckled.

"But you'll pardon me if I don't want you to practice on my feet or my eyes, right?"

Neve chuckled, too.

"Of course," she said. "But—"

Then she brightened.

"I'm sure Rhadaman would have some ideas."

"That mage?" Ash raised his eyebrows. "Guess so. What, you mean like teaching you?"

"Maybe," Neve said with growing eagerness. "Or maybe he could just suggest how I could use my magic—you know, properly." *And perhaps how to keep from using it IMPROPERLY.*

"Well, I suppose," Ash said slowly. "But he wouldn't know nothing about being a good Guardian, would he?"

"I *know* about being a Guardian," Neve said dismissively. "It's the magic I need to understand now."

"If you say so," Ash said, shrugging. "Guess we'd better go see him, then. Tomorrow?"

"I don't want to wait," Neve decided. "This afternoon, I think."

She glanced at Ash.

"You probably don't need to come," she said. "I imagine you'd find it pretty boring, waiting around while we talk about magic."

"Mmm." Ash gazed at her a moment, then shrugged. "Right, then. This place needs a few things, anyway. I suppose I'll go out and spend some of that money in the market."

"That's a good idea," Neve said. She didn't tell Ash that she could probably make whatever he wanted; he was obviously loving having money to spend. She pulled out her pouch and extracted two rubies, handing them to him.

"We said we'd share costs," she explained when Ash gave her a questioning look. "Whatever we need here, I'll pay for half of it."

Neve's heart was considerably lighter as she made her way

through town and back to Rhadaman's shop. The room was crowded with customers, and Neve leaned against the counter, out of the way, smiling at Rhadaman when he acknowledged her with a delighted smile and a brief dip of his head. Maybe by watching him she'd learn more about how magic should be used *properly*.

To her surprise, however, Rhadaman actually appeared to use his magic rather sparingly, dispensing potions and salves rather than spells. He did cast a minor divination for a noblewoman who wanted to know whether her unborn child was male or female, and cast a translation spell for an unfortunate merchant with no knowledge of Olvenic. On the whole, however, Neve was amazed at Rhadaman's restraint, especially when the last customer, a pretty young woman, was brought in with blistered legs, her husband explaining that a kettle of hot oil had spilled over on her. To Neve's astonishment, Rhadaman handed over a jar of ointment which, he assured the anxious man, would prevent any infection and speed healing. When Neve realized that that was as much as he was going to do, she cleared her throat slightly.

"Ah—maybe I could be of some help?" she asked tentatively when Rhadaman glanced at her.

Rhadaman raised his eyebrows.

"My lady?"

"I mean—I'm rather good with burns," Neve said awkwardly. She didn't want to make Rhadaman look inadequate in his own shop, but by the Nexus, how could he just hand out salves like any two-copper herbalist? Neve *knew* how much burns like that had to hurt; by the Nexus, she'd burned herself often enough at home.

"Well—" To her dismay, Rhadaman actually hesitated, long enough that Neve began to feel rather insulted. "If you're certain, my lady—"

Without a word, Neve knelt beside the woman's chair, pushing her skirt up to expose the burned skin. Neve fought down her distaste at having to touch the oozing blisters and ran her fingertips down the legs as gently as she could. *Don't think too much. Just help the skin remember wholeness, smoothness, health—*

The woman gasped, but with amazement rather than pain

as the skin smoothed, the redness faded. When Neve took her hands away, the woman ran roughened fingers up and down her legs, again and again as if she couldn't believe what she was seeing.

"Oh, thank the gods." The husband sighed with relief. He turned to Neve, bowing. "My lady, we didn't know a healer'd come to town," he said. "We're glad to have you, no doubt of it." He pulled out his purse. "I don't know your fees, my lady, but whatever it is, I'll pay it gladly."

Neve hesitated, rather taken aback.

"I'm not exactly—" she stammered. "I mean, I haven't actually thought about—"

She took a deep breath.

Value given for value received, she reminded herself. *That's the order of things.*

"I'll ask—uh—" *By the Nexus, I don't even know the local coinage!* "Five of those silver coins," Neve finished lamely. "I'm glad I could be of help."

The man's eyes widened, but he hurriedly fumbled out the coins, pressing them into her hands, then bustling his wife out of the shop as if fleeing. Neve stared after them.

"That was a ridiculously low price, you know," Rhadaman said gently after the door closed.

Neve swallowed, flushing with embarrassment. By the Nexus, what rudeness, to steal Rhadaman's customers right there in his own shop! Whatever must he think of her!

"I'm sorry," she said awkwardly. "I didn't mean to—I just thought perhaps—"

Rhadaman waved his hand dismissively.

"Oh, please, don't trouble yourself," he said, smiling. "I'm glad you could help that poor woman." He gazed at Neve more sharply. "You didn't find that difficult at all?"

"Well—no, not really," she said, shrugging. "The burns weren't that severe."

"That wasn't what I meant." Rhadaman leaned over the counter. "I meant the distortions in the aether hereabouts. I rarely risk using magic for such minor injuries, and even when I do, I find the proper preparations and rituals absolutely necessary. And yet you healed that woman so effortlessly, without even the structure of a spell. How did you manage that?"

"I'm sorry," Neve said embarrassedly. "I never really learned to use spells. My mother gave me a grimoire when I left the Crystal Keep, but it was lost when the *Albatross* sank. And I don't think it was much help even when I had it. I seem to do better without."

"Really." Rhadaman gazed at her a moment longer, then stepped out from behind the counter. He locked the door and pulled the shades over the window.

"Come," he said, holding out his hand. "We'll talk in my home, if you permit."

"All right," Neve said shyly. She took Rhadaman's arm and followed him through a door at the back of the shop.

To her surprise, Rhadaman's house was luxurious, bordering on decadent. Despite his rather ascetic appearance and practical manner, this man obviously enjoyed his comforts. Rhadaman gestured Neve toward an opulently cushioned chair, and he picked up a small silver bell from a table and rang it. A neatly dressed middle-aged man brought in a tray, deposited it on the table, and left as silently as he'd come. Rhadaman lifted the silver lid of the tray.

"Tea and spice cakes," he reported. "Can I tempt you?"

Neve was duly tempted. *Now, THIS,* she thought smugly as she nibbled a cake, *is how a powerful mage should live, with respect and comfort. So much for Mother and her turnips.*

"So tell me," Rhadaman pressed, "how your magic works. I'm very interested to learn what science of magic remains unaffected by the distortions in the aether here. I've consulted via farspeaking with other mages, but every system I've heard of seems vulnerable. The distortions are so severe that sometimes I believe the earthquakes are related to them, since the severity of both seems to increase together. I've never seen anyone work as easily as you did with magical energies anywhere in this area."

Neve hesitated. Science of magic? System of magic?

"I'm not certain how the magic of the Nexus works," she said apologetically. "You'd do better asking Kelara that. She created the Crystal Keep." She grimaced. "Not that she seems too eager to answer questions, about that or anything else."

Rhadaman gave her a sympathetic glance.

"As I said, I wouldn't call your elven friends precisely sociable," he said.

"Yes, well, I wouldn't precisely call them my friends, either," Neve said wryly. "What I *would* call them is odd and rude and maybe mad."

"Mad?" Rhadaman raised his eyebrows. "Rude? I admit I've had little opportunity to spend much time with them, but I never saw any indication of anything beyond simple eccentricity."

"Well, maybe they just don't like me, then," Neve said sourly. "I seem to have that problem with a lot of people." She shook her head. "Or maybe it was just the crystal."

Rhadaman leaned forward, taking her hand.

"Start at the beginning," he said gently. "Tell me what happened."

He listened quietly as Neve told him about her visit to Yaga and Kelara's house, nodding slightly when she mentioned Ash's explanation about dream dust.

"He may have been correct," Rhadaman said when she had finished. "May I see this crystal?"

Neve pulled the box out of her pocket and opened it, taking the crystal out. When Rhadaman reached toward it, however, she drew back instinctively, flushing when he raised his eyebrows again.

"I'm sorry," Neve said. "I'd rather you didn't touch it."

"Of course." Rhadaman smiled gravely. He held his hand up a few inches from the crystal, and his eyes unfocused slightly; then he drew his breath in sharply, rocking back in his chair as if he'd been struck, the color draining out of his face. He closed his eyes, pressing trembling fingers to his forehead.

"Pardon me," he muttered, his voice distinctly unsteady. "Would you mind terribly putting that away?"

A little alarmed, Neve hurriedly put the crystal back in the box, tucking it into her pocket.

"Are you all right?" she said anxiously.

Despite his shaking hands, Rhadaman poured himself a cup of tea. After a few sips he seemed to steady somewhat. At last he glanced at Neve again, and she wondered at the mixture of wariness and respect in his gaze.

"And you manipulate those energies," Rhadaman said

slowly, "as naturally as I sip this tea. No wonder the fluctuations in the aether here don't trouble you. Your power isn't anchored in the aether at all—or anywhere else that I can discern. The sheer power you wield is—awesome."

He shook his head.

"I can easily imagine how . . . intoxicating . . . such power must be," he said softly. "I can barely conceive, though, of how one long accustomed to wielding it might walk away from it. How painful it must be to see that power again, almost touch it, and still—"

He shook his head.

"Never mind," he said, smiling more naturally. "You came here with a purpose, and I doubt it was to enjoy my spice cakes or to heal that unfortunate woman or impress me with your particular brand of magic, however glad I am that you've done all of those things. How can I help you?"

"Well, you may have already done it," Neve admitted. She told Rhadaman what her father had said about Kelara judging her readiness to become Guardian.

"When she told me to come back in a month," Neve said, shrugging, "I figured I'd better spend that month proving I'd make a proper Guardian. And I thought you might be the person to consult about how to do that."

"Mmm." Rhadaman sipped his tea; he seemed to have recovered his composure. "If you want to learn how to develop your magical skills and to use them responsibly, yes, I can probably help you with that, and I'd be delighted to do so. But has it occurred to you, my lady, that your father may have sent you here not to be judged, but rather to judge?"

Neve grimaced.

"What do you mean?"

"I mean," Rhadaman said slowly, "you've lived all your life in the Crystal Keep, seeing your father wield the power of the Nexus in all its glory. He says he's paid a price for that power, but you can't see that price, feel it. Watching him, all you've seen is the summer side of that power. But he sends you here to visit Yaga and Kelara, past Guardians. Even in the briefest meeting you've seen what their time as Guardian has done to them—the storm side of the Nexus, if you will. You can see with your own eyes the consequences of that power. Perhaps that's the reason why you were sent."

Neve clenched her teeth. All along, she'd thought this journey was her mother's idea. But it would be entirely like her father, such a devious scheme. He knew she couldn't refuse such a journey if he couched it in terms of a test. Dara's motives, like Dara herself, were probably much more straightforward—she simply wanted her daughter to see the world she'd be giving up as Guardian, to taste the life mortal humans live, the life Neve would never know.

And perversely, for all of Vanian's cleverness, it was Dara's argument Neve found the most potent now. She'd resisted the journey, yes; in retrospect, however, her life at the Crystal Keep seemed as placid and smooth as the water of a still pond compared with the waves and tempests of the sea. Neve had created dragons, yes (if poorly)—but she'd never come close to being eaten by one. She'd climbed in trees, but never the rigging of a ship or the web of a monster insect. In the Keep she'd never bargain in the market for linens or sit in a tub while a bath boy scrubbed her back.

But her mother had never felt the Nexus pulsing in her blood.

"Well, whatever reason, Father told me to get Kelara's approval before I came home," Neve said wryly. "So either way I'm here for the next month. And if I spend that month idle in my rooms, *I'll* go mad. So I may as well do something useful in the meantime, if I can. If you can teach me, I'd like to learn."

She hesitated.

"I can pay you," she said. "I've got plenty of money."

Rhadaman smiled.

"Not necessary, my lady," he said. "I'll find the opportunity to observe your magic and the pleasure of your company recompense aplenty. And I'm sure the people of Zaravelle will be delighted to have a healer in town."

Neve scowled.

"I don't like to take away your customers," she said slowly. "Value given for value received, that's the rule of the Keep."

Rhadaman waved his hand.

"Oh, very well," he said negligently. "For the time you're here, I'll consider you my partner in business, and for the use of my shop you can pay me one third of what you charge.'' He chuckled. ''And in return, perhaps you'll allow me to suggest a more reasonable set of fees. There are only two genuine mages in Zaravelle, and they're both sitting in my parlor eating my spice cakes.''

It was more, far more than Neve had hoped for.

''All right,'' she said shyly. ''That sounds fair. But—you know, I really haven't done that much healing. I'm just a beginner, and I don't even know how it works.''

''Perhaps with the magic of your Nexus, the whys and hows aren't so important,'' Rhadaman said speculatively. ''The system of magic I'm familiar with is rather like building a ship—you choose your wood carefully, prepare it meticulously, build a good framework, and take it up one step at a time; simply dumping a huge wagonload of trees on the spot wouldn't accomplish much. In your case, however, your magic sounds rather like gardening—you plant the seed, tend it a bit, keep your garden trimmed back to be sure it doesn't get away from you, but mostly just stand out of the way and let it happen.''

Neve fought back a grimace. If the spider-creature and the rest were examples of weeds, she'd need a monstrous good hoe.

Which brought her to the point.

''Have you ever known a mage to do something—magically, I mean—without even trying?'' she said. ''I don't mean having a spell go wrong, more like—oh, I don't know, casting one accidentally?''

''Accidentally?'' Rhadaman smiled slightly. ''No. A spell takes a great deal of preparation and concentration, just as I've said.'' Then he hesitated. ''But it's not uncommon for mage-gifted youngsters to manifest involuntary magical phenomena.''

''Really?'' Neve said, trying not to sound too curious.

''Oh, yes,'' Rhadaman said, nodding. ''It's commonest in girls who have just reached womanhood, who have the mage-gift but don't know it and haven't received any training in controlling the energies. These manifestations are random outbursts of power sometimes confused with hauntings—objects flying about and smashing, doors slamming, furniture shaking, rocks falling out of the sky and suchlike. Why do you ask?''

"Oh—no reason," Neve said vaguely, disappointed. What Rhadaman described sounded vastly different than what she'd experienced. Her magical "outbursts" weren't random flares of energies; they were quite elaborate and tangible and, in a bizarre way, in response to her own wishes. No help there.

Father grants wishes, Neve thought miserably. *Now it looks like I'm granting my own without meaning to. But badly, like I made the dragons.*

"Well, I've never taught anyone," Rhadaman admitted. "But it sounds as though all you need is the opportunity to practice, and a little advice now and then. I'm sure I can manage that, regardless of the differences in our techniques. Why don't you come in tomorrow morning—I don't open the shop until about midmorning, unless someone comes to me with an emergency—and tomorrow you can take whatever cases you're comfortable with, and otherwise watch and learn." He grinned wryly. "As the only mage in Zaravelle until now, I deal with everything from bunions to termites, so you shouldn't lack for a variety of opportunities."

"That sounds perfect," Neve said relievedly. She stood. "Thank you ever so much—and for the tea and cakes, too."

"My pleasure, my lady, I assure you," Rhadaman said gravely. "Can I persuade you to join me for supper?"

Neve was tempted, but—no, she hadn't told Ash she'd be gone for supper, and he might be waiting for her.

"Not today, thank you," she said apologetically. "But we could go tomorrow, to celebrate my first day as a practicing mage?"

"Absolutely," Rhadaman said, smiling. The smile transformed his face, made him look less gaunt, and his green eyes sparkled pleasantly.

"And if we're working together," Neve said wryly, "I'd just as soon you call me Neve. I mean, I'm not really a lady by birth, I don't believe."

Rhadaman chuckled.

"Judging by the status of your family and its holdings, you're as entitled to the honor as any High Lord's daughter," he said. "But I thank you nonetheless—Neve." He held out his hand.

"Rhadaman," Neve said, taking his hand briefly, feeling

suddenly unaccountably shy. His fingers were warm and smooth, not calloused, and his nails neatly trimmed—a mage's hand, like her father's.

Ash was indeed waiting when Neve returned; to be more precise, he was sitting in the window sipping from a cup and staring moodily out at the sea. The cup and his breath smelled of brandy.

"Have you been here all afternoon?" she asked, raising her eyebrows.

Ash shook his head, not turning to look at her.

"Went out to get this," he said, raising the skin of brandy. He took a deep sip. "Took you a while," he said rather sarcastically. "Did you stay for your first lesson?"

"No, I stayed for tea and cakes," Neve said, annoyed by his tone. What in the world had Ash so upset? Then she looked at him again more closely, noticing what she hadn't seen before. Ash was wearing boots—rather hasty-looking ones made of soft leather with no real sole.

Ash glanced at Neve, followed her gaze.

"Takes a few days to get boots to my measure," he said tonelessly. "When I can find a cobbler who'll even make boots for someone looking like me, that is. Quite a few won't."

A spear of pain stabbed into Neve's heart, and she bit her lip hard. She stepped to Ash's side, took his hand.

"Come on," she said. "Let's go out and get some supper. It's a beautiful evening."

Ash drained his cup before setting it and the brandy aside, but he followed her without a word. Neve was silent, too; she strode straight to the market, pulling Ash with her. At the edge of the market plaza she stopped.

"Now," she said, feeling a cold and terrible rage running through her veins, "show me which cobbler wouldn't serve you."

Ash glanced at her, then shook his head slowly, folding his arms over his chest.

"Uh-uh," he said slowly. "I don't know as that'd be a very good idea. We've got to live here, girl, at least for a few weeks, and my memory of the inside of a prison cell's fresh enough."

"Either tell me," Neve said coldly, "or I'll find the cobbler who *did* make your boots and then curse all the rest.''

Ash sighed irritably.

''Over there,'' he said, pointing.

Neve strode into the shop, pulling Ash after her. The cobbler, who was fitting a pair of slippers to a richly dressed lady in his crowded shop, glanced up at her, startled; then he saw Ash and his eyes narrowed. He opened his mouth to speak, but Neve silenced him with a glare.

''My name is Neve,'' Neve said icily. ''Aside from my colleague and business partner Rhadaman, I appear to be the only real mage and healer in this city. You refused to serve my friend. It's your shop; you can choose your customers. But so can I. Don't bother setting foot in Rhadaman's shop, at least not as long as I'm in Zaravelle, and pray to whatever god you worship that that's as far as my anger goes.'' She stayed just long enough to see fear fill the cobbler's eyes; then she walked out of the shop. Ash followed her silently, but when they were out of earshot, he pulled Neve to a stop.

''That was decent of you,'' he said.

''Which?'' Neve said sourly. ''Taking him to task for it, or not rotting every piece of leather in his shop?''

Ash chuckled.

''Both, I guess,'' he said. ''Anyway, thanks.''

Neve smiled unwillingly, her anger fading. She felt satified. Proud.

This is what a Guardian does, she thought. *A Guardian uses her influence as well as her power.*

''Any others?'' she said, but Ash shook his head.

''Nah, the next one made these,'' he said, gesturing at the hasty boots he was wearing. He grinned. ''Seeing you tell him off like that kind of makes me wish there *was* more of 'em.''

Now Neve chuckled.

''After that little speech, I hope there'll be less, actually,'' she said. ''I doubt too many businesses want to make half the town's mages angry all at once.''

Ash took Neve's arm.

''Well, my lady mage, I know *I'd* rather not,'' he said, grinning broadly. ''So come with me, and I vow I'll buy you the finest supper that can be had in a port city.''

Neve laughed and followed willingly. When they were

seated on the dock, however, and Ash nonchalantly plunked a steaming bucket down between them, she wrinkled her nose.

"This isn't exactly what I had in mind when you said the finest supper in town," she said.

Ash patted the bucket smugly.

"Trust me, food don't get any better than this," he said. "Cold ale, fresh bread, and all manner of seafood cooked in butter and wine and spices. Come on, get your fingers greasy."

Two minutes later Neve was forced to admit that Ash had been correct. The setting sun gilded the sea, the cold ale tingled on her tongue, and the fine soft bread sopped up the rich juices in the bucket. She wiped her mouth on the back of her hand, licked her fingers, and tossed shells over the edge of the dock as Ash did.

"Yes, I suppose there's worse things than being stranded here for a month." Neve sighed, slurping down a succulent salt-sweet morsel of who-knows-what.

"Mmm. Enjoy it while you can," Ash said wryly. "See those clouds? That's storms moving in. You've had your last seaside supper for a while, I guess."

"Well, never mind," Neve said stoutly, although she dreaded the rain that would confine her indoors. She'd never been restricted to buildings before; in the Crystal Keep, it was always sunny somewhere. "We'll just take our bucket up to our rooms when it rains." She wiped butter from her lips, noticing with a grimace that she'd dripped on her tunic. "At least then we can have a bath afterward."

Ash shook his head amusedly.

"Not likely," he said.

"What?" Neve paused, unsure what he'd meant.

"Baths," Ash said. He tipped his head back at the town. "Isn't like we're in a fancy inn with lots of servants anymore. Got to go down the street to the well, draw up your water, and haul it all the way back and upstairs in buckets, not to mention heating it up. Lot of trouble for a bath."

Neve swallowed.

"But—but people do wash here, don't they?" she asked hesitantly.

Ash chuckled.

"The poor probably just jump in the river," he said. "Most folks have barrels to catch rainwater, and there'll be plenty of that. I noticed a few on our roof, so it isn't quite as bad as I said before. But those as can afford it go to bathhouses. I've seen four or five of 'em, some of 'em fancy places."

Neve grimaced.

"You mean in this heat people actually want to sit in steam like we did in Strachan?" she said.

"Nah, bathhouses are real baths," Ash said, shaking his head. "As you say, nobody wants to steam around here. We can go to one now, if you want." He glanced down at his boots. "Good thing I got these, or they probably wouldn't let me in."

"They'd let you in, all right," Neve said righteously, "or they'd be sorry they didn't."

But in fact it was Neve that got a rather curious and dubious glance from the attendant who took three silver pieces from Ash and escorted them past several closed doors to a small room that contained simply a couple of pallets on the floor, a tiny brazier now fragrant with incense, and a large tub of water set into the floor.

"My goodness," Neve said, dipping her hand into the tub. The water was pleasantly hot. "It must take forever to fill this."

Ash shook his head.

"Water's piped in from a central cistern over a big fire," he said. "Other pipes dump the water into the river when the tub's emptied."

He grinned.

"Come on, girl, you want to study it or you want to wash in it?"

"I want to know how it's done," Neve said enviously, "so that someday back at the Keep I can make one just like it."

"This is nothing," Ash said as he tossed his clothing aside and settled into the bath. "You should see the baths at Allanmere. Those come up from hot springs way under the ground. The water's always hot and clean and bubbly, too. Doesn't smell very good, though—kind of like eggs that've gone over."

Neve laid her own clothes aside neatly and slid into the water, sighing as the warmth enveloped her.

"You're right, that would be even better," she reflected. "And when I make one, it'll smell however I want it to."

"Turn around and I'll do your back," Ash suggested, and Neve sighed as his fingers dug into the muscles of her shoulders.

"So how'd your meeting with Rhadaman go?" he asked casually.

"Oh, perfectly," Neve said contentedly. "He said I could work as a partner in his shop, doing whatever magic I'm comfortable with. That way I can learn from him and from practicing both."

Ash stopped scrubbing momentarily.

"He made you a partner in his shop?" he said slowly. "Just like that?"

"Well, not 'just like that,' " Neve said defensively. "If I was working on my own, some of his customers would be coming to see me instead of him, and he'd lose business. Besides, I didn't want strange people coming up to our rooms, and how else would I have a chance to practice things like healing? Rhadaman knows I'll only be here for a while, and I'm to give him a third of whatever I make." She shrugged. "I don't need the money anyway."

"If you don't need the money, and I guess you don't," Ash said practically, "why charge anything at all? You could just do your magic for free, like some of the temples I've heard of that do free healing for the poor."

Neve thought about that for a moment.

"I don't know," she said. "Value given for value received is the rule of the Crystal Keep, and I always thought it made sense. Why should anyone expect something for nothing? And I *should* pay Rhadaman; he's going to be teaching me, and he's being very nice about losing customers to me—for a while, anyway."

"Well, what's the value to him, then?" Ash argued. "He's only getting a third of what those customers pay, instead of all of it, and he's teaching you for nothing, right?"

Neve was troubled; she hadn't thought about their bargain exactly that way, but Ash was right.

"Well, there *is* some value in it for him," she said slowly.

"He said the magic of the Nexus works entirely differently from any kind of magic he's ever known. He wants the opportunity to watch how it works, to try to understand it."

"Mmm." Ash was silent for a moment. "Look, don't get me wrong—I don't think getting help and advice is a bad idea at all, and choosing between him and those two elves, I'd choose the same as you. But maybe you ought to ask yourself why he wants to know about this Nexus and its magic. What good's it do him when there's no Nexus hereabouts? What'll he use it for?"

Neve hesitated, then shook her head.

"He just wants to learn because my magic isn't affected by those distortions he's talking about," she said. "If he could figure out how my magic works, maybe he could keep his own magic from being affected, too. What other use could it be to him? As you say, there's no Nexus here for him to use, and he wouldn't know how to open it if there was. If that's what he was wanting, he'd be better served asking Kelara and Yaga than me."

She smiled.

"You're more cynical and suspicious than even my parents," she said. "Father would admire your caution." Then she gasped as Ash's hands slid over her skin in a far less clinical manner. "But Mother wouldn't think much of your gentlemanly restraint."

"I'll leave noble games to the nobles." Ash chuckled. "I'll settle for reminding you there's more than one kind of magic, and some of 'em even common sailors can use."

Neve turned in his arms, flushed with more than the warmth of the water.

"Well, I'm still a bit of a beginner in the ways of magic." She laughed. "But I'm always willing to learn."

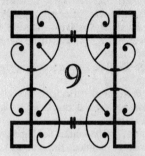

9

"IT'S NO DIFFERENT THAN THE BURNS, or the coral cuts on that child yesterday," Rhadaman said patiently.

"It *is*," Neve said anxiously. "Skin's easy. I can see the damage. Besides, those weren't as serious."

And there was no doubt in her mind that the injury she saw now in the boy who lay in drugged sleep before her was very serious indeed. The leg had been set, and the only sign of the fracture was dark bruising of the skin, but the break was high in the large bone of the thigh, near the hip, and Neve knew it would never heal properly on its own. The child would certainly be crippled for life if the bone wasn't healed correctly—or might even lose his leg.

"Try," Rhadaman urged. "Yes, the injury is serious, but the healing is straightforward—a difference only of degree, not of technique. Just help the bone restore itself as you did skin."

Neve hesitated a moment longer, then nodded. She took a deep breath and closed her eyes, letting the power of the Nexus uncoil. *Like gardening—plant the seed and trust it to know how to grow.*

She let the power touch the injury, guided it. She could

feel the break, like a dark, jagged chasm bisecting the bone, an interruption in the smooth line.

Remember wholeness, Neve thought. *Remember strength, smoothness, solidity. Like the ship.* It wasn't as difficult as she had thought; there was, after all, a perfect duplicate only a short distance away. It was only a simple matter of joining two ends that were never meant to be separate in the first place.

A touch on her shoulder; Neve jolted upright, startled, staring at Rhadaman.

"Good," he murmured. "Perfect. You did it."

"I did?" Neve glanced at the sleeping boy. Most of the bruising was still there.

"That's nothing," Rhadaman said gently, following her glance. "The bone is mended; the rest will heal on its own. In magical healing it's always safer to do too little than too much."

He helped Neve up and guided her to a chair.

"Just rest," he said. "I'll take the boy to his parents."

Neve *was* tired, and that more than anything surprised her. Using her magic hadn't wearied her for a long time; even making the rubies had become almost effortless with practice. She'd thought it would all be downhill from here.

But after a week of working in Rhadaman's shop, Neve began to wonder whether it was getting harder instead of easier—well, no, that wasn't exactly true. It was getting easier all the time; she could wave items into being almost effortlessly. Her healing was progressing rapidly. She could cast a light globe almost without thinking. No, it wasn't the magic that was difficult; maybe it was the cumulative effect that tired her so. She'd never spent her entire day, morning to night, working magic constantly before. Or was it just that she was using her magic in ways she'd never tried before, and the strain was beginning to tell on her? She'd slept for hours and hours last night but woke up unrested. That had been happening a lot lately.

Rhadaman sat down next to her, saying nothing, and Neve glanced up. She'd never noticed him carrying the boy out to his parents.

"Are you all right?" he asked softly.

Neve nodded.

"I'm sorry," she said. "I'm just—a little tired."

"Of course you are," Rhadaman said gravely. "Magic can be exhausting, especially such extensive healing. You need to rest and eat, replenish your energies. Shall I get you something to drink, some tea perhaps?"

Neve sighed, rubbing her eyes.

"I think I'll just go home, if you don't mind," she said. "Sleep sounds good right now."

"Of course," Rhadaman said understandingly. "No, just rest. I'll call a cart and take you home myself; I need to stop in the market for a few things anyway. Oh, by the way—" He pressed a pouch into Neve's hand. "Quite a handsome fee for that healing. More than I asked, even."

Neve shoved the pouch absently into her tunic. She didn't care about the money at all right now, but it was *her* fee, and after all she had to pay her share of the rent on the rooms she shared with Ash. And it was nice to have coins to spend without having to haggle with jewelers and moneychangers.

When she heard the wheels rattle outside the door, she got up wearily and followed Rhadaman out to the goat cart. Despite the late afternoon hour, the market was still full and busy. When Neve commented on the crowd, Rhadaman told her that now that the rainy season had officially begun, everyone took advantage of any dry day to sell their wares or stock their cellars against the inevitable long weeks of torrential downpours. The driver of their cart pulled to a stop when a gathering crowd blocked the road; Neve couldn't clearly see what was going on, but she thought there was a single figure, perhaps a bard or acrobat, at the center of the throng.

"What is it?" she murmured to Rhadaman.

"I don't know." Rhadaman stood up precariously in the small cart, peering over the heads of the crowd. He grimaced, shaking his head, and sat back down.

"It's just Sobel," he said, sighing. "Make yourself comfortable. We may be here awhile."

"Who's Sobel?" Neve asked. She stood up, peering as Rhadaman had, but she was not tall enough to see over the crowd in front of her.

Rhadaman shook his head again.

"A simple madman who thinks himself a foreseer," he

said. "I assure you, nobody who kept count of his predictions would call him a genuine seer, although some of the fishermen persist in consulting him about the weather. They're an ignorant and superstitious lot, sailors. As I keep telling them, if they'd stop patronizing these charlatans, frauds like Sobel would leave Zaravelle for richer waters and we'd all be the better for it."

Neve frowned at Rhadaman's comment about sailors—she certainly hadn't found Ash to be either ignorant or superstitious—but her irritation gave way to curiosity. She'd never seen a madman before, unless she counted Kelara and Yaga. Despite her weariness, she scrambled down from the cart and pushed her way impatiently through the crowd until she could see what was taking place at the center.

A man stood atop a small barrel, his arms raised to the sky as if invoking some sky god. To first appearances, he looked neither mad nor remarkable in any other way, not among Zaravelle's varied population. He was a slight, dusky-skinned young man with long black hair sheened with gold in the sunshine, dressed in ordinary clothes. The strangest thing about him was his startlingly pale gray eyes that seemed to focus on no particular point; for a moment Neve wondered whether he was blind.

"I tell you, this will be a storm season like none Zaravelle has ever seen, nor yet will see again!" he intoned in a pleasant, rather musical voice. "The earth will shake and groan beneath your feet, and water will run deep in Zaravelle's streets. I see disaster, cataclysm beyond description—"

"Mad as a dog with frothing-mouth sickness," one man muttered to his companion, shaking his head sadly.

"I dunno," a nearby sailor said, vulgarly cracking his knuckles despite the disgusted look Neve directed at him. "He predicted those early blows down to the day, and he spoke for sunshine today, didn't he?"

"Ah, that's just luck," the first man said loftily. "Three years of four we have early storms, then more sunny days. My wife's mum can predict as much with her aching elbow."

As if he heard this interplay—although surely he couldn't have over the other noise of the crowd—Sobel fell silent in mid-sentence, his head swiveling around in the speakers' direction, and they fell silent, too. Surprisingly, however, it was

Neve on whom that pale gaze fastened, and she immediately revised her opinion of Sobel's vision as he gazed straight into her eyes.

Abruptly the young man leaped down from his barrel, landing nearly at her feet and sweeping an extravagant bow.

"Well! I'm honored indeed," he pronounced. "Has the great lady mage come for counsel of the seer, or merely to jeer at the madman like the rest?"

Neve was neither embarrassed by the attention nor taken aback by Sobel's directness.

"I don't know," she said simply. "*Are* you mad?"

Sobel threw his head back, laughing deeply and long.

"Oh, most assuredly, my lady," he said. "But then, what is sanity to one who walks from world to world, from winter to summer in lands where time stands still?"

Neve froze.

"What do you mean?" she said cautiously.

"What do I mean? Ah, if only I knew! But you know, sweet duchess, the lord you seek will most assuredly ask for your hand by midwinter. And gold spent on marsh-cat furs will return thrice over when the pelts are sold in spring. If there is indeed a spring." He spun around as if forgetting Neve completely. "The sea! The sea! The sea is coming for Zaravelle!"

Neve scowled and retreated through the crowd, which was beginning to break up as Sobel danced off down the street. Rhadaman was waiting patiently in the goat cart, but he got out to help her back up.

"Well, did that satisfy your curiosity?" he said, smiling slightly. "Did you find our local seer entertaining?"

"Not especially," Neve said, still scowling. "I see why you call him mad. But some things he said—"

Rhadaman raised an eyebrow.

"What things?"

"Oh, never mind." Looking back on it, Neve was sure she'd misinterpreted what Sobel had said. The man certainly didn't have his thoughts in order; why, he didn't seem to know from one moment to the next whom he was speaking to! Rhadaman certainly wouldn't take such ramblings seriously, and she shouldn't, either. And she was too tired to try to sort it out anyway.

She sat silent beside Rhadaman until the cart pulled up in front of the chandler's shop; to her gratitude, Rhadaman got out to help her down.

"Eat a good supper and sleep well," he said kindly, kissing her hand. "That'll put you to rights. If you're not refreshed enough to work tomorrow, just send word."

"Oh, I'm fine," Neve said hastily. "I'll be there. Thank you for the cart, Rhadaman. And the escort."

Rhadaman waved negligently,

"Nothing of the sort," he said. "Good evening, my lady."

Neve trudged wearily into the chandler's shop and forced one foot in front of the other up the stairs. Hopefully she could coax Ash into preparing supper, or at least fetching something back for them to eat. She was simply too exhausted to conjure something up, or worse yet, actually try to *cook*.

"Ash?" she called as she unlocked the door.

No answer.

Neve glanced around the apartment. It was neat, clean, empty. Ash wasn't in his room, wasn't sitting and drinking in the window as he'd been most evenings when she'd come home before. Then again, she didn't usually come home this early. Likely he'd gotten bored and gone out for a spot of gambling or some such. It hardly mattered; Neve really didn't want conversation and companionship anyway, and even supper took second place to rest.

Neve stumbled into her room and wearily pulled off her tunic and trousers, then paused, staring at herself in amazement in the mirror.

She was pale, even paler than usual, with great dark circles under her eyes. Her cheeks looked hollow. Even her black hair was losing its luster. Neve glanced down at her hands. No doubt about it; she was losing weight.

At the moment, however, she was too exhausted to care. She collapsed on her bed in her linens and slept deeply.

She woke around sunset to the sound of the door banging shut. Footsteps clattered in the kitchen; there was the scrape of flint and steel, faint hiss as a lamp was lit.

"Ash?" Neve called out, sitting up tiredly.

The door to her bedroom opened and Ash peered in, leaning against the door frame, lamp in hand. To her surprise, he looked as tired as she felt—and a great deal grubbier.

"Ash?" Neve repeated dumbly. "What've you been doing?"

Ash grunted.

"Just a little loading," he said. "Brought back some meat rolls and cheese and cider. Want some?"

Her stomach rumbled loudly and she slid out of bed, padding into the kitchen without bothering to pick up a robe. She tore into the rolls and cheese with an appetite that surprised even her, although Ash ate heartily himself.

"What kind of loading?" Neve said.

Ash shrugged.

"Loading wagons," he said rather self-consciously. "In the market."

"Loading wagons?" She stopped eating. "What in the world were you doing loading wagons?" A nasty suspicion began to creep up on her. "You haven't gambled all your money away or something like that, have you?"

Ash chuckled wearily.

"No," he said. "Tell you true, I'm just damn-all bored, sitting around here. You're gone all day and there's nobody I even know in this city, so what's a fellow to do? Can't just sit around; I'm not used to it."

"Well, what did you do before?" Neve said practically. "Winters, I mean."

"Never was a problem before," Ash said, sighing. "I'd work the the northern river cities in the summers, southern in the winters. If I was working the coastal ships I'd go inland up one of the trade rivers for the rainy season. Even if I was stuck in port for a couple weeks, there'd be all my shipmates stuck there, too, so a fellow's got company. Or I'd find work of one kind or another. Can't say I've ever had a combination of money and leisure time all at once before."

"Oh." Neve didn't quite know what to say. She'd never been actually *bored* in her life, except when her mother had her doing housework or some such. The pocket worlds of the Keep had always offered plenty of diversion even when she wasn't experimenting with the magic of the Nexus.

"I can't imagine being bored enough to take a job loading wagons," Neve said after a moment. "I mean, there's plenty to see here. I saw a madman today in the market."

She leaned her elbows on the table.

"Have you ever looked in tidepools?" she said.

"Tidepools?" Ash chuckled, sipping his cider. "Why do you ask?"

"I used to do that," Neve said, sighing. "Walk up and down the seashore in one of the pocket worlds, just looking at things. My mother thought it was foolishness, but there was so much to see. I mean, there were animals that looked like flowers, that enticed fish in close with their beauty before seizing and eating them. There was a creature shaped like a pentagram with little suckers all over its bottom side, and it could pry open shells and eat what was inside—"

Ash put down his mug, grinning.

"Yeah, and long worms who live in shell tubes," he said. "The ends that stick out look like feather dusters in all sorts of colors, and if you wave your finger through the water close by, they pull in so fast you miss it if you blink. And clear creatures soft as jelly that float in the water, and if you get too close they sting like fury, worse than any bee."

"And the fish!" Neve marveled. "So many shapes and colors, like jewels."

Ash sat back in his chair, gazing at her.

"When I first saw the sea," he said, "I'd spend weeks on end walking the shores, just looking at things. I'd go out after every storm to pick up shells and see what else had washed up. Often as I had money to spend my days doing that, that is. But when'd you see the sea? And what's this bit about pocket worlds? You've said that before."

"Mmm—it's hard to explain," Neve said reluctantly. "Inside the Crystal Keep, there's hundreds and hundreds of little worlds. A new one's created every time a visitor enters there—usually something from their past. Most of them were created long before I was born. I've been in only a small fraction of them. Some of the pocket worlds are dangerous places, and others are just too nasty to spend any time in—swamps and volcanoes and the like."

Ash shook his head wonderingly.

"Guess you don't know what it is to be bored, then," he said. "Guess you never run out of things to look at, eh?"

Neve chuckled.

"Actually this city is just as interesting," she said. "All

the interesting things to see in the Keep, but there's no *people* to watch. Here there are all kinds of people to watch, every color and shape and size, just like the fish. Only they do even more interesting things.''

She sighed.

''I do think I like the fish better, though,'' she admitted. ''I'm trying—I honestly am, truly. But people are noisy and rude and annoying, and every time I'm in a place where there's a lot of them, I feel like I'm being crushed. Like I'm losing myself. There's no room for me to be *me,* if that makes any sense.''

Ash shrugged.

''I like cities well enough,'' he said. ''But I can't say as I'm fond of people for the most part. Most of 'em seem to love the sound of their own voices, but without anything much to say—especially nobles and merchants and the like.'' He grimaced. ''Besides, most of 'em don't much care for the likes of me for company. Nah—I prefer a ship where you do a good day's work in the fresh air and don't have to listen to much besides the wind.''

He glanced at Neve for a long moment, rather measuringly.

''You don't look like city life suits you too well, either,'' he said. ''You're starting to look kind of puny.''

Neve sighed.

''I know,'' she said. ''I *am* tired. I did a serious healing today. Rhadaman says it's only normal that I'm tired afterward.''

Ash buried his face in his mug, but not before Neve saw his grimace.

''What?'' she said. ''What's the matter?''

Ash shook his head.

''Nothing,'' he said shortly.

''What?'' Neve insisted. ''Just say what you're thinking.''

Ash set his mug down.

''I'm thinking this mage and his teaching aren't maybe so good for you,'' he said. ''All this time you've been a tough little thing. I've seen you summon up whirlwinds, fight monster bugs, pull me off a burning ship, hike through a jungle—and even in the worst of it, I ain't never seen you look so whipped as you do right now—not even when Warten and his mates beat you most to death. Seems like all this magic ain't so healthy for you. Maybe you ought to pull back a bit, let this Rhadaman get along without you for a while.''

Neve felt unaccountably irritated. What did Ash know about it? By his own admission he knew nothing at all about magic.

"I'm *learning*," she said sharply. "I didn't expect it to be easy. And Rhadaman doesn't push me. He's very understanding and patient—and polite, too."

"Well, pardon me, my lady," Ash said, just as sharply. "I didn't realize it was a killing offense to criticize your noble friend."

"What's the matter with you?" Neve demanded. "You know I've got to prove myself to Kelara; you know I've got to learn to use the magic of the Nexus. I'd think you'd be happy that I'd found a teacher, that I'm using my power to do good for people."

"Oh, yeah?" Ash said, raising an eyebrow. "And do those folk know how they're being used?"

"*Used*?" Neve bristled.

"Ah, look at you," Ash said disgustedly. "You don't give a damn about those people you heal. They're just something for you to practice on, or a notch you can put on a stick to show this Kelara. 'Look what a good little Guardian I am. Now please tell Daddy that so I can go home and get away from all these nasty and rude and annoying people.' Except for Rhadaman the Utterly Perfect, of course," he added sarcastically, "who heals the people of the city—at a hefty profit, that is."

Neve bolted to her feet, her cheeks flaming.

"You didn't sneer at his magic when you wanted to buy it," she said hotly. "You didn't sneer at my healing when I used it on your feet, did you?"

"Well, you notice that he didn't deign to use any of his fancy magic for the good of a simple fellow like me, eh?" Ash retorted. "And as for you and your healing, guess you had a use for fixing up my feet if that'd move me along that much faster. The two of you are quite the pair, aren't you?"

"You just can't bear it, can you?" Neve said between gritted teeth. "You can't bear it that Rhadaman's born of noble lineage and is a respected mage whose work is highly valued, while you're just an ex-thief and out-of-work sailor who's down to loading wagons. Oh, why don't you blame all *that* on your precious feet, too, as you do everything else?''

Ash jumped to his feet, his eyes blazing, and for an astonished moment Neve thought he actually might strike her. Then he turned without a word and strode out the door, slamming it resoundingly behind him.

Neve stood where she was, shaking with anger. How *dare* Ash speak so insolently to her! Why, if he'd spoken so to her father, Vanian would turn him into a swamp croaker or a newt and crush him underfoot. Ash was lucky Neve didn't—

Didn't—

Didn't transform his food into worms? a tiny voice in her mind whispered. *Make him vomit again and again and again until he dies?*

A sudden wave of fear utterly overwhelmed Neve's anger, and she collapsed back into the chair, trembling.

Oh, by the Nexus, please no, she thought. *Please, no. No magic, no curses, no harm. Not that.*

She crept to her bedroom and lay down, shivering with fear and exhaustion, waiting to feel that strange internal wobble that would tell her that once again she'd unintentionally struck out with her magic—and this time at Ash.

Not again, she thought desperately. *Please. Never, never again.*

She lay in the darkness, waiting for a sign, waiting for Ash to return. But neither happened, and at last she slept.

''You're not yourself today,'' Rhadaman said, shaking his head and passing Neve a cup of tea. ''You fidgeted all morning, and this afternoon you've hardly said a word. Are you still tired from yesterday?''

''I—I don't know,'' Neve said, sighing. ''Maybe. No. I quarreled with my friend Ash last night. We were both so angry. He left, and he wasn't there this morning when I woke up.'' She sighed again. ''He thought I should stop doing this.''

Rhadaman nodded sympathetically.

''You can't expect him to understand,'' he said gently.

"Someone who's never experienced the mage-gift can't understand the hunger for knowledge, the need to exercise your abilities so they can grow. He's just jealous of your power, of the respect you're earning."

"That's what I thought," Neve said miserably. "But—"

"Neve, he's a common sailor deprived of his trade," Rhadaman insisted. "Of course he's upset that suddenly you've found a place, a purpose, and he hasn't. But you have every right to exercise your magic and learn to use it more effectively, and I admit, I'm grateful for the help. I don't know why, but lately the distortions have gotten positively horrible. It's been nearly impossible for me to work with any accuracy. Thank the gods you've been here to help. Think of all the good you've done since you came to Zaravelle. Why shouldn't you share your power with the people of this city, who need it so badly? It's what mages are meant to do, Neve. It's not only our gift, but our destiny, our obligation."

"Of course, you're right," Neve said, chagrined. "It's just—I got so *angry* last night. And I said things, maybe cruel things—oh, I don't know." She leaned her forehead into her hands, sighing again.

Rhadaman patted her shoulder gently.

"I understand," he said. "Listen, why don't you go home now? The sun's setting anyway, and you're still tired. You need to settle your differences with your friend. Stop in the market and buy him something nice, then have a good dinner together and talk things out calmly. That'll put things straight between you, and tomorrow you can concentrate on your work again."

"Thank you, Rhadaman," Neve said gratefully. "You're right. I think I'll do that. Thank you for understanding."

Rhadaman smiled a little sadly.

"I do envy your friend," he said. "He doesn't appreciate you properly." His eyes grew warm. "In other circumstances—"

Then Rhadaman drew back his hand, shaking his head.

"Never mind," he said. "Go home and make peace with your sailor friend."

Neve hurried down the street to the market. What in the world could she buy Ash? Brandy? He didn't appear to like sweets, fancy clothes were a waste—wait! Didn't she see a merchant selling that *cai* he liked? Yes, that'd be just the—

A crowd had gathered at one end of the market; there were raised, excited voices. Curious despite herself, Neve touched the arm of a merchant standing in the street.

"Excuse me," she said. "Do you know what's going on?"

"Going on?" The lady turned to Neve surprisedly. "Nothing, now, although there was quite a commotion half an hour ago. Some fellows were loading wine casks into a wagon over there and the whole thing just collapsed on one of them—half a dozen casks, and the wagon itself. Strangest thing, it just sort of came apart. The horse flew into a panic and broke free—luckily it didn't trample anybody, thank Varak, but it knocked over several stalls and—"

Neve swallowed. Suddenly a cold sweat seemed to cover her.

"The fellow the wagon collapsed on," she said unsteadily. "What happened to him? Was he hurt?"

"Hurt?" The woman scowled. "I don't know. Probably. Knocked silly at the very least, I'd say. Some of the men carried him back to his house. Nobody said whether he was hurt or not. But there's wine simply *everywhere*. Terrible waste." Then she raised her eyebrows. "Oh, you're the lady mage, aren't you? Your pardon, my lady, I didn't recognize you at first."

But Neve wasn't paying any attention; in fact, she was already running down the street as fast as her feet could carry her, elbowing people aside, pushing heedlessly through the crowd without a word of apology.

Oh, by the Nexus, please no, she thought. She was panting, her lungs burning as her feet pounded down the street. *I didn't mean it last night. I swear I didn't mean it. I'll do anything, give anything, just don't let him be dead or maimed or crippled or—*

The chandler looked up from his molds in amazement as Neve thundered past, bumping a table and sending wicks and wax blocks tumbling to the ground without stopping. Then she was up the stairs and through the door, nobody in the kitchen, in the sitting room—

Voices from Ash's room, muffled by the closed door—

Oh, no, please, no—

Her heart in her throat, Neve pulled the door open—

"What the devil?" Ash snarled, hastily pulling the blankets up over himself and the buxom, fair-haired woman beside him. "By Peregard's balls, what do *you* want?"

Neve stood there in the doorway, utterly motionless for one heartbeat, two, three. Four. A great cool stillness settled around her heart.

"Nothing," she said emotionlessly. "Nothing."

She closed the door, unfeeling. She went to her room, found her pack, and stuffed her belongings into it. They didn't all fit; she had made and bought so much since she'd come to Zaravelle. She bundled the rest into a sack and slung it over her shoulder.

On her way out, she handed her key silently to the chandler.

Rhadaman's shop was closed, but he answered immediately when Neve knocked on the door. He raised his eyebrows, but took in the pack, the bundle, and asked no questions, stepping aside and opening the door wide.

"Come in, my lady," he said softly. "There's a spare room upstairs that—"

Neve looked him straight in the eye.

"That won't be necessary," she said.

It rained for six days without stopping. The market was empty now, but Rhadaman's shop was full. With the rains came the need for waterproofing spells, leak-sealing spells, spells to protect wood from rot and food from mildew and spoilage, spells to reinforce the flood levees around the city, spells to keep the city drains and pumps clear. Then there was the mud and its attendant injuries.

"Thank you kindly, Lady Neve," the elf said, pressing a pouch into her hand. "I beg you, please do stop by my bathhouse soon. It'll be my honor to treat you to my finest. I could hardly run my business with a sprained back, after all."

"Thank you," Neve said, rubbing her aching temples and forcing a smile. "I'll accept your offer soon, and gladly. A good long soak in hot water sounds good right now."

As soon as the elf was gone, Rhadaman brought in a tray, setting it on the table.

"Some willow-bark tea?" he suggested sympathetically.

"Oh, please, yes." Neve sighed, accepting the cup. The bitter taste of the tea was smothered under plenty of honey and spice.

"Enough for today, I think," Rhadaman said, latching the shop door. "If I have to seal another roof, I think I'll go mad—especially if it takes me five tries to get it right again. And you need to rest."

Neve sighed and let him lead her into the house and up to their room.

"Perhaps you've been working too hard," Rhadaman said gently. "You're so pale and thin. And I don't like these headaches you're having."

"It's nothing," she said, shaking her head and wincing. "I've got to learn. I've *got* to."

Rhadaman touched her shoulder gently.

"Tell me," he said softly. "You drive yourself so relentlessly. Tell me what's frightening you so badly."

Neve took a deep breath. Suddenly her secret seemed too dangerous, too burdensome to keep any longer. She buried her face in her hands and told it all in a monotone, hardly pausing to draw breath—the worms, the insects in the jungle, the spider-creature, and, forcing the words out, Captain Corell. Rhadaman sat silent, his hand on her shoulder, and let her talk without interruption.

"Oh, Neve," he said, very softly, when she fell silent. "Oh, my poor, poor lady."

Neve took a deep breath and forced herself to look up, to meet Rhadaman's eyes, dreading what she might see there. To her amazement and relief there was nothing but warm sympathy in his expression.

"Am I a monster, Rhadaman?" she asked nakedly. "Am I?"

"Of course not," he said immediately. He stroked her hair gently. "Here—take off your tunic and lie down. I know what you need."

Neve grimaced.

"Rhadaman," she said hesitantly, "I really don't feel like—"

"I know," he said gently. "Humor me."

Neve let Rhadaman draw off her tunic and coax her to lie

down on her stomach. To her surprise, his long fingers pressed gently against her spine at the base of her skull, then moving slowly downward, not massaging as Ash had done, only pressing gently. A cool tingling sensation radiated outward from his fingertips. Neve's headache vanished instantly and her body seemed to settle into itself more comfortably. She sighed contentedly.

"What in the world are you doing to me?" she murmured, not caring.

"Aligning your energy centers," Rhadaman said. "Elementary mage maintenance. Your problem is that since your power comes from this Nexus of yours, you're not grounded to the energy currents hereabouts; that's why the distortions don't bother you, but it also means that your centers have no natural orientation. I should have taught you to do it yourself from the outset, but I keep forgetting that you've never been properly educated. Just relax."

Neve didn't argue. She felt not a whit less exhausted, but her headache was gone and the sensation was marvelous.

"Now . . . about what you told me," Rhadaman said softly, still working his way slowly down her spine. "As I told you before, it's not uncommon for untrained mages—especially *powerful* untrained mages—to manifest involuntary phenomena. Ordinarily those phenomena aren't as . . . as specific as you've observed. Still, your magic is of an entirely different order."

"I suppose so," Neve murmured.

"From what you've told me," Rhadaman continued, "the magic of the Nexus is specifically designed to respond to the wishes of the Guardian, yes?"

"Well—yes," she said slowly.

"And in these cases, it appears to me that that's exactly what it has done," Rhadaman said. "You're not the Guardian, but neither is your fragment of crystal the true Nexus. You are the only . . . direction . . . it has. You wanted something, and in a moment of heightened emotion—specifically anger, it would seem—you wanted it very badly. Your magic simply and rather blindly responded to that desire."

"I suppose so," Neve said.

"But have you noticed?" Rhadaman said gently. "The

last time it happened was in the jungle, long before you reached Zaravelle.''

Neve thought about that.

''But—what about the wagon?'' she said.

Rhadaman chuckled.

''Neve, wagons collapse,'' he said. ''Especially wagons overloaded with heavy casks of wine. In this damp climate, and most particularly in the rainy season, wood rots quickly if it isn't preservation-spelled. Tell me, at any time did you specifically *wish* that a wagon would collapse on your friend?''

''Well—no,'' she said cautiously.

''Then I don't think you can claim responsibility for that, at least,'' Rhadaman said. ''As for the other incidents, they all occurred when you had no guidance whatsoever in using your magic, at times of high emotional stress. Since you've been practicing your magic here in Zaravelle, there have been no other incidents, correct?''

''That's right, I suppose,'' Neve admitted.

''Because you're learning to control your magic,'' Rhadaman said firmly. ''You're using it; it's no longer using you. You shouldn't have any further problems of that nature.''

''But—what if I really did those things?'' Neve asked in a small voice. ''What if I *killed* people?''

For a moment his fingers paused; then he started working his way down her spine again.

''Neve, if wishing ill on someone was a crime, magistrates would have to hang themselves, for there would be no one else left to do it,'' Rhadaman said gently. ''Everyone feels anger. No one can guard their thoughts every moment of their lives, least of all an untrained mage in very new and trying circumstances. Tell me, since you left the Crystal Keep, has every ill wish you've made against anyone come to pass?''

''Well—no,'' Neve admitted. Gods, the carnage she'd have left behind her if that had been the case!

''And of the harm you believe you *have* caused to others,'' Rhadaman said, ''would you willingly—deliberately—have done any of those things?''

''Of course not,'' she said hotly, pushing herself partly upward. Then, ''Well—maybe the insects,'' she admitted.

"Relax, relax," Rhadaman said soothingly, pressing her back to the bed. "I know. The point is, Neve, you're not a monster. You're not to blame. Blame your parents, if you like, for not teaching you to use your power properly. Blame the gods—or your Nexus, if you prefer—for giving you such power in the first place. If a newborn baby soils itself, there's no point in blaming the baby or crying over the mess; you simply have to wait until the child is old enough and then teach them not to do it."

Neve grimaced. She didn't precisely appreciate Rhadaman's analogy.

"So you don't think it'll happen again?" she said.

"I very much doubt it," he said firmly. "Of course you must learn to keep your anger under control; that's vitally important for any powerful mage. But I wouldn't worry about causing any more accidental misfortune to anyone. I'm probably more of a danger to others than you, since your magic doesn't appear to distort here. Now that you're learning to use your magic constructively, to shape it by your will, I strongly doubt that you will ever lose control of it again, especially as you're so determined not to let that happen."

Neve sighed, comforted. Rhadaman's explanation made sense. She *wasn't* responsible. She couldn't have helped herself, couldn't have controlled the magic of the Nexus. Now she could, and it would never happen again. It was that simple.

She rolled over.

"You were right," she said, smiling. "That *was* what I needed. Or maybe *part* of what I needed."

Rhadaman smiled, too, and bent down to meet her lips.

The storms grew more frequent, longer. Roofs needed leak-proofing and walls needed reinforcing; ships anchored at the wharf needed joints sealed and masts strengthened. And always there was the parade of injuries, large or small—sprains and broken bones, burns and cuts and infections—even more now as the frequency and severity of the earthquakes increased, too. Now Neve appreciated Rhadaman's salves and potions; there was simply too much to do, too many who needed help. There was never time enough and strength enough for everyone who needed her. And Neve was doing all the magic now. Rhadaman worried that the distortions in the aether were worse, much worse than he'd ever felt them; despite his care, more of his spells went awry than not. His reputation had begun to suffer, and finally Neve suggested that he concentrate on the salves and ointments that she didn't know how to make, and the scryings that caused no harm if they failed, while she handled the problems that could only be solved by magic.

And it was easy, deceptively easy. Neve could heal the most difficult injuries now; a little over a week after she'd moved into Rhadaman's house she had dealt neatly with a child's cracked skull and, a few days later, a carpenter's punctured eye. Since then she'd cured four cases of choking sickness, a girl's shaking fits, and a man with an arm paralyzed since childhood. Yes, it was easy.

But every morning Neve's pallor, her thin cheeks, her hollow eyes, her shaking hands, told her that not only her patients were paying a price.

Rhadaman comforted her, tended her, reassured her that this was the most difficult time of year in Zaravelle, the busiest for a mage. She was simply suffering under the strain of doing too much too soon. She'd adjust to the work as she became more accustomed to using her magic regularly.

Neve took comfort in that thought, but even more so in the realization that the end of the month was only a little over a week away. Then she could see Kelara again. Then this whole business would be over and she could return home. In the sanity of the Keep, with her father's teachings, her mother's steady practicality, there would be no more mistakes. No more danger.

In a way she'd miss Zaravelle. She'd never felt so powerful, so respected, so—well, so much like a Guardian in her life. She was doing good, helping people—maybe atoning, just a little, for all the people who had died so horribly on the *Albatross,* and that thought comforted her. And if she'd *had* to choose a city to be stranded in for a month, Zaravelle wasn't such a bad choice, despite the weather and the earthquakes which still frightened her. She was certainly never bored here. And of course there was Rhadaman. He was kind, patient, gentle, intelligent. He was a good friend and a good teacher and a good lover. She'd miss him, yes.

But somehow this city had soured on her.

Part of that, of course, was Ash. Neve tried not to think of him too much. He'd never come to the shop since she'd left, either to confront her or to insist that Rhadaman perform the transformations he'd wanted. She hadn't really expected Ash to come. She told herself that she was glad he hadn't. It would have only been uncomfortable, awkward. She told herself firmly that she certainly wouldn't miss *him*—but she repeated that to herself many times a day.

At last, a brief break in the rains, sunshine that Rhadaman assured her would be fleeting. Every citizen in Zaravelle flocked to the market to trade while they could, and Neve, desperate for fresh air, allowed Rhadaman to shoo her out the door for a day at leisure as well. She was so tired of the inside of his shop and his house and, though she'd never tell him, Rhadaman's constant company, that even the crowded and noisy market was a welcome respite, even though the streets were muddy and foul and she was so tired that just walking from stall to stall was exhausting.

She browsed nostalgically at the tea merchant's cart, hating herself for the involuntary pang of pain she felt when she saw the small sacks of *cai* beans. Despite herself, she picked up one of the sacks, pressing it to her nose and closing her eyes, sniffing deeply. Well, she'd always liked the *smell* of the stuff, if not the nasty taste. She sighed.

"I'll take this, I think," Neve said to the merchant, reaching for her purse.

"Well, if it ain't the marvelous noble-lady mage," a familiar voice said sarcastically, and Neve whirled, then had to seize the edge of the cart for balance as the world whirled, too—in a different direction. Ash was leaning indolently against the next cart over, arms folded.

Neve's head spun with emotion—joy, fury, relief, outrage—and she clutched the cart more tightly. Her hands were shaking.

"Can't imagine what your ladyship's doing in the market mingling with the likes of—" Then Ash's voice faded, along with his mocking expression, as he took in her appearance.

"Peregard's limp manhood," Ash said slowly. "What the—" Then he shook his head and took Neve's arm, dragging her to the nearest bench, which happened to be occupied by a burly young man eating a meat pie.

"Shove off, lout," Ash growled, pushing the man off the bench and helping Neve down more gently, squatting beside her.

"Gods above and below, girl, what's become of you?" he said, and the rough worry in his voice, the anxiety in his eyes, was the last straw. Neve opened her mouth to speak and found herself sobbing weakly instead. Ash fell silent, nudging her over slightly so he could perch on the edge of the bench beside her, his arm around her. He simply held her and let her cry for a while, waving aside several peasants who appeared quite stunned to see the powerful lady mage weeping in the arms of a common sailor in the middle of the market.

When Neve had cried herself out, Ash left her to herself for a moment, standing up and scanning the crowd of passersby. He strode up to a baker hawking his wares from two deep baskets over a mule's back.

"I'll buy that animal," he said brusquely. "Name your price."

To the baker's astonishment, Ash pulled out his purse and counted out gold there on the spot. He pulled the baskets off the mule and led the animal back to Neve's bench.

"Hop on up," he said shortly, helping her up. "Just hold on. I'll lead the thing."

To Neve's dull amazement, Ash led the mule neither toward his rooms nor Rhadaman's house, but toward the edge of the city.

"Where are we going?" she asked.

"Where the devil you think?" Ash snapped. A little farther and Neve realized he was heading for the path to Kelara's house.

"She said a month," Neve said hesitantly. "It hasn't been a month yet."

"Looking like that, you aren't going to last the month out," Ash said sourly.

"What if she won't talk to me?" she protested.

"She will," he said grimly. "By all the gods, they both will, or they'll dearly wish they had."

Neve hadn't remembered the walk to Kelara and Yaga's

house being so *long*, so tiring. She simply sat on the mule silently, letting Ash lead it. Ash, in turn, seemed no more inclined to conversation than Neve herself, although she heard him muttering darkly to himself as they walked. At last, however, the clearing and the cottage were before them, and Neve hurriedly put the crystal into the silver box Yaga had given her. To her surprise, she hardly felt the loss of it this time. Ash tied the mule outside the door, picked her up, and blithely carried her inside, depositing her on a chair at the table before he vanished outside again. He returned presently, dragging Kelara and Yaga bodily after him.

"Play in your pretty garden later," Ash snarled. "No more riddles, no more games." He pushed them toward Neve. "You talk to her now, or you can explain to her daddy, the big bad Guardian, why you let his daughter drop dead in your kitchen."

Yaga took one look at Neve and gasped.

"By Alaster," he breathed. "I had no idea."

Kelara knelt by Neve's side, taking her hand. Kelara winced as if in pain, hastily releasing Neve's hand.

"The Nexus," Kelara whispered. "It is feeding upon her."

"Feeding on her?" Ash repeated. "You mean that bit of rock?"

Kelara hesitated.

"Perhaps," she said. "The Nexus I opened was anchored deep into the earth, to draw its power from the energy lines running through the world. But this—"

Neve pulled out the little silver box, not opening it.

"But this is just a part of that nexus," she said. "Isn't it?"

Kelara shook her head.

"I have no way to know," she said. "You are a part of that nexus as well, are you not? But I know this—there is a powerful disturbance in the aether centering around *you*, the strongest distortions I have ever known, as if the Nexus reaches out wildly for a source of power upon which to draw. And having none, it is drawing upon *you*."

Neve froze. Hadn't Rhadaman said the distortions in the magical aether were worse since she'd arrived in Zaravelle?

And hadn't his own magic become increasingly ineffective since she'd worked in his shop?

"But there were distortions here even before I came," she said cautiously. "Rhadaman said so."

Yaga nodded.

"The power lines in this part of the world have no pattern, no center," he said. "They feed randomly into the aether. No one knows what caused such chaos, as if a powerful magical war was once fought here, disrupting the natural order. Once Kelara and I thought of opening another nexus here, to center the power lines and stabilize the aether. But—" He fell silent, glancing at Kelara, then down at the ground.

Neve understood. Another nexus meant another Guardian, the very power they craved most. But creating the Nexus had torn Kelara's soul from her, and Guardianship had imprisoned them both in the Keep for centuries. Yes, Ash was right. The temptation and the repulsion must be nearly unbearable for them. And then here came Neve, bearing her fragment of the Nexus to remind them of all they'd given up—or fled from.

"Well, what can she do, then?" Ash asked impatiently. "Get rid of the thing? Will that make her well? What if we hide it in the jungle, or throw it in the sea?"

Neve clutched the box desperately. Surely he couldn't be serious!

"That would certainly stop the Nexus feeding upon her," Kelara said slowly. "But there must be no chance the crystal could be found by another. I can think of no way to be certain of that."

"Well, can the two of you keep it?" Ash demanded.

Kelara went white.

"No," she whispered. "Never that."

"Well, what about destroying it, then?" Ash said. "What about crushing it, melting it?"

"No!" Neve pushed the box hastily back into her tunic. "Ash, you don't understand. It's part of the Nexus. So is my father. So am I, even more so. If the crystal is damaged, it might hurt him and me. It might even kill us both."

Yaga and Kelara exchanged glances.

"There's only one way," Yaga said softly. "Neve must return to the Keep immediately."

"Oh, thank you," Neve breathed, closing her eyes. At last!

"Well, that's easy enough to say," Ash said sarcastically. "How do you expect to do it? Not a ship can sail right now, and over land would take months. Going to Gate her back?"

Kelara frowned.

"There is the complication," she said. "With the increase in the distortions, there is no chance of safely casting a Gate—and even if we could, there is no way to know whether Neve and the fragment of the Nexus could safely pass through."

"The safest choice," Yaga said slowly, "is for Neve to keep the fragment isolated—in the box—and allow the disturbances in the aether to subside. Hopefully, when deprived of usage and energy, the fragment of the Nexus will become dormant, and the magical energies in the area will stabilize sufficiently to allow a Gate to be cast, while Neve conserves and regains her strength."

"Yes," Kelara said after a moment's thoughtful silence. "Perhaps that is best."

"So, what, she's just to keep that thing shut up and not do any magic?" Ash asked disbelievingly. "That's *all*? Can you at least get in touch with her folks, maybe, see if they can help?"

Kelara shook her head.

"No magic from outside can reach into the Crystal Keep," she said gently. "We communicate with Lord Vanian, yes, but only when he calls upon us. But he has called several times since you left, asking if we had any tidings of you. Surely he will call again soon. Perhaps from his end he could find some way to open a stable Gate, or—or suggest some other solution."

Ash gave a disgusted grunt and turned back to Neve. Abruptly he thrust his hand into her tunic, pulling out the box; before Neve could do more than gape in amazement, he stuffed it securely into his own tunic.

"What do you think you're doing?" she demanded hotly.

"Putting this damned thing where it's safe, even from you," he retorted. "Folks as might look for a powerful magical stone on a mage won't go looking on a common sailor, will they? Besides, I'm in a damn sight better shape than you to defend it right now." He slid his arm around her waist, hoisting her up from the chair. "Come on, we're going back. Not much to be gained *here*." He gave Yaga and Kelara a scowl of pure contempt.

Neve didn't protest when Ash loaded her back onto the mule—in fact, she was fairly certain she couldn't make the long walk back to Zaravelle—but she fumed nonetheless.

"Tired or not," she declared, "I'm perfectly capable of defending the Nexus."

Ash glanced at her narrowly.

"Yeah, well maybe you are, and maybe you aren't," he said sourly. "Guess it would all depend on who tried to take it, and how, eh?"

Neve scowled.

"You mean Rhadaman, don't you?" she said. "I tell you, he's been a good, true friend, he's always been honest with me, and there's not a chance in the world that he'd—"

"Fine, fine, the man's a model of virtue," Ash said, rolling his eyes. "Frankly, I'm more worried about keeping the damned thing away from *you.*"

"Me?" Neve ground her teeth. "What, now you think *I'm* going to misuse it?"

"Nah, I think you're going to *use* it," he said flatly. "Never been without that magic your whole life, have you? I guess you're worse off than them two elves, even, or those dream dusters I saw. So I'm just putting temptation right out of your reach for your own good, and there won't be no argument about it."

Neve subsided, confused. Ash was furious, that was plain enough, but she couldn't decide whether he was angrier *at* her or *for* her. Her own feelings were even more confusing. She'd thought she never wanted to see him again—until she saw him. Until her world and her heart had turned upside down at the sight of him.

Ash led the mule back to the city in silence; to Neve's surprise he took her back, not to Rhadaman's house, but to the rooms they'd shared. He picked her up and carried her upstairs without a word, simply abandoning the mule in the street to whoever might take it.

"But all my things are at Rhadaman's," Neve protested, unsure whether she should insist to be taken back there. *Why should I stay with him if he hates me? And I'm not so certain how I feel about him, either.* But Ash had the crystal, and she didn't like to let it get too far from her. "He'll be worried about me by now."

Ash grimaced.

"Never mind that," he said shortly. "I'll send a messenger to tell him where you are and fetch back your things." He plopped her down on the bed that had been hers, a little more roughly than Neve thought was strictly necessary. "You're going to lie right there and sleep, if I've got to tie you there."

"But I don't—" she began.

"Sleep," Ash said. He tossed her a blanket and walked to the door.

Neve flushed.

"Ash, I—"

"Sleep," he said again, flatly. He stepped outside, closing the door firmly behind him. Neve heard the scrape of a key in the lock.

She flushed miserably. Put to bed like a sick child, and locked in her room like a prisoner! But she *was* exhausted, there was no arguing it, and it was unaccountably comforting to have Ash looking out for her again, however rudely he did it. He'd always been loyal and trustworthy in his rough way, and if he said he would keep her and her fragment of the Nexus safe, he'd do that very thing beyond any doubt— whether she wanted him to or not.

And if he said "sleep," nothing would suffice but that Neve do exactly that.

Neve pulled the blanket up over her and could not quite suppress a small smile as she obeyed.

When Neve woke, the room was completely dark and her head was horribly muzzy. She sat up, groaning and rubbing her temples. She felt sick—for a moment she thought she might vomit—and weaker than ever. She pushed herself to her feet and stumbled to the door; it was still locked. From the door it was only a short step to the window, and she unfastened the shutters, flinging them open. Wind blew rain in on her face and she heard the rumble of thunder—another storm. The brief clear spell was over, then. Neve leaned against the windowsill, ignoring the rain simply because she had to rest before she tried to close the shutters again.

The door opened and Ash stood there, lamp in hand. He put the lamp down on the table and silently helped her back to bed, going back to fasten the shutters.

"If you're longing for fresh air, tonight's not the night for it," he said, chuckling slightly. "Seeing as you're awake, though, I'll bring you in some supper."

Neve's stomach flipped over at the thought.

"No, thank you," she said as steadily as she could. "I'm not hungry."

"You'll eat, if I have to pour it down your throat," Ash said flatly. "Nobody ever got strong lying in the dark starving."

He stepped out and returned with a bowl of soup on a tray. He set the tray in Neve's lap, giving her a stern glance.

"You cooked soup?" she asked disbelievingly, stalling.

"Not a bit of it," Ash said, shaking his head. "I've been paying the chandler's daughter to bring me up supper every day. Today I told her I needed something fit for a sick friend."

Neve swirled her spoon through the soup reluctantly. It smelled of goose and herbs. She glanced at Ash, but his gaze was merciless. At last she choked down a mouthful of the soup. For a moment the outcome seemed doubtful, but the soup stayed down. She risked another mouthful.

"So," Ash said, his eyes never leaving her. "Guess you've been busy this past couple weeks, eh? All I hear all over the city is about the new lady mage, the marvelous healer working with Rhadaman who can cure everything from broken backs to bad dreams. Hell, I've heard 'em speculating you can probably raise the dead. Made a lot of money, I'll bet. At least that was a pretty heavy purse with your things."

Neve forced down a little more soup.

"Yes," she said. "I made some money. And yes—" She met his eyes squarely. "I was a *good* healer. And I don't want to argue about this again."

She took a deep breath.

"Did Rhadaman come over?"

"Yeah." Ash was still watching her. "He brought your things, wanted to see you. I told him you needed to sleep."

Neve sighed.

"I'd like to see him."

"I'll bet you would," Ash muttered. "But it's rest you need, not a tumble."

Neve felt her cheeks heat.

"That's none of your affair," she snapped. "What right have you got to speak to me like that after what you did?"

Ash folded his arms, narrowing his eyes.

"Yeah, I brought a whore home to my bed," he said evenly. "I was as angry as you were. But at least I didn't hurry off to move in with her fast as ever I could scamper."

Neve dropped her spoon from shaking fingers.

"What did you expect?" she said bitterly. "Did you think I'd just go quietly to my room and listen to the two of you in there?"

Ash sighed irritably.

"No. I expected to have her paid and long gone by the time you got home. I knew it was just spiteful foolishness even when I hired the wench. Should've just gone to a whorehouse, I guess—not that it ever made much difference to you what I did most of the time, anyway, you were so busy polishing up that reputation you've got. What the devil were you doing home so early anyway?"

Neve stared down into the soup.

"I stopped in the market to buy you a present," she said faintly. "To—to make up. They said there'd been an accident, that a man loading a wagon had been hurt badly and taken home, and I thought—I thought you—" Her mouth had gone dry. "So I ran home as fast as I could."

Ash muttered an oath that brought new heat to Neve's cheeks; then he shook his head, rubbing his eyes tiredly.

"Peregard's drooping mustache, aren't we the pair." He sighed. "Go on, eat your damned soup."

Neve had even less appetite for the food than she'd had before, but she forced it down, spoonful by spoonful, until she'd emptied the bowl. Ash set the tray aside.

"Scoot over a bit," he said. He slid into bed beside her, pulling her down comfortably against his side, pulling the blanket up over both of them.

"Tell me something," he said softly after a long silence. "Why are you doing this to yourself? You always seemed

like such a sensible little bit, in your own odd way. I mean,
I know how much you want to be Guardian, but you didn't
seem the kind to half kill yourself to get it.''

Neve sighed. Ash wouldn't understand. His nights weren't
haunted by dreams of fire and sea dragons and little gap-
toothed boy-faces.

"I don't know,'' she said after a long moment. "Ash—
have you ever done something you felt really awful about?''

Ash was silent for a while.

"What, you mean that girl?''

"No.'' Neve wrinkled her nose. "Worse than that. Something—something you weren't sure you could ever forgive
yourself for.''

This time the silence stretched out so long that she wondered whether Ash had gone to sleep. At last, however he
spoke quietly.

"Yeah,'' he said. "Yeah, I did once. Back in Arawen.''

"What was it?'' Neve hesitated. "I mean, if you don't
mind telling me.''

Ash shifted slightly, settling her more comfortably against
him.

"I told you about Harod, and what he had done to me,''
Ash said, very softly. "Everything was different after that.
People looked at me funny—they'd back away from me.
There'd be this look in their eyes, I don't know, like they'd
look at a leper or a corpse swarming with maggots. I guess
they thought maybe I was part shifter or something, who
knows? Even the other children Harod kept around. We'd
been almost like a family before, but now it was different.
Wasn't nothing but Harod and the work and the money anymore. Harod had always been good to me—I can't say like
a father, don't rightly know what that feels like, but I'd liked
him, respected him. Suddenly I found myself starting to hate
him—just a little, maybe, at first, but every time somebody
would look at me that way, the hate would get a little bigger
and the respect would get a little smaller. I thought he didn't
really care about me, not if he could do that to me just so I
could steal better for him, you see?''

Neve took a deep breath. She couldn't imagine her parents
doing such a thing to her, not on the worst day of her life.

"It must've been awful,'' she whispered.

Ash shifted uncomfortably.

"One time he set up a special job," he said. "A lord was moving out of his town house to a country estate. He'd made a fortune in the wars and had weapons and loot hanging all over the place. He'd gone on to visit some friends while his stuff was being moved to his country house, but his belongings hadn't been moved out yet, and there was just a few servants and guards about the place. An easy job, we thought, but this fellow believed in locks the way priests believe in their god, and some of 'em was probably bespelled against tinkering. I didn't know nothing about magic, but Harod had a little magic-sniffing. So Harod said he'd go on the job with me. I'd go in from the roof, through one of the upstairs windows, and then I'd sneak down and let Harod in.

"Well, that part of it worked just fine. I got in with no trouble and let Harod in at the front—back would've been less obvious, but the servants' quarters were there and we might've been heard—and locked the door again. We knew this lord kept his valuables in a hidden vault in the library upstairs, so we went in there and started searching. What we didn't realize was that the minute Harod opened the lock to the vault, he set off an alarm spell down in the servants' quarters, and up come one of the lord's private guards with a damned big sword. The spell did more'n that, but I didn't know that—not then.

"Anyway, before we knew what was what, here's this big lout with the sword in the room yelling like thunder," Ash said ruefully. "He came straight after me, probably because Harod was mostly in the vault, stuffing jewels into his sleeve. Well, I dodged all over the place, and the fellow wasn't too quick with his big old sword, but after a minute he had me cornered by the fireplace and I knew it. I knew it was all up with me—and then I saw Harod with the jewels, heading for the door, and I thought he was leaving me there. But this guard saw me look, and he looked, too, and that gave me time to reach the poker. I bashed him across the head hard as ever I could."

Ash fell silent.

"Oh, gods," Neve whispered. "Did you kill him?"

"Oh, yeah," Ash said flatly. "No doubt about that. But at the moment I didn't much care, because there was other

things going on. For one, I thought Harod was abandoning
me. For another, I heard more guards coming out of their
rooms, so the back door was blocked good and proper. And
for another, I heard the city guard pounding at the front
door.''

Neve gasped.

"What did you do?'' she said.

Ash shrugged.

"What do you think?'' he said. "I went out the window
and up the wall to the roof. I jumped to another roof, shinnied
down the back, and got out of there as quick as ever I could.
I didn't know where to go, what to do, so I just hid in the
alleys. Thievery was one thing, but I'd committed murder.

"Well, I stayed in the alleys for a couple weeks,'' he said
slowly. "At last I started thinking I'd better get myself out
of town. But I ran into some beggars, and from them I found
out what'd happened after I left. The city guard had beat
down the door and caught Harod on the stairs with a mace
in his hand. He hadn't been running away. He'd been fetching a weapon to come back and help me.''

Ash's arms tightened slightly around her, but his voice
stayed flat.

"They didn't know whether to blame him or not for the
guard's murder,'' he said. "I'd left a footprint in the blood,
and it sure didn't match Harod's foot, so they were pretty
sure he'd had someone else with him. But he wouldn't tell.
So they questioned him—under torture.''

"Oh, Ash,'' Neve whispered.

"Way I hear it,'' Ash continued slowly, "he lasted about
three days. But he never told them nothing about me. I'd
hated him, but I guess he cared a hell of a lot about me. He
died in prison, of course; the local guild couldn't ransom
him, there being a murder involved. So I lit out of Arawen,
headed west, and took up another line of work.'' He fell
abruptly silent.

"Oh, Ash,'' Neve repeated. "That's *awful*. But—but there
really wasn't anything you could've done, was there? I mean,
by the time you found out, it was all over.''

Ash shrugged.

"I don't know,'' he said softly. "I keep asking myself
that. Maybe I could've gotten him out the window and up to

the roof with me. If I hadn't been such a bloody coward, hiding in the alleys, maybe I'd have found out what happened in time to do something about it—break him out of prison, maybe. Or maybe I'd have gone to the magistrate, told him the truth. I don't know whether I'd have been strong enough to do that." He rested his cheek against Neve's hair. "I'd like to hope I would have. You did, after all."

"That's not the same," Neve protested, digging her fingers into Ash's shoulder. "I mean, *I* wasn't risking any punishment."

" 'Course it's the same," he said roughly. "You gave away your secrets for me. What you told that magistrate could've cost you your freedom, even your life."

"Well, I didn't know that," Neve argued.

"Doesn't matter." Ash shook his head, rumpling her hair with the motion. "Everything we say and do, even when we don't mean to, has consequences, and we've got to stand up to them. That's the right thing to do. You did the right thing, I didn't, and I'll never forget it. It's as simple as that."

Neve grimaced. Ash's words were far less comforting than Rhadaman's glib dismissal of her responsibility for what had happened to the *Albatross*. Maybe killing all those people by accident wasn't as horrible a crime as doing it on purpose. But was that any comfort to the dead, or to their kinfolk? No, maybe it wasn't fair. But in her years in the Keep, Neve had learned that fairness didn't usually enter into it.

"Ash—" she whispered at last. "How do you learn to forgive yourself after something like that?"

Ash was silent for a long moment.

"I don't know," he said at last. "I guess I've never figured that one out myself."

Then he pulled her closer.

"Maybe you start," he murmured, "by getting somebody else to forgive you first. Like telling you how stupid I was with that woman. I was jealous of your friendship with Rhadaman, afraid he was getting too close to you. I meant to hurt you, I guess, but not as much as I probably did. But that doesn't make what I did any nicer. And even if you forgive me, I won't be forgiving myself anytime soon. Look what it's done to you, me driving you off like that. If I'd been the friend to you I should've been, you'd have been here and

I'd have gotten you out of the magic business a lot sooner.''

Neve sighed.

"I wish—"

Ash chuckled.

"No, don't wish," he said gently. "Just rest and keep warm. Sleep yourself out."

Neve sighed and closed her eyes. It was hard to believe she'd found it so annoying, sleeping beside a man. Perhaps she'd gotten more accustomed to it with Rhadaman. Now, though, it was Ash's shoulder under her head, Ash's familiar scent in her nostrils.

"Ash?" she whispered after a long silence.

He stirred slightly.

"Hmmm?"

"Ash, I—I'm sorry," Neve murmured. "For the things I said to you that day. And for not trying to make it right with you again sooner."

Ash chuckled.

"You know, I don't believe I've ever heard you say you were sorry for anything," he said. "Nothing'll surprise me tomorrow, not if the sun drops right out of the sky." His cheek brushed her hair. "Don't fret yourself. Foolishness breeds foolishness, and I'm the one who took it to bed. Don't bother about it. Just sleep now."

Neve closed her eyes, let all her worries leave her in one exhausted sigh, and slept.

Dim rainy morning. Neve felt worse than ever, sick and weak, and her head ached abominably. Dimly, she heard voices in the next room but couldn't distinguish words. She pushed herself up on one elbow, groaning at the effort, and the voices stopped. Footsteps, then the door opened. To her surprise, Rhadaman stepped into the room, lamp in hand, with Ash close behind him.

Rhadaman pulled up a chair and sat down at the side of the bed, and his gently sympathetic expression froze, then shifted to dismay as he gazed at her.

"By the gods," he murmured. "Your friend said you were seriously ill, but I never—" He shook his head.

"I'm not that bad," Neve said irritably. "Just worn-out, I suppose."

Rhadaman gazed at her intently, then reached out slowly and touched her forehead. He withdrew his hand, shaking his head again.

"No," he said. "This goes beyond mere exhaustion." He turned to Ash. "Tell me again what the elves said."

His voice flat, Ash repeated the entire story of their second visit to Kelara and Yaga's cottage, Neve prompting him occasionally. Rhadaman listened soberly.

"I never considered such a possibility," he said at last, sighing. "Magic is exhausting work, of course, especially in these parts, and occasionally I've worked myself almost to collapse, but it never occurred to me that we might be doing you actual harm."

He touched her forehead again and smiled rather wistfully.

"And your energy centers are misaligned again. At least I can do that much for you."

At that point Neve would have gladly rolled in dung if she'd thought it would make her feel any better. She pulled her linen shirt off and rolled over on her stomach.

"Now, see here—" Ash began. Neve glanced at him, grinning reassuringly.

"Not what you think," she said. "It's a mage thing."

This time, however, her headache subsided only slightly when Rhadaman had finished, and her nausea was no better at all. In fact, Ash appeared more relieved than Neve when Rhadaman took his hands away and helped her pull her shirt back over her head.

"I'm sorry," Rhadaman said softly. "I don't think that helped much, did it?"

"A little," Neve said as positively as she could. "Listen, a few days of no magic and a lot of sleep and I'll be fine. That's what Kelara said."

Rhadaman gazed at her steadily, then sighed.

"No," he said. "I don't think it's as simple as that at all."

Ash grunted contemptuously.

"I suppose you know more about this Nexus than the mage who created it," he said sarcastically.

"No, I know very little about this Nexus, except for what Neve's told me," Rhadaman said evenly. "Listen—in healing it's important to focus on the patient, not the wound; otherwise it's all too easy to see the broken knee and overlook the cracked rib. And since I know almost nothing about this Nexus, I can look at Neve instead.

"It's true that the distortions in the aether have improved dramatically in the last two days, since she left the shop— and so has the effectiveness of my magic," Rhadaman said ruefully. "And I can't deny that the magic she was performing was draining her; I could see the effects in her myself. But I can also see that she's noticeably weaker than she was when I last saw her, and according to you, she's rested, ate, and performed no magic since then. She isn't gaining strength; it's continuing to drain out of her. I think Kelara was right in one respect at least—it's vital that Neve return to the Nexus. But I don't think Kelara is correct about the Nexus draining Neve. I wonder if she simply can't bear to be away from it—the entirety of the Nexus, not the crystal she carries—for so long. I believe perhaps it sustains her somehow."

Ash gave a short bark of laughter.

"And I suppose *you* can open up a Gate to send her home?"

Rhadaman sighed.

"No. My own spells are still unreliable, even more so around Neve. I can feel the change in the aether right now, just sitting beside her. I've only dared a spell as strong as a Gate once or twice in my entire time here, and then the risk wasn't nearly so great." He sighed again. "Besides, I can't cast a Gate to an area of the world I know absolutely nothing about. There isn't even so much as a map showing the location of the Crystal Keep. And I can't scry it out; as Kelara and Yaga told Neve, the Crystal Keep protects itself from outside magic."

"I had a map," Neve said wearily. "But it sank with the *Albatross.*" Then she pushed herself up slightly as a thought occurred to her. "But Kelara and Yaga, they could make a map."

"It wouldn't help, even so," Rhadaman said gently, patting her hand. "As I said, I wouldn't dare cast a Gate now, especially for you. It would almost certainly fail. At best, it would drop you in some unknown place, even into the sea far from shore. At worst it could close with you inside it, and I have absolutely no idea what would become of you then.''

"Well, then, what the devil do *you* suggest?" Ash demanded.

"For now, exactly what you're doing," Rhadaman said softly, apparently unoffended by Ash's less-than-amiable tone. "Rest and food and no magic. But I do think you should give that fragment of crystal back to her immediately."

Ash gave a bitter laugh again.

"Well, since I don't hear any explanations from you better than Kelara and Yaga's, guess I'll go with their suggestions instead of yours," he said.

Rhadaman sighed.

"Well, I have only a belief, and no proof to back it," he agreed unhappily. "There's no doubt they know more of the Nexus than I do. So I suppose there's little I can do, except for this—"

He laid one palm against Neve's forehead, and Neve gasped as energy flowed into her in a warm wave. Ash bolted forward, eyes wide.

"Here, now!" he said, alarmed.

When Rhadaman took his hand away, however, Neve sat up, smiling. Her headache was gone, her nausea had subsided, and she felt considerably stronger again—almost normal. Rhadaman slumped back in the chair, eyes closed, his hands shaking.

"Oh, *thank* you." Neve sighed with relief.

Ash scowled.

"What the devil did he *do* to you?"

Neve chuckled.

"Gave me a magical recharge," she said. "I feel ever so much better—I think I could get up now."

Then realization struck—that magical energy had come *from* somewhere. Neve turned to Rhadaman, dismayed at his obvious exhaustion. He must have seriously drained his magical reserves.

"Oh, Rhadaman, I didn't think, or I wouldn't have let you," she said, wincing. "Are you all right?"

Rhadaman waved off her concern, smiling tiredly.

"Don't worry," he said. "Remember, I'm used to exhausting myself with magic hereabouts."

"But your customers," Neve said, troubled.

Rhadaman shook his head reassuringly.

"I'll take a carriage home," he said. "Unlike you, a hearty meal and a good night's sleep *will* put me back to rights."

He chuckled.

"My customers are ever so disappointed anyway," he said ruefully. "I'm afraid they've gotten spoiled by the powerful lady mage who can heal their ills and mend their roofs with a wave of her hand. Well, no matter. We managed before you came, Neve; we'll manage now."

Neve suddenly thought of the little girl with the cracked skull.

"Rhadaman—" She grabbed his arm. "Listen, if there's an emergency, you call me anyway. Promise me, if there's somebody seriously sick or hurt, if you can't help them, promise me you'll call."

Rhadaman patted her hand.

"Of course," he said gently. "If there's a true emergency, I'll call you. So rest and stop worrying about it, yes?"

Neve sighed.

"Yes," she said ruefully.

When Rhadaman was gone, however, she slid out of bed and dug through the bag Ash had slung in the corner, pulling out clean clothes.

"And what do you think you're doing?" Ash asked, scowling.

"I'm putting on some clothes," Neve said patiently. She was still tired, but she felt better than she had in days and that was good enough for her. "I feel like I've been stuck indoors forever, and I want some fresh air."

"You haven't been stuck indoors forever." Ash scowled. "It hasn't been that long since we went all the way down the coast to the elves' cottage. Besides, it's pouring down rain outside."

"Then I'll wear my cloak," Neve said adamantly. "Come on, at least we can go down the street and get some hot supper. Maybe we can find some of those spicy spiderclaws like we ate in Strachan."

"Last night you looked half-dead," Ash said disbelievingly, "and this morning now you want spiced spider-claws?"

"Well, I certainly don't want goose-gizzard soup again," she said, chuckling. "Come on, Ash. I'm starving. Find me some spiderclaws. I'll pay."

Neve was shocked to see what the endless rain had done to Zaravelle in the short time since she'd met Ash in the market. The streets were pure knee-high mud and the market was completely empty. The colorful ribbons that had festooned doors and windows hung draggled and dull now. The brightly clad and disparate citizens of Zaravelle now scurried from one doorway to the other in gray-cloaked similitude.

"Welcome to rainy-season Zaravelle." Ash sighed. "Come on, then. Let's go show the folks at the Oaken Barrel that their lady mage hasn't dropped off the edge of the world."

A few minutes' brisk walk through the rain and Neve was enjoying spicy stewed seafood and cold ale while Ash sighed at the excited murmurs that had started the moment Neve walked into the tavern.

"Be lucky if we make it out the door," he said glumly.

True to his prediction, Neve had barely finished sopping up the last of her stew with some rather chewy bread when, after a lengthy whispered discussion, a young fellow left his group of drinking companions behind and made his way to their table, ducking his head abashedly when Neve acknowledged him with a smile.

"Begging your pardon, Lady Neve," the lad mumbled. "I don't want to trouble you at your supper, but my friends and I were wondering—is it true what Sobel says, that there's a storm coming like to wash all of Zaravelle out to sea? Lord Rhadaman says there's nothing in it, that Sobel's just a faker, but he true saw the big flood last spring, and he saw the shaking getting worse, too, so we thought as we'd ask you your mind on it."

Neve turned to Ash.

"Have you heard anything about this?"

Ash shrugged.

"Not really," he said. "Way I hear it, this fellow Sobel's no foreseer; he's just plain mad."

"Well, he's mad, not much doubt of that," the boy said

abashedly. "And it's true he's wrong more often than right about most things. But weather—well, he hits it most always. A lot of the fishing captains consult him before they take a long trip out along the coast or go into the deep waters. I've seen half the fleet sitting at the docks if he says there's a bad storm coming."

Ash chuckled.

"Bet he's been predicting rain lately," he said.

The boy grinned.

"Well, yeah," he said. "But we aren't far enough along in the storm season for the really bad blows, except now he's saying the biggest ever's coming soon. He said the sea would swallow up Zaravelle and everyone in it. Most folks just laugh at him, don't put any stock in what he says, especially since Rhadaman says there's nothing to worry about, but there's some that—well, you know." He shrugged, gazing expectantly at Neve.

Neve flushed.

"I'm sorry," she said abashedly. "I don't know anything about foresight or weather, either." *The only thing I know is how to do a storm-turning spell completely wrong and bring a whirlwind down on myself. And I couldn't even do that now; Mother's grimoire's at the bottom of the sea somewhere. I haven't even learned to scry.* "But I saw this Sobel once in the market, and it didn't seem to me there was much to his predictions. If Rhadaman says there's nothing to it, likely he's right."

Neve's uncertain reply seemed scant comfort to the boy; he wrinkled his brow doubtfully and glanced at his companions, then back at Neve.

"So you don't suppose we'd be smart to get out of the city, head inland, just in case?" he asked.

"I'm sorry," Neve said again. "I really couldn't advise you one way or the other. But that does seem rather extreme, doesn't it, leaving the city on the word of a madman? Apparently Rhadaman thinks it's safe to stay." She glanced at Ash. "My friend and I aren't going anywhere."

That seemed to reassure the lads; their spokesman ducked his head again rather sheepishly and returned to his friends to resume their drinking.

"Sobel was talking about that before, the sea swallowing

Zaravelle,'' Neve murmured to Ash, accepting another mug of ale from the barkeep.

"Well, I hadn't heard it,'' Ash admitted. "But, then, last couple of days I been at home with you. But you know if Rhadaman thought there was anything to it, he'd've told you.'' He grimaced slightly. "I don't expect he'd stand for you being in any danger.''

Neve put her mug down a little more firmly than was strictly necessary.

"Now you're being ridiculous,'' she said, fighting down her anger. "If Rhadaman thought there was any danger to the city, he'd have warned me, yes. He'd also have warned the other people in the city, and he'd be working hard to protect them, not wasting his magic on me.''

"Hmm.'' Ash shrugged as if unconvinced. "Well, we've got a madman who apparently foresees weather saying go, and we've got a mage whose spells aren't working more than half the time saying stay. Too bad there's not a third mage in town to give an opinion.''

"There is,'' Neve said grimly.

Ash put down his mug, gazing at her.

"You're not thinking—uh-uh, no, sir,'' he said firmly. "You just said you don't know anything about foresight.''

"Everybody starts someplace,'' Neve said decisively. "Come on, there's a jeweler I want to visit on the way home.''

Ash followed her to the shop, but not silently.

"Look, this is damn-all stupid,'' he said hotly. "If you're so determined, why don't we go see Rhadaman? I bet he never did no scrying about this, just decided this Sobel fellow was mad and shrugged it off.''

"Maybe he did, and maybe not,'' Neve said. "But he's not doing any scrying now, that's for certain. He's probably resting after pouring all his magical energy into me. And I'm going to put it to good use.'' She picked up an ornate silver bowl and turned to the merchant, who had tactfully been ignoring the exchange taking place in his shop. "Is this bowl unused? I mean, are you certain there's never been anything put in it since it was forged?''

The merchant raised his eyebrows.

"I can't rightly speak as to that particular bowl,'' he said slowly. "It's been in the shop a few weeks. I couldn't swear nobody's dropped a few oddments into it. This one, though—" He pulled out a slightly smaller bowl from a box behind the counter. "My son just finished this. I haven't even had it on the shelf yet."

"That one, then." Neve paid for the bowl without bothering to haggle the price. She could have probably made one herself, but she could spare the money more easily than the magic.

"Look, where's the good in you using up what strength you've got?" Ash demanded as they walked back.

"Where's the good in the strength, if the city gets washed off the coast with me in it?" Neve said practically. "Listen, Ash—either Yaga and Kelara are right about the Nexus, in which case I'll regain my strength with rest and food, or Rhadaman's right, in which case all he's bought me is a little temporary respite. Either way there's no great damage done by a simple scrying."

"Well, before you go wearing yourself out, at least let's go have another look at this Sobel," Ash suggested. "Maybe you can tell whether there's actually some magic about the fellow or not, eh?"

Neve had to admit that that made sense. It took some time to find someone who would admit to knowing where Sobel could be found, but at last they got directions and slogged through the mud and rain to a tiny tumbledown shack near the docks. There was no sign above the door, and the shutters were closed, but Neve could see light through the cracks in the shutters and the latch string was out, and that was all the invitation she needed. She knocked on the door, but when there was no response she glanced at Ash, shrugged, and pulled the latch string, stepping inside.

The shack was as small as it had looked from the outside, and it appeared to be both business and home, impoverished but spotlessly clean. A rickety table near the front window held the lit lamp and nothing else; two overturned crates apparently served instead of chairs. A tiny fireplace housed an even tinier coal fire, which put out more smoke than heat, but to some extent dispelled the pervading damp and mustiness. There was a makeshift cabinet formed from old wooden boxes, a chamber pot, a crate of foodstuffs, and a simple pallet against the back wall. That was all—apart from the hovel's inhabitant, of course; Sobel was sitting on the pallet gazing at them calmly, his strange, pale eyes half-closed, apparently unperturbed at their entrance. Abruptly he rolled to his feet fluidly, sweeping a grand bow and smiling widely.

"Welcome to my humble abode, O most powerful lady," he said. His voice was soft and melodic, but his eyes didn't focus on her; once again she had the odd impression he was blind.

"I don't think we met properly before, in the market," Neve said cautiously. "Your name's Sobel, isn't it?"

"In this time and place." Sobel swept another bow. "And you are Neve, daughter of the lord who is as a god in his own kingdom, the lady who walks the worlds within worlds. Have you come to scoff and sneer, O mistress of life and death, of miracle and disaster, or to ask what the gods have destined for you?"

Neve froze, remembering suddenly what Sobel had said to her in the market. His words sounded more like farsight than foresight or madness either. But neither farsight nor scrying could penetrate the protections of the Crystal Keep. How could Sobel know so much about her? She'd only confided in Ash and Rhadaman, and neither of them was likely to have told anyone.

"To ask, I suppose," Neve said slowly. "I heard you speaking in the market of the coming of a great storm—"

"Oh, Zaravelle is bound for a wetting like none before!" Sobel chortled. He sprang forward and danced lightly around the room, twirling on the tips of his toes. "A bath for her dirty streets, to wash the squirmy little creatures from their dens." He seized Neve's hands, whirled her around. "Dance! Dance on the grave of Zaravelle!"

Neve pulled away, shaken and confused. Certainly this creature *was* mad, but there was more to it than that. She didn't like to touch him; he felt . . . wrong. Cursed, perhaps?

"Sobel—" She waited for him to stop dancing. "What exactly have you seen?"

Sobel whirled around once more, then stopped as abruptly as he'd started. He pulled a small clay jar from his pocket, opened it, and dipped out a little dark paste on his fingertip, popping it into his mouth. He put the jar back in his pocket and whirled again.

"A shaking deep in the bones of the earth," he chanted. "Then comes the water, leagues upon leagues. Land is over water until water is over land. Zaravelle, who watches from her lofty height, finds herself now in the depths, drowning in the airless blue—"

Sobel stopped again directly in front of Neve, and this time his eyes gazed flatly into hers, those pale grey eyes lost and bewildered.

"Who are you?" he asked in the soft and confused tones of a lost child. "Have you come to save us, or will you leave us lying broken in the depths like a bracelet cast aside—a bracelet of beads and one precious red stone?"

Suddenly a band of fear and dread tightened about Neve's chest, forcing the breath out of her in one wounded gasp. She stumbled backward as if she could flee from Sobel's words, colliding with Ash behind her.

"Steady on," Ash murmured in her ear. "What's the matter?"

Neve shook her head, unable to speak; a tight, shaking coldness had settled itself deep inside her. She forced herself to take a deep breath. It went down unwillingly.

"What—" She steadied her voice. "What must I do?"

Sobel suddenly laughed, whirling away across the room again.

"Not what you do, but what you are!" he chortled again. "Like the sea herself, all unbounded, life for some and death for others. How far is the reach of your hand or hers? What shield will you raise against the world? Not what you do, but what you are—" He dipped another fingerful of paste out of the jar and sucked it off his finger, then abruptly dropped onto his pallet, his back to them, and fell silent.

Neve turned, pulling Ash out of the little shack by main force. Suddenly she wanted nothing in the world more than to get away from those horrible pale eyes, that voice, those visions.

"Here, here, now, calm down," Ash said patiently, pulling her to a slower pace. "Don't let him get you so rattled, girl. Madmen, sometimes they say the strangest things, but it don't come to nothing. I've heard the likes of him a thousand times. Only difference is, folks hereabouts are gullible enough to give him coin to live on. Look, what's got you so spooked?''

Neve rounded on him.

''Didn't you *hear* him?'' she demanded. ''Didn't you hear what he said?''

''I heard a lot of hull-knocking nonsense,'' Ash said patiently. ''That was dreamweed resin paste he was sucking on. No wonder he ain't got his head on straight. Don't tell me you made something out of that babble?''

''But the br—'' Neve shook her head impatiently. Ash didn't know about Ruper's bracelet, the ruby. ''Never mind. Just never mind. We're going home and somehow, I don't know how, I'm going to manage to do a proper scrying before either of us is an hour older.''

Ash began to protest, but Neve forestalled him by stalking off into the rain as fast as her feet could carry her. Let him follow or not as he liked; crystal or no crystal, her mind was made up.

Back at their rooms, Ash remained moodily silent while Neve snipped a few hairs from her head and burned them to ash, trying to remember the preparations she'd seen Rhadaman make. She filled the bowl with rainwater—water simply didn't come any purer than that—and sprinkled the burned remains of her hair over the water, then dripped in three drops of her blood from a pricked fingertip.

''Listen,'' Ash said quietly but intensely. ''I won't say this again, but I got the feeling this is one devil of a bad idea.''

''Probably,'' Neve said wryly, holding out her hand. ''Now give me the crystal, please.''

Ash scowled but handed over the metal box. Neve opened it and took out her fragment of the Nexus, waiting for the familiar sense of homecoming, the resurgence of energy—

It was there, but less than she'd expected, much less, barely noticeable. Desperately Neve clutched the crystal tight, feeling a stab of real fear. Was the crystal going dormant, as Kelara had suggested, or was it something worse? Could a fragment of the Nexus actually die apart from the whole? Was that what was happening to her? If this fragment of crystal died, what would become of Neve? Of her father?

Neve resolutely cleared her mind. She'd seen Rhadaman

scry often enough. Unfortunately she hadn't paid any real attention to the spell he'd used; scrying was one area of magic he could handle well enough even with the distortions, so she'd left that to him. Still, she knew that her father and mother did their own kind of scrying, so it was within her power, if she could figure out how to do it.

And maybe the Nexus, though weakened, could still help her.

Father's mirror required questions, Neve thought. *But asking the wrong question can give dangerously misleading answers. Rhadaman doesn't ask questions, just looks for what he needs. Maybe that's safer.*

She closed her eyes, concentrating.

The future of the city? No, too vague, too dangerous. The weather? No, I'd just see rain, lots of rain. She grimaced, shaking her head.

No. Danger to the city. Show me the danger.

She opened her eyes.

For a moment when she saw nothing but water, Neve felt doubt, fear that she'd done it wrong. Did she have to use an actual spell after all? Then she realized that although she saw water rippling, she didn't see the bottom of the silver bowl. She wasn't seeing rainwater; she was looking at the surface of the ocean.

It was trembling.

Neve sensed rather than saw the vibrations, unsure exactly what she *was* seeing. An earthquake, but far out to sea? What difference could *that* possibly make? Even as the thought formed in her mind, however, a new image was forming in the bowl. The water of the sea seemed to dip inward, like the trough between ocean waves; then a wave formed, moving slowly across the surface of the bowl. Once more, Neve's confusion almost cost her her focus. It was only a wave, after all. Then in the bowl she saw the coast, and Zaravelle.

And realized what she was seeing—the *size* of what she was seeing. A wave unimaginably huge, as big as a hill, a mountain—

Oh, by the Nexus, if that hits the city, everyone—

And in response to the thought that barely took shape in her mind, the image changed—barely seen, through deep, dark water, the short white line of fish-cleaned bone, and around those bones, a pitiful little bracelet of cheap chipped beads.

And one single perfect ruby.

No. No. Please, no, never again—

"Ash—" The word was all it took to break her focus, and the horrible image in the bowl dissolved, but it was already engraved in Neve's mind. She didn't care about the bowl or her foresight now, nor did she care that the strength had drained out of her like blood from a mortal wound, leaving her weak and trembling once more. At that moment nothing existed to Neve but the horror of that small bony arm and its pitiful ornament.

Something in her eyes must have communicated itself to Ash, because the annoyance in his expression vanished instantly. He leaned over the table, steadying her in her chair without a word of I-told-you.

"What?" he said softly. "Did you see something? A bad storm?"

"I saw—something," Neve said, swallowing. "But it wasn't a storm. Ash, have you ever seen a wave so huge it could wash a whole city away?"

Ash went very still, very quiet.

"Gods preserve us," he whispered. "Seen? No, I never seen such a thing. But I've heard. Every sailor's heard. Fifty some years ago a wave the likes of that wiped Strachan right off the coast, and three or four smaller fishing villages with it. We've all heard of waves so huge they dwarf the tallest cliffs. You don't never mean—" He met her eyes.

Neve nodded slowly.

"I don't think I'm wrong," she said, her voice very faint. "I'd never even heard of such a thing. I *couldn't* have made it up, imagined it."

"Gods," Ash said again, just as faintly. "How long?"

"I don't know." Neve clenched her trembling hands. "I—I don't know how to ask *when*. I was lucky to even be able to see *what*."

Ash took a deep, shaking breath.

"Right," he said. "Come on, then."

Neve barely had time to empty the bowl before Ash grabbed her, crystal, bowl, and all, and dragged her out the door. She didn't have time to protest that she was too tired to walk across the room, much less across town; he had already swept her up in his arms and was bearing her down the street.

Ash waved down the first carriage he saw; Neve was too stunned and exhausted even to muster embarrassment when a brief but heated argument ensued between Ash and the carriage's occupants. The argument ended with the occupants quickly abandoning the vehicle, probably in fear of their lives, and the driver changing his route to Rhadaman's shop, probably for the same reason. Neve didn't care; she felt nothing but relief when Ash helped her out of the carriage and didn't even protest when Ash, ignoring Rhadaman's servant's adamant refusal to admit him, simply shouldered the door open.

Apparently Rhadaman was not too exhausted to respond to the crash of the door. By the time Ash and Neve were halfway across the parlor, he had appeared at the top of the stairs in his dressing gown, pale and drawn but very much awake.

"By the gods, Neve," Rhadaman said mildly, tying his robe. "Has something happened?"

"Not yet," she croaked.

There was a moment of confusion as Ash helped her to a chair and Rhadaman's manservant helped Rhadaman down the stairs. Ash told Rhadaman almost tonelessly what they had heard in the tavern, what Sobel had said, and what Neve had done. Neve rested, content to let Ash do the talking, until it came time to relate the details of her very first scrying. Rhadaman sat silently, listening intently, his eyes narrowing as she told him what she'd seen.

"A wave so large that it dwarfed the entire city?" he said slowly. "You're absolutely certain?"

"I'm certain what I saw," Neve said as firmly as she could. "I don't deny that was my first scrying, that it wasn't very specific. I mean, I have no idea of time or—or—maybe you'd better check yourself."

Rhadaman shook his head slowly.

"I'm afraid I'm a farseer, but not much of a foreseer," he said gently. "Very few mages have the talent for both. Even if I had my full strength about me, I doubt if I could accurately confirm your vision, much less scry out additional detail. We're better served consulting someone more likely to succeed.''

"What, go back to Sobel again?" Ash said impatiently.

Rhadaman shook his head again.

"No," he said. "If his visions had any more clarity, he would have given a time for the disaster he foresaw. And even if he could, we would have nothing more than confirmation. No, we will consult your friends, the powerful, if reluctant, elven mages.''

This time even Ash had to admit that being the most powerful (and only) mages in Zaravelle had its advantages—probably nobody else in the city could command the instant loan of three surefooted mules in such a rain as was pouring down over the city at that time. But nothing Neve or Rhadaman could do shortened the trail along the coast to Kelara and Yaga's cottage, and every passing minute made Neve more fearful. She couldn't tear her gaze away from the sea, scanning for the faintest hint of a gigantic approaching wave, but there was nothing.

"You won't see the wave first," Ash said, following her glance. "First thing, the tide'll go out—way, way out as all that water's pulled back out to sea into that wave.''

"Ash—" Neve swallowed. "What about up here? Will the wave reach this far?"

Ash nodded briefly.

"One way or another, it will," he said. "Even if it doesn't reach all the way up the cliff, the pressure'll crumble the whole coastline like stomping on a biscuit. Short of a Gate, I don't see how we could get far enough away to be safe. Even moving straight inland on horses, a big enough wave'll swell the river enough to wash out everything for leagues inward. That's not counting earthquakes and the like, either.''

A Gate. Neve swallowed, not wanting to seize on that faint hope. Even if Yaga and Kelara could manage to cast a Gate despite the distortions, could Neve herself pass through it? And even if she *could*—well, they couldn't Gate the whole population of Zaravelle to safety, could they?

Apparently that thought didn't hinder Kelara and Yaga, for when they reached the clearing and the cottage and stumbled through the doorway, incense was already burning in a brazier, Yaga leafing busily through a thick tome, and an outline of a door had already been chalked on one wall. For a moment Neve was appalled by the thought that the elves would Gate themselves to safety and leave—

Me!

—all those people behind to die.

"You can't," Neve whispered before Yaga could even speak. "By the Nexus, you can't possibly—"

"Zaravelle has welcomed you for decades!" Rhadaman protested, outraged. "You can't simply abandon its people now!"

"There is nothing else we can do," Yaga said stiffly. He turned to Neve and touched her hand more gently. "Neve, Kelara and I have no magic powerful enough to save Zaravelle and its inhabitants. You know we would if we could, but such a feat is far beyond us even were it not for the distortion of magic here. We have less than an hour, hardly enough time for a spell of any complexity. Opening a Gate long enough to get the five of us to safety is the very most we can hope to accomplish, and even that is far from certain, especially with—" He flushed.

"Especially with me here buggering up the aether, or whatever it is," Neve said grimly. "Listen, we have four powerful mages here. Surely between us there's *something* we can do. It's a wave, that's all, just *water*."

Ash chuckled wryly.

"Just water, yeah," he said. "And that monster we fought in the jungle was just a bug, right?"

"We have two completely exhausted mages," Rhadaman said gently, "and two elven mages who have never attempted strong magic in this region, and a completely unstable aether. Neve, as little as I like to admit it, perhaps Yaga is right. Even returning to warn the people would do no good, as your friend said, and we would only die with them. We couldn't even get back to Zaravelle before the wave hits, much less evacuate any of the people out of the city. Escape is better than death, and if there's nothing else we can do—"

Neve wanted to believe him, wanted it desperately. A Gate meant more than safety; it meant home. Family. The Nexus. A return to order, to sanity. But she couldn't get the image of that pitiful bracelet out of her mind.

That was one little boy. There are hundreds *of children in*

Zaravelle. Hundreds of children whose bones would litter the bottom of the sea like scattered sticks—like that little girl with the cracked skull or the baby with the scalded arm or—

"No," Neve said as firmly as she could. "There has to be a way. There *has* to." She turned to confront Yaga and Kelara, bracing her back against the edge of the table; it was all she could do to remain standing.

"If you had all the power you wanted," she said, "and if there weren't any distortions, what could you do about that wave?"

Yaga shook his head slowly.

"Neve, as I've told you, even the most powerful spells—"

"Forget spells," Neve snapped. "You used to be the Guardian of the Crystal Keep. What would you have done then?"

Startled, Yaga glanced at Kelara. Kelara frowned, shaking her head slightly.

"I never—" she said softly, hesitantly.

"Yes, you never actually wielded the power of the Guardian," Yaga said slowly. "But I—"

"You did it for *centuries*," Neve said impatiently. "What would you have done?"

Yaga was silent for a moment.

"There are three possibilities," he said thoughtfully at last. "Turn the wave, transmute it, or shield the city."

"Turning the wave would be nearly impossible now," Rhadaman said, sitting down at the table, folding his hands with a speculative expression. "So much weight of water, with such force behind it—"

"Transmuting it would be nearly as difficult, and less effective," Kelara said softly. "Even if one could transform such a huge quantity of matter, the sheer energy moving it would still mean disaster for Zaravelle."

"That leaves shielding the city," Neve said flatly. She raised a hand, forestalling Yaga's objection. "Don't tell me it can't be done. Tell me how it *could* be done."

"Well, it's not all that tricky," Ash interjected, startling all of them.

Neve turned to glance at Ash, almost falling from the effort.

"What do you mean?" she said.

"Look here." Ash squatted down on the dirt floor and drew his dagger, scratching lines in the packed dirt. "This is Colehaven, one of the eastern coastal cities. Bad seas thereabouts, rough weather. But see here?" He scratched more lines slightly out from where he'd marked the coast. "This here's a line of reefs. Ships can't come in too close to shore or the reefs'd tear out their bottoms, it's that shallow over top. But those same reefs take all the force out of the waves coming in to shore. Even the worst storms haven't done much damage to that city in centuries."

Of course, Neve thought wonderingly. *Maybe the wave can't be turned or changed, but take all the force out of it— like Father said, it's easier to work from the inside out!*

"Right," she said. "We know what needs to be done, then. All we have to do is figure out how to do it."

"We know what I could do when I was Guardian," Yaga said patiently. "But the Nexus and its Guardian are hundreds of leagues away. I cannot even call your father, Neve, and if I could, his magic cannot reach outside the Keep to help us. We simply do not *have* a nexus available to us."

"Well, what if you did?" Ash put in, scowling. "You made the first one, didn't you? Couldn't you just make another one here?"

Kelara gave Ash a gently chiding look, and Yaga shook his head.

"It is far from that simple," he said. "Kelara did not precisely *create* the first nexus; rather, she tapped an existing power point where many energy lines naturally converged, harnessed that power and—for lack of a better word—*grew* the Nexus and the Keep from that power. It took time and the most potent magic imaginable to simply start that process, to create the merest seed of what is now the Nexus within the Crystal Keep. Here we have no central convergence of power currents—quite the contrary. There is nothing to create a nexus *from*."

"No," Rhadaman said suddenly. "We have a Nexus already."

This time when Neve whirled she *did* fall, but Ash helped her up, pulling her to another chair.

"You mean that crystal?" Ash said. "The one that's part of the other Nexus?"

"No." Rhadaman smiled tiredly. "I mean Neve."

"Me?" Neve sat up a little straighter. "But—"

"Take it out," Rhadaman said, gesturing. "The crystal. It's simple enough to test."

Glancing hesitantly at Yaga and Kelara, Neve slowly withdrew the box from her tunic, opening it. She took the crystal out, clutching it tightly. It was dull, inert in her hand. A lump of rock, nothing more.

"I do not believe," Rhadaman said softly, "that the crystal was ever feeding upon Neve. Quite the contrary—I think it was feeding *her*. Serving the child of the Nexus, yes?"

"I don't understand," Neve said slowly.

"Of course!" Ash said suddenly. "*She's* a nexus! Or—or the start of one, maybe?"

Yaga's eyes slowly widened.

"Yes," he breathed. "I should have seen it in the way the energy flows changed around her, the patterns altering to her presence, yet not affecting her magic. She had no energy source to tap, nothing but the crystal—"

"And she has exhausted that," Kelara said wonderingly, taking the dead crystal from Neve's hand. "All of her life the Nexus fed her, sustained her—"

"As a parent does its child," Rhadaman said, nodding. "But that little fragment could not continue to supply the energy to meet Neve's increasing needs as she came into the fullness of her power."

"Wait a minute," Neve said weakly. "The Nexus is a— a *thing* that Kelara created or grew or whatever."

"As you were created," Rhadaman agreed. "By the Nexus and your father. A part of its substance, yes, but a living, growing child. And in time, a whole new life."

"But what does that *mean*?" Neve protested. "All right— assume I have a nexus inside me, or I *am* a nexus, or whatever you'd like. Obviously I don't have that kind of power— why, I can hardly stand up after one little scrying. What good does that do us?"

"The nexus Kelara created tapped into a natural convergence of energy lines," Rhadaman told her. "We have energy lines aplenty here, though disorganized, and you've been trying to draw them to you since the day you arrived. If we could do what Kelara did in reverse—not create a nexus where those power currents converged, but bring those lines together to feed an already existing nexus—''

"It could be done," Yaga said reluctantly. "Kelara and I had even spoken idly about opening a new nexus to stabilize the aether here. But—'' He glanced at Kelara. "I do not know whether she could do it again. What it did to her before—''

Neve took a deep breath.

"Yes," she said. "It tore her soul loose, and it was centuries before she got it back. But—listen, if this works and that happens, I'll give her back her soul myself. I promise.''

"Now, wait a minute," Ash said slowly. "This is starting to sound like a not-so-great idea. Nobody said anything about this nexus stuff being so dangerous.''

Yaga gave Neve a glance of pure exasperation, completely ignoring Ash.

"Neve, it is hardly that simple," he said. "The risk to you is even greater. We do not even know—''

"Now, hold on—'' Ash began, scowling.

"Well, I know *this*," Neve interrupted. "I know that in less than an hour we're going to have a city full of dead people. I know if we go off and leave them to die when we might have saved them—''

She glanced at Ash.

"—then we're responsible," she said flatly. "We're responsible because we should have *tried*. And I know I can't live with any more deaths on my soul. Can you?''

"What do you mean, any *more* deaths?'' Ash said, but Neve ignored him, her eyes on Yaga's.

Yaga glanced at Kelara. After a moment Kelara dropped her eyes, nodding slowly.

"Yes," she said, almost inaudibly. "We will try.''

"What do you mean," Ash said slowly, "any *more* deaths?''

"Nothing," Neve said brusquely, turning back to Yaga. "Whatever you need to do, let's get it started before I lose my nerve.''

"No, damn all!'' Ash exclaimed, grabbing Neve by the shoulders. "Just a minute here! What exactly do you mean, any *more* deaths?''

Rhadaman shook his head.

"She blames herself for the sinking of the *Albatross*," he said. "She wished ill on the captain, and the captain became sick, and Neve thinks it was a manifestation of her magic."

"Is that what this is about?" Ash demanded, giving Neve's shoulders a little shake. "Are you going to stand here and get yourself killed because you think you sank that ship? Listen, girl, I never heard such foolishness in my life as—"

Neve closed her eyes briefly.

No. He doesn't understand. And I can't let him stop me.

She laid her hand on Ash's shoulder, remembering what Rhadaman had taught her, pulling up the last dregs of her power.

Sleep. Sleep deeply.

For a moment astonishment, then realization, then outrage flickered across Ash's eyes, just before they rolled up in his head. He collapsed limply to the dirt floor, and Neve sagged back in her chair.

"All right," she said faintly. "Let's get this done fast. Before I lose my nerve."

To Neve's surprise, there appeared to be very little preparation—no incense, no candles, no powders or potions or oils, only a circle and a few odd designs scratched into the dirt floor around her, and lodestones at the four poles. Yaga pressed the spent crystal into Neve's hands.

"This will serve as a focus, at least," he said. "It is still a fragment of the original Nexus. It remembers the feeling of a center of power. Perhaps that will help you when the time comes."

Kelara traced a second circle in the dirt floor outside the first, broken only where the lodestones had been placed.

"As we bring each power line in to you, you must seize it, bind it," Kelara told her. "We will begin slowly, but there are many lines to harness to give you enough power to do what must be done, and little time to work. We cannot move slowly for long. You must stay ready, focused."

Neve took a deep breath.

"I will," she said. *I can guess what might happen if I don't.*

There was no ritual, no chanting, only Yaga and Kelara kneeling at opposite sides of the circle, eyes closed, silent.

But she did a ritual when she constructed the Keep, Neve

thought, confused. *Never mind, this is different. More improvised, maybe.*

Suddenly a sharp shock ran through her, as if someone had poked her hard, and instinctively Neve reached out toward the source of the sensation, not physically, and seized—something. She shivered as strength flowed back into her.

That must be one of those power lines Kelara mentioned. Better pay attention to what I'm—whoa! Another nonphysical poke, and Neve had to "reach" quickly to grab it. Then another. Another.

Now Neve could see something, vague and insubstantial at first but sharper as she focused on it—bright, narrow lines curving in, sliding through the circle at the open points—four of them now, but another was bending toward the circle as if seeking an opening. Then it darted toward her like a serpent striking, and instinctively she "reached" again, seeing a sort of tendril whip out from her body, seize the bright line, and pull the end to her.

Neve hardly had time to marvel on this phenomenon, however, because already another bright line was bending in toward her, this one from the air rather than the ground, and she could see others approaching as well. At the same time she realized that she certainly wasn't "seeing" these lines with her eyes; several were approaching her from behind, but that didn't alter her perception in the slightest, nor hinder her as she pulled them in almost instinctively.

As if I was meant for this. Neve marveled. *But of course, I was. This was always—ah, ah! You're mine!*

Now they were coming faster and faster, and Neve no longer consciously focused on each line and pulled it in; now she only kept up her concentration and let whatever perceptions she was instinctively using expand to detect and seize on those glowing lines. Each new line sent a jolt of energy through her, seemed somehow to anchor her, at the same time filling her with a strength she'd never felt before.

Yes. This is what I was always meant to do. This is what I am.

She was pulling in the lines of energy unconsciously now, not even waiting for them to bend toward her but somehow reaching out and seizing them, drawing them in herself unconsciously. There seemed to be a glow around her now from the dozens—hundreds?—of bright lines leading in to her, and Neve opened new eyes and gazed out to sea.

The line of the tide was receding back, farther than she'd ever seen even at the lowest tides. Boats that had floated solidly the day before now teetered unsteadily on wet sand and gravel. Stranded fish flopped and suffocated; coral heads' wet backs glistened nakedly in the sun. But she could feel the weight of the approaching water, still far away but coming fast, the sheer force of it.

No, she thought. *The sea almost had me once. But it didn't get me then and it won't have me now. And this time* I'm *in charge.*

She reached out and caressed the gleaming back of the distant wave with invisible fingers, sucking out the power of it, drawing it in as easily as she'd drawn in the glowing lines of energy that even now multiplied around her. Yes, the wave was losing force, momentum—but not fast enough.

Father never wanted to let me practice worldscaping—but Father's not here now.

Neve reached deep into the ocean floor and *pulled*.

The ocean floor split open and rock burst forth, pushed upward and molded by Neve's invisible hands, higher, higher—

Then she felt something she hadn't expected, a shifting under the seafloor, pressure, heat too near the surface—

Oh, by the Nexus, no, I didn't know, it's like a volcano and I've scraped off the top holding it down, what do I—

Desperately her hands, her body's hands clutched the fragment of crystal.

Remember how it feels, she thought frantically. *You're part of the Nexus, all its memories, its deeds, they're all there, REMEMBER.*

She tried to "reach" into the crystal as she'd "reached" for the lines of power, as she still pulled them to her, reach through the crystal to the Nexus—

And then there was *something* there, a presence, a familiar touch—the Nexus, yes, oh, yes, and—

Neve? Suddenly her father was *with* her, not there in body but still so close she could feel his touch. *What in the world have you done? All this power, I can feel—by the Nexus, what have you done?*

Neve fought down her fear; the mere presence, however unphysical, of her father was reassuring.

Renounced my claim to your kingdom, Father, she thought with a sort of frantic amusement. *But right now I could use a little fatherly advice, if you please.*

Now she could feel her father more clearly, even closer, as if he somehow looked through her eyes—or, more properly, that unseeing perception that even now seized more lines of force, drawing them inward even as Neve maintained her desperate hold on the seafloor.

An interesting problem, Vanian admitted. *Too much stress on the sea floor and you're going to break the lava shell, pull the whole city into the sea or burn it to cinders; but then there's the wave, and—*

Father, Neve thought a little desperately. *Discourse later. Help NOW.*

Oh, very well, Vanian thought rather irritably. *Just like your mother, so demanding. Look. Work from the inside out, remember?* Use *the lava, mold it, cool it and use it to seal the whole thing up. Like THIS.*

And Neve reached out fingers of thought, molding molten rock and cold rock and sand and coral—*No, watch the pressure there, yes, good; don't be so timid; give it a good push. Good, good, you're getting the way of it now*—and she pulled up a solid, thick wall, a wall that scoffed at water no matter how great its force—

Oh, wait. They have to get the ships through, don't they? All right, then, an opening large enough—no, over here, I think. Yes, that should do nicely. Good and strong and tall; it's a large wave, after all.

Then an unimaginable wall of water struck solid rock still hot from its birth. Rock groaned and cracked and split; water poured over, around, between, poured in to fill the harbor, tear some of the boats loose from their fragile moorings, dash others to splinters against piers that groaned and held or shattered. Water welled up to splash over the wharf, all the way up to the city—

And some, a little, spilled into the streets and puddled under scrambling feet, feet that paused in their flight, then stopped.

Done, Neve thought with satisfaction. *Well, too bad about *the boats. But at least nobody died and nothing exploded.*

A good job, Vanian, the Guardian of the Crystal Keep, admitted. *I couldn't have done better myself. Your mother will be proud—when she stops shouting at me, that is. When you've settled in, create a mirror so you can speak to her yourself. Make it soon, before she takes it into her head to storm out of the Keep and* walk *all the way down there.*

I will, Father, Neve thought humbly. Then common sense reasserted itself. *Well, not until Mother's had time to get over shouting about what's happened.*

Oh, thank *you.*

You're more than welcome. And how *many times did you spy on me despite your promise?*

The tone of Vanian's thought positively *dripped* self-righteousness.

I never promised. That was your mother. Then: more gently, *I'm proud of you, Neve. We both are. You'll be a good Guardian.*

Thank you, Father. She could feel his touch fading, growing more distant. *Thank you for everything.*

Then one final thought, just before their contact broke:

I wouldn't try dragons anytime soon, if I were you . . .

Somehow remote, she felt hands clasping hers, real physical hands, and as easily as that she was flesh again, flesh pleasantly tired but at the same time humming with energy. Neve opened her eyes. Ash was crouching in front of her, his expression unreadable.

"Is it over?" Neve asked hesitantly. Now that she thought about it, it seemed awfully like a dream. But she could still feel the power lines feeding into her, humming with energy, and if she focused on them, she could almost see those bright lines, steady now. Stable.

Ash chuckled.

"Oh, it's over, all right," he said. "Come look."

He helped her up and drew her outside, where Yaga and Kelara and Rhadaman were standing silently, gazing out at the sea.

Half of Kelara's garden was gone—well, not precisely *gone;* rather it was probably a couple hundred feet below. The edge of the cliff was considerably closer to the cottage now. The view, Neve noted, was spectacular.

"Just couldn't have cut that any closer, could you?" Ash asked mildly. "I mean, just look down there at Zaravelle. They're going to be all spring rebuilding their fishing fleet."

"Well, excuse *me*." Neve bristled. "It's not like I had a chance to practice ahead of time, after all. I think I did pretty well for a fast and dirty first try."

"Reefs, I said." Ash chuckled, gazing out at the jagged rock jutting up around the harbor. "Shallow reefs. Didn't say nothing about *mountains*, did I?"

"Well, fine, then," Neve retorted. "*Be* an ungrateful toad." She *reached* out, pushing the rock down, down, flattening the wall until the surf broke over the top of the rock. "Better?"

Ash turned, gazing at her with that strange expression.

"As easy as that, eh?" he said softly.

"Yes, as easy as that," Neve said, swallowing hard. *As easy as creating a few worms, or a giant spider, or*—She glanced down at her hands and realized they were trembling.

Ash took her hands again, firmly.

"You're no monster," he said, meeting her eyes. "Rhadaman told me what you'd told him, about the *Albatross* and such. Listen, you didn't kill anybody."

Neve dropped her eyes.

"I wish I could believe that," she whispered.

"Well, you can, 'cause I'm not nice enough to lie for your peace of mind." Ash chuckled. "Listen, maybe you had the captain puking down in her quarters, and maybe you didn't. Did you get around to cursing the bosun, too? Because he ate the same pork pies as the captain, and he was puking just as hard."

"Well—" Neve took a deep breath. "No. I don't think I ever even saw the bosun."

"So maybe you made Captain Corell sick, and maybe you didn't," Ash said again. "But you didn't put those sea dragons out there, and you didn't make lightning strike the ship, and you weren't the damned fool who loaded the ship full of flammables in storm season. What you did do is you worked damned hard to save the *Albatross* with everything you had, and you stood your ground and did what you could even when everybody else was fleeing for the longboats."

He grinned.

"Mind you, I won't say you can't be the most irritating, peevish bit I've ever met," he said. "But you got guts and you do your best. You're going to make a damned fine Guardian or Nexus or whatever the hell you are."

Neve smiled, her heart suddenly very light.

"What do you think, Kelara?" she said, turning to the elf. "Am I good en—"

She stopped. Kelara was standing very still, gazing silently at her ruined garden. Her eyes were wide and empty.

"My garden," she whispered.

"I'm sorry," Neve said, very softly. She'd seen Kelara's garden in the Crystal Keep, a small oasis of beauty in a tortured wasteland. Kelara had built a garden here, too, her tiny island of sanity amidst the chaos. Suddenly Neve could feel Kelara's pain, the wounds to her soul that perhaps would never heal.

She stepped closer to the elf, reaching out to her, then drawing her hand back when Kelara winced away.

No. I can't heal those wounds. I can only make them worse.

"I'm sorry," Neve repeated softly. "I can put it back, Kelara. Just exactly the way it was."

"No." Kelara looked up, meeting Neve's eyes. "This is your garden now. Make what you will of it. You will need it far more than I." She reached for Yaga's hand. "And we are not staying."

Neve took a deep breath, wanting to panic, to argue. But she knew better.

"What's with them?" Ash asked, shaking his head as Yaga led Kelara to a bench and sat down, taking her in his arms.

"The power of a nexus," Rhadaman said, joining Ash and Neve. "I don't think they can bear to be near it now. Zaravelle is safe, we're all alive—but everything has a price, doesn't it?" He was gazing at Neve as he spoke.

"Yes," she said quietly. "I suppose it does."

Ash scowled.

"What, I suppose that means you're staying here, then, if they can't?" he said.

"I have to," Neve said, realizing it for the first time even as she spoke. "I'm bound into the energy lines here. Which makes me the Nexus *and* the Guardian, I suppose.'' She swallowed, feeling invisible chains settle around her. Was this what her father had meant when he spoke of imprisonment? She *was* a prisoner—a prisoner of her own power, perhaps more so even than her father. His nexus was a part of the Keep, separate from himself. He could at least conceivably leave it. Not so Neve. She was a spider caught at the center of her own web. She could move only so far as the power lines would move with her.

''So if she's the Nexus and the Guardian, what's that make you?'' Ash said, glancing at Rhadaman.

Rhadaman chuckled resignedly.

''Redundant, I'm afraid,'' he said. ''For the first time Zaravelle has a stable aether—but under *her* control,'' he added, nodding at Neve.

''Oh, come on,'' Neve said, meeting his gaze. ''You don't mean to tell me a city as big as Zaravelle doesn't have room for *two* powerful mages, especially now that there's a stable aether or whatever?''

''You know what I mean,'' Rhadaman said quietly.

''I know I'll never love those people the way you do,'' Neve said, taking his hand. ''I know people need a mage who's there in the city and available to them, who isn't too busy pushing up the ocean floor to leakproof their roof or fast-ferment their wine. I know I've got a lot to learn. I could still use a teacher, too, you know.'' *One who doesn't find mortal suffering entertaining. Mother was right. When your body, your power becomes something other than human, it's all too easy for your soul to go with it.*

Rhadaman gazed into her eyes, then smiled sadly.

''A teacher?'' he said gently.

Neve squeezed his hand, feeling a pang of regret.

Yes. Everything has a price. And some prices I can't pay.

''A teacher,'' she said softly. ''And a friend.''

Rhadaman sighed, then smiled again.

''I suppose,'' he said, ''there are worse jobs than teaching the Guardian of Zaravelle.''

''You'd better believe there are,'' Neve said, turning to Ash. ''There's the poor fellow who has to put up with her bad temper and her sharp tongue and her cravings for spiced shellfish, even when the rain's pouring down.''

She held out her hand.

"But the pay's good and the food is fantastic," she said, raising an eyebrow. "What do you think?" She gestured at Ash's boots. "I could even throw in a free transformation or two."

Ash shrugged, wrinkling his nose as he glanced down at his feet.

"Ah, I'm getting kind of used to 'em," he said. " 'Sides, they do come in handy now and again, I guess."

Neve took a deep breath, suppressing a pang of fear.

"Is that a no?" she asked.

Ash rolled his eyes.

"Girl, you can be the *stupidist* little bit." He sighed. "Now come here and kiss me, will you, and convince me I'm not the biggest fool on the face of the earth."

Neve grinned, made an obscene gesture, and obeyed.

"So tell me," Ash said as they walked back to the cottage together. "Figure you can manage something better than this little hut?"

"Oh—just about anything." Neve laughed. "A castle, if you want it. Or we could live in town, if you'd rather. I think I can go that far, although I like the peace and quiet out here."

"Ah, people are a noisy lot," Ash said comfortably. "Here'll do fine, especially if you can wave up some of those fancy suppers."

"Anything you like." Then a thought occurred to her, and she laughed. "As long as you don't expect me to chop turnips."

Ash glanced at her, then grinned.

"Nah," he said. "Never could stomach the damned things, myself."

He waved at the cottage.

"Well, what are you waiting for, girl?" he said. "Where's that castle?"

Neve stopped in her tracks.

"It's *Neve*," she said flatly. "Not 'girl,' not 'little bit.' Neve."

Ash turned and took her hands, his eyes warm.

"Right, then," he said. "Neve."

Neve smiled and squeezed his hands, and glanced at the cottage.

She made a wish.

ANNE LOGSTON

Shadow is a master thief as elusive as her name. Only her dagger is as sharp as her eyes and wits. Where there's a rich merchant to rob, good food and wine to be had, or a lusty fellow to kiss...there's Shadow.

In the heart of one woman burned the flames of magic...the flames of passion..the flames of glory...

❏ FIREWALK   0-441-00427-X/$6.50
❏ WATERDANCE   0-441-00613-2/$6.50

Sharon Shinn————————